# CHAMPION

# CHAMPION

VICTOR OF TUCSON ✝ BOOK NINE

## PLUM PARROT

Podium

Podium

# CHAMPION

# 1

## GOODBYES

Victor stooped to pick up a smooth stone and threw it out over the ocean. It soared much farther than he'd intended, becoming a small black dot in his vision before he lost track of where it went. Kethelket chuckled and paused to sit on a large driftwood log. "So. You leave tomorrow, hmm?" They'd met several times during Victor's visit, even gone hunting once, but the weight of Victor's impending departure had given this visit a different, more somber, almost sullen tone.

"Yeah. I have to get back. There's so much I have to do, so much I have to learn." Victor sighed and reached up to run his fingers through his hair—too long by inches for his tastes.

"I'm sure you do. A world where kingdoms vie for power through dueling champions? It doesn't seem ethical."

"What part? The fighting and scheming, or the no wars killing the 'common folk' part?"

Kethelket narrowed his eyes but nodded slowly. "I suppose you have a point—I forget, from time to time, that while you're young, you've seen much. I concede that, while some will suffer in the machinations of those kingdoms and their dueling champions, it's perhaps better than peace for many years followed by bloody campaigns where thousands die."

"Or millions. Some worlds are far more populous than Fanwath, Kethelket. You've heard our stories about Sojourn—millions of people all clustered together in a single city. There are worlds far more ancient than that, worlds with dozens or hundreds of cities that size. Imagine the carnage of wars at that scale!"

"Yes. Yes, Victor, I'm all too familiar with the carnage of wars. I will say that having spent so much time slumbering away, lost to the advances of the Ridonne and the expansion of our network into other worlds, I certainly feel adrift, lost in a sea of information that I should have a much surer grip upon. Perhaps I'll make a visit to Sojourn soon. If I do, I imagine you'll be gone?"

"Maybe. I have a few months before Dar sends me off. Even so, Valla will be there—Lam, Edeya, and Lesh, too. There are libraries and, well, shit, anything you might want. You should definitely pay a visit; there's no reason for you to stop . . ." Victor let the thought hang, not wanting to spell out his borderline criticism any more clearly.

"Advancing? Learning? Lusting for life?" Kethelket chuckled. "There are other things in life, Victor. I take great pleasure in leading my people and seeing them made safe. I helped to build a school last month, and when the first class of newborn Naghelli attend it in a few years, I imagine I'll feel a swelling of my heart far fiercer than any victory I might win in a dungeon or dueling ring."

Now it was Victor's turn to feel attacked, but he took it in stride, nodding solemnly. "Point well received, Kethelket. This week, I felt a small inkling of that when I saw Cora making friends with the Shadeni children and learning to stalk huldii with Deyni. Her smile, the joy in her eyes—it erased some dark smear on my spirit. I could use more moments like that."

"Wisely said, young man. Well?" He sighed and stood, his strange mothlike wings fluttering softly as their ochre patterns flared with Energy. "I suppose this is farewell for now, then. It's been good to catch up. Any other plans before you go?"

"Nope." Victor shrugged and looked up the grassy slope to the wall surrounding his "retreat," which was really just a modest estate considering the size of his holdings. "Valla wants to have dinner; we, uh, have a lot to talk about."

Kethelket narrowed his eyes. "Is all well?"

"Yeah, I think so." Victor shrugged again and kicked a stone toward the lapping waves. "We were having a lot of . . . I don't know what to call it, but maybe 'friction.' We decided to put off fighting," he said, laughing at the idea, "until after this trip. Hopefully, she's feeling as relaxed as I am, and it'll go smoothly."

"Ah." Kethelket clapped him on the shoulder. "I have no easy advice for you there, lad. I've had many loves, but most were quite brief. One was profound, but she was Ghelli and royalty, to boot. This was before the great war split our people and before Kthella was ripped asunder and combined with the other worlds to create Fanwath. In any case, she died while I was locked away in Belikot's service. My greatest regret."

"Shit, man. Way to put my little pissant problems in perspective!" It was Victor's turn to clap Kethelket on the shoulder, giving him a comradely shake. "I mean that. Thank you, 'cause sometimes I build things up bigger than they are, you know?"

"Of course I know! Everyone does it." The older man laughed, shaking his head. He held out his hand, and Victor clasped it firmly. After a moment,

Kethelket nodded and then stepped away. "I'll leave from here; I'm due at Seaside for dinner."

Victor nodded. Seaside was the name Rellia had given her capital. "You think you can make it?"

"Oh, aye. My wings have improved much since I pushed my racial advancement into the advanced stages." He fluttered said wings, and they became a blur of ochre light that seemed to weave in a hypnotic pattern. Then he was in the air, calling down, "Just watch me!" Victor shaded his eyes and grinned as his friend streaked away to the south. It was true; he was two or three times faster than Victor remembered. Soon, he was gone, too small to track against the sun's light.

Victor turned toward the path leading up to his home, stuffing his hands into his pockets as he walked. He was eager to get back and get to work, but he knew he was going to miss Fanwath. He would miss the weather, the comfort of his home, and the heartwarming presence of his friends; Thayla, Deyni, and Chala had practically moved in for the last week, and he'd enjoyed having them close.

He could see what Kethelket meant, though, about watching your people grow and improving their lives. Nia and the other members of the Ninth who'd come to work for his "household" were completely different people from those whom he'd left behind. Some time at peace, some time helping others, had done wonders for them. He supposed things wouldn't always be so idyllic in the Free Marches or even his own lands, but he hoped it would last a long, long time.

One thing was certain—Gorro ap'Dommic was a hell of a governor. Victor's properties were already producing a revenue surplus. When Victor met with Gorro, the governor had been afraid Victor would empty the coffers, taking the surplus—as was his due. Victor had chuckled, though, and insisted they build up a management fund and reinvest in the community. He hadn't said it so eloquently—something more like, "Don't we need it here?" Still, Gorro had capitalized on his impulse for generosity and laid out his plans for expansion. Victor looked forward to seeing the results on his next visit.

He was only halfway up the path when he saw movement at the gate, and when he looked up, Valla stood there. She was tall and lithe, with a lustrous glow to her—the afternoon sun reflecting on the almost metallic sheen of her skin and feathers. Victor lifted his arm to wave, a big, lazy gesture impossible to miss. Valla's wings spread, and so did Victor's grin as he saw them light up in the sunlight—great, silver-teal things that made the Ghelli and Naghelli wings look like something you'd find on a toy. Valla snapped them down and leaped. With the slope of the hill, that single flap was enough to allow her to glide gracefully down to him.

She landed, light as a feather, on her tiptoes, and before Victor could utter a greeting, she leaned in and kissed him gently. "Shall we walk before dinner?"

"Yeah. Why not?" Victor took her hand, and they walked that way, arms swinging between them, down to the shore, adding to Victor's and Kethelket's earlier footprints. Victor had to admit he felt a weird twinge of nervousness in his gut and, hating the sensation, blurted his thoughts. "I thought we were going to talk at dinner, so I hadn't given myself a chance to feel the stress I was building up."

Valla giggled, and Victor took that for a good sign; he hadn't been sure his mention of stress regarding their meeting would be received well. "I, too, had buried some stress about this day," she said. "I haven't wished for time to slow down so hard in all my life!"

"It was a pretty nice time here, wasn't it? I think if someone told me I had to settle down and stop . . . *everything*, I'd be tempted to go along with it."

Again, Valla's laugh trilled out, and she slowed to a stop and turned toward him. "You're a liar."

"I . . ." After a short deliberation, he shrugged and agreed. "Yeah."

"I love you, Victor. I truly do."

"Well." Victor felt himself flushing with heat, not embarrassment, exactly, but suddenly wholly aware of how much Valla was scrutinizing him as she professed her feelings so plainly—so rawly. "Shit, Valla. I love you, too. I love you so much, it makes me stupid."

Her smile was so sweet, her eyes so open, that Victor felt that old rush, that old thrill he'd had the first time he tried to kiss her in Persi Gables. He leaned toward her, and they kissed several times, just sweet, little kisses that sent tingles through Victor's lips and down the nape of his neck like electricity. When she pulled back, she spoke words that hit him like a lightning bolt. "That's why I'm going to stay here for a while. That's why I'm going to step away from you and give us each a chance to live a little bit."

"Huh?" Victor didn't have to feign his idiocy.

"I've been thinking about this a lot; we're both young. Neither of us has ever had another meaningful romantic relationship." When Victor opened his mouth to protest, she held up a hand. "Not *really*, Victor. You know it's true." As he clamped his mouth shut and narrowed his eyes, she gestured an arm toward the sky. "We might live thousands and thousands of years! How long do you think our romance will last if we stay together now? We've been together, what? A year?"

Victor shrugged, his heart hammering too hard, his mind racing too much for him to formulate a proper response.

"Tell me you didn't think about how it might not be working when we were back in Sojourn. Tell me!" She wasn't yelling, but her voice was pleading, and where she clutched Victor's wrists, she tugged gently in emphasis.

"I was worried."

"So, suppose we do better. Suppose we cross this current hurdle of you being gone for—who knows how long. What if we make it five years before we decide it won't work?" Again, Victor didn't reply. "What's five years in a lifetime that stretches into millennia?"

"Nothing," he finally grunted.

"So, let's live some of that life. Let's build experiences—meet people, go places, accomplish things. And let's do it out of each other's shadows." That last sentence hit Victor like a hammer, and suddenly, things were clarifying in his mind. Valla was admitting that she hadn't been happy lately—dwelling in his shadow. Could he blame her? What a shadow he'd been casting! He'd had the same worry, hadn't he? He wanted to be angry, hurt, and reactionary, but he forced himself to take a deep breath, and contemplating the cool, reassuring Energy of his inspiration, he slowly began to nod.

Though Valla smiled at his positive body language, Victor's first words were an objection. "And if you meet someone you truly love, the person that makes you forget all about me?" With a deepening frown, he added, "Or if I do?"

"Victor, how many people stay together for a decade? A century? Do you know? Because while you were in the Iron Prison, I spoke to many ancient cultivators in Sojourn. People just don't last that long together, or if they do, their relationship evolves over time. Heated love becomes warm companionship. I don't want our heat and passion to be over yet, and when we do come together, I want it to last a very long time!"

Victor stood there, feeling stupid, or slow, or something along those lines, and he stared at her, every second adding to the panic that he was about to lose the best part of his life. Valla must have seen some of it in his eyes, because she didn't wait for him to figure out what he wanted to say. "I started thinking about this a while ago. I think it was after I hurt my eye. After we made up, and you told me about going to Ruhn for Dar's granddaughter. I remember us talking about me staying in Sojourn, which was perfectly reasonable, but I wondered why that was the extent of my ambition."

"It's not, though—"

Valla gently squeezed his wrists. "Sweet Victor. Let me finish, please?" Victor nodded, embarrassed to realize he had some moisture gathering in his eyes. "Of course, it would be *smart* to take advantage of Sojourn! What did I want, though? When we came here and Thayla told us about Chandri, these thoughts came up again. I know I deny it, but Victor, I *am* in your shadow. What's more, I'm planning the next months or *years* around what you're doing! I don't want to stay in Sojourn and grind away at levels with Lesh. I enjoy Lesh, don't get me wrong, but I have other interests! I want to *explore*. I want to meet new, strange people, and I'd like to do it without all the stress that comes along with doing it by your side!"

Victor thought of Coloss, and he snorted a soft chuckle. "You have a point, but it had nothing to do with me when War Captain Blue decided he had to have you."

"Suffice it to say I'll plan my destinations more carefully than when we went to Zaafor!" She grinned and twitched her wings. "Besides, I think *little* Lord Blue would sing a different tune if he ran into me today." Her eyes flashed briefly with dancing static energy.

Victor grinned at the thought, but his levity faded rapidly. "Why are you staying here, though?"

"You're leaving at Dar's command, but I'm not subject to Dar's whims, Victor. I'm not done visiting yet! I want to spend time with my mother and learn from her as she builds this new nation! I want to spend more time with our friends and explore these new lands a little. When I'm ready, I'll travel. I may go through Sojourn, or I may fly to Tharcray and see where the Ridonne's City Stone can take me."

Victor's frown hadn't faded. "So that's it for us, then? I go my way, and you go yours, and—"

"Oh, hush! Don't be so dramatic! We both consider this home, don't we? We have a Far Scribe book we share, and if we fill it, we'll need to meet to exchange new ones, won't we? We'll see each other from time to time. After we've spent some time living our lives, perhaps we'll come together again, and our love can bloom into something stronger, something with durability that the centuries will have to struggle to wear down."

Victor took a deep breath and forced his reeling thoughts to slow and solidify. He pushed away petty urges to lash out. He fought down the words on the tip of his tongue about what she'd do if one of those times he showed up on Fanwath with a new wife. Instead, he slowly exhaled through his nose and stared into her eyes, digging as deeply as he could, willing the truth to come to him as he asked, "Are you just saying all of this to let me down easy? To send me off without hurting my feelings? It seems like an easy way out—a way to hope I'll forget about you so you never have to say how you'd decided you didn't *really* love me."

"Oh, you absolute *idiot*! You *know* I love you! I couldn't deny it enough to convince a child! Do *you* value our love? Do you value it enough to make it stronger by fulfilling your potential? Do you think our love can last while you're climbing that pinnacle?"

Victor shrugged. "I don't know. I could end up like Dar; I don't think that dude's interested in love anymore."

"Dar isn't you! His passions are different. You may not have love as an Energy affinity, Victor, but you know you have a heart bigger than most normal people."

Victor gestured to himself. "I'm not much bigger than you right n—"

"Stop making light!"

Despite his earlier resolve to be understanding and mature, he blurted, "This is kind of what she said, you know."

"She?"

"Tes."

Valla's eyes widened, and then her brows drew down severely. "You mean about waiting for you to grow before you have a relationship with her?"

"Yeah. I mean, I'm just being honest. Valla, what *if* one of us finds a real love elsewhere, something stronger than what you and I feel right now?"

"Then . . ." She frowned, and Victor saw moisture pooling in her eyes, and his emotions responded. He felt his blood rushing and his throat tightening as she continued, "Then I suppose it wasn't meant to be."

"Bullshit!" Victor growled, reaching out to grab her and pull her close, kissing her again. She kissed him back, but then she pushed him away.

"Stop." Victor reached for her again. "Victor, really!" He growled and dropped his hands.

"This is stupid! If you love me, you love me! Why tempt fate?"

"I have faith that we'll come together again, Victor. My mind is set."

Victor stared at her for several long seconds. He knew her face too well to miss the determination in her eyes, the firm set of her lips, the slight upward tilt of her jaw—they all told him that he wouldn't be changing her mind with mere words. Could he do something dramatic? Could he beg or plead? He almost scoffed at the idea as it flashed through his mind; he had a good feeling that such a display would only assure her that she'd made the right decision. "So," he finally said, folding his arms over his chest. "What do I have to do to be 'ready' for your love?"

"It's not just you! It's me, Victor! Was I not plain enough? Was I too soft-spoken when I mentioned your shadow? You are driven, and that's one of the things I love about you, but I don't want to sit by, doing the sensible thing, putting my dreams on hold while you pursue anything that inspires you. I won't be kept safe like a figurine on a shelf."

"You don't have—"

"Victor. Please. Don't fight me anymore. Let me go and make my own—" She clamped her lips together, and a soft growl escaped her as she fought to think of the right word. Victor thought he understood, though, and he risked jamming his foot in his mouth by helping her complete the thought.

"Glory?"

Valla surprised him by chuckling. "Maybe. Maybe that's part of it, aye. You're going to be something great—that or you'll die. Either way, I won't be happy as I am."

"Is that what this is about? That duel I had with Cora's father? Are you worried about the duels I have to fight on Ruhn?"

"That's a piece of it!" Valla growled, balling one of her hands into a fist and thumping it against his chest. "Yes, that's a piece of it. I also want to be someone who achieves great things, though, and I don't want to do it by walking on the path that you make smooth with your efforts."

Victor unfolded his arms and took her fist in one hand, gently worming his thumb under her fingers until she relaxed them. "Listen, I want to scream and rage. I want to pick up that boulder over there and hurl it into the ocean. I don't want to end this time with you like that, though. If you're so determined, then let's enjoy this last night together. The hours I have before I enter that portal tomorrow have just become enormously valuable to me, and I don't want to spend them throwing a fit or fighting with you. Can we do that? Can we savor each other's company for a few hours more?"

Valla's eyes filled with tears again, and she sniffed, nodding quickly before falling into his arms, folding herself against his chest in the way only she knew how. Victor forced himself to take deep, even breaths, pushing his Energy back into his Core as it constantly tried to win free—his rage and fear were especially restless, and he knew, someday in the distant future, he might make a powerful cultivation template out of the memory of that moment.

# 2

## CHECKING IN

When Victor stepped out of the coach he'd hired in the city, he was a little surprised to find the lake house dark and quiet. A single lamp illuminated the front door, and only a dim, ambient nighttime glow shone through the windows. When he opened the front door, a startled servant looked up with wide eyes and hurried to take the door from his hands, motioning him in with a hasty "Welcome home, milord."

Victor frowned and fished his watch out of his pocket—every time he put it in a storage container, the time got messed up. He'd last used it in Sojourn, so he assumed it was accurate when it told him it was an hour past midnight. "Hi, Ranal. Everyone asleep?"

"I believe Sir Lesh is in his quarters, aye, but your other companions left two days ago intent on delving into a dungeon."

"Oh. Well, that's good, I suppose. Darren doing okay?"

"He's a bit out of sorts but eager to improve his bloodline advancement, sir. Excuse the gossip, but from what I hear, he's rather unhappy being in a . . . well, an in-between stage."

"Yeah, I can't blame him. What, uh, all changed?"

"Well . . ." The servant paused, looked left and right, and spoke in an even more hushed voice. "His head is adorned with lustrous feathers, and his eyes are quite large and, if I'm honest, fierce-looking. The biggest change, though, milord, is the beak. He's certainly adopting a type of avian bloodline."

"Huh. Yeah, I guess that would freak me out quite a bit—he probably doesn't look anything like his old self."

"Correct, milord. His long, handsome hair is gone, but I think his feathers are quite nice; they have a certain sheen to them—much finer than some of the other avian folk I've seen."

Victor chuckled, looking at the servant a little more closely. He certainly seemed to have a lot to say about Darren's appearance. After a moment's consideration, he shook his head and let the matter drop. "And Lord Dar?"

"He has anticipated your arrival and intends to have breakfast with you. Shall I wake the staff? Are you hungry now?"

"Nah. Thank you, Ranal. I'll plan for breakfast at the usual hour." Victor nodded to the slender, green-skinned man, then moved past him and into the house. He hadn't slept the night before and was eager to rest, but his first priority was to check on Lifedrinker. His boots, in their non-armor form, were comfortable and the soles soft, so he didn't make much noise as he moved through the house to the kitchen cellar and then down into the tunnels. He noticed a particular dampness to the air down there and, not for the first time, wondered if he'd find underground access to the lake if he took the time to explore.

His lack of knowledge regarding the extent of the tunnels would have concerned him or even dissuaded him from leaving Lifedrinker down there, but he knew Dar wouldn't let anything happen to the axe. Even so, he felt a little nervousness in his gut, a twinge of worry that he strangely welcomed—it took his mind off Valla and the fact that he'd returned to Sojourn alone.

He didn't use a light as he stalked through those tunnels; Victor's eyes were good, far better than he could have ever hoped. He saw great distances with ease, could focus on the tiniest of details up close, and in the dark, the faintest of glows served to provide him with clear, faintly sepia-tinted vision. When he'd first descended, the soft, pale illumination of the storage ring Dar had given him was enough to outline the tunnel walls and corners, but as he neared his destination, things grew brighter and tinted with a ghostly blue light. Victor inhaled sharply in anticipation as he saw the outline of the opening leading to his cultivation chamber.

It was limned in pale blue light, and a faint mist hung in the air, further adding to the mysterious appearance of the space. At first, he frowned, trying to remember what he'd left behind that glowed so, but a quick glance into his storage ring confirmed that he'd picked up his cultivation objects. Had he left behind a glow lamp? Victor knew he hadn't, but he supposed Dar might have stopped by to check on the axe and left a light. Still holding his breath, he put his fingers on the rough cold stone of the opening and peered inside.

"Holy shit, *chica!*" he gasped, for Lifedrinker sat alone in the space, and it was immediately apparent that she was the source of the illumination. Victor stood still, frozen in wonder, as he took her in with his eyes. Lifedrinker's haft, once dark and alive—wood that hinted at untold depths as tiny motes of light winked in the impenetrable grains—had grown to nearly eight feet in length. More than that, the ancient living-wood haft had taken on the metallic qualities of the "soul ore" Victor had left behind. It gleamed with a profound, lustrous sheen, and just as before, little blue stars twinkled in its depths, their number uncountable.

The change to her haft was only the beginning. Lifedrinker's axe-head had grown in size tenfold. A massive yard-long blade with an edge that bent the air with waves of radiated heat rested on the floor where the soul ore had once sat. The edge of that lethal-looking blade was buried several inches into the stone. Behind her edge, Lifedrinker's axe-head flared severely, broadening to several inches of heavy-looking dense dark metal that somehow seemed translucent and opaque at the same time—as if Victor could look through the top layer into a depthless expanse of darkness—a metallic window that could swallow light, matter, or even souls.

"*Chingado!*" he hissed through his teeth, approaching the massive weapon. Even giant as he was, the axe seemed like too much. He could see, if he stood her on her head and rotated the haft upward, that she'd be taller than his ten-foot frame. Even so, he reached a hand toward her haft and was rewarded by a surge of recognition, welcoming joy, and excitement when his fingers closed around the cool, surprisingly pliant, metal-wood hybrid material.

"*I did it, Victor! I conquered that ore and incorporated it into myself. I hope I've pleased you!*"

"Are you kidding me? You're fucking *amazing!*" Victor's smile only broadened as he wrapped his other hand around her haft and, with a grunt and a muscle-popping strain, lifted her off the floor. Her head was unwieldy for him, and he had to lean back for balance as gravity pulled it down. "Holy shit, *chica!*" Victor choked his grip up to the halfway point on the haft and found he could manage her better. "You're heavy, beautiful." It was true—if he were to make a guess, she was a good deal denser and heavier than Karl's gigantic axe.

"*When you're mad with the lust for battle, I'll be just right!*"

"Haha, true." Victor smiled and realized he was beaming from ear to ear when his cheeks began to feel the strain. "You make a good point. Shit, though, you're not going to fit in your harness anymore."

"*Try me in that magical container where you store your vile spirits.*"

"My cultivation objects?" Victor shrugged; Dar had assured him that the geists were safe within the device. Would a conscious weapon be different? "If you're sure. I'll . . . I'll just put you in for a second, and you can tell me how it feels, okay?"

"*Yes!*"

Hesitantly, Victor mentally selected his storage ring where his most valuable objects sat and *sent* Lifedrinker into it. He forced himself to count to two aloud and then summoned her out. "Are you okay?"

*"It's fine there, Victor. I can feel the outside—a trickle of ambient Energy drifts into the space constantly. While I love to have you hold me, is it not nice to know I can be with you even when your hands must be free?"*

"Yeah," Victor sighed and hefted her again, holding her crossways. He wanted to swing her around but didn't want to mutilate the tilework he'd done if he misjudged her weight and followed through a little too much. "Yeah, this is great, Lifedrinker. Shit! Imagine if we fought Lira now! I bet you'd shred her damn armor."

*"I would!"*

Victor lifted the axe so the edge was closer to his face, and he could feel the heat rippling away from her glossy, glass-like metallic edge. *"Damn,* you look sharp. I bet I could shave with that edge."

*"The heat of depthless, mountainous pressures bleeds from my edge, my battle-heart. Don't scald yourself!"*

"I won't! It was just a thought." He wondered if she was right; his feats and bloodline made him rather resilient to high temperatures. Still, it was with a wary, hesitant, feather-light movement that he quickly touched a finger against her edge. It stung immediately, despite his haste, and when he held his finger up, he saw flesh burned white with a sliver-thin cut at the center. *"Shit!"* He chuckled, watching his regenerative flesh slowly repair the damage. "Okay, beautiful, I'm putting you away for now. We'll get some practice soon."

*"Goodnight, blood-mate."*

Victor's eyebrows shot up at the new moniker, but he shrugged, taking it in stride. It wasn't the first time Lifedrinker had called him something like that. He sent her into his ring, and then, feeling a good deal lighter in his heart, he made his way up to the house. When he entered his room, he felt a veil of darkness close over his mind again when he looked at the bed and unconsciously pictured Valla lying there. Grumbling and growling, he hastily threw his clothes off and lay down on the rug, stretching out on his side with his head resting on one arm. He shoved the melancholy memories away, instead focusing on the positive things in his life.

With thoughts of Lifedrinker and imagined adventures on fantastical, distant worlds, he closed his eyes and quickly found sleep. To him, it felt as though a mere moment had passed when he heard the knock at his door and the soft, too-polite voice of Wensa, one of the younger staff members, calling, "Victor, sir, are you awake? Lord Dar requests you on the deck for breakfast."

Victor rolled over onto his back and put his hands under his head as he stared at the ceiling. He was stiff from lying on the floor, but his Quinametzin constitution wouldn't allow that to last long. Another knock on the door sounded. "Victor? Um, sir? Are—"

"I'm awake and on my way. Thank you!" With a grunt, Victor hopped onto his feet, pulling his clothes on. He swished a "cleansing draught" he'd picked up while shopping for odds and ends in Sojourn. When his gums began to tingle, he swallowed the apple-flavored fluid. Before he left, he used the restroom and checked his smile in the mirror. For some reason, he felt much lighter in spirit after only a few hours of sleep. He proceeded to the deck, where he found Dar sitting on a broad orange cushion at one of the low wooden tables.

The master Spirit Caster wore one of his usual loose-fitting, bright teal, silken pajama-like outfits. This one had a sigil stitched onto the breast that reminded Victor of a hippopotamus. "Good morning, Victor." Dar gestured to a matching cushion on the other side of the table. Victor folded his legs and sat.

"Good morning."

"I see you're back as scheduled and seem well rested." Dar paused while a pair of servants deposited a large glass of fresh-squeezed purple-colored fruit juice and a plate of eggs and sausages before Victor. "We're going to be very busy for the next few months. I'm not surprised your lady decided to stay back—I'm assuming that's the case, as she's not here."

"Yeah, Valla's back on Fanwath." Victor didn't feel the need to delve deeper into his personal matters.

"Mmhmm." Dar nodded and bit a fat sausage in half, chewing it noisily in his square-jawed, stony mouth for a moment. "While we dine, I'll tell you a bit about Ruhn's customs. Consider it your first lesson in etiquette."

"Okay." Victor took a sip of the juice; it was equally tart and sweet, providing a strangely addictive tang that had his taste buds flooding his mouth with saliva.

"First, it's customary to show more affection on Ruhn than on many civilized worlds. Don't be alarmed if a gentleman or lady leans in for a kiss on the cheek when they greet you or bid you farewell." Victor's eyebrows arched as he took a bite of eggs, but he didn't say anything. "Secondly, honor is paramount on Ruhn. To question a person's honesty is a dire insult. People will challenge each other to death duels for less."

Victor nodded. Considering they fought their wars with duels, it made sense to him. He was curious about one thing, however. "Is everyone like that, or just the nobility?"

"An astute question—the noble folk of Ruhn do not allow the common folk to slay one another out of hand. If a challenge is issued, the two parties must come before a magistrate who will determine the fairness of the contest. If one party is grossly outclassed, a suitable champion must be found, else the dispute must be settled in another way."

"I see. But, like, does crime still happen? Murders and whatnot?"

"Oh yes. People are people, Victor. Laws are not always adhered to." When Victor only nodded, Dar continued. "Let's see." He paused to sip his juice. "On Ruhn, feasts have a bit more ritual to them than you might be used to."

"Yeah?"

"Yes. They're seen as a time for entertainment as well as fine food, and all the guests at the high table will be expected to perform." Dar chuckled when Victor's eyes widened. "Relax, you'll be permitted to contribute in many ways—poetry, singing, playing a bit on an instrument, and even storytelling. I imagine you have a few battle stories you could share, no?"

"Um, I guess so." Victor shrugged. He hadn't ever considered himself a public speaker, but the speeches he'd been required to give during the campaign for the Untamed Marches had broken him of any fear in that regard.

"A pity you don't sing; such a voice—"

"Not really my thing, sir."

"Well, we'll see. For now, think of a few stories you might share; you'll need a repertoire, as I'm sure you'll be invited to many dinners." He glanced at Victor for another long moment. "Feats of skill are also considered entertainment. If you could bring forth the Paragon of the Axe . . ." Dar trailed off as Victor ate another sausage, then cleared his throat and changed the subject. "Gift giving is important on Ruhn. You should have a gift ready when you meet anyone of note. You should, likewise, be prepared to offer a valuable gift if you offend someone—an apology with no gift is considered more insulting than no apology. I'm sure Kynna will assign an assistant to you, someone to help remind you when such a thing is required."

"Kynna? That's your granddaughter?"

"Oh, aye. Haven't I said so before now? You should address her as 'Queen' or 'Lady Dar,' however. Hard to imagine that after all these centuries, they still bear my surname, don't you think?"

"How will they view me? I mean, coming from Sojourn at your request. Do they love you there? Hate you?" Victor had long since stopped worrying about Dar's emotions; the man only ever showed hints of anger—never sadness.

"Ah. I suppose most of my distant kin will be indifferent, though there are a few who seem to view me as a sort of deity—a, um, celestial ancestor who birthed a dynasty." Dar chuckled, and Victor was certain he looked a little embarrassed. "Though, a fallen dynasty, to be sure." He sighed heavily. "I certainly have neglected them. They're not my only kin, however, and there are people with no relation to me who require much of my time. Then there are my studies and research, my odysseys and conquests—" He snorted a short laugh and cut his words off with a wave of his hand. "Suffice it to say that some will love you immediately, some will hate you, and many will simply find you an oddity."

"Um, not to be rude, but will your kin look like you?" Victor cleared his throat and looked from side to side a little nervously before blurting, "I mean, your race?"

"Igniant?"

Victor's eyes bulged at the word. "Are you calling me ignorant or—"

"No, fool boy. Igniant is my species. To answer your question, I was the only one of my kind on Ruhn, and I'm sure my descendants will bear a small resemblance to me but lean more toward the natives of that world. Ruhnians are a race of giants who have close ties to the Fae. Well, they did a few tens of thousands of years ago. You'll find they look much like your own kind, though"—he chuckled—"perhaps a bit fairer."

Victor snorted. "Fairer? As in prettier?"

"Aye, lad. You're a handsome fellow, but your face is always declaring your intent to kill and slaughter." Victor just snorted again and put an entire sausage into his mouth, masticating it savagely. "That's another thing we'll need to work on. Table manners."

Victor swallowed his bite with a gulp, then drained his juice. "Okay, I get that I need to learn to behave myself in, um, Kynna's—"

"Queen Kynna's," Dar corrected.

"Right, Queen Kynna's court, but, Dar, I'm going to be fighting some tough *hombres*, yeah? Shouldn't we, like, get me ready? I need to learn how to advance some of my spells that have been stuck for ages. I need to practice with my axe. I need to get my armor upgraded. I need—"

"Enough!" Dar chopped his hand through the air. "I won't be hounded with your list of needs. Step one: Get to your cultivation chamber and don't come out until your cultivation technique is no longer 'advanced.' After that, we'll speak about your next lesson."

"Seriously?" Victor frowned, but he pushed his chair back from the table.

"Seriously. You'll figure it out. If it takes more than a month, I'll come to check on you." Dar grinned, displaying his large white teeth, then, to Victor's dismay, he stood, summoned his dragon-spirit mount, and flew away. Victor watched his diminishing form with his mouth hanging open.

"You kidding me? What the hell, man?" Grumbling with frustration, he stood and walked toward the cellar. If he had to improve his drill in order to get Dar to teach him what he wanted, then that was what he'd do.

# 3

## BALANCE

Darren looked at his plate, then up at Edeya, and made clicking sounds deep in his throat. She narrowed her eyes. "I forgot, Darren—is that one a happy sound or an annoyed one?"

"Happy! It's like a smile. I love chicken!"

"It's a chottle hen, according to the woman at the market." Edeya smiled, then returned to her spot beside Lam on the other side of the fire. Lam mock saluted with a drumstick from her own little roasted bird, then took a large bite. It had been Edeya's turn to cook, which Darren thought was lucky for her; they weren't yet in the dungeon but camped a short way outside, eager to enter as early as possible the next day—the soonest their entry slot allowed.

Trin cleared her throat. "It doesn't bother you that it's a, uh, bird?"

Darren *clicked*—a sound distinct from his earlier one with a longer windup and a more resonant final thump followed by a sort of hum. "I'm a thunderbird, Trin! A raptor! Haven't you ever seen a hawk take a quail?"

"I see. No, that makes sense. I've certainly seen hunters using hawks to kill game birds." While she spoke, Darren pulled the meat from the bones with his fingers and deposited huge hunks of flesh into his beak, swallowing the mouthfuls whole. He closed his eyes in pleasure, and a deep, thrumming hum sounded from his broad chest.

Licking some grease from her fingers, Lam commented, "I thought birds didn't really taste their food."

Darren opened his eyes and clicked happily. "First of all, I'm not exactly a bird. I'm an *avian* species now, or, well, on my way to being one. According to Brimi, we're different from birds in quite a few ways. Anyway, eating is . . . different. I feel a wave of pleasure with each bite. It's not exactly a taste so much as a . . . I don't know how to describe—wait! I do. It's very similar to an early buzz from alcohol! I get this warm feeling that spreads through me and makes me a little giddy. Different foods give it a different feel, too."

"Not veggies, though?" Edeya asked because Darren had explicitly asked her to leave her stewed carrots off his plate.

"Nah, I get nothing from 'em. Mostly meats."

Edeya nodded. "It's so strange how much deeper your voice is, Dare."

"Eh, it's still me, though, Dey-dey." Darren put an entire drumstick in his beak and crunched it to pieces before swallowing it down. His beak was incredibly durable, and he'd found that if he guided food with his fingers, he could efficiently masticate hunks of bone that would've given a Rottweiler a challenge.

"I know." Edeya smiled and took another dainty bite. Darren leaned back and watched the three women eat for a moment, giving them a chance to catch up. He'd been dismayed, at first, by his new physiology, but after a few days at the lake house, experimenting with food and practicing his speech, he'd begun to warm up to the new features. Not every change had been alarming; some had been immediately positive. His newfound height, his sturdier body, and his fantastic vision had done a lot to make up for the utterly foreign face he saw in the mirror. Putting those things aside, he was also excited by the prospect of growing powerful wings and learning more about his bloodline.

After a while, he grew tired of waiting and tossed the remainder of his bird into his beak, swallowing it whole, bones and all. It was a mouthful, and he felt it going down, but something had changed in his neck; he felt as if he'd never choke anymore, and the sensation was pleasurable, like having an itch scratched, but on the inside. He stifled a burp, then pulled out his Sojourn guidebook, a crystalline tablet enchanted with all sorts of interesting information. He was particularly interested in the section about the dungeon they would be entering the next day.

When he found the correct page, he read the section he was interested in aloud for the benefit of his groupmates. "Ahem. 'The Fungal Fortress is known for its daunting challenges for Tier Two iron rankers, but even more so for its healthy list of rare growth treasures. While these treasures are rare, and only one in every dozen dungeon runs results in a single drop, their value makes up for the infrequency. If your party is able to claim a slot, it's certainly an investment in time that has the potential for excellent payoffs. See the table below for a list of the known growth item drops.'"

He looked up. "Want me to read the table?"

"You already showed us yesterday, Dare." Edeya walked over and took his plate. "You're cooking breakfast, right?"

He nodded. "Easy." He wasn't hurt that no one wanted to hear the list again. He'd pored over the tablet for days, trying to find the dungeon with the best chance of providing another racial advancement item. Everyone knew why; Darren was desperate to get his wings and push past his awkward, in-between status of half-human, half-avian. The Fungal Fortress had the best chances, and though Trin was the only member of their party who'd reached Tier Two, they were all close.

Lam handed her plate to Edeya, then nodded to Trin. "I'm just glad Trin's brother got us on the entrant list. The usual wait time is nearly two months."

"My father might be an evil sociopath, but some of my kin are redeemable." Trin produced a fancy wine bottle with a gold-embossed label. "Shall we?" Everyone scrambled to agree, furnishing their own glasses. Darren summoned a glass, but when Trin got around to him, she took it, filled it up, and then handed him the bottle, still nearly half full. "I'll take your glass, Darren. You'll find it easier to pour the bottle into your beak."

"Oh." Darren took the bottle, then cocked his head to the side, his throat clicking the way it always did when he felt like smiling. "That's considerate of you, Trin."

"I've had many avian friends, Dare." She poked him in the chest. "Cheers." She held out her glass, and Darren knocked his bottle against it. Lam and Edeya hurried over to clink their glasses against his bottle.

"Cheers!" everyone echoed, and then Darren poured a good portion of wine into his gullet, laughing as he swallowed it down, and a warm buzz began to tingle in his chest and face.

Victor stood and stretched. He'd just spent his eleventh night sleeping on the floor of his cultivation chamber. Most of his time during those eleven days had been spent doing exactly what the chamber implied—cultivating. However, even though it wasn't exactly a physically taxing activity, he periodically found himself feeling exhausted to the point where he'd lie down, close his eyes, and immediately drift away. He didn't resist those urges to sleep; something in him was worn out from the cultivation, and he always felt better, more hopeful, and less frustrated when he awoke.

"Frustration," Victor muttered, retrieving some bread, sausages, and honey from his storage ring. The word went a long way toward describing how he'd felt during the last ten days. He knew he was doing the cultivation technique that Dar had taught him correctly. He could pull large currents of attuned Energy into his Core, and watch it absorb and become part of his Core, but for whatever reason, he couldn't see what he was doing that wasn't . . . optimal, he supposed, was the right way to describe it. According to Dar, the technique was capable of epic tier cultivation, but it had to be done perfectly.

Part of Victor's frustration was with the master's hands-off teaching style. He knew Victor wasn't doing something quite right, but he wouldn't show him what it was. Of course, Victor was no ancient master with thousands of years of experience, so he couldn't really argue about the man's teaching methods. Maybe he knew what he was talking about. Maybe when Victor finally figured it out, he'd learn as much from the discovery as he would from the proper technique. He chuckled and stood, intent on doing some stretches and calisthenics to warm himself up for the day's work.

As was his routine, he first summoned a Globe of Insight, filling the chamber with clarifying, white-gold light. Then, he cast Inspiration of the Quinametzin—probably the most significant factor in his maintained sanity. As the spell filled his body and mind with optimistic, steady inspiration, the dreary despondency he'd begun to dwell upon fled before its clarifying light. He nodded confidently and started to go through his routine of stretches and body-weight exercises—everything from planks to pushups to air squats. It wasn't something he *had* to do—his Quinametzin constitution and enormous vitality would keep him fit for tremendous periods of inactivity—but it still felt good, and, with his blood flowing more vigorously, he felt more confident in success.

After a while, he sat down at the center of his chamber, his four cultivation objects arrayed around him—he'd left his magma-attuned cultivation treasure in his storage ring. He wasn't sure how, but he felt as though he *knew* the added step of cultivating his Breath Core while he worked on his Spirit Core would only muddy the waters. "One drill at a time." He chuckled, as though confirming to himself that he'd made the right decision. He spread his arms, closed his eyes, and, with his fingers outstretched and loose, wriggled them, willing his inner eye to feel the way the thick currents of Energy in the chamber danced along his fingertips.

After a few minutes of breathing, watching the Energy tendrils around him course through the air on their currents, rebuffed by the enchanted stone lining of his chamber as they tried to drift away, he slowly began his drill. He pushed a weave of his Core's four different Energy types out through his pathways, sending it out through the chamber, circulating, coiling, and weaving its way around as he pulled more and more of the ambient Energy into it. The coil thickened, and the weave tried to pull apart, but he held it tight with his will, guiding it along a perfect path back into his pathways and his Core.

As the Energy flowed into the construct at the center of his Core space, Victor watched the weave pull apart as each constituent Energy type found its home: Bright, cheerful inspiration sank into the orb at the heart. Brilliant, enthusiastic glory wrapped into the golden band closest to the center. Baleful, bloodthirsty rage found its home in the equally furious deep red ring. And, finally, the glowering, doom-filled, purple-black tendril of fear-attuned Energy found its home in the dark ring that encircled them all.

As the Energies found their homes, his Core brightened, and the rings moved more quickly. Victor watched them, intent on finding the key to his cultivation technique that he'd missed so many times—hundreds or thousands—since Dar had taught it to him. Once again, he failed to see what he'd missed. The Energy settled in, his Core resumed its usual pace, and Victor, fighting the usual frustration, began the process anew.

Twelve hours later, after nearly thirty more cultivation cycles, Victor didn't feel any closer to solving his problem. One thing he was near, though, was ranking up his Core. He could tell it was close because its usual, slow, deliberate pulse had quickened, and he could feel the palpable *thump* of pressure as it throbbed. He paused to watch it, wondering if the next cycle would push it over. It would be his first new rank in the epic tier of his Core's development.

The pulse was almost hypnotic, and perhaps because of its increased intensity, Victor noticed it wasn't a single beat, but that it had a transient quality. The pulse began at the heart, in the center of his inspiration-attuned Energy sphere, but it traveled out through the rings of other Energies. With the more rapid, frenetic quality it had taken on as his drills had made the Core heavy and swollen with Energy, one pulse began before the previous one propagated the whole. This constant stream of beats made it clear that what Victor had taken for a simple flash was actually a sort of shift in the position of the Core; it moved ever so slightly as the *thump* of Energy went through the rings, especially when it hit the heavy, dense, fear-attuned one.

Victor focused his entire attention on the process, watching as the next pulse flashed at the center of his Core, then moved up through the rings, first inspiration, then rage, then fear. With the pulse, it almost seemed that the rings of rage, fear, and glory around his inspiration sphere had taken on an orbiting quality. Glory and rage were separated by something like twenty degrees and rotated near the horizontal axis of the inspiration globe, while fear stood alone, rotating nearly diagonally, twenty or so degrees from the vertical axis.

When the pulse moved through the thinner, closer bands of glory and rage, the entire Core shifted toward them slightly. When it passed through fear, however, the Core noticeably surged toward that ring. For the first time, Victor wondered if the problem with his drill had nothing to do with his gathering of Energy but rather how it flowed into his Core. Was it out of balance? Could he move those rings?

With an effort of will, Victor grasped ahold of his fear-attuned ring of Energy and *pulled* it toward the vertical axis of his Core. It resisted, heavy with Energy as it was, but Victor was resolute, and his will was like an implacable force of nature as he bore down. Eventually, the ring shifted to where he wanted it, circling his Core at the dead center, straight up and down from his point of view.

Now, as it pulsed, the Core shifted massively, jerking up and then down, snapping back into place as the pulse ended, but immediately bouncing again as the next pulse fired. It was dizzying to watch, and Victor felt unwell deep in his being. Fearing he'd done something stupid, something that would prove his undoing if he didn't figure it out quickly, he grasped ahold of his rage-attuned ring and pulled it toward the horizontal axis. As he did so, he immediately felt some relief; it was balancing his fear-attuned ring, if not perfectly, then much better than it had been.

Victor shifted his attention to his glory-attuned ring. If he was right, all he needed to do to balance the "gravity" of his Core was to find the perfect position between his rage- and fear-attuned rings for this third one. Sure enough, as he pulled it toward the center of the diagonal axis between rage and fear, he felt the shudder of his Core reduce more and more. Now, the pulses flashed through his Core, and the strange *thump* was nearly gone. With careful precision, Victor tugged on the glory-attuned ring, balancing his fear by moving it just a tiny bit closer to his rage-attuned ring.

As he found the perfect balance, Victor wasn't rewarded with any System message or sudden tangible award, but he knew it was right. He could *feel* the balance, and moreover, he could see the flashes of his Core's pulsing, throbbing beat flow through his Core without even the slightest wobble. He likened it to tuning an engine—the idle was smooth and steady. Smiling, pleased at the balanced aspect of his Core, he began another cultivation cycle.

Nothing seemed all that different as he went through the motions, but when he brought the streams of thick woven Energies into his Core, they separated and flowed into his Core much more evenly. Before, he'd often have strands of rage and glory left over before his fear-attuned Energy was fully absorbed, but this time, they all entered his Core evenly. More than that, as the streams of Energy flooded their respective rings, they began to spin rapidly, rotating around his Core and creating a sort of draft.

Victor immediately recognized what was happening and seized the opportunity, cycling through another cultivation round, pulling more Energy into his Core space that was instantly snatched up by the pull of his Core's newfound rotational gravity. As that new stream of Energy began to absorb, Victor began a third round of cultivation and had it ready, already entering his pathways as the previous was pulled in. His mouth spread in a triumphant grin as his cultivation cycle took on a life of its own. All he had to do was weave the Energies; the current his Core had created in the chamber was enough to pull them into his pathways.

Victor lost himself in the giddiness of his success. He'd emptied the ambient Energy from his chamber and pulled streams of attuned Energy directly from his cultivation treasures. He wove them as fast as they could provide the Energy, and his Core pulled them in. Soon, though, the pressure in his Core space became almost agonizing as the pulses intensified into a steady stream, one after the other. They bled into one another, and soon, the density and brightness of his Core made it hard for him to observe it with his inner eye. Just as he contemplated stopping and taking a break, it broke through.

With a tremendous spike of Energy that surged through his body, his Core seemed to *crunch* down on itself, and the backwash was so intense that his cultivation chain broke. Victor fell flat on his back, panting and staring at the ceiling as System messages flashed across his vision. Ignoring them for the moment, he turned to his inner eye and observed his Core. It pulsed almost lazily now, a steady, heavy wave of Energy propagating through the somehow heavier, denser rings. Even without reading the messages awaiting him, he knew it had ranked up.

"All right," he grunted, turning his attention to the messages:

*****Congratulations! You have learned a new skill: Spirit Core Cultivation Drill, Epic.*****

*****Congratulations! Your Spirit Core has advanced: Epic 2.*****

"Damn," he grunted when he realized that he only had two messages; it had felt like more. He'd hoped the advancement would be enough to push him to the next level. Nevertheless, he pulled up his Energy statistics to see how much he'd gained from the Core rank-up:

| Breath Core: | Elder Class: Improved 3 | | |
|---|---|---|---|
| Core: | Spirit Class: Epic 2 | | |
| Breath Core Affinity: | Magma: 9 | Breath Core Energy: | 2200/2200 |
| Energy Affinity: | Fear 9.4, Rage 9.1, Glory 8.6, Inspiration 7.4, Unattuned 3.1 | Energy: | 35045/35045 |

"A thousand, huh?" Victor pushed himself back into a sitting position. He'd gained five thousand when he broke into "epic," and now it seemed he'd earn another thousand for each rank therein. He supposed that was better than the one hundred he'd gained in previous tiers. Still, for all the work he'd done over the last eleven days, it felt a little underwhelming.

"Well, apprentice, I certainly felt that!" Dar's voice sounded from the entrance to his chamber. "It seems you managed that more quickly than I'd feared. Excellent. Let's celebrate with a meal, and perhaps I'll teach you a bit about proper spirit walking. How does that sound?"

Victor hopped to his feet, turning to see his master in a migraine-inducing set of magenta pajamas decorated with hypnotic yellow swirls. "What the hell are you wearing?" Victor cleared his throat and held up a hand. "Sorry, that was rude. I mean, but seriously, Dar. That suit's making me dizzy."

Dar lifted the hem of his shirt and frowned. "You don't like it? The saleswoman said it was the latest fashion on Foh." He saw Victor's confusion and clarified, "That's the homeworld of some of Sojourn's more influential citizens. I bought it to attend a gala at Lord Drok's estate last night. Is it so bad?"

"I mean, to me, but . . ." Victor trailed off, shrugging. He moved closer to his master and clapped him on the shoulder. "What do I know?"

"Indeed. You're young and have hardly traveled. Come, Victor, let's eat—I've been drinking and carousing for twenty hours."

# 4

⸎

# FRIENDS AND ENEMIES

After they emerged from the catacombs beneath his home, Dar led Victor into the main parlor and said, "Why don't you take a shower and freshen up, and then we'll go out. Tell your dragonkin friend that he's welcome to join us. I had plans to dine with Lo'ro, but when I felt your breakthrough, I thought it a good opportunity for you to let off a little steam. He won't mind the extra company."

"At his home?"

"Ha, no." Dar chuckled. "He may be a friend, but I've no taste for death-attuned environs." He glanced down at his hypnotic attire. "I'll get myself cleaned up—too much powerful drink can wear a man out. I'm in need of some hearty food. Meet me back here in twenty minutes."

Victor nodded, squinting at the windows. He'd utterly lost track of the days, let alone the time while he'd been down in the cultivation chamber. The setting sun was bright in the sky, and it felt good on his face as he looked out toward the lake. "I'll let Lesh know." As Dar nodded, Victor walked toward the front door where he could be sure a servant was always on duty. He didn't have to go that far, though, before Mr. Ruln approached from the direction of the kitchens.

"Looking for something, Sir Victor?"

"Do you know where Lesh is?"

"Ah! Sir Lesh is currently sparring with a guest on the recreation field."

"Oh?" Victor's eyebrows shot up. "That's good! Thanks, Mr. Ruln." As the steward nodded, Victor hurried out the front door and down the path toward the outdoor recreation area where he and Lesh often practiced. Long before he arrived, he heard the grunts and *thuds* as two very large men exchanged blows and grappled. When he rounded the corner, Victor was thrilled to see Lesh grappling with Drobna, the turtle-like berserker he'd battled in the Vault of Valor. He paused on the edge of the sand-covered field and watched, waiting for the two men to notice him.

Victor could see that Drobna wasn't berserk; his muscles were swollen with power, but he was clearly not enraged. Watching them exchange blows and struggle to throw each other, Victor wondered if Drobna's Berserk ability differed from his own. He wondered if he'd advanced it to the epic tier and, if so, whether or not he'd gained Iron Berserk as an ability evolution. He watched and contemplated such things for nearly five minutes, but when the two showed no signs of pausing their struggles, he finally called out, "Lesh! Do you want to join Dar and me for dinner?" When the two fighters looked his way, he added, "Hey, Drobna! You're welcome to join, of course."

"Victor!" Lesh laughed, releasing Drobna and jogging over the sand toward him. "You've finally come out of your cave!" Drobna followed him over, brushing his large greenish-brown hands together.

Victor laughed. "I did! At long last, I've come out of hibernation!"

Drobna stood beside Lesh, clapping the black-scaled dragonkin on the shoulder. "I'm pleased to see you, Victor. When can I claim that promised sparring match?"

"Soon. In fact, I'll corner Master Dar at dinner tonight to get him to commit to some kind of schedule. I need regular practice." He reached out a hand, and Drobna took it in a firm grip. "Join us?"

"It's a wonderful offer, and I'm sure I'll be gnashing my beak in frustration later tonight, but I must decline. My wife's parents are hosting a small event, and if I don't attend, I'll be sleeping outside for a month."

Lesh chuckled, a deep, almost growl-like sound, and elbowed the Berserker. "You'd miss a chance to dine with a great master? Your wife must have a weighty hand."

"Ha!" Drobna shrugged. "She does, I can't deny. I fear her wrath a great deal more than I value the attention of even the great lords of Sojourn."

"Don't worry about it, man." Victor gave his hand a final squeeze and let go. "I'm glad you've been keeping Lesh busy. I'll reach out with our training schedule for the next few months, okay?"

"Yes! I'm eager to see if we might have a secret or two to share with each other." He turned to Lesh. "I suppose that brings our session to an end?"

"Yes! I'll not miss a dinner with Victor and the mighty Ranish Dar!"

"Until next time, then." Drobna waved and started down the path. Victor grabbed Lesh's shoulder and pulled him along behind the shelled warrior.

"We need to hurry. Dar's leaving in about fifteen minutes."

Lesh nodded, quickening his steps. "I must rinse this sweat and blood from my scales, and then I'll be ready!"

Eighteen minutes later, Victor and Lesh, both freshly washed, climbed into Dar's coach. The master Spirit Caster was already inside and, to Victor's relief, wore a fresh set of silken pajama clothes. These were solid emerald green and much easier on his eyes. As he and Lesh took their seats, Dar smiled and gestured to a tray of drinks—large tumblers filled with rich amber liquid. "Have a drink, men. I'm pleased you joined us, Lesh!"

"Thank you for the invitation, Lord Dar." Lesh picked up one of the tumblers and drained it in a single gulp. Victor chuckled and took a more restrained sip, well aware of how strong Dar's liquors were.

"I have something for you. I was waiting until Victor was finished with his seclusion in the cultivation cave, and I think now would be a good time to present it."

Victor looked into Dar's fiery eyes and raised an eyebrow. "Is this the—"

"It is! Lord Roil was loathe to hand it over; he was rather irritated that you slipped away before the council could question you, but I pointed out that you were not obligated to do so." Dar chuckled, shaking his head. "Oh, you should have seen him fume when Lady Rexa wrested control of the dungeon from him."

"Wait, what?"

"I spoke to her in confidence about what was taking place in the dungeon. After you told me of the children's plight and your promises to aid them, I felt obligated to seek her advice."

"But what about Ronk—"

Dar held up a hand, shaking his head. "Remember your promise, Victor. Lesh is an ally, but he's not part of that man's trust. Rest assured that I wrung a promise out of Lady Rexa; she will aid the children and not interfere with other matters." Again, he chuckled, a deep sound like large plates of stone grinding against each other. "To be honest, I believe she prefers it that way." He turned back to Lesh. "That's all beside the point, however. The council owed Victor another prize, and he chose to request a cultivation item for you."

"What?" Lesh's eyes opened wide, and he looked from Dar to Victor. "You didn't have to do that, Lord Victor!"

"Come on, Lesh! Just Victor. Don't worry about it, anyway. I promised I'd help you figure out how to cultivate your Breath Core, and you can't do that without something to cultivate from."

Dar nodded. "Exactly so." He held out his hand, and a heavy-looking metallic box with a rounded lid appeared in his broad palm. "When I demanded your prize, I thought the council would open its coffers and purchase your friend an Energy heart attuned to acid. I was rather surprised when Kreshta Griss provided this treasure instead. Fear not; she was reimbursed by the council." Dar lifted the top of the dull-gray box, revealing an interior filled with dark, moist soil and a single sprout of green rising from the center. As soon as the lid was clear, the little sprout began to exude green vapors that hissed in the air as they climbed toward the ceiling.

Dar quickly replaced the cover, but not before everyone got a whiff of the caustic gas. Victor's eyes immediately began to water, and he leaned back, holding his breath. Lesh, however, leaned forward, eyes alight. "It's potent!"

"Aye, very." Dar nodded, holding the box out to Lesh. "A venom petal orchid. It's something of a misnomer; there's no venom involved. It exudes pure acid-attuned Energy vapors." As Lesh gingerly took the box, he added, "You may find a place in my gardens to plant it—distant from the house, please."

"Thank you, Lord Dar!" Lesh tried to bow, sitting down, but his bulky body didn't accommodate such a maneuver easily, and he almost tumbled out of his seat.

"Thank Victor. He gave up a treasure of his own for this."

"We already went over this!" Victor laughed, again clapping Lesh on the shoulder. "It's nothing." He turned to Dar. "Thank you, though, Dar, for keeping the council honest and for going to Lady Rexa for help with the children. I made a promise to a kid—young man—in there, and I'm pleased to see he'll be getting some help. I, uh, hope it didn't cost you anything."

"Cost? No, rather, I *gained* something in the bargain. Rexa has a soft spot for children. She may be Fae, but she's a Summer Fae, and they love life. She was pleased that I shared the secrets of that place with her."

Victor nodded, and they rode in silence for a few minutes. The coach was Dar's best—swift and smooth—if Victor couldn't see out the window, he wouldn't have realized they'd even taken flight. Lesh put his treasure away, but only after having Dar inspect his storage container to ensure it was suitable. Victor thought about the little sprout inside the box and pictured himself and Lesh planting it. Then, an idea occurred to him. "Should we build some kind of cultivation chamber around that plant?"

"The Energy is in the form of a mist, so I would think a canopy would suffice. Something domed with open sides so the flower can still get light when the sun rises and sets. I'll have Mr. Ruln collect the supplies—I'd like to ensure they're aesthetically pleasing since you'll be building it in my garden."

"Thanks." Victor grinned and elbowed Lesh, who was also grinning. His snout made it look more like a hungry leer, however. "Getting excited? Soon, your Breath Core is going to rank up!"

"I'm more than excited. I'd like to get started immediately—"

"Tomorrow will be soon enough." Dar chuckled. "Victor and I are hungry." Lesh began to reply, but Dar spoke over him, pointing out the window. "We're here." Victor followed his pointing finger with his eyes and saw that they were coming in for a landing near the top of one of Sojourn's enormous crystalline spires. This was the first time Victor had been up to those heights while in the downtown area. The spectacle was enough to strike him dumb.

High Sojourn, as the heights were colloquially known, was off-limits to the likes of Victor and Lesh. At least, he'd thought so. Looking out there, he could see the nearly invisible walkways with their faint, iridescent sheen, stretching from spire to spire, arching over and under one another in a weirdly beautiful tangle. They weren't crowded—there were only a few thousand veil walkers in Sojourn—but the people Victor saw were interesting enough to make up for their small numbers.

A woman with a great bulbous black spider's body marched by, descending an arching crystal span toward a round-capped tower with gem-studded stars and moons adorning its dome. Passing above her, a blue-fleshed man strode— he was easily thirty feet tall and moved his long, slender legs ponderously. He wore a toga that seemed to be crafted of silvery mist. Before Victor could closely examine any of the other folk passing nearby, Dar jostled him and gestured toward the door.

"Come, Victor. We should hurry into the restaurant before I have to defend my right to bring you two here."

Victor nodded, blinking his eyes rapidly and chuckling as he exited to stand near Lesh. The dragonkin was similarly dumbstruck, staring over the edge of the crystalline pier where their coach had set down. Victor followed his gaze and felt a spinning sense of vertigo when he saw the towers stretching down toward the distant ground where ant-like people crowded the streets. He quickly looked away, grasping his friend's shoulder. "Holy shit," he laughed. "Didn't realize how damn high these towers go."

"Come." Dar, leading the way, gestured to the nearby tower. The crystal walkway expanded near the tower into a wide ring. Victor immediately felt strangely out of place when he saw the floor-to-ceiling glass windows and brightly lit signage; it reminded him of a sci-fi movie more than anything else. They'd stepped out of Sojourn's luxurious, high-fantasy medieval setting and into a weird alien city from a futuristic film. At least that's what his imagination told him, even though he knew that Energy and enchantments powered everything around him.

The sign that hung above the doorman's station, glowing in bright neon oranges and yellows, proclaimed the restaurant as Sunset's Rest. As they approached the door, the man standing ready to open it leapt into action, bowing stiffly before pulling it wide. "Welcome, Lord Dar. Your table is ready."

Dar flicked something to him that glimmered, and he deftly caught it. Before Victor could wonder what it was, they were inside, and the door was swinging shut behind them. Dar turned to regard Victor and Lesh and gestured to the wide open dining room. Black tables that gleamed like cut and polished opal dotted the midnight-blue floor. They were almost all occupied by interesting folk, but Victor couldn't focus on the people; he was too taken by the fact that the walls surrounding the dining room were wide open to balconies with crystal-clear railings, allowing for an unobstructed view of the High Sojourn skyline.

Just as he'd stared from the coach, Victor found himself doing so again. His eyes traced the crystalline walkways, the colorful spires, and the strange, fantastical people walking about in the distance. Lesh gave him a nudge, and Victor started walking, following Dar through the dining room to a table where Lo'ro sat, adorned as usual in black robes and sipping from a tall glass of blue fizzing liquid. Standing close, Victor realized the table was high, suited for a man of Dar's or Victor's stature, but Lo'ro's chair was tall and allowed him to sit at a comfortable height.

"Lo'ro," Dar greeted the Death Caster with a nod. "Apologies for our tardiness."

"No need, no need." Lo'ro smiled and regarded Victor and Lesh. "I didn't realize you were bringing your apprentices."

Dar chuckled and sat down, then gestured to the two empty seats. "Sit, men." He turned back to Lo'ro. "I'll claim only Victor. Lesh'ro'zellan is his companion."

"Lesh'ro'zellan, is it?" Lo'ro openly stared at Lesh as he took a seat and pulled his chair in. "Well met, dragonkin." Lesh hurried to stand again, but Lo'ro waved him back down. "Relax, young man. How interesting! Dar, you always surprise me. I had no idea you had someone from Ashenshoal at your house."

At that moment, Victor wished he had a camera pointed at Lesh's face. The dragonkin's mouth hung open, and his eyes bulged as he practically choked. He coughed to cover his surprise, then asked, "You know of Ashenshoal?"

"Naturally! The birthplace of Zoh'ka'drul? He violently conquered a few worlds in allegiance with the Bloodmoon Triumvirate before succumbing to the Dread Scourge. He almost won through, but those were Vesavo Bonewhisper's most bloodthirsty years, and his undead legions were merciless." He laughed and sipped his drink. "I'm sorry, Dar—I'm already a bit drunk. Forgive my rambling."

Victor had watched Lesh during the little exchange and saw only confusion in his friend's eyes; he figured it was a safe bet that Lesh had never heard of Zoh'ka'drul. He wanted to ask Lo'ro more about the story; he was interested in Vesavo's history, if only because he was helping Arona to escape him, but Dar spoke first. "Nonsense. We're celebrating. Victor had a breakthrough today." He waved a hand, and a server hurried over. She was a petite, elfin-looking young woman wearing a shimmering black dress that clung to her figure—all the servers seemed to be women, and all were similarly dressed.

While Dar ordered drinks, Victor leaned closer to Lo'ro. "What's the 'Dread Scourge'?"

"That was the teeming mass of undead Vesavo led from world to world, conquering in the name of death and revenge. I was one of his lieutenants back then. Some might say I was his right-hand man, but they'd be wrong; his infatuation with Shivana kept the rest of us firmly on the periphery. Those days are long over, however. We've been rather lazy these last few centuries, idling about Sojourn. I wonder how many of his worlds he still holds."

"Seventeen," Dar said immediately.

"Is that all?" Lo'ro laughed and shook his head. "He was so hell-bent on conquering the Greensap Ascendancy—I swear he held more than a hundred at the height of his power."

Dar chuckled. "Don't downplay your part. I believe he handed off a dozen or so to you during that expansion."

"True, true. Though I was never one for ruling—I'm more at home in my laboratories." Lo'ro sighed, then finished his drink. As he set it on the table, Victor's eyes were drawn to his long, corpselike fingers with their polished black nails. He didn't realize he was staring until Lo'ro cleared his throat and startled him by saying, "Victor! You've recently come out of a harrowing experience, haven't you? I heard both the Volpuré boy and dear, lovely Arona Moonshadow perished, yet you emerged hale." Victor experienced a moment of panic at those words; he'd forgotten that Lo'ro had been somewhat obsessed with Arona.

Dar saved him, though, thumping the table and proclaiming, "That's right, he did! Now, a toast!" Victor hadn't realized the server had returned, but she was there, reaching up to deposit tall, slender, fluted glasses before each of them. They were filled to the brim with steaming orange liquid, and Victor caught a faint whiff of something like vanilla as he leaned close to inspect the drink.

Dar picked up his glass and held it out. "I'm inspired by Lo'ro's ramblings about empires and great wars. I, too, have conquered a place or two; in fact, my army's destruction of Lo'ro's forces led me to befriend this dastardly rascal. How many years in my prison did you languish, old friend?"

Lo'ro's skeletally thin face always looked angry to Victor. Even when he smiled, it looked as if he was preparing to devour someone alive. Still, even with that evil rictus grin, his voice was light when he replied, "Seventy-nine years, Dar. Seventy-nine years in which we played at least a thousand games of Fortitude. We became fast friends over that marble table, didn't we?"

"We did. So—to friends!" Dar held his glass up, but before anyone could join in the toast, he added, "And enemies." Victor suddenly felt like a child having dinner with a couple of old tigers, as if they might destroy him with a careless swipe of their paws. Hearing them talk of conquering worlds and fighting world-spanning empires was a little daunting, not to mention that they'd apparently been mortal enemies in the past. Victor locked eyes with Lesh and raised an eyebrow. He could tell the dragonkin was thinking similar thoughts.

"To friends," Victor said, touching his glass to Lo'ro's and then to Lesh's and Dar's.

"And enemies, Victor." Lo'ro leered as he leaned close. "Never forget to thank your enemies. They make you what you are." He nodded to Dar. Victor downed his drink, and it burned like acid. In fact, both he and Lesh belched loudly, and smoke erupted from their mouths.

"Ha!" Dar laughed. "Another!"

# 5

## SPIRIT WALK

Victor jogged along the lakeshore, loping easily over the scattered rocks, driftwood, briar tangles, and other obstacles in his path. It was late afternoon on the day after his celebratory dinner with Dar, Lo'ro, and Lesh, and Victor was feeling good, though pleasantly weary after a long day of sparring in the circle with Lesh and Drobna, who'd come early after a last-minute invitation. Now, though, Victor was heading to a spot where Dar had instructed him to await his presence.

His mentor had refused to elaborate on the purpose of their meeting or why Victor had to make his way through the seldom-traveled parts of Dar's property to meet in a secluded grove on the far side of the lake. The demand had come up when Victor asked about a regular training schedule. Dar had been drunk—as they all had been—and had put off the conversation, saying simply that Victor would have the day to exercise his weapon skills but that he must be in the "fath" grove across the lake at sundown. Luckily, when Victor asked Mr. Ruln what a fath tree was, the steward could point one out on the property—a tall, white-barked deciduous variety with hand-sized, fan-shaped leaves.

So, Victor ran along the lakeshore, eyes peeled for a cluster of similar trees, enjoying the light exercise in the cool late-afternoon air. As he ran, he couldn't stop his mind from wandering, and despite his efforts to the contrary, it often found its way to subjects he'd rather avoid; chief among them was Valla. He'd been doing well, he reckoned, considering his nearly two weeks of seclusion in the cultivation chamber, to avoid those melancholy musings, but now, for some reason, she kept coming to mind as he ran.

He had a strange hollow feeling every time she came to mind. He felt a little like he'd done something wrong or that he'd lost something precious, even when he reminded himself of Valla's words. He tried to keep in mind that she was just trying to see what she could accomplish outside his shadow, exploring her own interests and giving them both a chance to grow and learn and become the people they were meant to be. Still, every time he remembered that she wouldn't be back at the house or ready to accompany him to dinner or whatever adventure came next when he finished with Dar's business on Ruhn, it felt final.

The other half of the matter was that Valla hadn't argued enough—for his tastes—about what would happen if either of them met someone they fell for. Victor, obviously, was more concerned about the idea of Valla loving someone else. The thought rankled something deep in his spirit and reminded him of how he used to feel when he couldn't control his rage. He kept picturing Valla with a faceless man, someone holding her hand, kissing her—loving her. It made his gut twist, and he had to remind himself that he didn't *own* Valla. If they were apart for years or decades or—God forbid—centuries, how could he expect her to spend all her time alone?

As he spied the tops of tall white-barked trees on a nearby hillside, he tried to conclude his ponderings on his relationship by telling himself that the answer to his unrest was to throw himself into training. The discipline would be good for him, and when he went to Ruhn, he knew he'd have plenty to keep him occupied—people to meet, the wonders of a distant world to see, and best of all, duels to fight. He found a path meandering up the hillside and slowed to a walk as he ascended toward the grove.

His feet crunched on gravel, and birds by the dozen chirped in the nearby treetops, helping bring Victor back to the present as he grounded himself with slow, steady steps and deep breaths full of amazingly clear, rich air. As the sun dipped below the horizon and stars and moonlight guided his steps, he walked between the first of the white-barked trees. It felt as if a curtain had been drawn—everything grew dimmer and quieter. A gentle breeze blew, rustling the leaves high overhead, and Victor felt peace like he hadn't in a long while.

The glow of a lamp brought his eyes ahead and to his right, and he recognized Dar's hulking shadow as he moved around in its circle of illumination. As he approached, he wanted to call out, but something told him it would be wrong to be noisy in that place, so he padded up the slope to the small clearing where his master sat on a patch of soft, rich loam. When he stepped into the clearing, Dar looked up and smiled and, as softly as he could with his rough, grating voice, said, "Welcome, Victor. Sit down here with me."

The master Spirit Caster wore a loose black silken shirt over gray pants of a matching style. Looking at him as he sat down, Victor contemplated Dar's habit of always wearing something loose and comfortable. "Do you ever wear armor?"

"Not these days. I have some—armor that could withstand the destruction of a mountain—but I've learned abilities that make it . . . redundant." He gestured to the ground before him, and Victor saw that he had a few items arrayed there beside the softly glowing orb-shaped lamp. The first was a smooth, normal-looking river rock. Beside it was a carved ivory figurine that reminded Victor of a chess piece, and next to that was a small terra-cotta pot holding a delicate green plant with beautiful star-shaped blue flowers. "Have you ever wondered why your Spirit Walk spell is still in the basic stage?"

The question surprised Victor, as it seemed to have nothing to do with the three items arrayed on the ground. He blinked, thought for a moment, then nodded. "Yeah, of course."

"Spirit walking, at its most basic level, is the ability to project your conscious spirit onto the spirit plane. You've mastered this quite well—you've learned to find places you've seen or visited before, and you've also learned to visit other spirit walkers. What you don't know is that, with practice, you can learn to bring physical objects onto the spirit plane with you. Once you've mastered that, you can also learn to bring your physical body there. It's the first step to learning how to travel through the spirit plane from one location on the material plane to another."

"I—" Victor paused, considering his words, ensuring he was right, then finished his thought. "I've brought Lifedrinker onto the spirit plane with me before."

Dar nodded. "You've brought Lifedrinker's *spirit*. She manifested as an axe there. It's also possible that you've brought some small item with you before, subconsciously tapping into the spell's greater potential. However, you won't evolve the spell until you learn to do it with intent."

"Ah. All right."

Dar gestured to the stone. "We'll start with this simple rock I picked up from the shore on my way here. Pick it up." Victor took the stone in his hand, weighing it in his large palm as Dar continued. "Bringing something with you on a spirit walk requires an effort of will. You must concentrate on the object and, just as you might move Energy about with your will, you must *command* the object to accompany you as you cast the spell."

Victor frowned and looked up from the rock he'd been studying. "I've never tried to exert my will on something other than Energy or a spell or person using Energy."

"Open your inner eye, Victor, and contemplate the stone in your hand."

Victor did as instructed, closing his eyes and opening that inner sense that allowed him to see his Core, pathways, aura, and the Energy in the world around him. As he moved his gaze away from his Core and out of himself, he had a hard time even seeing the stone at first. As he concentrated, though, he began to see tiny swirls of dim, gray-brown Energy. He continued to focus and saw that the swirling loops of Energy were contained, and that's when he realized they were bound by the shape of the stone. "I see it! It's full of Energy!"

"Good! And now you see how you will influence the stone; like all things, Energy is part of it. When you cast Spirit Walk, wrap that stone in your will and *pull* it with you. Do you understand?"

"Yeah, I think so." In theory, Victor thought it seemed simple and was eager to try. He began to gather his Energy into the pattern for Spirit Walk, but Dar leaned forward, and suddenly he felt a knife-like fragment of Dar's aura reaching out and erasing the pattern before he could complete it.

"Patience! Did I say to cast your spell?" Dar didn't sound angry, but Victor couldn't help scowling at the intrusion into his personal Energy space.

"Can any veil walker do that? It feels like bullshit. I mean, I'm helpless before you!"

Dar chuckled and leaned back, shaking his head as his broad smile demonstrated his good temper. "It's a frustrating realization, isn't it? I know what it's like to think of the obstacles you've overcome, the trials you've faced, the hard work you've put in, and to know that there are those who can swat you like a bug."

"Yeah, it's not so much *you*, Dar, but what if Lord Roil wanted me dead?"

"Yes. If he hadn't been worried about the code of conduct for our kind here on Sojourn, he might have struck you down shortly after that challenge dungeon showing." He sighed and shrugged. "Listen, Victor, the secret to resisting the likes of me is to build your aura to a point where it can resist my intrusion. You've learned to veil your Core, and that's the first step. Your aura is heavy for someone at your tier, but you can make it heavier. Build your Core, continue to advance your bloodline, increase your attributes, and continue to win contests. Nothing can build an aura like deeds accomplished. They become part of your *weight* in the universe. No wallflower who learns every spell and swallows a thousand rare treasures will ever have the weight of one who's entered hell and come out the other side."

Victor liked the way that sounded. He clenched his fists as he asked, "Can someone who hasn't passed their test of steel resist a veil walker?"

"Oh yes. There are steel-bound cultivators who would pose a serious threat to me. I'm not so sure it would be possible in the iron ranks, but there are prodigies of all sorts that I've yet to meet. In my many years, Victor, I've met few with the potential you show. Let's focus on keeping you alive so you can reach further heights, though, shall we? Leave off your thoughts of challenging veil walkers for now." Dar finished the last sentence with a chuckle and reached over the glow lamp to jostle Victor's shoulder.

"All right. I mean, honestly, that makes me feel better. It's nice to know what I need to work on."

"Oh, there is *much* you need to work on—"

"Yeah, about that, Dar. Can we please set up some kind of schedule until I leave for Ruhn? I'd like to be able to arrange for regular sparring partners and also spend time doing Breath Core cultivation with Lesh and—"

"Enough!" Dar laughed, shaking his head. "You're the first in centuries to demand so much! Fine, heed me well: The mornings shall be yours, but you must be prepared to receive my tutelage at half past noon each day. Further, there will be times when I'll set a task before you that will require several days or weeks of effort—your 'partners' will need to make do without you during those times. Understood?"

"Yes! Thank you, Lord Dar." Victor figured using the honorific might earn him a little leeway for being a demanding student.

"Good. Now, let's see how well you listened. Cast Spirit Walk and bring that stone with you."

"Right." Victor reflexively clutched the stone, suddenly hyper-aware of his senses—the smooth cool surface in his hand, the tickle of the soft breeze on his freshly shorn hair, the distant trill of a nightbird, and the mesmerizing rustle of the leaves high overhead. He took a deep breath, centering himself, then closed his eyes and *saw* the stone again, focusing on its shape containing the tiny swirls of earth-attuned Energy. He built the pattern for Spirit Walk and, as he sent Energy into it, *willed* the stone to come with him.

When he opened his eyes, he and Dar sat in a dark, twilight forest. It was the spirit plane version of the grove where he'd left his body. Here, though, the trees were much taller, with vast trunks. They were limned with ethereal light, and the dense boles stretched away as far as he could see; it was a massive forest. Dar looked exactly as he did on the material plane, but he was no longer seated, and Victor could see that his feet hovered above the loamy soil. "Can you fly here?"

"Easily. Look to your hands, apprentice."

Victor looked at his open palms resting on his knees, and when he saw they were both empty, he groaned. "Shit! I thought I had it, for sure!"

"It's not as trivial as it seems. The stone *wants* to be in the ground on the material plane. You must overcome its primitive desire with your will. Next time, when you've wrapped your intent around it, try to hear its voice, its whispered desire. You have to have a closer connection to it than surface level."

"All right." Victor reached into his pathways and severed his connection to the Spirit Walk spell, plunging himself back into the material plane. Once again, the stone sat heavy in his palm. "You want to be here, huh?" Victor chuckled and hefted the stone, peering at it as though he could see into it somehow. "Come on, *hermano*. Don't be an asshole, all right? I'll bring you back." Victor closed his eyes and built the pattern for Spirit Walk. Then, before he filled it with Energy, he turned his inner eye on the stone again.

He stared at those tiny whorls of gray-brown Energy. They were dim and, in his estimation, weak; an Earth Elementalist would struggle to cultivate anything of note from this stone. Still, it was evident the stone had a will; it wanted to stay where it was. Victor tried to do what Dar said, staring hard at it, but he couldn't see any indication of its primitive desire. Then he remembered Dar had said to *listen* for its "whispered desire."

Victor inhaled deeply and willed himself to stop hearing the noises of the world around him. He shut out the birds' trilling song, the leaves' rustle, the breeze's whisper, and Dar's slow, steady inhalations. When he'd imposed his will upon himself to the point where he sat in utter silence, he stared at the stone again, and this time, he caught it—the faintest, strangest sound he'd ever heard. It was like a distant muffled conversation of which he couldn't make out a single word. The muttered, droning sound was without intelligence, without design, but it held a definite *intent*. The stone wanted to be part of the earth—part of the world.

Victor wrapped his will around it, and this time, as he *pulled* it with him into the spirit plane, he ground out a single word, directed toward the stone, and pitched so it overwhelmed its strange intent-filled drone, "Come!" When he opened his eyes, he looked at his hand and was rewarded to see the gray stone there, solid and real, not limned with the weird phantom light of spirit things. Victor's lips split in a wide grin, exposing his bright teeth.

"Congratulations, apprentice. You did well, though I feel compelled to inform you that I managed to pull a stone with me onto the spirit plane with my first attempt. Still, success on your second try is an admirable feat. I've taught apprentices who required weeks of constant effort to achieve the same."

"Uh," Victor chuckled, "thanks, I guess."

"Back to the material plane, now." Dar winked out of existence, and Victor quickly canceled his Spirit Walk spell. When he opened his eyes, Dar was hefting the ivory figurine.

"This was once a living thing. A piece of ivory from a tavahawk's horn. Because of its former existence as a piece of something powerful and alive, you'll find its will somewhat more . . . tumultuous. For reference, Victor, it took me several hours and close to a hundred attempts to pull a similar object into the spirit plane with me. I was a child, however. Hopefully, you'll prove yourself more capable." He stood and held the figurine toward Victor.

Victor took it, and when Dar stepped away toward the lake, he raised an eyebrow. "Oh, are you leaving?"

"I won't go far. I'll feel it if you succeed because I'm quite certain it will rank up your Spirit Walk spell." He pointed toward the lake. "I'll just step over to the house for an early dinner. Pay attention, Victor; if you were wondering how a veil walker like me might move great distances quickly, this is one method. I'll bring myself onto the spirit plane, walk quickly to my home, and then emerge back on the material plane."

"Will I be able to do that?"

"Eventually. First, you must master these three objects. Then, Victor, the fun begins, and you will work to master yourself. You might not realize it, but your body—down to your very cells—has desires. Once you've learned to exert your will over yourself, many doors will open to you." He gestured to the ivory figurine in Victor's hand. "Focus on what's before you, however. After you succeed with the piece of horn, move on to the plant—a complex living thing. When you've emerged victorious, I will return, and we will speak of the next step."

"Okay, but—" Victor snapped his mouth shut as Dar shimmered and disappeared with a potent swirl of brilliant golden Energy. Victor wanted to be annoyed, but he was too busy feeling excited. How incredible would it be to use the spirit plane to move around? He could walk from the lake house to Sojourn in seconds. Back on Fanwath, he'd covered a thousand miles on the spirit plane in minutes. Could he learn to travel between worlds? "Yes!" He laughed as he recalled Dar talking about "walking" to Ruhn. With a grin, excited to prove he could do it, Victor closed his eyes and turned his attention to the strange golden Energy swirls inside the figurine he held.

# 6

SUCCESSES AND WARNINGS

Victor managed to bring the carved piece of ivory with him onto the spirit plane after two difficult, aggravating hours. The plant, however, took him nearly a week. After he succeeded, he was awarded with System messages declaring his Spirit Walk spell had ranked up to improved and that he'd be able to "more easily bring lesser beings and objects with him onto the spirit plane with an increased Energy expenditure." The message felt as though it had been a long time coming, and Victor's relief and pleasure at seeing those words was on par with when he'd pushed his Berserk into the epic rank.

Dar was there to welcome him back to the material plane with words of praise and encouragement. They sat together in the grove of tall quiet trees and enjoyed a meal together that Dar provided. They spoke about Sojourn, the political scene, and then, at much greater length, about the goings-on around the lake house. Lesh had been entertaining sparring guests in Victor's absence, just as he had been while Victor had been on Fanwath and secluded in his cultivation cave.

Victor nodded as Dar described Lesh's guests—Drobna and Dovalion Boarheart, the plate-wearing giant swordsman. He was glad Lesh was keeping up with his practice and also maintaining relationships with some of the stronger fighters in Sojourn. It alleviated some of his guilt for, once again, disappearing for days on end. In truth, he'd tuned out those feelings of guilt along with his recurring despondency regarding Valla. "And what about Lam and the others?"

"They've yet to return from their dungeon expedition." Dar watched him polish off the last hunk of smoky, tangy boar meat. "Well? Are you ready for the next task?"

"I guess. I feel like I learned a lot from my struggles with that stubborn little plant."

"I'm sure you did! The plant's lesson will serve you well as you struggle to convince your physical form to join you on the spirit plane."

"Yeah, I figured that was the point of it." Victor sighed and handed his polished silver plate and fork to Dar. They disappeared into some hidden storage vault as Dar nodded and stood. Victor frowned. "You're leaving? No words of advice?"

"Ha! You know what to do. It's the same task as before, just . . . harder."

So, just like that, Victor's struggles began anew. Dar hadn't lied; the task was the same, but it was strange as hell—in Victor's colorful opinion—to be battling his own body. Beyond the strangeness of it, he found that his "self" was unreasonably stubborn. It wasn't until three days later, with no sign of success, that he finally had a breakthrough in his thinking; if he couldn't convince his entire body to come with him to the spirit plane, perhaps he could force part of it through.

"What the fuck would that look like?" he asked himself, staring at his hand, wondering what would happen if he dragged his little finger with him into the spirit plane. Would it simply be gone on the material plane? Would a void appear? Would his stump bleed, and would his regeneration begin to grow a new finger? He laughed at the idea and realized his most prominent fear—that he'd somehow permanently remove a piece of himself—wasn't such a terrible worry; his ability to regenerate would make short work of a pinky.

So, with renewed excitement and inspiration—he'd constantly been operating under the influence of his inspiration-based spells—he began to try anew, this time simply focusing on the stubborn flesh, bone, and blood of his left pinky. The battle of wills was still there, but he could feel the difference. Those living cells put up a fight, but they were not, collectively, as strong as his entire body. When he appeared on the spirit plane and looked down at his hand, he laughed uproariously when he saw a solid, living pinky jutting out from his faintly ethereal, luminescent hand.

When he returned to the material plane, his fears of spattered blood and a stubby, slowly regrowing finger were for naught—the pinky was there, and he could find no evidence of bleeding. Whatever strange magic allowed him to bring just a part of himself onto the spirit plane seemed to defy the rules of physical flesh. With his confidence renewed, Victor got to work trying to bring more and more of himself onto the spirit plane. He managed his hand right away, but his arm defied him.

That resistance drew out Victor's stubbornness, and he doubled down, focusing his will with long hours of meditation. He *listened* to the Energy in his body and worked to understand its desire to remain where it was. It wanted to be part of the light of the sun and stars. It wanted to be grounded to the planet. It wanted to be surrounded by air and to taste the moisture in the breeze. It wanted to feel the waves of sound bouncing against and through it—sounds of animals, plants, people, and things. Victor used each of those desires against himself, making levers out of them and pressing his will against them.

The hours bled into days, bled into weeks, and it wasn't until sixteen days later that Victor finally achieved victory over himself, dragging his stubborn, recalcitrant flesh and blood—his entire body—with him onto the spirit plane. When he finally did it, when he opened his eyes and saw his solid living naked flesh sitting on the luminous loam of the magical ghostly forest of the spirit plane, Victor tilted his head back and howled at the stars.

He stood and danced, howling and crowing, struggling to believe his battle was over; those weeks had been the most frustrating, annoying, mind-bogglingly boring days he could recall, and it was as if a wave of constant relief and newfound excitement kept rolling through him every time he looked at his hands, flexing his fingers into fists in front of his very real, very solid eyes. Only after he'd howled his lungs out several times did he notice the heavy drain of Energy on his Core. When he looked inward, his eyes bulged when he saw he was nearly drained and that Energy was pouring out of his Core at an astonishing rate.

Before he ran himself dry, Victor hastily ended his Spirit Walk spell, and as soon as the material plane snapped into existence around him, he was bombarded with System messages:

*****Congratulations! You have learned a new spell: Spirit Walk, Advanced.*****

*****Spirit Walk, Advanced. Prerequisite: Any spirit-based Energy affinity. Using the fundamental primal nature of your Energy, you send forth and sustain your spirit on its essential plane of existence. You've mastered the innate resistance of your flesh and can now walk physically upon the spirit plane. Be warned that your body will be vulnerable to harm in ways your projected spirit would not. The duration of this spell is dependent on your Energy stores. Manifesting a physical presence on the spirit plane is extremely costly. Energy Cost: Minimum 50, scalable. Cooldown: Short.*****

*****Congratulations! You have achieved Level 69 Herald of the Mountain's Wrath and gained 12 strength, 17 vitality, and 12 will.*****

*****Congratulations! You have earned a Class spell: Voice of the Angry Earth, Basic.*****

*****Voice of the Angry Earth, Basic. Prerequisite: Titanic, colossal, or gargantuan bloodline. Channel the volcano's fury, projecting it in a roar that will brutalize the senses of your foes. Drive them to their knees with the power of your voice, reminding all who stand before you that just because it slumbers does not mean the mountain is at peace. The power of your roar will be influenced by the strength of your aura and the amount

**of Energy you pour into the spell. Energy Cost: Minimum 2000, scalable. Cooldown: Medium.*****

Seeing those messages made Victor feel as though the many days he'd spent struggling against his own body had been worth it. A broad smile split his face, exposing white straight teeth, and he laughed, clapping his mighty hands together. "Yes! *That's* what I'm talking about!" With eager anticipation, he looked at his attributes:

| Name: | Victor Sandoval | | | |
|---|---|---|---|---|
| Race: | Quinametzin Bloodline: Epic 2 | | | |
| Class: | Herald of the Mountain's Wrath: Legendary | | | |
| Level: | 69 | | | |
| Breath Core: | Elder Class: Improved 3 | | | |
| Core: | Spirit Class: Epic 2 | | | |
| Breath Core Affinity: | Magma: 9 | | Breath Core Energy: | 2200/2200 |
| Energy Affinity: | Fear 9.4, Rage 9.1, Glory 8.6, Inspiration 7.4, Unattuned 3.1 | | Energy: | 433/35458 |
| Strength: | 478 | Vitality: | 628 (691) | |
| Dexterity: | 190 | Agility: | 213 | |
| Intelligence: | 172 | Will: | 661 | |

He laughed when he saw his current Energy level; he really had almost drained himself by bringing his physical form onto the spirit plane, and he'd only been there for a couple of minutes. He turned toward the lake, thinking it might be amusing to try out his new spell, but Dar was already standing there.

"That was well done, Victor. I was pleased when I saw you work on bringing your body through piece by piece. I thought I might give you that guidance, but my master did not do so for me, so I thought it might be wise to follow his example. It seems I was right; you gained much from the effort." He stepped closer, resting his large heavy hand on Victor's shoulder. "While you were on the spirit plane, I noted the Energy infusion hanging heavy in the air—you gained a level?"

"Yes!" Victor was too exuberant to hold back. "My Spirit Walk is now advanced! And I gained a new class spell—Voice of the Angry Earth."

"A shout ability? This will pair well with your feats and bloodline boons!" He nodded, tugging Victor's shoulder. "Come, let's walk toward the house.

You've secluded long enough and accomplished the only thing that was absolutely necessary before your journey to Ruhn."

"Oh?"

"Yes. I have the strength and reserves of Energy to pull a being like you onto the spirit plane, but I would have struggled to pull you all the way to Ruhn. Now, you can do the lion's share of the lifting where you are concerned."

"Um, I don't know about that; I ran dry on Energy after only a couple of minutes—"

Dar waved his hand. "You'll work on that over the next few months. Each day, before you rest, you'll project your physical form onto the spirit plane. With practice, you'll extend the time you can hold yourself there. Our journey will take less than an hour. As long as you can hold yourself on the spirit plane for that duration, I can do the work of moving us."

Victor nodded. If there was one thing he understood, it was grinding out incremental gains. "So I have time?"

"Yes. The hardest part is getting yourself there. Imagine how much work it was to do that; now imagine doing it for another person. You'll be able to, eventually, but it's taxing." As he spoke, Victor and Dar descended the path to the lakeshore, where a small wooden boat bobbed in the shallow water, bumping into the shore with each gentle wave. Dar pointed to it. "Climb aboard, and I'll ferry us back to the house. Tomorrow, you'll begin that routine you pestered me about."

"I can't begin to tell you how ready I am to get some sparring in, Lord Dar. I was going nuts sitting in that grove day after day." Victor sloshed through the shallow water, his boots and pants sloughing the water off like a seal's skin. He climbed onto the little boat and added, "If I hadn't figured out how to bring myself over to the spirit plane little by little, I would have gone mad. Seeing the progress day by day kept me going."

Dar nodded. "You've earned some exercise. The mastery of your body's will and the ability to physically walk on that plane are both keys to greater powers." Dar nudged the rudder, and the boat turned and began to speed silently over the water, leaving a long, deep wake as it rushed toward the center of the dark water. Dar continued, "For example, you can now move, unseen, unfelt, and much more quickly, from point to point on the material plane. When you've gained more Energy and an even stronger will, I'll teach you how to bridge worlds. The spirit plane doesn't have 'worlds'—it is all-encompassing—but the expanse between planets is too vast for a normal walk."

"I was wondering about that!" Victor took in the stars and moon, enjoying the rush of cool lake air against his face and through his hair.

Dar was quiet for a minute, but as the lake house came into view, he said, "You'll spar in the mornings, as I promised. Your follower has arranged for new partners each day for the two of you. After sparring, you'll be given two hours to cultivate your Breath Core. After that, I'll have lessons for you. I've decided that a course on runic structure will serve you the most at this time. Many rituals—like the one we did for your friend Lam—require knowledge of sigils and runes. They serve as a way to channel and direct your Energy, giving it purpose much the way that a spell pattern does."

Victor nodded emphatically. "I've wanted to learn about that stuff!"

"Good! Moreover, the knowledge will help you on Ruhn. If you're victorious in your duels, you'll be given treasures and gifts, and many will likely be enchanted. It would be dangerous to expose a gap in your education by relying on others to explain those treasures. Never mind that you wouldn't know if you could trust the person aiding you."

Before Victor could check himself, his tongue got away from him. "What about elder magic?"

Dar looked at him and frowned. "What of it?"

"Do you know how to read it? The spell patterns and sigils and—"

"Better to avoid curiosity about that, Victor. Many have found their downfalls dabbling with pre-System rituals." He sighed, and as the boat sped toward the pier outside his home, he turned his blazing eyes on Victor and, in a much sterner voice, said, "People more powerful than I have destroyed themselves pursuing elder magic—literally and figuratively. I've seen a man rip himself apart, atom by atom, and I've seen a woman go mad to the point where even a racial advancement treasure was wasted on her, unable to salvage her wits."

"Really?" Victor frowned. "I had it in my head that maybe part of being a steel seeker or becoming a veil walker was learning to do elder magic. Like, it was a time for us to learn to grow without the System guiding—"

"That's not correct." Dar turned the rudder, slowing the boat and bringing it up alongside the pier. "The System will still be there. It will still award you and provide guidance, but you'll have more freedom to direct your development—this all begins at level one hundred when you build your class."

"Ah, I see. Yeah, I knew about that—the class building, I mean. I just thought maybe it was the first step of being free of—"

"Turn your mind from such fantasies, Victor." Dar stepped out of the boat, hardly causing it to dip into the water, and it took Victor a moment to realize the huge, weighty man must be adjusting his weight somehow—how else could he keep the little vessel from shifting in the water? By contrast, Victor had to use every ounce of his agility to avoid falling as the boat tipped and rocked under his feet. When they were both on the solid planks of the pier, Dar clapped his shoulder and walked with him toward the stairs leading up to the house. "Tell me, what got you so interested in elder magic?"

Rather than be caught out in a lie, Victor shared part of the truth: "When I was on Zaafor, in the city of Coloss, I met another traveler who claimed to be from a world where the System had been rebuked; she said the people there used elder magic."

Dar stopped and pressed Victor's shoulder, turning him until they were face to face. "Is this one of the secrets you've held back from me?"

Again, Victor didn't want to lie. He knew better. "Yeah. She made me swear not to reveal her identity."

Dar nodded. "It's good that you understand the weight of such a promise. Well, you've heard my words of caution. You're no child. I do hope you'll heed me, however. Now," he said, turning back toward the house, "let us feast and share your good news with your follower."

As they walked up the steps, Victor thought about Dar's warning and his earlier assumptions about elder magic and the System. There was certainly *something* that he was missing. He didn't believe that Dar knew nothing about elder magic; it simply didn't make sense. The man had been around for millennia, and Victor had only been walking in this part of the universe for something like two or three years if he were guessing—he really didn't know. How could he know more about such a subject than Dar? He could believe he knew more than the other iron rankers in Sojourn; they'd led sheltered existences. But Dar had been places—conquered worlds.

He supposed Dar's admission that he'd seen people ruin themselves pursuing elder magic was enough to spell the truth: His master knew much more but wanted to shelter Victor from dangerous knowledge. As they made their way into the house and Dar sent one of the servants to look for Lesh, Victor sat down, still deep in thought. His mind kept returning to the book he'd found in the Iron Prison. He was sure it contained writings in the same script of the spell Tes had taught him. Despite Dar's warnings, he hoped his lessons with the master Spirit Caster on runes and glyphs would help him wring some secrets out of that book.

"You seem very lost in thought, Victor. Are you still dwelling on our earlier discussion?" Victor looked up to see Dar, a drink in hand, taking a seat on one of the plush couches.

Victor smiled and tried to steer the conversation to a safer topic. "I was, but now I'm thinking about my class and the spell I just learned. I'm going to be choosing a new refinement at the next level. Do you think there's any chance I'll reach seventy before I leave for Ruhn?"

"Not likely. Not unless you kill someone—or many people, depending on their strength." Dar chuckled. "The last level in any tier is always the steepest, and gaining levels through cultivation or skill and spell improvement is a slow way to go about doing it. You did so tonight, thanks to the fact that you were already on the cusp."

"Right. Yeah. I suppose that makes sense."

"I've been thinking, Victor. We should talk about your strategy when you get to Ruhn. I'll keep it brief for now since you've had a long day and deserve some rest before tomorrow's tribulations, but consider this: My granddaughter has two kingdoms practically laying siege against her. They've been pressing her for duels, so they'll be quick to receive her acceptance of their challenges. I believe it would be wise for you to win those battles using very few of your abilities, perhaps even using a weapon other than your precious axe. The less you show, the easier a time she'll have when she moves to consolidate her new position and challenge other neighboring kingdoms."

"Wait a sec." Victor chuckled, shaking his head. "You want me to fight some steel seekers without Lifedrinker? Without using my abilities?"

"They'll likely not be steel seekers. Those kingdoms are small and weak—not far above Kynna's in terms of might and prosperity. In my estimation, it won't be until you've had a few victories before you begin to find yourself faced with a steel seeker." When he saw Victor's scowl, he added. "It's just a thought. Think about it as you train; the less your enemies know about you, the better." He nodded his head toward the hallway leading to the foyer. "I hear your draconic follower approaching. Enjoy the night—tomorrow your training will be . . . intense."

# 7

## A REVIEW

On the third day of the fourth week of Victor's new "routine," Dar called him into the library late in the evening and asked him to sit down. Dar stood facing out toward the lake, but Victor saw a tea service arranged on the small table between two chairs, so he chose one of those two seats, wondering what the late-night meeting was regarding. This was the hour Victor usually reserved for reviewing his lessons on runic structure, writing correspondence to his friends and loved ones, and occasionally cultivating Energy in his chamber beneath the house.

He hadn't done much cultivation for his Spirit Core, but he didn't feel guilty about that; Dar had instructed him to put it lower on his list of priorities simply because Victor gained so much Core development from eating hearts—a boon most Energy cultivators couldn't fathom. He *had* been working on his Breath Core, however. After sparring each morning, he and Lesh gathered Energy in the garden. Victor kept his magma-attuned Energy heart next to Lesh's acid-emitting plant, and by the time they sat down to cultivate each day, the canopy they'd built over the plant was thick with roiling Energy. His Breath Core had gained two ranks and Lesh's nearly four—only to be expected, considering Lesh was starting from the base ranks.

"Pour yourself a cup of tea, Victor." Dar didn't turn away from the windows, but his voice seemed relaxed, so Victor's budding unease about the unscheduled meeting receded. He did as Dar suggested and poured himself a cup of steaming, slightly green-tinged liquid. "It's an herbal mix from the world of Jovir—one of the twelve Radevian Empire worlds. The Radevians discovered Sojourn nearly a thousand years ago and established robust trade channels with other worlds under Sojourn's influence. There are some beautiful freshwater seas on Jovir, and their agricultural exploits are renowned in this part of the universe."

Victor sipped the tea and found it slightly bitter with an odd ginger aftertaste. Rather than profess his less than enthusiastic reception to the flavor, he asked a related question. "Do you know how many worlds are . . . I guess I don't know the right term. Subjects? Of Sojourn, I mean."

"Sojourn doesn't rule other worlds, at least not directly. However, many of the veil walkers who call Sojourn home have led conquests—military, financial, humanitarian, and even evangelical—of nearby systems. It's more accurate to say that many worlds are *influenced* by Sojourn and not ruled over. Last time I heard the matter discussed, there were nearly two hundred thousand worlds under Sojourn's influence." Dar turned and walked over, sitting in the other chair by the tea service.

"That sounds like a lot to me." Victor frowned. "I suppose you'd be including Fanwath in that number, considering Sojourn was the first 'hub world' the System provided a teleportation to?"

"Indeed, not to mention the rulers of Fanwath have been coming to Sojourn for hundreds of years, absorbing our culture and sharing bits of yours."

"Not *really* mine." Victor chuckled.

"You understand my meaning." Dar didn't wait for Victor to acknowledge the fact. He poured himself some tea and said, "Let's review your progress. Start with your sparring. How go things with the various brawlers you've brought in from Sojourn?"

"Um . . ." Victor gulped the rest of his tea, set the delicate cup on the table, and leaned back, crossing one ankle over his knee and clearing his throat. "They go well. One thing I've come to learn, being immersed in the System, is how much we all come to rely on it to measure progress. Fighting with Drobna, Valeska, Sora, Brontes . . ." Victor paused and held out his fingers, running the names through his mind as he counted. "Oh yeah, and Dovalion—they each have different styles, and I've learned something from them all. The System doesn't reflect that. My axe skill is still epic; my strength, vitality, and agility are all the same as they were a month ago—but I *know* I'm better. Does that make sense?"

"Indeed it does, Victor, and now you begin to unveil the truth of levels and tiers—the reason you have pounded the blood and shit from men and women more than thirty levels above you is because what you've noticed doesn't just stop at weapon skills. Talent, heart, drive, muscle memory, bloodlines—I could go on and on; all the little intangibles add up to something very tangible indeed. You aren't the first to feel that way. Tell me, can you think of a single person you've met recently who reminded you of yourself, perhaps uncomfortably so?"

Victor's answer was immediate. "Ronkerz."

"Ha!" Dar slapped his hands together. "Just so! Ronkerz was much like you in his youth—challenged at every turn, hardened in a crucible of suffering and opposition. Unlike you, he didn't have the benefit of a Spirit Core or the wise tutelage of a kind master." Dar smirked. "Still, there's much about you that evokes his memory. I've made contact with him, you should know."

"Really?"

"Oh yes. He's determined to have vengeance against the great masters of Sojourn, but I'm working with him to think of a wiser plan. Even if he raised up a hundred veil walkers in that dungeon, he'd be outnumbered twenty to one if he assaulted the city or the Council Spire."

"How do you communicate with—" Victor grinned and leaned forward. "The spirit plane?"

"Indeed, lad. No place is beyond the bounds of the spirit plane. When you learn to bridge worlds through that misty realm, you too could come and go from a place like the Iron Prison. Of course, wards could be put up, making such travel impossible, but the Iron Prison wasn't meant to hold the likes of me—or you, once you have the Energy and will to travel that way."

"It's not something an iron ranker could do?"

"Only a tiny percentage of them might be able to. I won't be surprised if you pull it off before you become a steel seeker. We'll see." Dar drained his tea and poured a new cup. "Now, you've mentioned your axe skill, but didn't I suggest you begin your duels on Ruhn with something other than your beloved weapon? Have you practiced with another weapon?"

"Oh!" Victor snapped his fingers. "Yeah! My Spear Mastery is up to improved."

"Good. Focus on that until you leave; it would be wise to have the forms and knowledge granted with advanced mastery at your disposal before your first duel." Dar took a sip, sighed heavily, and looked toward the window where the moon hung large in the star-filled sky. "So your sparring goes well. Tell me of your Breath Core cultivation."

"It's good. I've gained two ranks—halfway to advanced now."

"Good. You should see a large increase in magma-attuned Energy when you break through to advanced." He reached up to straighten the collar of his flowing purple tunic. He *tsked* as he pulled a loose thread away. "We both know how you're doing with runes. You've mastered two alphabets and can decipher basic System enchantments and the most common Artificer script. I've decided that I'm going to teach you a set of elder glyphs."

Victor's eyes bulged. "I thought you said—"

"I know what I said, and I stand by it. Elder magic is dangerous. If you don't harm yourself, there's a good chance the System will mark you and label you a disruptor."

At those words, Victor's heart began to pound, and he had to look down so Dar couldn't read the guilt in his eyes. Wasn't that what the strange duo, Fox and Three, had called him on the spirit plane when he created his Wild Totem spell? He coughed to cover his reaction, then, clearing his throat as though his tea had gone down the wrong pipe, he asked, "What happens if the System decides I'm a disruptor?"

"It will try to weed you out, issuing quests to powerful folk to remove you. So, I will teach you, but I must stress caution."

"Why?" When Dar looked at him and scowled, Victor hastily added, "I mean, why will you teach me, not why should I use caution."

"Because you are not a child, and I know that, were I in your shoes, I'd likely seek the knowledge on my own, and then my risk would be magnified." Dar shrugged. "So, we'll learn a bit about elder scripts, starting with a set of glyphs used to enchant items by people who lived in this section of the universe a hundred millennia before I was born."

"That's . . ." Victor fumbled for words and decided to turn his filter off for just a moment. "That's fucking awesome, Dar! Thank you!"

"Ha! There's the enthusiasm I was looking for. I've meant to ask you, Victor, how fares your heart? Are you sleeping well? Do you keep a journal?"

Victor fidgeted, suddenly uncomfortable. "Journal?" He chose the least troubling of the topics Dar mentioned.

"Do you write how you feel each day? It's a routine that has served me well over the years."

"Not exactly, but I write in Far Scribe books—to friends back home and Edeya when she and the others are out in dungeons. I have a book I share with my cousin, Olivia, and I have one with Valla." He didn't mention the fact that Valla had written to him twice and he'd yet to respond.

Dar narrowed his eyes, clearly not buying it. "If that is so, I applaud your ability to process feelings. Of course, I say that without reading what you write, but it's good that you confide in people you feel close to. If you find it difficult to share some things, even with those loved ones, you might try a journal, however. I write in one each night before I sleep."

"Really?" Victor had difficulty imagining the master Spirit Caster would need any such mental therapy.

"Yes, 'really.' You say that word far too often." Dar chuckled, shaking his head, then added, his voice a good deal sterner. "You'll begin writing in your journal each night. I don't care what you write, but you'll write something. If you only describe your day, that's fine. If you begin that way and find yourself writing more heartfelt things, all the better. This journal will be private; I won't ever expect you to share it with me. Understood?"

Victor felt himself grinding his teeth together, but he nodded and asked, "Is there some reason? Am I acting . . . bothered?"

"You're acting a bit too *unbothered*, in my estimation. I believe using a journal to express your feelings will be good for your spirit. Enough about that for now. Tell me about your spirit walks. How long can you hold your physical form on the spirit plane now?"

"Last night, I managed nearly fifteen minutes."

"Excellent! Another example of how one can improve without any notification from the System. What you're doing is strengthening and widening the tiny pathways in your body where the Energy of that spell takes root, pulling your flesh onto the spirit plane. Keep it up, and the System will eventually notice and rank up your spell. At the epic tier, you'll be able to hold yourself there with ease."

"That's encouraging." Victor poured himself more tea—it was beginning to grow on him.

"Have you given thought to your gift for Kynna?"

"*Ahem* . . ." Victor coughed, sputtering tea into his cup. "Gift?"

Dar chuckled. "Didn't we speak about this? Didn't I say—"

"That I should have a gift ready when I meet someone of note." Victor sighed and knocked his knuckles on his forehead. "Yeah, of course, meeting the queen would qualify."

"Don't despair; I know you have much on your mind. That's why I've reminded you. I would provide the gift for you, but she's crafty; she'll know if it came from me."

"Dar," Victor groaned, leaning back, "I don't know a thing about her. Does she like weapons? Tea?" He gestured to the delicate white kettle with its fanciful blue hand-painted flowers.

"Let's see. Like most people on Ruhn, she's of giant proportions, not unlike you and I. She's a skilled huntress, and her preferred weapon is a greatbow. From the letters she's sent me recently, though, it's clear her duties at court have taken the forefront in her life. Every spare moment is spent countering the schemes of her besieging neighbors. When you arrive to replace her current court champion, I'm certain there will be much fanfare; it will be seen as the kingdom's last chance to climb out of ruination. I'm afraid she's already done much to advertise your impending arrival."

Victor groaned again and waved a hand. "I'm nervous enough already! You're supposed to be giving me ideas for a gift!"

"Oh, yes. Where was I?" He began to tick qualities off on his fingers. "Tall, hunts with a greatbow, spends her time trying to save her kingdom—queendom, really—I believe she wears dresses, appreciates fruit and flowers, and—" Dar cut himself off as he began to laugh, shaking his head. "I'm no help, Victor. Half of those qualities are guesses. I don't know her at all. Her letters talk about the kingdom, its dire straits, and the things she does to counter the undermining efforts of her neighbors."

"All right, hold up. We always talk about Kynna's 'kingdom' or, yeah, 'queendom,' but what's it called? What are her neighbors called?"

"An excellent point, Victor. It's time you began to learn these things. My erstwhile kingdom was called Gloria. Can you guess why?"

Victor smirked. "Because, like me, you have an affinity for glory?"

"Precisely!" Dar slapped his knee with a cacophonous report. "Kynna's neighbor to the north is Frostmarch, a kingdom that spans her entire border and half again as far to the east and west. It's a country rich in acreage, but most is rather bleak. Frostmarch is ruled by a man named Wil Vennar, and his champion goes by a single name: Obert."

"Obert?" Victor raised an eyebrow.

"A giant, hairy, hard-headed man who cut his teeth fighting hordes of snow ogres along Frostmarch's northern border." Dar tilted the teapot to fill his cup, and Victor realized the thing must have a dimensional container built into it; they'd drained more than a gallon of the stuff since he'd been sitting there. "The Kingdom of Xan occupies Kynna's southern border. Bors Groff is Xan's king, and his champion is Qi Pot, of whom I know very little."

"Kee?"

"Yes, but it's spelled with a *Q* and an *i*. Kynna says he's formidable, and her current champion, Foster Green, is terrified that he'll have to duel him."

Victor nodded, rubbing his chin, visualizing a map in his head. "So those two countries are larger than hers, and they sandwich her?"

"More than that—Xan has conquered her neighbor to the east, and Frostmarch, her neighbor to the west. Between the two, she is utterly surrounded. Her people starve, and soon, barring intervention, she'll be forced to yield her lands or force poor old Foster to duel, in which case he'll die, and she'll lose her lands anyway."

"Damn. Are you being literal? Are people actually starving? I feel like we should send me over there right fucking now!"

"The risks involved, should I fail to hold you on the spirit plane while traversing worlds, are too great. No, you must be able to hold your spirit there long enough to make the journey. You've worked hard and done your best; any delay is on my shoulders. Recall that I've had Kynna's request for years. Though, in my defense, the perfect solution wasn't apparent until I knew you better." Dar waved his hand, dismissing the notion. "Now, let's get to the point of this meeting."

"Oh, this wasn't it?" Victor waved a hand between himself and Dar, indicating their conversation.

"Partially, partially, but I wanted to tell you that I'll be gone tomorrow, so our lesson will be canceled. I have an alternative assignment for you: Go into the city, find a gift for Kynna, and purchase the armor upgrades you've been pestering me about."

Victor grinned. He'd been wanting to go to the Sojourn City Stone and upgrade his set pieces since getting back from Fanwath and simply hadn't had the opportunity. "Is there anyone else I should purchase a gift for?"

"Yes! Good question, student! Foster Green will retire when you arrive, and you should give him a token. For him, I'd suggest a fine aged liquor. Don't skimp."

"Got it."

"Good. As soon as you finish your morning practice and cultivation, you may have Mr. Qwor drive you into the city. Any questions?"

"You'll be back the day after tomorrow?"

"Yes, and we will begin your lessons in the elder glyphs." Dar stood and, as he smoothed down the front of his silken tunic, added, "Now, go and practice your Spirit Walk. When you finish, write in your journal."

Victor stood. He smiled, and it came easily; he was a good deal more relaxed after his talk with Dar than he had been coming into the meeting. "All right. I'll do that."

Dar reached a hand to his shoulder, grasping it firmly. "You know, Victor, I would never eavesdrop on you in your private room. I might have dominion over this house, but I respect your privacy. I won't watch over your shoulder, just as I wouldn't listen to your voice. Whatever you put in that journal, whatever you mutter aloud in your sleep—those things are yours alone and will never leave the walls of your chamber."

"I . . ." Victor frowned, then sighed and nodded. "I appreciate that, Dar. I think I get why you're saying that. I'll write in my journal tonight, and I won't hold back." When Dar released his shoulder with a nod, Victor left, walking down the short hallway to his quarters. He closed the door behind him with a resounding *click*, then looked at the bed and his nest of blankets beside it on the floor. Despite his bravado and denial, it was true that *something* was up with him. Why else could he barely summon the courage to look at the empty bed?

With a growl, he dug around in one of his storage rings for a blank notebook, and then he stomped over to his writing desk, stacked high with books about runes and magical scripts. If Dar thought he should write about what he was feeling, he supposed he could do that. Scowling, pressing much harder than he needed to, he began to write, and the first words that came to mind surprised him:

*Dear Valla,*

# 8

## IDEAS

Drobna laughed—an exhausted, wheezing laugh, but a laugh all the same—and fell to the sand, rocking side to side on his leathery shell as he clutched his sore shoulder. "Old gods, Victor! I've had enough!"

Victor grinned and leaned against his spear, the butt firmly planted in the practice ring sand. It was a bright, sunny morning, made brighter still by the glowing orb of inspiration-attuned Energy that hung over their heads. He watched Drobna lying there, rocking side to side, using his "inner eye" to observe the rage fleeing the man's pathways and retreating toward his Core. Drobna had been berserk during their last match—Victor hadn't.

It said a lot that he could beat the warrior, enraged as he'd been, even though he'd only used his inspiration-based spells and a spear. It was a matter of toughness, he supposed. Add to that his uncanny ability to heal and his potent secondary abilities like Sovereign Will, and he was just too much for a guy with nothing but brute force going for him. Drobna was tough and had a great attitude, but Victor had learned the secret to beating him was simply to outlast his rage, and surprisingly, the spear made that even easier. It was an excellent weapon for creating distance between himself and his foe.

He stepped forward and held out a hand, hauling Drobna to his feet. "I take it you haven't broken through with your Berserk yet?"

"Nah. Still advanced." Drobna bent to brush the sand off his legs. He looked toward the edge of the ring. "Lesh? Up for a rematch?"

Lesh was seated on the ground, Belagog, his massive cudgel, resting on his shoulder. "Thanks, Drob, but I'm eager to head to my cultivation garden. I'm close to a breakthrough of my own."

Drobna looked at Victor with his smooth brows arched. Victor shook his head. "I've too much to do today. When's your next day on the schedule?"

"Five days hence," Drobna sighed. "These sparring matches are wonderful! I wish I could come every day."

"Well . . ." Victor looked at Lesh, frowning for a moment as he contemplated. "Why don't you get the names of the other people on the schedule? I think Valeska's coming tomorrow—check with her; if you two want to spar when Lesh and I are done, I don't mind you using this space."

"Ah, thanks, Victor, but it's just not the same without your inspiration Energy thick in the air like this. My time between sessions is better spent in a dungeon or cultivating."

"All right." Victor shrugged. "I'll be gone in a couple of months, though. Might be good for you to make some connections. Lesh will be wanting to do some dungeons, and I bet between you two and the other folks we've been sparring with, you could build a solid team."

Lesh grunted his agreement. "I'll write up some plans, Drobna. Don't worry, I won't forget about you."

Drobna nodded, and that conversation marked the end of their sparring for the day. Victor, still leaning on his spear, watched him leave. The spear was one of the better-made mundane ones he'd taken from Karnice in Coloss. He had a few very nice spears but had yet to pick his favorite. The terror-attuned spear was potent, but it didn't have the proper heft for Victor's robust frame. A couple of others, though, like the fourteen-foot one he currently held, must have seemed enormous to Karnice. Still, he had a mind to trade it and some others for a spear made for a giant like himself—something heavy and long and with an oversized, nigh-indestructible blade that he could use in situations where Lifedrinker wasn't ideal.

As Drobna turned the corner and his footsteps faded with distance, Lesh asked, "You're disappointed?"

Victor frowned in puzzlement, turning his gaze back to the darkly scaled, hulking figure. "About?"

"Drobna. I can tell you'd hoped to learn more about your Berserk, but it seems you are the one doing the teaching."

"My *abuelita* always said, 'The best way to learn is to teach what you know.' It's funny because she didn't say it to me; she said it to my older cousins who didn't want to let me play football in the street or join them playing other games." Victor barked a short, loud laugh. "Even video games!"

"It seems you've taken her lesson to heart, however it was initially intended." Lesh stood with a grunt. "To the garden?"

Victor thought about it for a moment, then shook his head. "Dar gave me the afternoon off, and I just thought of another thing I want to do in town. I think I'll skip cultivation today. I'd ask you to come, but I know you're close to breaking through to improved . . ." Victor left the statement hanging, giving Lesh the chance to object. The dragonkin didn't, however.

"Yes, I'd prefer to stay here. Thank you, though." He frowned—a fearsome expression on his fang-lined snout. "Speaking of staying here, have you had word from Lam and the others?"

Victor nodded, stepping closer to his friend. "I heard from Edeya last night. She said they're having a lot of fun. The dungeon they're in is enormous. It's set up like a perpetual war between two factions—pirates and a beleaguered city-state. The city provides missions, and the party in the dungeon has to carry them out. They have a week-long access window, but inside the dungeon, there's some time dilation—to Edeya, they've already been inside for two months."

Lesh's eyes bulged. "I should seek such a place!"

Victor laughed. "Yeah, I think there are a few dungeons with dilations that severe, but they're hard to get into. Trin's connections made this one happen for them. I bet if you build a team with some of the folks we've been sparring with, you'll have the clout you need to swing something like that."

"Yes!" Lesh nodded enthusiastically. "Dovalion is something of a local hero, and Valeska was once teamed with Arona—everyone in Sojourn knows her name."

Victor clapped Lesh on the shoulder. "Exactly, my friend. You're going to do well here while I'm gone. I'll see you this evening, yeah?"

"Indeed. I hope I'll have good news for you." Lesh thumped his chest, indicating his Breath Core. Victor nodded, gave his shoulder another punch, then walked up the path leading to the house. When he reached the front door, he looked at the servant standing there and smiled. "Hey, Wensa, can you let Mr. Qwor know I'll need him and the coach in about twenty minutes? I'm heading into the city."

"Yes, sir!" Before he could reiterate that it wasn't urgent, the girl sprinted down the path toward the coach house.

"Thanks!" he called after her, chuckling as he pulled the door open, intent on taking a quick shower before leaving. Just about fifteen minutes later, after washing the blood and sweat from his hair and body, he was back outside, striding toward the coach where Mr. Qwor stood, ready to open the door.

"Into the city, sir?"

"Yeah. We'll head to the Council Spire first; I have business with the City Stone."

"Excellent." Mr. Qwor opened the door, and Victor hopped inside, grateful to Dar for having giant-sized things. He slid into one of the plush leather seats and watched out the window. As soon as the coach was airborne and streaming away from the lake house, he pulled the heavy silver-runed black bone from his storage ring and held it in his hand. "Arona?"

With a shiver of cold air that seemed to blow from nowhere and everywhere, a luminescent blue apparition took shape in the coach with him. Looking much as he remembered her in life, Arona stood before him, her small black-booted feet failing to make any impression on the plush carpeting. "The ether feels . . . the same. We're still on Sojourn?" Despite the lack of flesh, her voice was as raspy as ever.

"Yeah. Still a couple of months before we leave. Lesh mentioned you earlier while we were sparring, and it got me thinking about you. I figured it would be safe to talk to you while flying through the air; we're not in any lord's domain, right?"

She nodded. "Certainly not any undead lords."

"So? Are you doing all right?"

"I am. My phylactery is spacious and contains many of my favorite things, as I told you before. I've been studying and reading for pleasure. I listen to music and while away the hours dabbling with my spell patterns." She tried to rest her ghostly hand on his knee, but it passed through, failing to do anything but give Victor a slight, chilly sensation. "And you? Are you faring well?"

"Yeah. I'm learning a lot from Dar. I haven't told you much about where we're going or what I'll be doing. Aren't you curious?"

"Of course! But our time was short while I stood whispering to you in Dar's garden. It's a miracle he didn't suss us out!"

Victor smiled crookedly. "I dunno. Dar's oddly respectful of privacy for an old master." He pointed to the seat to his left. "Can you sit? I might as well tell you a little about what's coming. We have a half hour or so before we get to the city."

Arona looked at the plush couch and shrugged. "I can't feel discomfort, but if it will make you more comfortable . . ." She floated over to the seat and sat down, though the leather didn't move, and it seemed she was floating slightly above it.

"So, Dar's got some extended family he left behind on a world called Ruhn. His granddaughter is a ruler there, and . . ." Victor tried to abbreviate the situation as much as possible, hoping to leave room to talk to Arona about other things before they reached the city. As he wrapped up the tale with Dar's explanation of Gloria's besieging neighbors, she nodded and gently tapped her chin.

"It seems you'll be well situated to request meetings with high-ranking individuals in Kynna's court. I would think you might be able to meet with a Death Caster without raising any suspicions."

"That's what I wanted to talk to you about. There's something else I haven't told you, something I can do."

Arona's dark, angular brows shot up on her ghostly forehead. "Oh?"

"Yeah. I had a friend, back on Fanwath, who picked up an artifact that 'granted' her a death-attuned Core. It's a long story, but she ended up getting infected—possessed, really—by a Death Caster without a body. I chased him out of her with my spirit-attuned Energy, and, in the process, I gave her a spirit affinity. Since then, she's been cultivating spirit Energy and slowly altering her Core, minimizing the death-attuned Energy and—"

"Could you do this for me?" Arona leaned forward, her dark eyes wide and intense, glimmering with the strange inner light of her spirit form.

"That's what I'm wondering. I wonder if it would be a mistake to have a Death Caster help you. Maybe there's another way to get you a, uh, body."

"There are . . ." Arona's eyes grew distant as she contemplated things. "Some Death Casters have created vessels out of magical materials—golems or constructs. Even so, they maintained their Death Core, which was likely due to how they created their vessel. Some treasures can be used to form a Core in such a vessel, and I'm sure the materials impact the type. If I were to do as I originally planned and have a Death Caster prepare a dead body for me, then my spiritual essence would dictate the Core's type and strength; it would be just like the one from my former body. This is all beside the point you made, though—there may be a way for you to help me, regardless of the type of vessel."

Victor nodded. "I'd like to do that for you. I know you aren't happy being a Death Caster."

"You've given me much to think about, Victor! With the resources you may have available to you on Ruhn, and with the knowledge that you seem to be able to impart spirit-attuned Energy . . . yes, much to think about and research!" Her excitement was evident; her tone had lightened, her eyes shone, and she leaned forward with an intensity to her gaze that Victor wasn't used to. "Thank you!"

"You're welcome. I mean, I know you wanted to get away from Ve—"

"Don't say it!" Arona reached as though to put a hand over his mouth, but he only felt a waft of cold air.

"Right. Anyway, I know you want to get away from him, but I think you'll be even safer if you somehow figure out how to *not* be a Death Caster, you know?"

"Yes! I agree wholeheartedly!" She glanced at the bone, still clutched in Victor's hand. "I'll return to my phylactery and study. Perhaps I'll have some ideas when next we speak."

"Wait!" Victor's exclamation halted her sudden attempt to dissolve back into formless ghostly energy. Her features solidified again, and she looked at him questioningly. "Should I buy any books on the subject? Is there any way I can get them to you in the phylactery?"

Her smile was bright, something he'd never seen from her in life, as she shook her head. "Thank you for the kind offer, Victor, but only I can send things into my phylactery and only when I'm in a corporeal vessel. I'm afraid I'm stuck with what I have for now."

"All right. One more question. I told you what Dar said about Kynna and—" Victor chuckled at himself and ran his fingers through his hair, a little embarrassed. "Well, do you have any idea what kind of gift I should get her?"

Arona's ghostly lips continued to smile as she regarded his words. "A queen? Whom you've never met? I don't envy you. Perhaps a piece of jewelry—no!" She shook her head, chuckling. "She's a ruler at war. I think, as a gift, you should present a weapon and swear to use it in her defense."

Victor's eyebrows shot up as the idea hit home and set off a lightbulb in his brain. "So my, uh, *service* is the real gift?"

"Yes. Though she may consider the weapon as the material representation of the gift, so I'd not offer her your lovely axe, just in case she wants to keep it for sentimental value someday."

"Nah, this is perfect—I planned to get a new spear anyway. Thank you, Arona!"

"You're welcome, Victor. Anything else?" The edges of her spectral form began to blur as they faded to a ghostly, blue haze.

"No—talk to you soon, I hope."

"*Soon . . .*" The word hung in the air as she faded to mist and streamed back into her phylactery.

Victor moved to the other side of the coach compartment and slid open the window between himself and Mr. Qwor. "Do you know of a weaponsmith who might specialize in spears?"

"I may know someone like that. Allow me to consult the guidebook while you're in the Council Spire, and I'll have a destination for you."

"Perfect." Victor slid the panel closed and sat down, still smiling at the idea. He was killing two birds with one stone—a decent spear, fit for a titan, and a gift for Kynna all in one. "She's pretty smart, wouldn't you say?" he asked the empty coach. Catching himself talking to the air like that made him feel very alone. He wished Lifedrinker wasn't so unwieldy that he had to keep her in a storage container. He took her out at night and spoke to her often before he slept, but it wasn't quite the same as it once had been. He was tempted to bring her out inside the coach, but she was large and incredibly heavy, and her blade was as sharp as a shard of obsidian glass—he didn't want to slice one of Dar's lovely leather seats in half.

Perhaps because he was feeling so alone, he brought out the Far Scribe book he shared with Olivia, his distant cousin—possibly from another timeline or universe—and opened it to the most recent message she'd sent him just the day before:

*Victor,*

*I recently traveled to Rellia's budding city in the Free Marches—Seaside. While there, I was regaled by tales of your adventures in the city of Sojourn. I'm jealous! It seems that the people of Fanwath have, indeed, been intentionally kept ignorant of the greater universe around us. Of course, the Ridonne are to blame for that, though my investigations into similar matters have led me down strange paths that indicate that some of the blame is on the System itself. It seems that when a new "System" world is formed, it makes certain demands on the ruling factions. I don't hold the Ridonne blameless—regardless of the System's demands, they took things too far. Still, it's an interesting topic to my mind, and I would enjoy learning more. The travel cost to Sojourn is steep, and I have many demands on my time here, but I intend to make the journey sooner rather than later. I wonder: Will I see you there?*

*I look forward to hearing from you,*

*Olivia*

Victor thought for a moment, then with a shrug, he took one of his favorite pens and began to scrawl out a neat reply:

*Hey, Olivia. Things are good here, and I'd love to show you around, but my mentor, a very powerful and influential man here, is sending me on some pretty important business soon. Don't get me wrong—I'm not trying to sound like a big shot. It's just that Dar has some family who are in trouble; their kingdom is under attack, and he thinks it will be a good learning experience if I help his granddaughter kick a little ass around that place for a while.*

*Anyway, I have a lot of friends and connections here, and I'll give you their names. Shit, I'll leave a letter of introduction for you at Dar's place. Any coach for hire in the city will know how to get you there. If you're hurting for money, I can leave you some funds, too—enough to purchase some books or buy you access to one of the better libraries. Just let me know.*

*I'm not sure what level you are now, but be careful while you're here. There are people on Sojourn who could flatten you with a thought. Don't worry too much—laws here prevent the powerful from squishing us mere mortals. You'll love it, by the way; there are tons of opportunities for growth for "iron rankers." That's what you are, by the way—everyone under level 100 is called that. Shit! I just thought of something: Lam, Edeya, and Darren—ha! Remember him from First Landing?—are all closing in on level 20. They might be over that by now, in fact. If you're not too much higher than them—I'd say under level 40—you might have a good time adventuring with them in the dungeons around the city.*

*I'll write you again with more instructions about how to get in touch with everyone. Stay safe!*

*Your cousin, Victor*

Victor was smiling hugely by the time he put the pen down. It was nice to remember the people he cared about were still there, even though he was alone at the moment. He figured it would be even more important to remember that when he was on Ruhn, separated by billions or trillions of miles from all those people. As he stowed the Far Scribe book away, the coach set down, and he heard Mr. Qwor climbing out of his compartment to open the door. Victor climbed out with a heavy sigh, looking up the steps to the massive crystalline heights of the Council Spire. "Time to get some shit done. See you in a few minutes, Mr. Qwor."

# 9

## DEPARTURE

Victor stood in his room, staring at himself in the mirror. The figure looking back at him was monstrous—huge, dragon-faced, with scales, leather, and thick metallic plates hiding all but his muscular right forearm and strong clenched fist. His armor had taken on a new kind of vibrancy since he'd fully imbued it at the Sojourn City Stone. He'd spent more than two million beads to get the enchantments, and each one had altered his armor-clad appearance.

Of course, he'd already had some "class A" enchantments: self-cleaning, repairing, sizing, and disguising. The two "class B" enchantments he'd chosen were a bit more combat-oriented. He'd decided to shore up his resistance to electrical damage, largely because he'd been shocked and stunned in battle more than once. The second enchantment was a boost to his fire-attuned damage— why not capitalize on one of his strengths?

His armor also had slots for one "class C" and one "class D" enchantment. The C choice was easy—between enhanced mass or a Lava Blast ability, he'd taken the one he felt would always benefit him. Enhanced mass meant that he'd be harder to move, he'd resist physical damage more efficiently, and his own attacks would have more weight. Looking at himself in the mirror, he, once again, marveled at the enchantment's visual effect. The metal of his helm and gauntlet looked weightier. The scales and plates were denser and more prominent, and the horns and fangs glimmered with golden undertones. His leather pants, belt, and boots were now decked in red-gold scales that complemented his wyrm-scale hauberk's dark red-black ones.

The class D enchantment was another story altogether. Once he'd selected the one he wanted—Flight of the Lava King—his armor had begun to glow with an inner fiery illumination that was subtle but present enough to catch the eye. It was almost as if it smoldered—as if always on the verge of bursting into flames. He'd tried the ability a few times over the last couple of months, and while it wasn't true, limitless flight, it was incredibly useful. When he activated it, great fiery wings sprouted from his shoulders, and they carried him wherever he focused his gaze, ripping through the air on currents of fiery Energy. The wings only lasted about ninety seconds, but, in Victor's estimation, that was plenty of time to bring down a flying foe.

He turned left and right, inspecting himself once more. The draconic lava king maw that obscured his face did so via some kind of magic. He only saw shadows within, no matter the angle from which he peered into the maw. Meanwhile, the fierce, ruby-red draconic eyes looked alive and seemed to focus on whatever Victor stared at. It was an imposing visage. The reason he studied himself so was that he was torn, unable to decide if he should wear his armor when he traveled to Ruhn, or if he should keep it hidden until he needed it. He hadn't asked Dar, but he had an idea what his mentor would say.

Inside his helmet, he grinned as he spoke to himself. "Something like, 'Victor, only reveal your cards when you need to play them.' Ha!" He laughed at his near-perfect impression. His mind made up for him by an imaginary Ranish Dar, Victor sent some Energy into the runes that converted his armor to simple, fine clothing. He touched the key and marble-sized vault hanging from the chain around his neck, almost as if he wanted to ensure it was still there, and then he looked through his rings, reviewing the things he was taking with him to Ruhn.

Dar had given him nearly a library's worth of books to study. Victor had sorted them as neatly as he could, but he still felt overwhelmed by the stacks of books in the enormous high-quality storage space he'd taken from Fak Loyle. As the thought crossed his mind, Victor thought about Cora, and his lips spread into a smile; he'd received a note from Efanie just the day before describing the girl as "increasingly happy and making fast friends with Deyni and Chala." He shook his head, pushing the happy thought aside, and refocused on the books.

Foremost among them were his tomes on runes, sigils, and glyphs. He'd made much progress with Dar over the last few months, but there was still a lot to learn, especially where elder magic was concerned. Dar had, begrudgingly, taught him one set of glyphs, but he'd also given Victor tomes on two others, again urging caution and patience in their study. Beyond those books were ones on spell patterns, enchanting, and artificing. Dar had expectations for Victor to study them while he was away, along with several accounts of military history and other general areas of study like—to Victor's dismay—math, poetry, literature analysis, and even philosophy.

The enormous list of study materials and lessons Dar had given him— enough to fill a small leather-bound book—drove home the point that Victor would be on Ruhn for a while. In his estimation, Dar had given him at least two years' worth of study materials, and that only accounted for the academics. Victor would also be expected to continue to practice his martial prowess between duels, maintain his daily Spirit and Breath Core cultivation, and, of course, pursue his social duties and goals among the elite of Gloria.

After several minutes of perusal, Victor felt satisfied that he had everything he needed packed away in his storage rings, and he began to feel a twinge of nervous energy as he realized he'd run out of excuses to stall. It was time to say his farewells and meet with Dar. With a heavy sigh, he gave his room a final lingering look and then left, walking quickly down the hall and into the main parlor. Just as they'd promised they would be, Lam, Edeya, Darren, and Lesh were all there, ready to see him off.

Edeya was first on her feet, fluttering her blue shimmering wings as she raced across the large area rug to wrap her tiny arms around his waist, hugging her cheek against his stomach. "Promise you'll visit when you can!" she said as he gently pressed her close.

Victor laughed and nodded. "Dar says it's cheaper to stop here on my way to Fanwath if I want to visit home, so you can believe I'll spend a day or two catching up with you all." He directed his words to the others who'd all stood and approached. Darren cocked his head, eyeing him down his beak with his predatory, perpetually angry-seeming eagle face, and Victor couldn't help a chuckle as the tall feathered man made deep, resonant *clicks* in his throat.

"Oh?" Lam asked, arching an eyebrow. "You'll only stop here because it's *cheaper*?" At her teasing tone, Edeya tightened her squeeze, and Victor laughed.

"No, of course not. I suppose I was just saying I could kill two birds—" He stopped abruptly, glancing at Darren with wide eyes.

"Oh, very funny!" Darren chuckled and folded his arms, putting on a show of being offended. Victor could tell he wasn't, though, because he was still making that happy *click* in his throat. He and his groupmates, including Trin, had been running through dungeons nonstop over the last few months. They were all well into Tier Two but had, thus far, failed to pull any treasures to advance Darren's bloodline further. Victor had offered to help him buy one, but, to his credit, Darren insisted he wanted to earn it.

Lesh stepped closer, holding out a hand. "If it weren't so many jumps, I'd travel with you to see you settled in, Lord Victor."

"Oh, come on, *hermano*! Don't start with the 'lord' this and 'lord' that again." He grasped the dragonkin's hand and squeezed.

Lesh chuckled and returned the pressure. "I'm feeling formal, seeing as you'll soon be gone. Rest assured that Darren and I will continue to make a name for your household here on Sojourn."

"Hey!" Edeya released her grip around Victor's waist and turned to glare at Lesh. "We're *all* making our names known here, and, of course, we know it reflects on Victor."

"I didn't mean—" Lesh floundered.

"Well, you big, scaled—"

"Whoa!" Victor laughed, wrapping an arm over Edeya's shoulders and pulling her into his side. "I'm proud of you all, and I know one thing: There's nothing any of you can do to mess up whatever reputation I have around here. Ha! That's the last thing on my mind. I'm just going to miss you all, but I know you'll be doing great things while I'm gone." He turned to Darren. "Did the page I gave you work?"

"Yes! I messaged Olivia, and she's aware that if she writes on that page of the Far Scribe book, I'll see the note. So far, she doesn't have a firm date for her arrival, but I'll be checking the page daily."

"Good." Victor looked at Lam, met her eyes, and smiled, then at Lesh and nodded his head. Finally, he squeezed Edeya's shoulders one more time. "I guess that's that. I gotta meet Dar down in the catacombs."

Lam's wings flickered, and golden motes sprinkled to the carpet like fairy dust. "Where he helped me?"

"Yep. I guess the veil is thinnest there."

"Bye, Victor," Edeya said, turning into his embrace so she could look up into his eyes. "I love you, you know?"

Sudden moisture sprang into Victor's eyes, and he blinked, looking up. "I love you too, dummy."

"Hey! That's my name for *you*!"

With a chuckle and a sniff, Victor looked around the room one last time. "Stay safe." He turned and started toward the hallway, but plenty of well-wishes chased him as he made his way to the kitchen.

"Be safe, yourself!" Lam called. "Take care!"

"Thanks for everything, Victor!" Darren's newly deep voice rang out.

"We'll speak soon! Good luck, brother!" Lesh boomed.

Only Edeya was quiet, but her earlier words still rang in Victor's ears. She *loved* him, and that felt wonderful. Of course, he knew it before then. He knew there were people here and on Fanwath who loved him, but it felt good to hear it just the same. He was surprised to find most of the staff lined up in the kitchen, waiting to watch him pass through on his way to the cellar. Several of them called out fond farewells and urged him a speedy return, and Victor could only smile and wave as he hurried past.

Dar was waiting for him in the cave where they'd done Lam's ritual. Victor, as always, had a sneaking suspicion that the master Spirit Caster could somehow sense his location on his property and would use the spirit plane to travel quickly ahead of him. Victor grinned when he saw his mentor in his orange and teal flowing silken outfit and sketched a formal bow. "Good morning, Lord Dar."

"Ah, excellent form on that bow, Victor. You'll make me proud on Ruhn." He gestured to the stony ground before him. "Come close. You should find it easier than usual to pull your physical form onto the spirit plane from here. Are you ready? Have you meditated on the toil ahead of you?"

Victor nodded. "I've been holding myself on the spirit plane for nearly an hour a day these last few days."

"Good. Perhaps, after some study and advancement, when you visit me next, you'll be ready for me to teach you the secret to bridging worlds on the spirit plane." He chuckled and shook his head. "It depends on how long you wait to come for a visit. Don't expect me to teach you if you come running home after a week or two."

"Nah, I won't." Victor smiled, inhaling deeply through his nose. "I think it'll do me good to be on my own for a while. I've got my Far Scribe books if I need to hear from some familiar people."

"Good. You have everything? Your books? Your weapons? Your gift for Queen Kynna?"

Victor nodded. "All set."

Dar looked him up and down, nodding. "I'm pleased you chose to keep your armor concealed. Best to avoid using it until you must. I won't be joining you for an introduction. Instead, I'll deposit you outside the city walls. My welcome will be very short-lived; the veil walkers who watch over Ruhn will not tolerate my presence for more than a few moments. It's best that I don't attempt to interact with any of my descendants or those poor people foolish enough to worship my memory."

"Will I stand out?" Victor gestured to his clothes. "Like this?"

"Not especially. Your attire is suitable, and your Quinametzin blood makes you resemble the primeval Fae quite a lot. Some of my kin will be darker or lighter, depending on the amount of Igniant in their blood, but the primary ancestral heritage of the people of Ruhn is, as I told you before, one of giantish Fae."

"Is that a word? Giantish?"

"Did I not use it? Could I utter it otherwise? It means descended of, related to, or appearing like a giant."

"Am I giantish?"

"Ha! Until you grow to your full potential, aye. When you're enraged and fully in your titanic aspect, people will know that 'giantish' doesn't measure up when it comes to your description." Dar grinned and grasped Victor's shoulder. "Well? Have we dawdled enough? Are you ready?"

Victor returned the gesture, clapping his hand on Dar's shoulder. "I'm ready! Let's do this."

"Right. See you on the spirit plane." With that, Dar faded from sight. Victor steeled his will, looking inward as he built the pattern for Spirit Walk. He wrapped his aura around himself, grasping hold of his every component cell, and as he cast the spell, he *willed* his body to come with him. He'd done the same every night before sleeping, holding himself longer and longer on the spirit plane each time. As Dar had promised, it was almost effortless by then, especially from inside the cave beneath his home.

When he appeared on the spirit plane, Dar stood there, solid and real, just like him. "Good! Now, concentrate on keeping yourself whole. Don't let your body try to slip away from you. Moving will burn your Energy faster than simply standing still, but not by much. If my estimation is correct, we'll reach Ruhn long before you run dry."

"How will I guide myself? Usually, I have a destination in mind—a person or place I know."

"Leave the guiding to me. Focus on my presence and simply move with me. This will be another test of your will: You must not let your gaze wander. If you see something that takes your attention, you will fall away from me, and then we'll have to waste precious minutes looking for each other. Where we're going—between worlds—vast distances can be crossed in a single heartbeat, and it wouldn't be impossible to become lost. Even I would have trouble finding you."

"And if I run out of Energy out there?"

"Then you'll be pulled out of the spirit plane onto the material—in the void of space. Even a sturdy Quinametzin couldn't last long in such a state." Dar grabbed his shoulders and focused his blazing eyes on Victor's. "Stay with me!"

With that, Dar turned and began to walk, and Victor fixed his gaze on a spot of teal fabric on his mostly orange tunic as he followed. The spirit plane passed in a blur as they gained momentum, but Victor refused to break his gaze from that spot. He didn't blink; he hardly breathed as he focused on following his mentor. Soon, his vision tunneled as their speed became immense. They raced through the spirit plane as Dar guided them, and Victor focused on keeping up with him.

They never ran; it was always a normal walking pace, but that was the magic of the spirit plane; it wasn't properly tangible. It was a place of Energy and light and the stuff between the material and the metaphysical. With an act of will, a *desire* to be somewhere, a spirit walker could bend the reality of distance and move great distances with a thought.

Victor never noticed when they moved beyond the bounds of Sojourn into the space between worlds. He couldn't tell if Dar had changed directions or performed some action to create a bridge between the worlds. All he knew was that spot of teal on orange and the blur of the universe speeding by on either side.

He was acutely aware of his Energy levels; he could feel how his reserves dipped below half, then a quarter, and when he began to get nervous as he lost half of that again, Dar suddenly stopped. "We've arrived," he announced, gesturing around the spirit plane. They stood in a meadow of ethereal grass dotted with shimmering blue flowers. The stars above were brilliant and clear. Looking around, Victor saw distant luminescent trees and the faint purple outlines of mountain ranges in nearly every direction.

"The city walls are a mile or so distant; you'll see them when you look around. I won't cross over. This is where we part for now."

"Um . . ." Victor nodded, licking his lips. "And Kynna? Do you have a message for her?"

Dar waved a hand. "Your arrival is message enough. Victor, I know I speak flippantly about duels and family and . . . well, many things. Listen to me now, though, as I impart some final, serious words." He stared at Victor, waiting for a response.

"I'm listening."

Dar nodded. "Good. One: a final warning about elder magic. Tread lightly. Two: I've put much faith in your ability to win lopsided contests. If you get to a point where defeat seems inevitable, I will not hold it against you if you counsel Kynna to cease her attempts to expand her nation. I'd rather you back down than die." Those words were the first sign of any doubt Dar had that Victor could win his fights on Ruhn, and they tickled his spine like cold fingers.

"She's expecting to force a war of succession, though."

"I haven't pressed that issue yet in my correspondence with her, but once it's begun, she will understand if you don't believe you can win against the great nations. She'll have to. Remember, her original request was for a champion to fight off her neighbors. This expansion is entirely my idea—a plan to gain you worthy hearts for your ritual. I didn't want to fill your mind with doubt, but I feel I must tell you that the length of this campaign is entirely in your hands. You will be the judge of how far to push things."

Victor wasn't sure what to say, so he stood there, clenching and unclenching his fists. After a moment, though, he nodded. "All right, Lord Dar. I'll try to be smart about it. Is there anything else?"

"No. I'll look forward to your weekly reports. Farewell, Victor." With that, Dar was gone, and Victor stood alone on the ethereal grassy plain. Looking inward, he saw that his Core was nearly drained dry, so he reached into his pathways and severed the connection to his Spirit Walk spell. The world shifted, flashing brightly as his eyes adjusted to the sunlight, and then he felt the cool breeze, smelled the fresh air with a distant odor of woodsmoke, and heard the steady trundling rumble of a massive wagon rolling on nearby cobbles.

Victor turned toward the sound and saw, down a grassy slope, a broad brown-brick paved road leading toward a tremendous city wall in the distance. Dar had said he was a mile from those walls, so Victor took a moment to appreciate their size. They had to be a hundred feet high with an outward flaring base that made the gatehouse tunnel look deep and cavernous. Squat ballistae towers lined the wall, and, as he squinted to look more closely, Victor counted more than a hundred soldiers patrolling just the area above and near the gate.

"If they settle wars with duels, why the hell do they need walls like that?" He looked back to the wagon he'd heard earlier and saw that it looked almost like a rolling fortress. It had four axles, was plated with heavy-looking metal, and looked to be propelled by some kind of Energy engine that hummed and glowed with orange light, belching black smoke out of a chimney stack near the rear. Half a dozen guards lined the top of the wagon, all wielding glowing crossbows.

Victor could only assume that the roads and wilds of Gloria weren't safe. He didn't see any other traffic on the road, but looking away from the city, he saw massive forests and looming mountains in the distance. One of the peaks was enormous, with smooth white shoulders and a rounded top shrouded in black, dark clouds. "A volcano?" He grinned at the idea. Maybe he'd get a chance to visit.

He turned back to the wagon and watched it approach the gate. Despite the size of the vehicle, it easily disappeared into the gaping maw of the gatehouse tunnel. Victor saw a couple dozen guards form up ranks behind it, facing outward toward the road, apparently awaiting the next traveler or perhaps a hostile force. "Or maybe a damn monster." Victor shrugged and strode down the grassy slope to the road. "All right," he sighed, squaring his shoulders. "Time to meet the people of Gloria."

# 10

## A GIFT

As he approached the gray stone city walls, Victor realized his earlier estimation was off; he'd been gauging their height based on the size of the people he saw. His mind had let slip an important detail Dar had given him about the folks on Ruhn—they were almost all giant-sized. With that realization, he figured the walls were closer to two hundred feet high. The soldiers standing in the shadow of the gatehouse were loosely arranged in two ranks of ten, and they all watched the road through the eye slits of heavy plate helms as he approached.

The soldiers in the back rank were armed with long spears, and those in front wielded heavy metal pikes. To Victor's eye, their uniforms made them look sort of like conquistadores—black uniform pants, polished boots, and shiny helmets and breastplates. They each wore a sky-blue sash emblazoned with a yellow rose—the sigil of Gloria. Of course, when everyone was a giant, no one really seemed like one, so it wasn't particularly imposing for Victor, who was easily a match for the soldiers when it came to bulk, to step toward the armed, combat-ready men and women.

"State your business in Gloria!" the centermost soldier shouted when Victor was no closer than thirty yards from the gatehouse. The term "Gloria" referred to both the nation and the capital city of Dar's descendants, so Victor wasn't sure of the spokesman's exact meaning, but he supposed it didn't matter.

"I'm here to see the queen."

Murmurs and even a few snickers broke out among the soldiers, and the speaker turned to shout, "Quiet!" before addressing Victor again. "The queen is quite busy. If you've no other business in the city, then it would be best to turn around; we've little room or charity to spare for a vagabond."

Victor chuckled and stepped closer. "That's quite an assumption. 'Vagabond'? Why not wanderer or stranger? It seems you've chosen to label me with negative connotations." Victor laughed inwardly at his words; if the man he'd been a few years ago had heard those words come out of his mouth, he would have lost his shit laughing. What a poser!

"Whatever you call yourself, we've no room. Do you wish to declare yourself? Are you from Frostmarch? Xan? You had to come through their blockades! Turn around or be seized for questioning. This is your final warning."

In unison, the guards took a stomping step forward and lowered their polearms so the points aimed toward Victor. He wondered what hidden signal the leader—captain?—had given. He didn't back down, in any case. Instead, he stepped forward again, closing the distance between himself and the soldiers to just a few long strides. He sighed, shaking his head. "Is this the welcome I'm getting? I expected more." The guard began to speak, but Victor held up a hand. "You asked me to declare myself, so I will. I'm here at the behest of Ranish Dar to serve as a champion to Queen Kynna, and I'd appreciate you guiding me to her. If you can't do that, then at least get the fuck out of my way."

To his amazement, a good third of the soldiers fell to their knees at the mention of Ranish Dar. As he continued speaking, many of the other soldiers lifted their polearms, perhaps loath to seem threatening to a man making claims like the one Victor just had. The captain, though, stepped closer, his pike still leveled menacingly. "Have you any proof of these claims?"

Victor held up his right hand, displaying Dar's signet. "I have Ranish Dar's signet. Maybe you could recognize that? If not, just take me to the queen, and she will verify my words. I would have thought she'd put out word that I was on my way, but . . ." He trailed off, sighing, as he looked past the soldiers into the depths of the cavernous gatehouse tunnel. His gaze drifted down to the now quiet soldiers, especially those kneeling. Did they worship Dar like a founding ancestor, or was it something more? They certainly *seemed* pious in their bowed obeisance.

"Will you demonstrate your strength to back up your claim? A show of your aura, perhaps?" The captain had stepped even closer, and now, if he wanted to lunge, Victor felt sure the man could bring his gleaming pike into play.

"That's an odd thing for a captain of the queen's soldiers to ask. Why would I display my strength so that spies could run tattling to the borders and alert the kings who hold this nation under siege?" Victor stepped toward the captain, allowing his pike to brush against his hip as he held out a hand. "I'm Victor, and I come from a place called Tucson. Ranish Dar has seen the plight of his nation on Ruhn, and he wants me to help set things right. Now take my hand and then guide me to the queen." He'd rehearsed such words with Dar so much that they were starting to feel natural on his tongue. He hoped he was convincing to the soldiers.

Something about his tone and the sureness of his body language must have convinced the captain, because he slung his pike onto his shoulder and then clasped Victor's hand. He had a firm, strong grip, and when he nodded, look-ing through the slit of his visor, Victor saw hard pale eyes. The soldier released his grip. "I'm Captain Wash. Red Wash—if we meet again while I'm not on duty, please call me Red. The queen has people who can verify the signet you bear. Please follow me to the palace." With that, he turned and began striding through the ranks of soldiers, who were either bowing or kneeling by that point.

Victor could tell the soldiers were struggling to remain disciplined, and by the time he'd marched halfway through the gatehouse tunnel, one of them, a woman, called out, "Is it true? You've seen Ranish Dar?"

Victor smiled and turned, walking backward as he waved. "It's true! He's doing well and sends his regards to the people here! He's proud of your hard work!" Dar had never said such a thing, but Victor thought it wouldn't hurt to boost morale a little. As he turned and continued to follow Red, he could hear the excited chatter behind him, and his grin grew.

As they exited the tunnel, several soldiers approached Captain Wash, but the man waved them off and hurried onto the street that ran parallel to the wall. Victor followed, his neck craning to give him a view of the tall stone structures. Gloria reminded him of what he'd always imagined a true medieval metropolis would look like. The buildings were mostly built from stone blocks like the great wall surrounding them, and they were tall, with many towers and minarets capped in glittering metallic- and glass-studded tiles. Those tiles and the many crystalline windowpanes picked up the light of the pale yellow sun, bringing the heights to life with their reflections.

More than that, pennants and tabards flew from nearly every structure. They bore coats of arms and fanciful designs and added splashes of color everywhere. On every corner and in the courtyards of every great building, rose bushes bloomed, and their pleasant aroma was ever-present as he and the captain made their way through the clean, orderly streets. The populace was another story.

Everywhere Victor looked, he saw gaunt, hungry faces—mostly among the young. He'd been prepared for this; Dar had explained that while Ruhn's popu-lation was largely of a high iron-rank average, the children would be the ones who suffered the most when there was a shortage of supplies. The adults, who'd had time to gain levels, didn't require as much food to survive; the Energy was rich, and their bodies would sustain themselves on it. The children, however, were still low tier, and the Energy in the air did little for their mostly normal, mortal constitutions.

When he saw those groups of sickly children with wan faces and wide star-ing eyes, he felt warring emotions—anger at those responsible and pity for the pathetic individuals before him. He wanted to stop and hand out food, but he knew it would cause a riot and that he'd, at best, put off their suffering for a day or two. Instead, he steeled his resolve to end the stranglehold Gloria's neighbors had on the nation's supply lines.

As for their looks, Dar hadn't been wrong; for the most part, the people of Gloria looked like large humans. Here and there, Victor saw signs of Fae bloodlines—large bright eyes, pointed ears, and a general beauty and grace that outshone some of the more mundane-looking folk. He and the guard captain didn't draw many stares; Victor was dressed nicely but plainly, and he wasn't so out of line with his looks that he stood out. Plenty of the Ruhnic folk had dark hair and tanned skin, and as he'd observed earlier, the people who weren't "giantish" were few and far between and obviously not native to the world.

The palace was an imposing and beautiful structure, and it reminded Victor that, while Gloria was down on its luck as a nation, it had a proud heritage. It was a sprawling compound with many courtyards, gardens, wings, and outbuildings. He saw minarets domed in turquoise and glittering precious metal, stained glass windows, and structures built entirely of seamless polished marble. Everywhere his eye went as he followed Red through the echoing corridors, Victor saw liveried servants but only caught glimpses of the nobility through archways or around corners. He wasn't sure if Red was trying to keep him away from those folks or if they were just very thinly spread out on the palace grounds.

After a while, they came to a room with a vaulted ceiling, plush carpets, and many antique-looking high-backed chairs lining the walls. Red pointed to one of the chairs and said, "Please take a seat, and I'll fetch the chamberlain."

"If you must." Victor sat down and folded his arms over his chest, glaring as the captain hurried to a closed door. He then paused and looked back.

"Please don't wander."

Victor's frown deepened. "If you thought I meant harm to the queen, it would be foolish to leave me alone here."

"I don't." Red cleared his throat and spoke again. "I mean, I don't believe you're lying. Having the chamberlain inspect your signet is merely a formality, um, sir." With that, he bowed briefly and then departed. The gesture reminded Victor of his lessons on Ruhnic tradition, especially those regarding honor. If Red had indicated that he thought Victor was being dishonest, it would have been within his right to call him out, forcing an honor duel. He shook his head, *tsking*, as he thought it through.

It wasn't two minutes later when he heard the click of bootheels on marble, and then the door swung wide, and Red appeared with another, older man. He was dressed in attire similar to the servants but finer: black pants, a sky-blue silken shirt with a yellow rose embroidered over his left breast, and polished black leather shoes. He looked very sharp—everything was pressed to perfection, and his curly gray hair was coifed as though he'd just come out of the barbershop. Victor stood, and though he too was nicely clothed, he somehow felt sloppy as the man stepped toward him, looking down his long, sharp nose at Victor's hand.

Red cleared his throat and announced, "Chamberlain Thorn, may I present Victor of Tucson, emissary of the great Ranish Dar and prospective champion to Queen Kynna Dar."

At his words, Victor grinned. He wasn't sure why he'd said he was from Tucson, but it was nice to hear the name again. He'd learned the customs well, so he bowed deeply at the waist. Chamberlain Thorn also bowed, then stepped forward and held out his hand. "May I see Lord Dar's signet?"

Victor held up his hand, making a fist so the signet ring stood out proudly among his plainer storage rings. Thorn leaned forward, and Victor felt a small surge of Energy as his gray eye glittered with silvery sparkles. A moment later, he straightened, and his smile was enormous as he said, "Welcome to Gloria, Champion." He sharply about-faced and barked, "Hurry! Assemble the court. I'll present Victor to the queen personally!"

Red turned and bolted, his clomping boots loud at first, then fading with distance. Chamberlain Thorn's smile never faded as he slowly studied Victor from head to toe. "It's truly a miracle! I can't tell you how wonderful it is to see you, sir! There have been rumors, of course. The queen's attendants whispering about secret correspondence. Of course, we all dreamed. Surely, the great Ranish Dar wouldn't let his first kingdom come to ruin. Still, it's many a generation since anyone has seen or personally heard from him. Yet here you are, bearing his signet, with a promise to fight for us! Queen's mercy!" The man had tears in his eyes, and Victor struggled to maintain a little distance between them as the fellow kept encroaching into his personal space.

"Well, it's good that you're happy, Chamberlain. Now, since I seem to have you in my corner, can you give me any information about those who might wish to see me fail?"

Thorn's eyes shot wide at those words, and he nodded emphatically. "There are those among the nobility—landholders and distant relatives of the queen— who would benefit if they made underhanded agreements with the kings of Frostmarch and Xan. I'll draft you a document, sir, an accounting of Gloria's great lords and ladies. Will that be suitable?"

Victor nodded. "Yes. That's one thing Ranish Dar couldn't properly prepare me for; he's lost touch with the political scheming of the noble houses of his former home."

"I will be your guide, milord." He opened his mouth to say more, but just then many stomping boots sounded from the corridor outside, and soon Red was striding through the door, flanked by four other soldiers in matching attire.

Victor didn't love that all the household guards seemed to wear full helmets; he liked seeing a person's facial expression when he spoke to them. Still, he couldn't argue that it made for a more imposing presence.

"Lord Thorn, Her Majesty awaits in the throne room."

"Very well." Thorn turned to Victor. "Please accompany me to meet the queen, milord."

Victor nodded and gestured for the man to lead the way. Dar had driven home that it would be fruitless to insist on informal titles in the court of Queen Kynna. The Ruhnians put a lot of weight on the formality of rank. Chamberlain Thorn led the way through a new corridor, this one very broad and with a soaring ceiling. Paintings of stern-looking men and austere ladies lined the walls above the fanciful pale-blue wainscoting, and Victor occupied his mind wondering who they were as they approached a junction. He saw servants scurrying in the distance and imagined they were scrambling to do whatever servants did when the queen called an impromptu gathering of the royal court.

Red and the other soldiers stomped in near unison behind them, and when they turned the corner, Victor saw four more similarly armed men standing guard outside a massive ornate double door. Two guards pulled the doors wide as they approached, revealing a picture-perfect fairytale throne room. The cynic in Victor remembered the hungry, haunted faces of the children in the city outside, and he wondered if some of the opulence on display before him could be somehow traded for food.

The silver-flecked marble floors shone with a high gloss, reflecting the dazzling sunlight streaming in through high cathedral windows, and at the center of their focal point, a dais rose to support a massive throne of blue crystal. Victor lost track of everything else—the nobles lining the sides of the room, the elegant furnishings and art, even the softly playing string quartet in the corner. All he could focus on was the incredible vision of the queen sitting atop that crystal throne.

Queen Kynna was, as Dar had supposed, far more Fae than Igniant, but Victor could see traces of her ancestor in her visage. Her skin looked like flesh, unlike Dar's stony appearance, but it was a lustrous pale-gray color with hints of something beneath the surface that sparkled like glitter or maybe diamonds. Her eyes drove home her relation to Ranish Dar, though; they shone like two tiny suns, brilliant nuclear reactions beneath heavy black brows. Victor couldn't deny she was beautiful, if a bit severe and cold.

Kynna had high cheekbones, a regal countenance, and full lips, painted a shade of blue that picked up highlights in her dark eye shadow and the midnight blue, gem-studded, form-fitting gown she wore. As for the crown, five sharp, black crystal spires rose up through her thick, curly black hair, gleaming with some kind of inner light. She looked statuesque—too perfect to be real—even as she leaned on one elbow on the arm of her throne and gazed down at Victor and his procession.

As Victor stood, a little dumbstruck, Chamberlain Thorn stepped forward and bellowed, breaking the spell, "I present to you Lord Victor of Tucson, disciple of Ranish Dar, whose lineage and wisdom are reflected in the grace of our queen and whom we revere for the founding of this great nation." Thorn bowed so low that he continued down onto his knees and lay prostrate by the time he finished speaking.

Victor took the hint and performed a perfect, formal bow at the waist. He didn't wait to be given permission to stand, however. He straightened and moved into the suddenly silent hall. He could hear the nobility breathing to either side of him, but not a soul uttered a word as his boots *clicked* on the marble. Kynna straightened, shattering the illusion that she was a statue carved from crystal. He stopped a few strides away from the dais where her throne sat and waited, locking his eyes with Kynna's blazing ones.

After a few heartbeats, her voice rang out, strong, strident, clear, but utterly feminine, "You may approach."

Victor stepped forward to the edge of the dais and fell to one knee, summoning the spear he had crafted for this occasion. He held it aloft on the palms of his hands—no easy feat, for the thing weighed several hundred pounds. The haft was crafted from something called ebon oak and was sturdy enough to withstand everything Lesh and his other sparring partners had been able to dish out. They'd tried cutting it, smashing it, and snapping it with a hundred different methodologies, but just as the weaponsmith had promised, it was very sturdy stuff.

The top three feet of the spear were taken up by the blade—a length of magically hardened steel that the weaponsmith had staked his reputation on. Victor wanted something sturdy, something he could drive through a hunk of similarly hard metal, digging for a gap without worrying about snapping the blade. It had held up to the demand through quite a lot of testing. The blade gleamed and winked in the light, a shimmering length of razor-sharp, mirror-finished metal that ended in a point so needle-sharp that Victor felt confident he could use it to dig a splinter from a child's foot.

Edeya had given him a charm to loop around the butt end of the spear haft—a couple of Darren's thunderbird feathers fastened by a thin lock of Lam's golden, wire-hard hairs. It didn't do anything except make the spear look cool, and Victor figured, knowing the way he fought, that it'd be ruined soon, but he liked it. The weapon was heavy for two reasons: The materials were tough and dense, and it was enchanted to grow with him, doubling in size if he took on his titanic form.

With all that being said, the gathered nobles—and Queen Kynna herself—could not deny the quality of the spear Victor held aloft as he knelt. He let the anticipation hang heavy in the air before speaking. "Queen Kynna, I offer you a gift for this auspicious occasion. I present this spear and vow to wield it in your name, vanquishing the champions of Frostmarch and Xan. The time has come for your house to ascend to its rightful place of prominence on Ruhn."

# 11

❦

# FAITH

As Victor's words rang out in the hushed anticipation that hung heavy in the throne room, Queen Kynna's eyes flew wide at their implication—a promise far beyond simply defending her beleaguered borders. The room was silent for several heartbeats—the assembled nobles seemed to be holding their breath—and then it erupted in a buzz of excited whispers, though Victor's ears detected a good amount of grumbling. When Kynna stood, the room grew silent again. Victor looked up at her, his golden-brown eyes peering up from beneath his heavy brow, his arms steady though the muscles strained to hold the dense spear in its awkward position.

The queen stepped down from her throne's dais, looming over him as she ran her gaze from one end of the great spear to the other. Victor could smell her perfume—something floral that tickled a memory he couldn't quite grasp. Her deep-blue gown glittered as if a million stars were woven into the fabric, and as she reached out a long slender arm to touch the weapon, lightly grazing it with her fingertips, Victor couldn't help noting the many glittering jewels adorning her fingers and wrist. "You come, warrior, to stand as my champion?"

"I do."

"And what of dear, brave, loyal Foster?" At her words, Victor heard boots click on the marble, and he knew Kynna's champion had stepped forward. He didn't look at him, though; he kept his eyes trained upward at Kynna's face beneath the wild tangle of her curly black hair and the high glittering spires of her crystal crown.

"Let him rest." Victor knew the question was for show, a way for Foster Green to save face and be acknowledged.

"What say you, Champion?" Queen Kynna asked. Victor, still looking up, saw her chin turn to the right.

"I am ever ready to serve, my Queen, but it has been many long years since I rested." Foster's voice was gravelly and deep, and Victor could hear deep emotion behind the words. He hadn't really considered that—how it might feel to be asked to step down after a lifetime of service. Dar had made it seem that Foster would be relieved, knowing he wouldn't be asked to fight the battles he and his queen had been avoiding—knowing he wouldn't win. Still, it had to sting his pride a little, being pushed aside by a young stranger.

"You have earned your rest, Foster, but make it short; my close council has room for another chair." As she spoke, Victor heard dozens of murmured conversations pick up. He caught words and phrases here and there, primarily people speculating about the implications of another seat on Kynna's council. He also heard a few exclamations of disbelief—how could she take on an untested stranger when wolves were at the gates?

Kynna looked down, her bright eyes finally falling on Victor's face as she traced the spear with her fingertips. For a moment, he wondered if she'd grasp it and try to lift it, but she withdrew her hand. "I accept your gift, Victor, disciple of Ranish Dar. Though I must insist you hold this weapon ready until such time that you no longer need it to fight Gloria's battles." She lifted her hand and rested her fingertips on Victor's forehead. They were cool to his hot flesh, but he could feel the thrum of some kind of potent Energy in them; he wondered what affinity or affinities she had. "Rise, Champion of Gloria."

Victor did so, straightening in a fluid motion, snapping the spear around in a half twirl, thudding the feather-adorned butt against the marble. He'd gained much understanding of the weapon over the last few months of practice—not only his own experience but the knowledge the System granted him when he broke through into the advanced stages of mastery. He knew he had a long road to walk before he attained epic-tier mastery of the weapon, but he felt good with it in his hands. His guilty conscience was quick to remind him that Lifedrinker would be better, but he pushed the feeling down, knowing she'd come out when the time was right.

The crowd lining the sides of the throne room began to clap—not a raucous applause or boisterous cheer but a gentle, polite patter of fingers against palms. Victor frowned, glancing side to side for the first time, taking in the assembled nobility. They were, like their queen, austere in posture and expression. The women and many men wore makeup, darkening the skin around their eyes and brightening the red of their cheeks and lips. Their clothes were fine—silks and satins, capes and capelets, jewels on necks, fingers, and brows, and not a single one of them looked as if they'd missed a meal or suffered during the years-long siege of their nation.

Victor's burgeoning disdain was interrupted by the queen's words. Her words were directed at him as she spoke, but she projected them, ensuring all could hear. "My ancestor's most recent missive indicated a man named Victor would be coming. He didn't say how soon, though, and I'd honestly begun to lose hope."

Victor had become distracted in his study of the nobles, and as she spoke, his eyes fell on the man who had to be Foster Green; he was tall, swarthy, and lean and had steel-gray hair, cut short in much the style that Victor preferred. He was the only person in the room who looked like a fighter without the armor and livery of the queen's guard. When their eyes locked, Kynna was just finishing her statement, and Victor exchanged a solemn, knowing nod with the old fighter. He turned to regard the queen, pressing his lips together to avoid frowning as he replied. "Ranish Dar is a man of his word—I am here."

"My people suffer, though you wouldn't know it looking around this room, Victor." Her eyes flared briefly, and Victor wondered if she'd read more in his expression than he'd intended. "How soon will you be ready to accept a challenge?"

Victor, perhaps a foot taller than Kynna, took a step back off the dais to more easily look her in the eyes. He nodded slowly and then turned to more deliberately regard the assembled nobility again. This time, he allowed some of his scowl to enter his expression as he locked eyes with any who dared to meet his gaze; only a few did so. When he finished his more obvious perusal, he turned back to the queen. "I'll be ready after a bit of rest. The journey was arduous." Finally, some of the gathered nobles reacted with more than whispers, titters, and tepid clapping.

He heard exclamations of relief and, unsurprisingly, fear. One man called out, "My Queen! I beg your caution! Should he lose, we all will suffer!"

"Be still, Rannick," Kynna snapped. "Did you not hear what was said? Lord Ranish Dar has sent this man! He is here to elevate us, not to sit and fawn while we slowly wither! While our *children* starve!" Looking at the man in his finery, Victor had a feeling his children weren't lacking food. He had a feeling these nobles had storage devices holding years and years' worth of sustenance for the people they loved.

His scowling gaze didn't quiet the murmurs. In fact, they grew louder, and a woman from the other side of the room cried out, "Have you no eyes? No senses? I can read this man's Core like a child's! I'd wager most of us outrank him!" Her words were almost enough to get a reaction from Victor. He wanted to unleash his tightly held aura, wanted to swell his pathways with rage-attuned Energy and expand to his true titanic form, but he didn't.

Dar had instructed him well on his strategy; he was to play all of his cards close to his chest, including the strength and weight of his aura. He might be able to hide his Core from most of these folks, but there were, indeed, many people on Ruhn in the high iron ranks. Even if he wanted to block them from viewing his Core and guessing his tier, it wasn't a battle he should fight. Their guesses were immaterial; whatever they thought they knew was only that—a guess. Dar's strategy involved people underestimating him, and letting them see his Core was part of that plan.

He glared at the woman who'd spoken and growled, "Is that a challenge?" A sudden silence fell over the room. Nearly everyone ceased even breathing, and Victor was sure he could hear the quick, nervous pants of the woman he focused his scowling countenance upon.

As Victor continued to stare, she held a hand to her silk-covered bosom, glancing around nervously and stammering, "N-no! I'm not a fighter!"

"Outrageous!" someone muttered loudly enough to draw Victor's gaze. As he stared toward the voice, inviting the speaker to elaborate on his outrage, everyone grew very still. The tension grew thick as Victor's heart thudded slowly and steadily in his chest.

"Well," Queen Kynna said as she gracefully returned to her throne, "if no one would like to challenge Victor for his new position as my champion, perhaps you all should leave. He and I have much to discuss."

"You heard Her Majesty! Clear the throne room!" Chamberlain Thorn bellowed, still standing near the doors. Victor sent his spear into a storage container and stood, arms folded, watching the nobles clear out. The musicians, who'd long ago stopped playing, gathered their equipment and scurried out a side door, which drew his eye to a row of servants holding trays of drinks and hors d'oeuvres vying for the same exit.

"I see your nobles don't deprive themselves." He nodded toward the last of the servants who hastily rushed through the door.

"I . . . must find a balance between currying favor among the nobility and succumbing to my desire to throw every last scrap of food we all have to the masses. You must understand that the palace storehouse would only feed the city for a day or two, no? Many nobles are opening their personal stores; our people will not starve today or tomorrow. No, they'll last months and maybe years, though the discomfort on the children's faces will bring daily shame to those of us who feast mostly on the ambient Energy. For that reason, many nobles will shun the populace, hiding away behind these walls or in their own keeps."

Victor regarded her, pleased that she was so open about the subject. Though her skin was smooth and flawless, she struck him as being experienced; she didn't seem young. "You have to curry favor?"

"There are many among my kin with ties in our neighboring kingdoms—family members bonded through marriage, for instance. If I push them too far out of their comfort, their disloyalty might move beyond simple spying and missives regarding the state of our capital and into true treachery. Gloria would have fallen years ago if I hadn't been working to appease the nobility."

Victor nodded. His arms were still folded over his chest, and he lifted a foot, resting it on the edge of the queen's dais. "Well, that ends today. Schedule the first duel. We'll get one of your enemies off your back, and then, with a little breathing room, we'll start eliminating the nobles who aren't cut out for the struggle to come."

"*Excuse* me, sirrah?" the queen arched an eyebrow, tapping one of her blue-polished nails on the arm of her crystal throne. The sound it made was almost musical—*ting, ting, ting.* "I appreciate your confidence, but Embry wasn't wrong; you seem to lack the weight of a high iron ranker. You certainly are no steel seeker!"

"Listen, my, uh, Queen: Ranish Dar has given me a strategy to follow. Do you trust your ancestor?"

"I don't . . ." She frowned and sighed. "I don't know, Victor. When I first wrote to him, it felt very strange; imagine praying to a long-dead ancestor, and you'll know what I mean."

"Yeah, you'd be surprised." Victor chuckled and added, "Anyway, Dar ain't dead." He frowned as he caught his tongue running away, forgetting all the lessons on etiquette Dar and Mr. Ruln had put him through.

Kynna leaned forward, her black crystal crown tilting precariously. Something must have held it in place—magic or something mundane like clips attached to her thick, curly black hair. "He may as well be, for all the interest he's shown in our plight!"

Victor smiled grimly. "I know, but I'm here now. What do we need to do to arrange a duel?"

"The challenge was issued; I've been avoiding it. It shouldn't be difficult to get Vennar or Groff to agree to terms."

"Good. The sooner, the better, Queen Kynna. Now, is there someone who can show me around this place?"

"We have much to discuss, Victor. There's more to your role than fighting duels." She shook her head, forcing an almost delicate smile. "I'm sorry. You must be exhausted from your journey. I'm sure Foster stayed near at hand; I'll have him introduce you to the staff and show you the palace grounds and your quarters."

Victor rubbed his chin. "Is he going to be . . ." He let his words trail off, leaving Kynna to make assumptions about his meaning.

"He's eager to retire, Victor. He only stayed on to avoid one of my cousins trying to claim the throne. I have many asps and adders in my court, as I'm sure you'll soon learn." She touched something on the side of her throne, and the large double doors opened almost immediately. One of the helmeted guards stepped into the opening, staring intently at Victor and the throne. "Fetch Chamberlain Thorn and Foster Green."

Victor was tempted to say he wasn't tired at all and that they could chat for a while, but he had an image to uphold; being exhausted from travel was natural for a "champion" out of his depth. "I hope you don't mind me taking some time to get my feet under me, Your Majesty."

"No, I understand. It's only . . ." She frowned, an expression that made her look like an angry goddess come down from Olympus. "Are you sure you're up for this? Are you certain we should schedule the duel? I'm sure Ranish Dar told you that if you lose, my throne is forfeit."

"Just like you, my Queen," Victor said as he grinned, enjoying the roleplay, "I must put my faith in Ranish Dar. He said I was ready, so I must assume he is correct." Part of him wanted to reassure her and display some of his strength, but another part was profoundly enjoying the game he played. He knew she had advisors and that she'd speak to them. If any were disloyal—and Victor believed that was likely—then word of her concern would travel, making it easier to schedule the duels. He just hoped he wouldn't have to blow all his cards in the first fight.

Bootheels clicking on marble signaled the arrival of Foster and Thorn, and Victor turned to regard them as they approached. Foster moved like a dancer, and Victor figured he was a formidable fighter. The fact that he was avoiding the challenges from Gloria's neighbors was a little worrying, but Victor had to remind himself that Foster wasn't hiding anything. The people here knew him. If Victor were enraged, with his aura flowing freely and his axe in his hand, he didn't think Foster would be very intimidating.

"Goodman Foster," the queen said, gesturing to Victor. "Would you kindly show my new champion around the palace? Put him in the purple rooms."

"I could vacate my suite—"

The queen chopped her hand in the air, cutting him off. "I'll not hear of it! You'll stay at the palace until we've won free of this siege and your family is home safe."

"As you say, my Queen." Foster bowed deeply. Seeing his excellent etiquette reminded Victor of his manners, and he turned to face the throne again.

"I'll await your call, my Queen. Will it be early?"

"I am an early riser. Will two hours past dawn suit you?"

Victor rubbed his chin—freshly shaven—and slowly nodded. "I think I can be ready by then." He inwardly snickered, wondering what they all thought of his need for rest. Fighting to hide his grin, he bowed low, holding it until the queen dismissed him.

"Very good, Victor. You may take your leave."

"Until tomorrow." Victor slowly straightened, then turned and descended the steps, nodding to Foster, who turned on his heel and guided him out.

He heard the queen say, "Stay a moment, Thorn. I've a matter or two to discuss—"The doors clicking shut cut her voice off, utterly masking any sound from within the throne room.

Foster turned to look over his shoulder and nodded briefly. "This way, Victor. We'll start with a tour of the grounds . . ."

Kynna looked down her nose at Thorn, her oldest confidant—the only man her father ever trusted. "Are you absolutely certain of his signet's authenticity?"

"It is genuine. I'm certain. My Truth Sense is infallible. His confidence is also true. He *believes* he will win the duels, and when he says he intends to bring Gloria to a place of prominence, he means it. Now, whether he's a deluded fool . . ."Thorn shrugged, putting on a face that said he wished he knew.

"Would Ranish send me a lunatic? Would he send a man to his doom, thereby dooming us?"

"I have only the records of your great ancestor's time here to go by, and I fear there are more than a few accounts of Ranish Dar acting impulsively and without logic. He was young then, or so the story goes, so much might have changed in the intervening millennia. Was his letter not reassuring?"

"He hardly spoke of Victor! He said his name and said he was a man of high potential with a courageous heart! When I described Foster Green, I thought that Ranish would at least send us someone sturdier than that good man!"

"He did seem rather . . ."Kynna saw Thorn struggle to find the right words. His eyes narrowed, and he pursed his lips. Finally, with an explosive sigh, he blurted, "Mundane! His attire, his appearance, his demeanor—I've seen Obert fight, my Queen, and his presence sends shudders down a man's spine! This man, this *Victor*—he's tall, he's strong-looking, but I don't sense any *weight* behind him. Embry wasn't wrong, either. Did you sense his Core? He can't be much beyond Tier Seven. How will he face a Tier Nine champion? If he truly means to elevate Gloria, he'll face much worse than that!"

Kynna nodded, tapping her nails on the crystal of her throne. As they chimed melodically, she thought about the plight of her people, about the children in the city and the feeble trickle of her nation's economy. Thorn stood still, patiently waiting, knowing she was weighing matters. She ran through the many risks of trusting Victor, and she weighed them against the scant few options at her disposal. After a time, she looked up. "We could test him."

"A challenger?"

"Someone to question his strength. Someone to cast doubt on his claims." Kynna didn't like her own idea, and it showed. Her frown felt as if it might become permanent as the corners of her mouth twisted down and her brows narrowed.

"And if he takes the insult and fights? If he's *not* boasting a strength beyond his means? Whose life would we throw away to make that test?" Thorn stepped close and hissed, "My Queen, you wrote to Ranish Dar! Victor arrived with his signet, just as your progenitor said he would. When does faith come into play?"

Kynna snorted, shaking her head in disbelief. "My dear Thorn, did you just counsel me to have faith? I'm stunned!" Thorn started to sputter a response, but she held up her hand. "No, don't be chagrined. I'm rather pleased by your advice; I grow weary of this gilded cage. I grow weary of seeing my father's great kingdom brought low. Our borders have shrunk for a dozen generations. Our coffers have shrunk along with them. We once boasted the greatest champion on the western continent! I rather like the idea of 'faith,' my dear, loyal chamberlain. Let's put Victor into play and see what fate has brought us. Arrange the first duel."

# 12

## TERMS

Victor stood behind Queen Kynna's high-backed, hand-tooled, gold-filigreed chair and listened to her and King Vennar hash out the terms of the duel. The king sat in a similar chair on the opposite side of an equally ornate table. It was Victor's job to appear imposing, and he did his best. Still, with his aura tightly in check, his armor all stowed away, and his Core locked down like a bank vault the day before payday, he didn't think he was imposing anyone, least of all Vennar or his champion, Obert.

Obert, on the other hand, was putting on a show of deadly force and barely restrained potential for destruction. He was an eleven-foot-tall man built like a ballet dancer. He walked more gracefully than a panther and projected a ferocity that would make a tiger seem cuddly. His long, lithe limbs were corded with hard muscle, his skin was tan and glistened as though oiled, and he wore armor consisting of a shiny breastplate, an eagle-visored helm, shiny bracers, and rune-inscribed greaves. Victor considered it "shiny," but the armor was more than that. It shone with the inner light of dense enchantments and radiated with a lustrous greenish-blue tint.

Victor forced his face into an unimpressed, almost lackadaisical expression as he regarded him. Still, inwardly, he was impressed, especially by the man's eight-foot longsword that hung from a scabbard on his back. Victor could only see the hilt and pommel—a glowing tiger's eye gemstone—but the thing had a *presence* he couldn't deny. Still, Victor didn't react. He didn't smile or glower. He didn't let his gaze linger. He constantly surveyed the room, the table, the monarchs, and even the motes of dust gently drifting through the beam of sunlight streaming through the high window.

He could tell his inattention was bothering Obert. The man stared at him as though he could melt Victor's heart with his gaze. Victor almost smirked at the thought—maybe he *could*! He let his eyes drift past Kynna's crown to King Vennar, a very different sort of man. Short for a Ruhnian, with very dark, nearly black skin and eyes that glowed much the same way as Kynna's and Dar's. Was he a distant relation? His flesh certainly reminded Victor of Dar's. It wasn't quite the same—it didn't look exactly like stone, but it had a porous, uneven quality that made it difficult to imagine how it would feel.

The king's voice was certainly far smoother than Dar's. "I understand you feel backed into a corner, Kynna—may I use your given name?"

"We're both monarchs here, Wil. I won't complain if you don't."

"Very good. First, let me thank you for responding to me before King Groff. I assure you, Frostmarch will offer better terms than Xan." He glanced at Victor and ran his eyes up and down his figure, from his well-polished boots to his freshly cut hair. Victor thought he saw a smirk hiding behind his bright eyes. "I'm pleased you've found yourself a young champion willing to stand for you. I'd heard rumors but hadn't let myself fully believe them." His lips curled into a more pleasant smile, and he leaned closer to Kynna over the table. "I'm not ashamed to admit that I loathed the idea of a great old warhound like Foster dying to save a lost cause. Will your new man take the knee, as Foster never would?"

"Oh no. You mistake me, Wil. I'm not here to negotiate a surrender. Today, we will agree to the terms of the duel."

Chamberlain Thorn and his counterpart—a small woman Victor hadn't caught the name of—sat at the left-hand sides of their monarchs, and it was the woman who reacted first to Queen Kynna's words. She audibly choked and had to hold the back of her hand to her mouth and look down, coughing softly to clear her windpipe. Everyone ignored her as the king once again looked at Victor.

"You're serious?"

"Quite so. Shall we begin?" Victor couldn't see Kynna's face, but she sounded very prim.

King Vennar, still staring at Victor and attempting to make eye contact while Victor continued to study the empty space in the air between himself and the far wall, could barely contain the lascivious expression on his face—a dog eyeing a child's abandoned hamburger. He slowly nodded, cleared his throat, and elbowed the woman beside him. "Certainly. Let's discuss terms."

Kynna inclined her head slightly, her tall crystalline crown glittering in the light as it dipped forward. "Have you any thoughts about sovereign succession?"

King Vennar brushed the back of his hand over his lips, almost as if he had to physically push away the hungry grin. "I see no reason to be overly harsh. I would think banishment will suffice."

"Of only the monarch or their entire lineage?"

"Oh, I would think the entire lineage." He *tsked* and, again, leaned forward with an earnest expression. "You could avoid that if you'll just have your new champion take the knee. I'd keep you on as a duchess."

"No, King Vennar, I believe we should do this properly. I have my ancestor's reputation to manage."

"Ah yes, the great Ranish Dar." Vennar smirked, shaking his head. "So. Are we agreed then? Banishment for the ruling family?"

Kynna nodded. "I believe that will suffice. No need for a grisly display of beheadings." At her words, both chamberlains began to write on the documents before them. She tapped one of her hard nails on the table—*click, click, click.* "And the Oaths of Submission?"

"One hundred years," Vennar spoke firmly, and Victor saw Obert shift in the corner of his eye, but he refused to look at the other champion to see his expression. Instead, he continued to let his eyes wander around the room, staring at the art, the furniture, and even the tiles along the far wall.

Kynna glanced to her left, looking at something Thorn had written, then nodded. "Very well. All nobility, minor and major, shall swear peace and allegiance to the victor for a term of no less than one hundred years. We're in agreement?"

Vennar nodded. "We are. Tribute and taxation?"

Again, Kynna looked to Thorn. "What is our proposal, Chamberlain Thorn?"

Thorn cleared his throat and lifted his notebook, speaking clearly, as if he was presenting to a room full of people, not just the three at the table with him. "We propose the following: The vanquished shall be bound to deliver tribute unto the victor in the form of wealth, crops, and provisions. The amount paid shall be no less than thirteen percent of each season's surplus, verified by the Crown's agents, who shall be given full access to all records upon request."

Vennar frowned, looking at his chamberlain. She didn't speak but tapped something in her notes as she nodded. Vennar looked back to Kynna. "I agree."

"This has been painless, Wil!" Kynna sounded borderline patronizing, but Victor couldn't see her face, so he couldn't be sure. Vennar didn't look angry, though; in fact, he looked as if he'd just been given a gift. "There's just the matter of the Right of the Chosen Blade."

Vennar barked a short, harsh laugh. "Forgive me, Kynna, but do you even have a cadre? I thought Foster was your last champion until . . ." He glanced at Victor again, this time doing nothing to hide the smirk on his face. ". . . recently. Still, I'll bite. How many champions should the victor claim?"

Kynna stiffened her back, squaring her shoulders. Victor imagined she was putting on a show of indignation at Vennar's dismissive attitude. Even so, she spoke very precisely with perfect decorum, "I would think a single choice will suffice."

Vennar leaned back in his chair, pushing away from the table as he waved a dismissive hand. "Very well." He looked to his chamberlain. "Is there aught else?"

"Just secondary terms, Your Majesty—things like hostage exchange, judicial authority, cultural exchange—"

Vennar sighed. "You can handle this with Goodman Thorn here, yes?"

Kynna spoke before the diminutive woman could reply. "I'm in agreement. These lesser matters can be handled by our people. However, we have one final matter to discuss. I'm assuming the duel will be held here, at the ring at Westhome. Have you looked at the schedule?"

Vennar nodded, reaching up to adjust his golden, diamond-studded crown. It wasn't a bulky crown, but it gleamed and sparkled impressively. "It's clear for months. Not many duels these days."

Kynna's response was immediate. "Sunrise, then?"

"So eager?" Vennar chuckled, glancing over his shoulder at Obert. "What say you, Champion? Will you be ready at dawn?"

"To slay this whelp?" Victor could feel the heat of his stare and the sloppy, or perhaps deliberate, slip of his aura that felt like iron and blood and somehow made Victor think of burning flesh. Even so, he refused to look at him and kept his face fixed in his simple, almost idiotic half-smile. "Aye, I'll be ready," the champion growled.

Vennar nodded and pushed his chair back. "We're agreed, then?"

Kynna also stood. "We are."

"So witnessed," Thorn and the other chamberlain said in near unison. For the first time, Victor let his eyes drift over to Obert's face, and he locked his gaze with the fierce golden eyes behind his eagle-beak visor. He didn't do anything more than smile, a genuine, eager grin that exposed his bright straight teeth. Still, Obert took a step back, perhaps caught off guard by the idiocy suddenly fleeing his opponent's gaze. Or, Victor reasoned, maybe Obert saw something in his eyes that was at odds with his display of weakness. Victor continued to stare and grin as the man turned on his heel and led the king and chamberlain out of the room.

"You did well, Victor," Kynna said as soon as the door clicked shut. "Assuming your intentions had anything to do with your . . . less than significant bearing. If King Vennar thought there was any chance he'd lose, he would have bargained much more viciously."

Chamberlain Thorn gathered up his papers and nodded. "Yes! These terms are wonderful." He looked at Victor and inclined his head. "Ahem, assuming you win, sir. Do excuse me, Your Majesty; I'll need to catch up with Lady Foi to finish the negotiation."

Kynna nodded. "Go on then." She watched him exit, then turned to Victor. "If you fail, you realize my entire family, from my son to my fifth cousin, thrice removed, will be forced to leave Ruhn, yes?"

Victor shrugged. "Well, my Queen, if I fail, I'll be dead."

Kynna's face, never exactly cheerful, fell into such a dour expression that Victor instinctively wanted to proclaim his innocence, though he'd done nothing wrong. "You're awfully flippant about this whole ordeal. You saw Obert! I'm sure you *felt* him, too. Tell me this now, Victor, is there more to you or not?" She gestured to him in exasperation, indicating his current state, no doubt—dressed in the same clothes he'd worn the day before, only this time he'd tweaked the colors of his attire to be more complementary to Gloria's heraldry; his shirt was pale yellow, his pants and leather pieces black.

"I am what I am, my Queen." When Victor saw her irritation fall away, only to be replaced by something closer to despair, he almost confessed his game. He settled on a compromise, saying, "Maybe you fear that your ancestor has sent me here to fail, maybe to teach you a lesson or to play a cruel game. Maybe you're wondering if he wants your family to be forced to leave Ruhn—that he has some sort of plan for you beyond this world." Kynna took a breath to speak, but Victor rushed to finish his statement. "You should know that he's a prideful man, and he wouldn't enjoy seeing his descendants chased off their homeworld. I also don't think I've done anything to deserve being sent to my doom." He finished with another shrug. "Try to stay confident, Kynna."

"Your enigmatic nature is rather maddening, Victor." She sighed and pointed to the door from which they'd entered. "Our portal awaits. By the way, I'll put aside your lack of propriety for now, but do remember to address me properly in the future." With that, she turned and marched to the door, and Victor followed, trying to replay his words in his mind. When had he addressed her inappropriately? It took him a minute, and by then, he was already through the door and marching down the hall to the portal chamber, flanked by four of Kynna's guards. "Ah!" he said, as he recalled calling her simply "Kynna" after telling her to be confident.

She turned to regard him as they walked. "Something amiss?"

"No. My apologies, Your Majesty." He turned to the guard on his left, meaning to grin or wink, but thought better of it when he saw her stern eyes through the slit in her helmet's visor. When they entered the portal chamber, the magical gateway was already active, glowing with deep blue Energy that hummed and buzzed as it crackled faintly. It would take them straight back to Gloria. The two delegations had met on neutral ground—a city called Westhome, which was the seat of the Ruhnic Empire on the western continent. Victor had seen it on a map and knew it was close to two thousand miles south and east of Gloria.

Part of him wondered if the place would still be neutral after he began to enact Dar's plan—pushing Kynna into kicking off a succession war. There were many rules, laws, and customs he had yet to master in this strange, new world, but so far, he was rather enjoying himself. Kynna interrupted his thoughts by striding through the portal without hesitation. Victor hurried to follow her, cringing slightly as he anticipated the portal's hot, shocking embrace. When he stepped out on the other side, Kynna stood facing him.

"You've only about twelve hours before you'll be fighting for your life. Is there anything you need to prepare? Anything you'd like to put in order?"

Victor rubbed his chin as he looked around the dim circular chamber. The portal crackled behind him as the guards followed them through. And then it sizzled and disappeared, throwing the room into deeper shadows. "I'll take some time to myself, I suppose. Do you mind if I go to my chambers to write some correspondence?"

"By all means." She stepped closer and spoke in a less imperious tone than usual, "I am *worried*, and it makes me unpleasant. I understand you're putting your life on the line tomorrow, and while the consequences would be dire for me and my loved ones should you lose, I want you to know that I understand the point you made earlier. You may die tomorrow. It's not a small thing you do for me, and—"

"Um, my Queen?" Victor grinned at the wide-eyed disbelief on her face after he interrupted her out-of-character attempt at sympathy. "I certainly don't mind helping you, but there's no need for any guilt. I'm not doing this for you." He grinned wickedly and winked at her. "I'm doing this for the glory."

Kynna scowled and pressed her blue-painted lips into a thin line as she glanced at the nearby guards. Victor wondered what was running through her mind. How ruthless could she be? Would she banish these soldiers because they'd witnessed him interrupting her? He didn't believe she was a tyrant, but it was kind of fun to test her. If he wanted to gauge her response, he was left disappointed because she just nodded and turned to stride out of the chamber, followed by three of the four guards. "Well," he muttered several seconds after the door had clicked closed, "I guess, technically, not responding *is* a response."

The remaining guard didn't comment. Victor looked at her, standing at attention just behind him. "What's your name, soldier?"

"Bryn, sir."

"You're the same guard who was waiting for me at my chambers this morning, right?"

"Yes, sir."

"Assigned to me permanently?"

"Until you die or leave, I suppose."

Victor laughed. "I like you, Bryn."

"Thank you, Lord Champion. May I speak freely?" Her voice echoed from inside her helm—stern, husky, and confident.

"I'd be angry if you didn't."

"I don't reciprocate your feelings. I think you're awfully rude. I think Queen Kynna ought to have your tongue stabbed through with a hot poker, and I think you're probably going to die tomorrow."

"As my auntie would say, '*qué encanto!*' Ha! Did that translate? I can never tell what the System's going to make sound like English—er, Rhunish?"

"You said I'm charming," Bryn replied in a tone that made the words wonderfully ironic.

"*Perfecto!*" Victor laughed and started for the door. "I'll need your help finding my way back to my chambers. This is a big palace."

"Take a right after the door."

Victor grinned, pleased that he'd scored a blunt-speaking, no-nonsense escort. As they walked, he slowed and gestured for her to hurry beside him. "Tell me about Obert. You ever seen him fight?"

"I have. He's a devil with that longsword of his. Most people agree he's deep into the epic tier of mastery."

"Mmhmm. And what sorts of affinities does he have? Any spells that stand out?"

"I don't know how true it is, but I've heard his strongest affinity is for momentum, but I've also heard he has a touch of the void. I don't know much about his abilities, sir, but I'll say this much: The longer you fight him, the more deadly he becomes."

"Hmm." Victor nodded, sighing as he pressed his hands into his lower back, stretching as they walked.

"You're not concerned?"

"Sure, but I figured he'd be good with that sword. I mean, it's no secret that he's dangerous. I guess, if anything, your words make me feel a little better. Now I've got the beginnings of a strategy: Kill him quickly." As he spoke, his lack of sleep got to him, and Victor yawned hugely. "Sorry about that. I didn't sleep much last night."

"Nerves?"

"Hmm? Oh, no. I was reading. My mentor sent me with a huge list of topics to study."

"Your mentor?" For once, Bryn sounded respectful. "Do you mean Ranish Dar?"

"Yeah. I tried to get him to cut out some of the more boring-sounding stuff, but—"

"Boring? You have books from *Ranish Dar*, and he *personally* told you to read them? *Boring?*" Her voice rose stridently as she hurried to keep pace with him, so much so that a pair of housekeeping staff looked up from the cabinet they were dusting, staring after them with wide eyes.

"Easy, Bryn. You're going to get me a bad reputation around here."

Bryn scoffed. "Too late to worry about that!"

Victor smiled again, genuinely enjoying her acerbic nature. "Yeah? People are talking?"

"Do you want the truth, or do you want me to be 'easy'?"

"The truth, but don't yell about it!" Victor recognized the stairway down a long gallery of stately portraits to his right, so he turned that way.

"Well, most everyone thinks you're a madman or a criminal paying penance to the great Ranish Dar. People are getting their affairs in order and packing their belongings. Most agree that we'll be released when Her Majesty, Queen Kynna—long shall she reign—is ousted and banished. Not many are happy with you for forcing the duel; there was some hope that another neighboring kingdom would put pressure on one or both of Gloria's enemies, thereby granting us a reprieve. That hope is dashed now that—"

"All right, all right. I get it. Listen." Victor pointed down the hallway toward the purple-black pair of doors at the end. "There's my room. I'm going to go in there and write some letters to people who don't hate me. Then I'm going to try to get a little sleep. Can you make sure I don't—"

"Oversleep?" Bryn slammed a fist against her shiny, silvery breastplate. "It'll be my pleasure, Lord *Champion*."

"Jesus, *chica*," Victor laughed. "Do you have to make it sound like an insult?"

"Win tomorrow, and then maybe I'll change my tune."

"Ha! Right on. Say it like it is! You know I like it." Victor turned to face her more squarely, then stood to attention as though he was back in the Free Marches preparing to address his troops. He slammed his fist to his chest in salute, stared into her eye slit soberly for a moment, and then smartly turned on his heel and strode to his room. He had a lot of letters to write.

# 13

### PLAYING THE FOOL

Victor sat on a stone bench, one of several in the ready room of the arena at Westhome. He'd only caught glimpses of the city as they traveled from the portal hall, but he'd been rather impressed by its austere beauty. The streets were wide and cobbled with smooth stones laid so closely together that the carriage had hardly rumbled as it rolled through the city. The buildings were spaced apart from each other, and they all had matching marble facades; it was like riding through his imagined version of an ancient Greek or Roman capital. Everything was clean, gardens and parks abounded, and most striking of all, he only saw a handful of citizens; the place was a ghost town.

Kynna had explained the lack of populace as a byproduct of every kingdom having portals to the true imperial capital on the eastern continent. This city existed as a formality, a foothold for the Empire on the western continent where parades, ceremonies, and celebrations could be held for the nearby population. She'd indicated that duels between champions were one such ceremony.

Victor wondered if he'd see any representative from the Ruhnic Empire attending his duel. Surely they were interested in such a thing. There may be nearly a hundred kingdoms in the Empire, but it wasn't every day that a war was settled. "Damn," he sighed, squeezing his spear in his hands. He was nervous and desperately wanted to talk to someone he could trust.

He'd been true to his word the night before, crafting letters to most of his loved ones. He didn't want people to worry, however, so he hadn't exactly confided in them. What he *wanted* was to talk to Valla. He wanted to hold her and have her stroke his hair and tell him he would be fine, that he hadn't overdone his playacting, and that he'd be able to beat this champion without showing all his cards. She wasn't there, though, and he had to accept that. He'd been trying. He'd written to her half a dozen times in his journal; he just didn't have the guts to put any of those words into the Far Scribe book they shared. "If I win," he promised no one in particular.

He looked at the fancy bronze clock ticking away on the wall near the portcullis that would let him into the arena. "Twenty minutes." Victor stood and began to rehearse his battle plan. He thrust with his spear, parried an invisible sword, dodged, and even rolled on the hard marble floor, trying to build up a sweat. When he looked at the clock and saw it said five minutes, he stood before the gilded iron bars and went through some calisthenics, keeping his heart rate up as he waited.

He did that for several minutes before a crystal mounted near the clock glowed orange, and a man's voice resonated from it. "Champion of Gloria?"

Victor stopped moving. "Yes?"

"Apologies, but the Grand Judicator has requested a late start. Please remain ready; the duel will begin in half an hour."

Victor sighed heavily and turned back to his bench. "Okay."

"Thank you. Do you require anything?"

He waved a hand in the air dismissively. "No." The crystal stopped glowing as he sat, and he was once again alone. He scanned the room, ensuring no other crystals were mounted on the walls, and then he summoned Arona's phylactery bone from his storage ring. As soon as it was in his hand, her ghostly, ethereal form began to coalesce in the air, raising goose bumps on his arms as the temperature near him plummeted.

"Victor! We're no longer on Sojourn!"

"Yep!" He smiled and shifted his spear so it leaned on his shoulder. "We're on Ruhn. I haven't got any news for you, but I have a few minutes to kill and thought maybe you could stand a little company."

"I'm happy to be out of that bone for a while!" She turned in a small circle, observing the room, her gaze lingering on the portcullis. "I'd ask if you were imprisoned, but you're armed."

"It's a ready room. My first duel is coming up."

He might have thought she paled at the words if her face wasn't already ghostly and near-translucent. Her eyes widened, though, and she drifted closer. "Are you worried?"

"Honestly? Maybe a little. If I'm going to pull off Dar's strategy, I have to hold back most of my abilities, and this *pendejo* seems pretty tough."

"Strategy?"

"I have to come off as kind of a dipshit for a while, I guess." Victor shrugged. "It'll make it easier for the queen to get people to agree to duels and then to get the terms she wants out of them. Dar wants her to have 'momentum' before people realize I've been sleeping on my skills."

Arona frowned. "What do you mean 'sleeping on'—" Her lips curled into a smile as understanding lit up her eyes. "You mean downplaying."

"Right. And this *pinché* asshole seems like he's going to be a real bastard. Rumor has it that his main affinity is momentum. I was told that he gets stronger the longer he fights, so it seems like my strategy of bleeding him out, bit by bit, might be problematic."

"Well, you know I'm not a martial expert, but I've seen many physical contests. Might I suggest something?"

"It's why I summoned you, *chica*. I've got ideas, but at this point, I'm kind of just planning to go with the flow and see how things shake out."

Arona nodded. "Well, if you've already been playing the fool, why not lean into it? Struggle. Barely escape his deadly blows but let some others through. Fumble your attacks; fail to show any rhythm or grace. Let him build his confidence and goad him into trying to humiliate you. When he thinks he's won, when he's so cocksure that he lets his guard down, *destroy* him."

Victor chuckled. "Just let him carve me up for a while, huh? Easy for you to say! You haven't seen his damn sword."

Arona nodded. "True. I doubt I could perform such a strategy, even if I were inclined to fight with my hands."

"Yeah, well . . . I'm sure there are some things you can do that I wouldn't even think of trying."

She smiled, drifting toward the gate and then back. "I'd like to see what this world looks like. Is it large?"

"Yeah, I can show you a map sometime. There's a detailed one in Kynna's palace. There are four continents. Something about the way it orbits the sun makes the southern continent a harsh desert, and the northern one is mostly ice. The two in the middle are broken up into almost a hundred kingdoms."

"Are there mountains? Forests?"

"Oh yeah. It's a big damn world. Bigger than Fanwath, from what I can gather. When I get done here and get back to the palace, I'll show you the vista from my balcony. It's pretty great."

"I'd like that." She drifted over to the bench and sat beside him, though she didn't actually touch the surface. "I don't suppose you've had time to look into my . . . *situation?*"

"No. Believe it or not, I've only been here two days. Things are moving kind of fast, but I'm not surprised; the queen's people are suffering, and she's trying to get this blockade situation resolved."

"Yes, understandable."

"I'll ask around, though. Assuming I pull this fight off, I think people around the palace will be a little friendlier to me. I mean, some are already kind of . . . *strange*; it's weird as hell, but I think they kind of worship Dar. Some of them, I mean—plenty others think of him as kind of an asshole."

"And your lady? Valla? Is she getting along well?"

The question felt so far out of left field that Victor felt his heart lurch into his throat—as though he'd been caught doing something wrong. "Um, huh? No, Valla's not here. Didn't I tell you that? I came alone." When Arona raised an eyebrow, he clicked his tongue and added, "Almost alone."

"Well, you must be missing her."

Victor didn't have to pretend when he replied, "Yeah, actually, I miss her a lot." When he'd summoned Arona, the last thing he'd wanted to do was talk about Valla, so he cleared his throat and stood up. "Anyway, I should get ready—fight starts soon. Thanks for your advice."

"Good luck, Victor. I know you'll win." Her voice, strangely hollow and slightly delayed from the movement of her lips, echoed oddly in the room as she broke up into mist and streamed back into the bone. Victor put it in his storage ring and then, as before, stood before the gate, trying to keep warm and limber.

It wasn't long before the crystal lit up again, and the same voice said, "Champion of Gloria, please proceed into the central arena. Stay within the black section of sand. If you cross to the red before the Grand Judicator gives his approval to the fight, then you will forfeit, and your nation will lose the duel. Do you understand?"

Victor gripped his spear and nodded. "Yes." At the sound of his voice, the portcullis slid noiselessly upward, and Victor stepped into the well-lit, very clean passage. After just a dozen steps or so, he noticed black sand under his feet, and another dozen steps brought him to the arena. His breath caught in his chest when he saw what awaited him.

The city's empty streets hadn't prepared him for the size of the place—it was like a college football stadium back on Earth, only crafted of white marble and gleaming metal. The arena floor was round and had to be seventy-five yards in diameter. One half—Victor's—was covered in black sand, the other half with red. The walls around the perimeter were probably fifty feet high, and rather than plain marble, they were reinforced with straps of gleaming metal. Above those walls rose maybe a hundred rows of stadium seats, and they were filled with people.

The rumble of the crowd felt distant, like subdued thunder in the background, but when he stepped onto the sand, the noise grew to a steady roar as he realized most of the people in his half of the arena were cheering, and most of the people on the other half were booing. So many people being so vociferous was a sound he'd never experienced. He'd come close, sure, in the Coloss arena, but this place was ten times the size! He figured there were fifty thousand people or more up there, and as the noise got to him, he felt himself swelling. Victor straightened his shoulders, lifted his heavy spear over his head, and walked back and forth on the black sand.

He saw, on the top edge of the wall, at the very center of the arena, two boxes, one on his left and one on his right. They were like miniature stages with a railing, and Victor recognized the two monarchs and their retinues. Queen Kynna sat on his left, and King Vennar on the right. Victor moved toward the center, wondering where his opponent was.

He'd just formed the question in his mind when he saw him striding out of a gate on the red side of the arena. He looked just as Victor had seen him at the meeting between monarchs—clad in his shiny breastplate, eagle helm, bracers, and greaves. The only difference was that his enormous longsword was naked, held in both hands before him.

Obert's sword flickered with pale white flames as he held it in the air, and the blade gleamed like liquid silver as it shifted in the light of the sun. It was a beautiful weapon. However, Victor had tested his spear against the edges of many powerful weapons, and he felt confident it would hold up against Obert's. If Dovalion Boarheart couldn't chip the dense wood, surely Obert couldn't cleave through it.

Obert played up the crowd, raising his sword high and turning to glare into the stands. If Victor had thought they were loud before, he learned his mistake. The ground shook, and the sand danced as if it were layered atop a snare drum.

Victor wanted to summon his banner and go berserk. He wanted to summon Lifedrinker and wave her massive axe-head through the air with great *whooshing* cleaves. He didn't, though; it was still time to "play the fool," as Arona had said. He waved up at Queen Kynna, Chamberlain Thorn, a little boy he'd yet to meet, two other nobles he recognized but didn't know the names of, and the guards arrayed around them. He thought he recognized Bryn among them; she had a certain judgmental posture that was hard to mistake despite the visored helmet.

"Citizens!" a voice boomed out, and Victor looked up to see a disc of perfectly clear glass or crystal floating in the air above. A man rode the disc like a surfer on a board as it swooped around the arena. He was tall, with flowing silvery hair and a robe that shimmered like spun silver as it fluttered in the breeze behind him. "I am Grand Judicator Lohanse, and I am here to ensure all rules of law are abided by, that the agreed-upon terms are upheld, and that no outside interference mars the sanctity of this most venerated ritual of succession. Do any dare challenge my authority in this place?"

A hush fell over the arena, and Victor lowered his arm as he recognized the man for what he was—a veil walker. He'd assumed the "Grand Judicator" would be a representative from the Empire, but he'd apparently underestimated the level of participation the veil walkers of Ruhn took in the political affairs of the Empire. He supposed it made sense; there were a lot of rules and ceremonies these people abided by, more so than seemed likely for people of great power. The only thing he'd ever known to control men and women like the kings and queens of the Ruhnic Empire was fear. He chuckled softly to himself. "Always a bigger fish."

"I have read the terms of this duel of succession. Queen Kynna of Gloria, do you agree to abide by them?"

"I do!" Victor was surprised by how Kynna's voice rang out. Was the veil walker amplifying it? Was she? He shrugged. For all he knew, it was just a function of the box seats.

"King Vennar of Frostmarch, do you agree?"

"I do!" the dark, stony man boomed.

"Champions! You will not be permitted to access storage devices or use potions, tinctures, salves, or other consumable aids during this duel. Are you each equipped to your satisfaction?" He swooped down close to Obert. "Champion of Frostmarch?"

"I am ready!" Obert howled, hefting his massive sword.

The Judicator circled him once, examining him closely with his bright, pale eyes, and then he swooped over to Victor. "Champion of Gloria?"

"Um, one moment, sir." Victor held up a finger and shrugged sheepishly as he looked up at Queen Kynna's box. "Bryn!"

One of the soldiers jerked her head down toward him, and despite the distance and the narrow gap in her helmet, Victor imagined he could see the mortification in her gaze. She turned to Queen Kynna. When the queen nodded, shielding her eyes, perhaps embarrassed, Bryn leaned over the railing and called down, "Yes?"

"Can I borrow your, um, bracer? The left one." Again, Bryn looked to the queen, and again, Kynna nodded; this time, she shrank down in her seat as the crowd began to murmur.

"What's the meaning of this?" the Judicator boomed, swooping toward Victor. He was a very tall, very imposing man. His skin glowed with inner light, and his hair flowed in a mystical breeze that only it could feel. Victor felt himself being weighed and dismissed behind that severe gaze.

Victor set his spear down, leaning it against his shoulder, and slapped his wrist with his open palm. "I saw that guy's sword and figured I should have something to block with."

The Judicator looked from Victor to Bryn and then back again, narrowing his eyes. In a voice pitched so that Victor was fairly certain only he could hear, the man growled, "Don't make a mockery of this ritual, *titan*."

Victor replied in a normal voice, figuring the veil walker would mask it if he didn't want others to hear. "The only person I'll be mocking is myself, sir." He glanced at Obert and added, "And I guess that cocky *pendejo*."

"I recognize your game. It's within the bounds." He nodded solemnly, then drifted up to the box seats where Bryn still stood, staring uncertainly, gripping her silver bracer. The Judicator took it from her and then tossed it to Victor.

Victor grinned and held it up. "Thank you, Bryn!" While the crowd began to murmur, laugh, and even applaud, he snapped the bracer around his wrist. It wouldn't resize, thanks to likely being bonded to Bryn, but he shoved it on, bending the metal so it clung to his forearm like an oversized bracelet, not the heavy length of armor it was intended to be. He nodded to the Judicator. "Ready, sir!"

Victor gripped his spear, stepped to the middle of the arena, facing Obert, and readied himself. He lowered his center of gravity, renewed Sovereign Will to boost his agility and vitality, and then cast Inspiration of the Quinametzin. It was a potent spell, but not a flashy one. Only Obert would experience its effects and only secondhand as it boosted Victor. Even if he survived, he wouldn't be able to explain it. The world became a little brighter, Victor felt lighter on his feet, and Obert didn't seem so intimidating—he was just a man—a man with a deadly sword, an unknown number of magical abilities, and a hunger for Victor's blood, but still, just a man.

The Judicator swooped high into the sky, and his voice reverberated through the enormous arena: "Fight!"

# 14

## FIRST DUEL

Obert moved through the sand like an adder. He kicked up sand with each step, weaving and feinting, but Victor just stood still, aiming the point of his enormous spear at the man, bracing himself. In a fight between equals, minus the interference of Energy abilities, Victor didn't doubt that a competent fighter with a spear could kill a master swordsman. It was simply a matter of reach. The problem was that this wasn't a match between equals, and energy *was* a factor. Obert didn't try to dart past Victor's spearpoint; he surged with hot, tingly Energy and then exploded with speed.

He ripped through the sand, throwing it up in a red wake, and darted to Victor's flank. Victor was no slouch, and he spun, tracking the man's movement, but Obert didn't try to close further; he hacked his sword through the air, and again hot Energy flared, and a blade of cutting, brilliant light tore away from his sword and straight at Victor.

Victor figured he could dodge it; it wasn't *that* fast. He also figured he could knock it aside with his heavy, sturdy spear. He didn't, however. He stepped to the left, just enough to avoid *most* of the blade, then he feigned a stumble and cried out as the hot Energy sliced into his ribs and over his back, biting deeply into the thick muscles beneath his shirt.

Hot blood sheeted down his side and back, and he made a show of rolling over his shoulder and wincing as he scurried to avoid a follow-up cleave. He'd taken a risk with his armor; he wasn't wearing his disguised clothing for the battle. He'd put on a simple yellow shirt with short sleeves and a pair of soft, pale gray trousers. He fully intended for them to be red with blood before long.

The cut on his back was a good start; it was a real gusher and took several seconds to close despite his enormous vitality and inherent regeneration. Obert wore a grin as he watched the blood soak the fabric, circling him. Victor grinned back, but he did it in a lopsided, idiotic manner.

"What a fool." Obert closed with him again, driving forward with big sweeping cuts that batted aside his spear. Victor could have pulled the spear back, avoided the cuts, and then thrust into the man, breaking up his momentum, but he couldn't appear too competent. Instead, he widened his eyes and took far too long correcting his spear's guard as Obert fought his way in and, quick as a wink, thrust his blade into Victor's chest, just beneath his right shoulder.

Victor saw the blow coming and stepped back just enough so the sword didn't impale him more than a couple of inches. Still, he cried out and scurried away, whipping his spear around to prevent Obert from following up. A new sheet of blood ran down the front of his shirt. "Come on, *pendejo*," Victor hissed. "You can't hit harder than that?"

He wasn't sure if he'd wanted Obert to hear him, but the man did, and fury ignited in the golden eyes within that eagle-mask helm. Obert went wild, surging with Energy, blurring as his momentum began to mount, and he pounded great flaming hacks into Victor's spear as he kept him at bay, but just barely.

"This is the end, isn't it?" Kynna hissed. She looked away from her beleaguered champion and locked eyes with Thorn. "Get Tomorran away from here. I don't want him to—"

"I'll not leave, Mother!" Tom jumped up, dodging her attempt to snatch his wrist. "If this is the end of our house, I'll see it with my own eyes!"

Kynna stared at him for a moment, listening as the crowd gasped, cheered, and jeered as the sounds of weapons colliding rang through the arena, accompanied by Obert's fierce grunts and Victor's belabored breathing. Finally, she nodded. "Very well. You *should* bear witness. You'll be a man soon enough." She looked back to the arena floor and her blood-drenched champion. Had he delivered a single injury to Obert? "Dead Gods! How much blood can he have? If the sand weren't red and black, we'd see the path of his progress."

No one responded to her words. The mood in the box was grim, and why shouldn't it be? Most of the staff—the guards, the soldiers, the bureaucrats—would be dismissed. She and her kin would be shipped off-world. Would they get a say in their destination? She'd failed to look into that detail. Thorn would know—a hoarse scream from below jerked her thoughts back to the debacle of Victor's battle, and she saw him rolling away, cradling his right arm. "What happened?"

"Obert near took his arm off, Your Majesty," Bryn, the one who'd given her "champion" a bracer, replied.

"It's over then. He could barely stand against him with two good arms."

Thorn nervously clenched his hands together. "Don't lose hope, my Queen." Even he sounded unconvinced. Kynna watched Victor, saw the pain and fear in his eyes as he crouched, his spear loosely gripped in his right hand, while his left hand seemed to be holding his gushing right arm together. Obert stalked toward him, a hungry smile on his face.

Kynna groaned. "He's going to finish him. Watch, then, Tom. Watch and see our nation crumble." Kynna followed her own advice, sending Energy into the pattern for Clear Sight and filling her vision with a view of Victor as though she stood but a stride away. His chest heaved for breath, his face was drenched with bloody sweat, and his clothes—his clothes were shreds of crimson-stained cloth. She looked to where blood gushed between the fingers of his right hand as he held his ruined arm together. Kynna stared and frowned. Something wasn't right.

Nothing gushed between those fingers, and she was sure she could see the biceps beneath his shredded shirt flexing as his hand adjusted itself on the spear. Even so, he still crouched there, his footing all wrong for a man in a deadly battle. He *looked* defeated, but—

Thorn gasped as Obert surged with Energy and streaked over the sand. His passage was difficult to track as he wove left and right, leaping and redirecting himself. He flanked Victor, streaked up, into the air, and then down, like a fisher eagle going for a carp in the Cray River. In Kynna's heart, she knew it was over. Obert was about to impale Victor, about to cleave his mighty sword, Brightfire, through his body, spilling his insides out onto the sand—*clang!* The sound rang out, and blood fountained into the air.

Kynna's eyes struggled to make sense of the scene. She stared at Victor, trying to see where Obert's sword had cut him, but the image didn't match what she knew she should see. Victor stood tall. His spear was thrust into the air, and dangling from the blade was Obert's lifeless body—his head fully impaled on the spearpoint. Victor had driven the spear under his chin and out through the top of his skull! Brightfire lay in the sand, her flames flickering faintly, and Victor slowly turned in a circle, displaying Obert's corpse to the suddenly silent crowd like a grisly banner.

"Dead Gods!" Thorn cried, leaping to his feet. "He did it!"

Kynna couldn't believe what she was seeing. She'd utterly *missed* it. How had that dolt moved so quickly? How had he moved so *perfectly*? What was the *clang* she'd heard? Staring at Victor, looking to where his muscles bunched on his shoulders as he held Obert's tall corpse in the air on that heavy, ugly spear, she saw what she'd missed: Bryn's bracer was bent nearly in half, barely hanging onto Victor's wrist. He'd blocked the killing blow and driven the spear up—a perfect kill with Obert helpless in the air, descending to put his hapless foe out of his misery. "Maybe not so hapless," she whispered, earning herself several glances from the celebrating members of her delegation.

Celebrating! Kynna felt her lips spread in a smile as she listened to the crowd's roar. Everyone liked a good upset. Everyone wanted to see an underdog come up from behind and take the win. Victor's flawless blow was a reminder that, no matter how powerful and proud you were, this life was not guaranteed. Anyone could die in an instant. Kynna stood and moved to stand beside Tomorran, resting her hand on his shoulder. He looked up with wide, bright blue eyes—he'd failed to inherit the fire eyes of his Igniant ancestry.

"He did it! Our house won't fall today!" His voice was bright with excitement, and Kynna nodded, smiling as she stroked his hair. She turned her gaze to the other side of the arena where King Vennar stood. He was pacing and fuming; she could see his mouth moving as he jerked his hands this way and that. No doubt, he was struggling to believe what just happened. Soon enough, he could struggle in another world.

"What world?" she asked, glancing at Thorn.

"Hmm? 'What world,' my Queen?"

"Where will they send Vennar and his kin?"

"It's at the discretion of the Grand Judicator. Speaking of whom . . ." Thorn pointed as the Judicator's sky sled drifted down.

His voice boomed out. "Champion of Gloria. Release the corpse of your tormentor."

Victor heard the Judicator's words and realized he might be going a little too far. He lowered his fourteen-foot spear and with it Obert's dangling corpse, letting it fall into the sand. The Judicator's floating disc descended to the arena floor, and he stared hard at Obert's body for several seconds. He then turned to Victor. "I pronounce the Queendom of Gloria victorious!" Everyone had grown quiet when the Judicator first spoke to Victor, but they erupted in cheers again.

His pronouncement wasn't necessary; Obert's corpse began to glow as thick orbs of rainbow-hued Energy coalesced around it. They rapidly multiplied, flowed together, and streamed into Victor as the crowd roared. He held his arms wide, grinning, soaking in the euphoria of the thick rush. His lingering wounds closed, his Core flooded with Energy, and a sense of well-being entered his mind as he tingled from his head to his spine to the heels of his feet. He could hear the Judicator speaking but couldn't make out the words.

As soon as it started, it was over, and Victor fell to his feet, dazed as System messages filled his vision:

*****Congratulations! You have achieved Level 70 Herald of the Mountain's Wrath and gained 12 strength, 17 vitality, and 12 will.*****

*****Level 70 Class refinement is available. Class refinement is permanent. Quinametzin Energy cultivators will next be offered a Class refinement**

**selection at Level 80. To view your options and make your selection, access the menu through your status page.*****

He pumped his fist in the air, excited by his message, and the crowd reacted, roaring in response. Victor's glory-attuned Core flared, and he wanted to let it loose. Again, he yearned to summon his banner and pump his fists in the air, but he simply turned to Queen Kynna's box seats and bowed. "Champion." The Judicator stepped into his line of sight. "You may claim a prize from your foe. The rest of his belongings will go to his heirs."

Victor looked long and hard at the sword, flickering in the sand, but ultimately decided not to take it. It wasn't a matter of impulse; he thought hard about it. When he considered holding that sword, though, he imagined someone who killed him holding Lifedrinker. She wouldn't like it. More than that, Victor wasn't skilled with the sword; he could learn, true, and it was a fine weapon, but he didn't need it. Instead, he stomped over to Obert's corpse, grasped his thick shiny breastplate, and pulled until the strap broke and he could hold it out of the way. Then, Victor summoned a sharp blade, drove it into Obert's corpse, and—

A hand like a metal vise gripped his wrist. "What are you doing?" the Judicator asked.

"I'm claiming his heart."

"You'd take that over the conscious weapon in the sand, there?"

Victor nodded. "Wouldn't his heir be served better by that sword than this lump of flesh?"

"Very well." The Judicator let go of his wrist, and Victor plunged his hand into the still-hot chest cavity, wrapping his thick, strong fingers around the organ. He pulled it out with several wet, visceral *pops*, and then he stood, holding it aloft. The Judicator's voice rang out above the crowd's hysteria, "The champion of Gloria claims his opponent's heart!"

Again, the crowd erupted, but this time, there was a mixture of sounds— some cheering, sure, but also gasps, laughter, screeches, and outraged curses. There were too many sounds for Victor to discern them all; to him, it was just a crowd roaring, and that made him smile.

"Leave the arena, Champion. I must see to the house Vennar and their removal from this world." With that, the Judicator climbed atop his flying disc and whisked through the air to Vennar's boxed seating section. It was vacant. Victor glanced over to Kynna's section, and it, too, was empty. He shrugged, waved the heart through the air one more time, basking in the noise from the enormous crowd, and then stomped over to the tunnel that would lead him to his ready room.

When he stepped out of the sun and the crowd's noise, he breathed a heavy sigh of relief and sent the heart into his storage container. He flexed his shoulders, rolled his neck, and looked at his arm. "That son of a gun almost cut you off!" It had been a close thing; Victor had misjudged a glancing blow and caught almost the full brunt of Obert's magical sword strike. If not for his hard-as-rocks titan bones—

"Victor!"

He looked up to see Kynna and his usual escort, Bryn, standing in the ready room. "Oh, hello, my Queen." He bowed low, his shredded shirt hanging in bloody tatters, dripping on the ground.

"Stand, Champion." When Victor complied, she folded her arms over her chest. She was dressed in a lovely yellow gown that really made the deep blue crystals of her crown pop with color. "Tell me now, was it luck? Did the grace of a sleeping god touch you? How did you win when all was so dire?"

"Oh, hrmm." Victor frowned and rubbed his chin. "I guess it was mostly luck—"

"Ha!" Bryn cried, striding forward to yank her bent bracer from his arm. "I suppose you 'accidentally' blocked his killing blow with my bracer?" She put it on her arm, and the metal smoothly reformed to its original shape.

"Guard Bryn!" Kynna's voice was sharp, and Bryn whirled to face the queen, falling into a bow that nearly had her on the floor. "I'm so sorry, my Queen! He frustrates me so—"

"Be still." The queen stepped past her to confront Victor. "I'll not have you play games with my family, Victor—my house. Was it a lucky accident or not? If you say yes, I'll remove you from your position and put in the champion I earned today—my pick from Vennar's cadre."

Victor sighed and shook his head. He looked from the queen to Bryn, still on her knees. "Do I need to worry about my words leaving this room?"

The queen glared down at Bryn and flicked her fingers to the door. "Leave us." Bryn scrambled to her feet and hurried out, joining a small group of people waiting in the hall. When the door clicked shut, Victor said, in a low voice, "No accident. I wasn't going to lose, but did you want me to trounce that guy? Do you want the negotiation with Xan to go well? If I didn't look like a lucky idiot, King Groff wouldn't negotiate so easily—"

"You . . ." Her eyebrows rose, and she regarded his shredded, bloody clothing. "You went through that torture for . . . for *easier negotiations?*"

Victor lifted his sleeve and rubbed the dried blood covering his shoulder and biceps. "I heal fast. See?"

"But it must hurt . . ." She stepped back and ran her eyes up and down his figure.

"I mean, in the middle of a fight, all pumped up with adrenaline—it's not that bad."

"What . . . how . . ." She clenched her fists and took another step back. "Who are you, Victor? What are you hiding? Obert was Tier Nine. Don't tell me you're so high." She tapped her temple behind her right eye. "I can see your Core's Energy levels."

"My Queen," Victor sighed, stepping toward the door, "there are many factors to a person's strength. You must know that. It's not all about level." He turned to her and grinned. "Besides, I don't think I'm *that* far below some of these guys." In his mind, he chuckled at the idea that he had a heart to eat and a Class refinement to go through. "Now, Your Majesty, if you wouldn't mind, I could use a bath, some clean clothes, and a quiet place to reflect on the strange customs in this world."

Kynna's crown glittered and twinkled in the light as she shook her head, pressing her dark, blue-stained lips together. "*Our* customs are strange? I feel I should ask what you intend to do with that man's heart, but . . . I don't want to know. Come, then, Champion. Let us return to Gloria; we have much to celebrate. The entire city will feast tonight."

# 15

## ALL IS WELL

Victor sat alone in his quarters at Queen Kynna's palace. He was tired—tired from the stress leading up to his duel with Obert, tired from the fight, and tired from the aftermath. When he'd gotten back to the palace, it had felt as if a blanket of dread had been lifted off the city, and everyone had been given leave to live and celebrate—something they'd been denied for, apparently, years. Of course, Victor had been expected to attend the queen's celebratory banquet. He'd had to stand at the high table and tell a story to entertain the guests—another reason for his current mental exhaustion.

The dinner had gone fine, of course. He hadn't had any trouble coming up with a story to tell; he had a thousand fights he could describe, but feeling alone among all those strangers, he'd chosen a story about the Greatbone Mine and how he'd first seen Lam fly, descending among a horde of mad beetles to save him and the other delvers. The feat itself wasn't impressive to the nobles gathered around Kynna's table, but the way Victor described his awe and how the event became the key to unlocking his inspiration-attuned Energy had kept their rapt attention.

The dinner had taken hours and hours, and as far as Victor knew, the feast was still ongoing; Kynna had proclaimed a week-long national holiday. He'd finally begged off, claiming exhaustion, and though his many new fans among the nobility had protested, Kynna excused him, and now he sat alone. His chair was comfortable; the little parlor in his suite was luxurious with fine, high-grade leather furniture that fit his frame like a glove. His little bar was stocked with potent liquors, and his view was incredible.

Through the floor-to-ceiling windows, he could see over the city's rooftops below and beyond to the rolling green countryside. Great forests covered much of Gloria, and to Victor sitting there, the expanse of tree-covered hills looked almost primeval, so unmarred was their wild majesty. He could see the road leading away from the city, but in just a few miles, it was swallowed by the forests. From there, he saw nothing but green all the way to the distant, towering purple mountain ranges. For someone who grew up in Arizona, Victor found himself easily enthralled by a view like that.

Still, his mind wandered, and he found himself wishing he had someone to talk to, someone familiar. He was half tempted to summon Arona from her phylactery again, but she wasn't the voice he wanted. He knew Bryn was standing guard outside his door, and the thought of making her take a drink with him and suffer through some teasing was an amusing proposition that he toyed with for a while but ultimately set aside. It was bad enough that the poor woman had to stand guard and watch over him; he shouldn't torment her to boot.

No, he had to admit, the truth was, he missed his friends, and, most of all, he missed Valla. When he sat down with a glass of something called Turnback Rye, he'd intended to go through his class refinement, but his mind kept returning to the simple promise he'd made before the duel: If he won, he'd write to Valla. So, with a troubled heart and a not-insignificant buzz, he took out his Far Scribe book and turned to the latest message she'd sent him:

*Victor,*

*I wish you'd write to me, but I know you need time. At least, that's what I keep telling myself. In any case, I have something I wanted to share with you. I'm leaving for a new world tomorrow—an ocean world populated by aquatic people who live on islands and swim and breathe freely under the water. It's called Crydagh, and there are rumored to be creatures living in those waters that rival dragons! Fantastic beasts called booraghi roam the oceans, unafraid of anything—even your mentor, Ranish Dar, would think twice about crossing one of them. If treated with respect, they're peaceful, though, and will sometimes speak to lesser beings who visit them. I'm going to seek one out; rumors have it that they'll grant boons to visitors they take a fancy to. Even if they refuse to speak to me, which I'm told happens often, I believe the trip will be worthwhile. Wouldn't seeing such a creature be a reward in itself?*

*Despite my excitement, I'm sorry to leave Fanwath. Uvu found his way home shortly after you left, and I've been spending time with him daily. He's gotten a bit feral, though; I think he has a mate out in the wild, so he'll likely be fine when I leave again. Of course, I'll miss Rellia, but she's so busy governing that I doubt she'll remember I'm gone most of the time.*

*Please write soon,*

*Love,*

*Valla*

Victor had received the message nearly a week ago, and reading it again, he felt a surge of guilt for putting a response off. He knew he'd feel worse if he went back and read through the other four messages she'd sent him. With a resigned sigh, he took up a pen, and, mustering courage on par with what it took him to face the lord of the dungeon near Greatbone Mine, he began to write:

*Valla,*

*I'm sorry I've taken so long to write to you. It's not right, I know. You probably know from Lam or Edeya that I've left Sojourn, but—*

Victor groaned and put the pen down. He didn't know how to do this. Grimacing, he returned to the note, skipping a line:

*Look, I'm not going to sit here and write a bunch of bullshit about how nice the world is, or how the people here are all giants, or that we had a big feast after I won my first duel. None of that really matters for shit. The truth is that I'm still raw as hell on the inside. I think about you all the time. Before my duel, I wanted to talk to you. When I saw my quarters, I thought about how much you'd like how everything was in shades of blue and purple—the sheets, the wallpaper, the vases, even the upholstery and carpet. When I was training back on Sojourn, I couldn't sleep in the bed 'cause I kept picturing you in it. I couldn't enjoy the lake 'cause I kept seeing you soaring over it.*

*I don't know if I'll ever get over you and the missing piece of my heart that you took with you, but I'm going to try. I'm going to try to remember that no matter what, I love you, and I don't want you to be gone from my life. So, yeah, I'll try to be better about writing, but I can't do it every day, every week, or even every month. I have to give myself room to breathe, to experience life without you, 'cause that's what you wanted, and it's too hard to let you go if I'm constantly reminding myself about how much I miss you.*

*It sounds like an amazing place you're going to, and I hope you really enjoy it. I hope you'll write to me about it after you're done, but let's wait until then, all right? In the meantime, I'll try to live my life and experience something worth sharing, too.*

*Victor*

Victor closed the book with a heavy sigh and a feeling of finality that he wasn't sure he liked. "Well, it's done." He could go back in and cross out the words, but there wasn't any guarantee Valla hadn't already read them. Even if he ripped the page out, it would still be there in her book. "Doesn't matter, anyway. I meant it all." He tucked the book back into storage, sat back in his chair, and downed his glass of, if he were honest, extremely potent whiskey.

He *wanted* to keep talking to himself, but he felt strange doing so without his usual crutch, so he reached into his high-quality storage ring and summoned Lifedrinker, allowing her massive, incredibly heavy axe-head to rest on the carpet before him while tilting the handle so he could grasp it as he reclined. "Hey, *chica.*"

*"Is it time, at last? Will you carry me into battle again?"*

"Sorry, not yet." Victor chuckled at how his tongue felt thick in his mouth. Whatever else you said about Ruhn, they made good booze. "I still have to fight with that *pinché* spear for a while. It's a tough weapon, but nothing like you. I'm saving you for when the fights get hard."

*"I yearn to feel your hands as I smash bones, spill blood, and drink the Energy of your foes."*

Victor arched an eyebrow as he looked down at the enormous axe. Her dark blade was like glass with its depthless black mirrored sheen, but as he stared, he saw the thousands of tiny motes of light deep in those unknown depths, almost as if he was looking through a window into space. It was mesmerizing, and he nearly forgot what he was going to say. As her handle vibrated with impatience in his hand, he startled out of his reverie, chuckling and reaching for the bottle of whiskey to refill his glass. "I miss fighting with you too. It'll be soon, though. Things are going to keep getting crazier and crazier around here."

She was quiet after that, and Victor enjoyed the simple comfort of her presence for a while. He sipped his whiskey, watched the view outside, and after a while, he opened his status sheet and selected the class refinement option, looking over his new options:

*****Class refinement option 1: Warlord, Legendary. Prerequisites: 1. Prior Class levels in Battlemaster, Martial Sage, or Combat Savant. 2. Sufficiently advanced bloodline. 3. Sufficiently advanced weapon skills. 4. Sufficiently advanced attributes. 5. A sufficiently advanced Core with appropriate affinities. 6. A history of leading followers into large-scale conflicts and achieving victory. Class attributes: Vitality, Intelligence.*****

*****Class refinement option 2: Colossal Spirit Champion, Legendary. Prerequisites: 1. Titan, giantkin, leviathan, behemoth, or colossus bloodline. 2. A significant portion of your total Energy earned from solo combat. 3. An affinity for glory, valor, justice, or honor. 4. Sufficiently advanced will attribute. 5. Sufficiently advanced Spirit Core. Through your many victories against difficult odds, you've gained the favor of your ancestors, and they see you as a living champion of their ideals. You embody titanic power, standing for glory, justice, and honor. Through your Spirit Core, your ancestors will unleash their fury on those who defy the might of their bloodline. Class attributes: Will, Vitality, Intelligence.*****

*****Class refinement option 3: Berserker of Unstoppable Momentum, Legendary. Prerequisites: 1. Epic-tier bloodline with a storied history of warriors or berserkers. 2. Rage, fury, or related affinity. 3. A significant portion of your total Energy earned from combat with heavy melee weapons. 4. Berserk or berserk-like ability. 5. Sufficiently advanced strength and vitality attributes. So long as you hold this Class, your strength, speed, and resilience will be fueled by combat. Every wound you take, and every blow you strike, will drive your battle lust to new heights. The enhancements of this "battle**

**momentum" will stack with traditional berserk-type abilities, but so will the madness. Class attributes: Strength, Vitality, Agility, Dexterity.*****

*****Class refinement option 4: No Refinement. You are pleased with the path on which you find yourself and choose to continue until your next refinement option.*****

"Damn, *chica*, three legendary options." Lifedrinker pulsed under his hand, and Victor took that to mean she was listening. He read the options aloud, and though he could feel Lifedrinker's presence and attention, she didn't speak. It didn't bother him; she was an axe of few words, and her company was enough for him.

Part of Victor wanted to seek out advice. He wanted to write to Dar or Kethelket. He wanted to break out the ancestor shard and speak to Khul Bach. Still, another part of him rebelled at the idea. He was alone on a massive world, about to embark on a series of brutal single combats. He'd be tested physically and mentally as he struggled to navigate the murky waters of negotiations, subtle deceit, and overt hostility. Wasn't it time he began making decisions for himself? He chuckled, shaking his head. No one ever made him choose a class, but he'd certainly always felt he had to hear other people's opinions.

So, determined to figure out the best choice on his own, he thought about each option, beginning with number four—should he keep his current class? It was something he'd never done before. He didn't even know what would happen; would he gain further class abilities if he kept it beyond the requisite ten levels? The question reminded him of the veritable library he had in his storage ring, so Victor perused his books, looking for a title that might give him the answer.

He found several promising candidates, spent another hour skimming through the pages, and came up with a resounding "maybe." Sometimes, when kept beyond the first ten levels, a class would grant more class-specific abilities, but sometimes it wouldn't. That same book took Victor down a rabbit hole, reading about how difficult it was to predict what unfamiliar classes would grant in terms of skills, spells, passive abilities, and even titles.

There were some well-documented classes, like the basic "fighter." He read the account of a man named Goh, who took sixty levels as a fighter, always forgoing a class change. He gained a few skills in the first ten levels but didn't begin seeing new ones until he'd reached his forty-second level as a fighter when the System granted him something called "martial mastery," which boosted every single one of his weapon abilities by an entire tier. As he closed the book, Victor told Lifedrinker about what he'd read. "So, that would be cool, but I'm not sure I want to stick with the same class for that long. I couldn't, really—I have to start building my own at level one hundred."

*"Class this, and class that—all you need is me."*

Victor snorted, choking on a sip of whiskey. She had a point. After he'd cleared his airway, he looked back to the class refinement screen. It seemed the System wasn't done offering him Warlord. It was tempting, but considering his current situation, he didn't feel it was the best option; he wouldn't be fighting many—or any—large-scale conflicts. If he was reading them correctly, the other two, newer options, were both geared toward the kind of fighting he'd be doing.

"Well, my first instinct is that the Colossal Spirit Champion is the smart move here. The Berserker of Unstoppable Momentum is another rage-based class, I think, and I've been working to keep my head during fights. Do I want a passive ability that will force me to build up to a berserk state? If I need to cast Iron Berserk or Volcanic Fury on top of that, how insane would I get? I can't even imagine being more crazy than Volcanic Fury already makes me."

Lifedrinker remained reticent, and since no one was there to do it for him, Victor voiced the contrary opinion. "But that passive 'battle momentum' sounds damn nice when you think about a duel. When you think about the fact that I don't want to be using many abilities until I have to, wouldn't it be nice to have one that just sort of made me stronger and faster the longer I fought? What would it look like to other people? Would they think I went berserk, or would they just think I was getting pissed off?" He supposed it wouldn't matter; if they thought he was berserk, they'd have a big surprise coming when he *actually* did.

In the end, the fact that he was Level Seventy helped him make the decision. He'd learned from Arona and Arcus that levels got progressively slower and specifically that gaining levels in the seventh tier took a fraction of the Energy for levels in the ninth. If he was going to experiment with a dangerous-seeming class choice, it was probably now or never. The thought of that battle momentum in a one-on-one fight was too tempting, and Victor reasoned that if he hated it, he only had to make it to Level Eighty to change it out.

So, perhaps a little impulsively and perhaps a little too loose of inhibition, thanks to the strong whiskey he continued to sip, he selected the option he had initially dismissed.

*****Congratulations! You have refined your Class: Berserker of Unstoppable Momentum.*****

*****Congratulations! You have earned a Class Feat: Furious Battle Momentum.*****

*****Furious Battle Momentum: Every wound you take and every blow you strike will drive your battle lust to new heights. Your strength, vitality, and speed will increase with your lust for battle, as will your fury and hunger for violence. These enhancements will stack with traditional berserk-type**

**abilities, but so will the madness. Unless altered or improved, this feat will be removed if your Class changes.*****

For the first time, Victor *felt* his class change as it occurred. He felt something *inside* him changing, burning from his Core out through his body. It was almost painful, but he could feel the euphoria of Energy masking the pain, twisting it into an almost pleasurable experience. Looking inward to see what was happening, he saw a slender pathway running parallel to his thick, well-developed Energy pathways. Intuitively, he knew what it was; it was meant to carry his rage into his body without interfering with his other spells and abilities. It was meant to feed his Furious Battle Momentum.

When he tried to push Energy into the new pathway, he couldn't, driving home the point that this "ability" wouldn't be something he could control. "Shit, *chica*. I hope I didn't just mess up."

*"Can you still wield me?"*

Victor downed the last of the Turnback Rye and laughed. "Hell yeah, I can."

*"Then all is well."*

# 16

## HELP FOR A FRIEND

Victor slept until nearly noon the next day, and when he opened his eyes, blinking in the diffuse light coming through the partially closed curtains, he was surprised by the silence and the fact that nobody had felt the need to wake him. With his head propped up on his plush feather pillows, he yawned and stretched, enjoying his room's calming, purple-blue color palette. Even the gauzy curtains were tinted a soft blue, which, in turn, tinted the light coming in. He enjoyed it and found it a nice change from the reds and burgundies of his quarters at Dar's lake house.

He took his time bathing and grooming himself, dressed in his usual disguised-armor clothes, and then prepared to leave, intent on finding some breakfast. He paused near the door and, thinking it over, decided to return to his suite's little parlor, where he'd spent the night drinking and making impulsive choices about his class. He sat in front of the little coffee table where his empty bottle of whiskey and dirty glass awaited—evidence of his crimes. A blue crystal bowl also occupied the table, piled with various fruits.

Victor scooped the plums, apples, and pears out of the bowl, setting them on the table, and then he reached into his storage ring and pulled out the heart he'd taken from Obert. Thanks to the magic of his dimensional container, it was still warm in his hand, the blood tacky and damp. Victor set it in the crystal bowl and stared. His body's physiological reaction to the raw hunk of, if not human, then at least *humanoid* flesh, was a stark reminder of how much he'd changed. He wasn't just Victor Sandoval from Tucson anymore. He was a Quinametzin titan, and his mouth filled with saliva at the thought of chomping down on a person's raw heart.

Worse, Victor didn't feel ashamed or dirty or even bothered by the idea. He knew without a shadow of a doubt that if he presented Victor, the teenage wrestler, with this heart and told him to eat it, there was no way it would happen— not without a fight. "Well," Victor chuckled, "I guess some shit's different." He summoned one of his cooking knives, a very sharp narrow-bladed one meant for deboning a piece of meat but that he used far more universally; he liked how it cut, and it was sharper than most of his proper "chef's" knives.

Fighting to contain his eager hunger at the sight of the bloody organ, Victor sliced it into bite-sized cubes. Then, one by one, he speared the hunks of flesh and chewed them down. He could feel the Energy in the meat, and it was potent, but it wasn't anything like the hearts of the great beasts he'd claimed. The wyrm and the gargantuopod, for instance, had overwhelmed him with their potency. This heart felt more like the giant spiders he'd slaughtered on Zaafor. It infused him with Energy, and he could feel his Core swelling, climbing toward the next rank. He also knew the Energy was infusing his flesh, inching him closer to Level Seventy-One.

Victor wouldn't deny a bit of disappointment; he'd believed the rumors that Obert had a "momentum" affinity, and he'd thought it too much a coincidence that his new class featured a type of battle momentum—surely the fates or karma or just the System had conspired to grant him a boon. He was embarrassed to admit that he'd begun to believe that Obert's heart would infuse him with some sort of momentum Energy and help his new feat to improve in some way. Unfortunately, when the waves of euphoria faded and he looked inward, all he was sure of was that his Core was heavier and denser, scraping the surface of the next rank.

Victor carried the bowl into his bathroom and rinsed it before returning it to the table. He felt good—well-rested, energized, and eager to see what lay next for him. Even if he tried, he couldn't be disappointed in the heart; an ordinary cultivator would have to work day after day for weeks or months to advance their Core by a single rank in the epic tier. Victor had nearly just skipped an entire rank by having a delicious snack.

So, it was with a grin on his face that he opened the door and stepped into the hallway. Bryn was there, her face, as always, obscured by her helmet, but he could see her eyes, and they looked stormy. "Something the matter?" The act of speaking triggered a yawn and a stretch, and Victor almost laughed as Bryn's dark brows furrowed behind the slit in her visor.

"Why would you ask that, milord?"

"Oh," Victor said, shrugging, "no reason." He looked down the empty hallway, admiring how the high windows reflected on the polished marble floor. "Is anyone waiting for me?"

"Sir, I do not have your appointment book."

"Well, Bryn, while you were standing watch here, did anyone come calling?"

"No, milord."

"Has there been any talk of the next duel?"

"I believe an emissary from Xan arrived last night."

Victor smiled, chuckling at her reticence. "But no one's been looking for me?"

"No . . ."

"Okay, well, I'd like to have a look around the city. Can you direct me to—"

"Milord, I don't think that would be wise." After a moment's pause and perhaps in response to Victor's arched eyebrow, she added, "I apologize for interrupting, sir."

"Why wouldn't it be wise?"

"There are factions in the city who worship Ranish Dar, and there are factions who view you as the harbinger of an apocalypse. Were you to wander the streets, I fear it would be akin to pouring water on a grease fire."

"Well, we'll need to ensure people don't recognize me, then." Victor grinned as an idea came to him. "You're going to have to lose that armor."

"Sir, I'll need to report our outing to my captain, and I think—"

"Bryn, do I, technically, outrank your captain?"

"As the crown's champion, sir, you hold the highest military office in the nation."

"In that case, we'll keep this outing between us. Now, can you go ahead and change into something less conspicuous?"

Bryn looked around, then nodded. "I'll go to my quarters and return after—"

"Nah." Victor opened his door and held it for her. "Go ahead and use my room. I'll wait here."

Her helmet inclined briefly, and then she stepped through. Victor pulled the door shut and looked through his storage rings for a hooded cloak. He had a few, though he rarely wore them; thanks to the constant heat produced by his Quinametzin blood and his feats, he couldn't remember the last time he'd felt chilly or even the need to protect himself from the elements.

When he pulled forth a dark gray cloak with silky rust-colored lining, he remembered when Valla had given it to him and felt a surge of melancholy that threatened to send him back to his room to curl up on the bed. He shook it off, though, and was just slinging the cloak over his shoulders, pulling the hood up, when Bryn emerged from his room. She'd changed out of her gleaming armor and wore a simple blue tunic over black leggings tucked into sturdy-looking boots. Of course, her belt sported not one but two heavy-looking swords, one a little shorter than the other.

As Victor fastened the clasp, securing his cloak, she frowned, and Victor got his first good look at her face. He liked it immediately. She looked like an athlete who spent a lot of time messing around with sharp objects. Her jaw was strong, her nose was a little flat, her lips were thin, and her brow was heavy and dark. Altogether, she looked healthy, strong, and dependable, especially with all the tiny scars on her cheeks, chin, and forehead. He almost commented on them. He nearly said, "You like to practice without your armor, I see." But he caught himself at the last minute, realizing not everyone might be proud of their scars.

Luckily, Bryn had her own acerbic comment, saving him from second-guessing himself. "I don't think a cloak and hood will suffice to keep folks from noticing you."

Victor held up a finger, grinning as he cast Alter Self, reducing his height to just around six feet. He was positively tiny by Ruhn's standards. "How about now?" he asked from the depths of his cowl.

"Ah, well, um . . ." Bryn took a step back to look him up and down more easily. "I suppose folks will think you're a traveler, but I don't think they'll suspect you're the queen's champion. You feel reduced in more ways than simply size. Have you hidden your power?"

Victor waited until the cloak's resizing enchantment caught up to his smaller body, and then he nodded. "It's part of the spell. Anyway, let's go. I'll follow you. Maybe avoid people who will ask us questions."

"Um, milord . . ." Bryn reached up to scratch at her very short, stiff brown hair, narrowing her perpetually scowling dark eyes. "Where are we going?"

"Oh, right! I need to speak to someone knowledgeable about magical . . . stuff. Someone who knows a thing or two about Death Casters and phylacteries, but hopefully a lot more."

Bryn's scowl didn't relent. If anything, it deepened. "Is there something more about you that—"

"It's just some information I need, Bryn." Victor chuckled, shaking his head within his deep cowl as he looked up at her. "I'm not planning to turn into a lich or anything—at least, not yet." He laughed and reached up to clap her on the shoulder. It felt like slapping a brick wall.

Bryn continued frowning for a moment, and Victor thought she was angry or was trying to think of a response without cursing, but after a minute, he realized it was just her regular expression. Just when he thought he'd need to prompt her again, she nodded slowly. "I believe I know someone who might have the knowledge you seek." With that, she turned and began striding down the hall. Victor had to double-time it to keep up with his much shorter legs.

They didn't encounter many palace denizens; the passages were broad and convoluted, and though they walked by several guard stations, Bryn just nodded at the men and women on duty, and they let them pass without a word. Victor chuckled at one point when he had the stray thought that maybe the other guards thought he was Bryn's kid. When she looked down at him with her usual stern expression, he couldn't help laughing. "I wonder if they think I'm your son."

"Don't be ridiculous! You don't move like a child. My comrades simply know I can be trusted, so they don't ask questions." After a minute, she looked down at him again, and this time, her thin, stern lips were curled into a smile. "Besides, I'd be too embarrassed to bring such a scrawny child to the palace!"

Victor's laugh renewed and, in high spirits, he and Bryn made quick time out a side entrance, then through the gate where, once again, the soldiers waved her through and Victor too after she jerked her thumb his way and said, "I'm escorting this one out."

Things were different in the city. The palpable pall of despair was gone, and the evidence of the night's revelries was everywhere. Victor saw people passed out in parks, empty kegs, and tankards on nearly every garden wall, and the folks who were up and about cradled their heads and moved very slowly. Seeing those things, he had to bark another laugh as he attempted to jostle Bryn's shoulder—his small hand was rebuffed by the meat of her muscles. "I can see why no one came looking for me! I wasn't the only one sleeping in!"

"Yes, well, some of us have duties."

"Was that a complaint?" Victor crowed. "My stoic guardian wanted to be partying last night?"

"I had a few drinks. You didn't know it, but one of my fellow guards relieved me for nearly four hours."

"*Four hours off?* What did you *do* with all that time?"

"Ha, ha." Bryn waved a hand dismissively, further improving Victor's good mood. He was happy to be getting some personality out of her. She surprised him further by asking, "Why the heart?"

"Huh?"

"It's one of the things everyone is asking me about. It's no secret around the palace that I'm your escort, so people think I know things. Everyone wants to know why you took Obert's heart."

Victor thought about the question, and it reminded him that he didn't really know Bryn. He was trusting her, in a way, because he had a—perhaps unhealthy—lack of fear when it came to people harming him. If he were being clever, he might have considered the fact that he'd just let a single individual lead him out into the city, unbeknownst to anyone. If Bryn were a traitor, she might be leading him into quite a trap, and no one would even know to look for him. No one would even know he was missing until, probably, the next day.

He shook his head as the paranoid thoughts began to spiral. "Why do you think I took it?"

She shrugged. "Perhaps to make you seem mad. Perhaps as a show of intimidation. Perhaps you have some sort of grisly ritual passed down by your primitive ancestors—"

Victor couldn't help the growl in his voice as he snapped, "My ancestors would think you were the primitive."

Bryn clamped her mouth shut and held up a hand. "I overstepped. I'm sorry, milord."

Victor sighed, tamping down his Quinametzin pride with a frustrating effort of will. "Nah, don't be like that. I'm sorry I bit your head off. My, uh, bloodline carries a lot of baggage—I have to fight the pride of my ancestors constantly."

"Is your bloodline so potent?" She glanced at him as they walked, and he could see the confusion in her eyes.

He figured a half-truth wouldn't hurt. "Yeah, my distant ancestors were great beings, and I don't think they really exist on this plane any longer. I guess you could say that when I claim an opponent's heart, it's a way to honor the rituals of my ancestors and also my foe. When I take that piece of an enemy, it's not about disrespect; it's the opposite. I wouldn't take the heart of an opponent I didn't respect."

Bryn's scowl turned contemplative, and she sounded sincere when she said, "I see." They walked quietly for a while longer, and Victor's earlier paranoia kept him alert, watching for signs of ambush or betrayal. They traversed busy streets, though, not back alleys. Bryn stopped before a large building with a tavern and tailor on the ground floor and pointed to the upper level where a sign read *Trobban's Enchantments, Rare Books, and Artificing.*

Victor had a hard time imagining the shop could be a trap. "This is the place?"

"I hope so. Troban is well respected by many, at least among the guards."

Victor started up the stout wooden stairs on the side of the building, chuckling at his own awkwardness as he stretched his legs between the wide steps. When he reached the top, he looked down to see Bryn hadn't followed. "Not coming in?"

She shook her head and sat on the bottom step. "I'll await you here."

Victor shrugged and pulled the heavy door open. A chime sounded from within, and a voice called out, "Welcome in." The shop was neat, with a sitting area in one corner, a sales counter on the rear wall, and a workbench taking up the left half of the room. A giant-sized man stood at the workbench, deftly using a wood chisel to smooth the contours of something that looked a lot like a doll's head. "Come around the bench, will you? I can't look up right now; this is a critical step."

"Sure." Victor walked around the workbench, feeling kind of ridiculous with just his head and shoulders clearing the surface, but he'd chosen his disguise, and he meant to stick with it. He watched for a minute while the man worked. He had curly white hair and bushy white eyebrows, but his face looked young, and his golden eyes were very sharp as he scrutinized his work.

"What brings you in, stranger?"

"I'm trying to find some help for a friend of mine, but the nature of the information I'm seeking is kind of a specialized topic. I also think she'd appreciate it if I kept my inquiries discreet."

"Well, discreet I can be, especially if I don't know the topic." For just a fraction of a second, the man looked up and locked eyes with Victor despite his deep cowl. Victor felt as if the man measured him with that brief look. When he broke the gaze and looked back to his work, he said, "I'm Trobban, by the way."

"I'm Victor."

"Ah, the name is familiar, though not your . . . stature."

"I told you, discretion is important to me."

"A disguise!" Trobban clicked his tongue. "Intriguing!" He carefully smoothed the wooden head—Victor had seen enough of its features to name it so—and nodded. "That'll do for now." He looked at Victor, smiling as he blew some wood dust from his fingers. "Now, what's the topic I can help you with?"

"Are you familiar with death-attuned magic? With phylacteries?"

"Certainly. How could a well-learned man not be? I've read a dozen books on the topic at least."

"That's encouraging." Victor wanted to lean on the table, but it was too tall for him. He settled for moving around to the end near the wall and leaned on that, folding his arms over his chest. "I have a friend who's a Death Caster. She had to flee into a hastily prepared phylactery because her body was . . . destroyed. Now she's kind of trapped in the phylactery with no vessel prepared to house her."

"Ah! Do you seek my help in preparing a vessel? I've read of several ways to do so. There are rituals from—"

"There's more to it," Victor interrupted, holding up a hand. "You see, my friend, she's never loved death-attuned magic. She hates her former masters and loathes the idea of becoming like them. We're hoping this transitory state she's in might lead to something of a rebirth, a way to help her change her path, avoiding something she'd feared was inevitable."

Trobban mimicked Victor's posture, folding his arms over his chest. "Death Casters and their apprentices are a complicated subject. I'd hate to come between a master and his—"

"She's free from her master. He believes she was destroyed."

"Truly? And you have access to your friend's phylactery? Her, um, master isn't aware of it?"

"I can access it, yes. And no, her master isn't aware. He's not even on this world or even close to it."

Trobban nodded, stroking his chin, picking at some flecks of sawdust he found in the stubble there. "In that case, there are some options we could explore. If I could speak with this friend of yours . . ." He trailed off, arching an eyebrow in question.

"I'll need to run it by her. Listen, Trobban, it's not convenient for me to wander the city. Do you think you could come by the palace?"

The crafter's eyes widened, and he leaned across his worktable, staring hard at Victor. "I would be honored! I have a wagon constructed just for such a cause—a mobile workshop! Why, it would do wonders for business if people saw me driving it through the palace gates!"

Victor moved back around the side of the table, holding out a hand. "In that case, let me extend a formal invitation. Can you make it this evening?"

"Ah, but the revelries . . ." Trobban shook his head. "I think it would be safer in the morning hours, sir. I'd hate for my wagon to be caught up in the mayhem, not if it's going to be anything like last night."

"All right. Tomorrow morning, then. I'll let the guard captain know." Victor shook the man's hand, then let himself out, and as he descended the steps, he called out, "Bryn, let's grab some food! Aren't you hungry?" Before she could respond, he added, "Also, there's no trouble with me inviting this guy to the palace, is there?"

Bryn stood and squinted up the steps to him, shading her eyes from the sun. "Um—"

Victor hopped down the steps, stopping on the third from the bottom so he could look her in the eyes. "It'll be fine, don't you think?"

"I'm sure it will be, but you should check with Queen Kynna about your schedule. You may have term negotiations tomorrow."

Victor nodded, frowning. "Yeah. Yeah, all right, Bryn. Let's get some food, then it's back to the palace for me." He continued to the ground, gesturing to the people moving about on the street. "Looks like folks are waking up! I'm in the mood for soup. You know any place that's good?"

After a bit more back and forth, Bryn settled on an idea for a restaurant, and Victor followed her through the streets. On the way, he thought about how he was using the poor woman, basically an employee who was forced to spend time with him, for company, and he decided it wasn't probably healthy for either of them. He needed to make some friends in Gloria, and though he was working to help Arona escape her bodiless state, it probably wasn't wise to put all his eggs in that basket. Still, it was something, and he was looking forward to telling her that help was on the way.

# 17

## A SUITABLE VESSEL

Seems these terms are amenable." King Groff folded his fingers together, peering at the document his chamberlain pushed before him. Behind the king, Qi Pot, the champion of Xan, stood. He wasn't as feared for his martial prowess as Obert, but he looked competent enough to Victor. He was a wiry, lean fellow who wore a rapier that seemed to exude shadows. They drifted out of the tooled scabbard like smoke, obscuring the weapon's hilt and darkening the air around him.

Qi Pot wasn't particularly tall, but he had a way of leaning forward that emphasized his lean, predatory posture. He didn't glower or try to intimidate Victor, which, if Victor was honest, was more intimidating than outright hostility. Still, the man's seeming competence made it all the easier for Victor to look the fool. Queen Kynna had done her part to make that job easier, too.

It seemed that, during the celebratory feast, she'd "had too much to drink" and had gone on and on to anyone who'd listen about how she was eager to replace Victor with a new champion claimed from Frostmarch. Apparently, she wasn't happy with his "lucky" victory. As one might expect, word of her disgruntled displeasure with Victor spread rather rapidly. So, Xan had come calling, offering favorable terms to move up the duel before Queen Kynna traveled to Frostmarch to claim a champion from the former king's cadre.

As the delegation from Xan stood and departed, Queen Kynna dismissed Chamberlain Thorn and then turned to Victor. "That went very well."

Victor nodded. "If I understood things correctly, you only stand to lose what you gained from Frostmarch? You'll remain queen of Gloria even if I lose?"

"That's correct. So, whether you win or lose, Victor, you've saved Gloria. At least for the immediate future." Smiling, she tried to push her chair back, but it was heavy, and the feet were caught in the plush rug that ran the length of the table. Victor hurried forward and lifted the back, helping her to slide it out. "Thank you."

"It's nothing."

"No, not the chair. Thank you for risking your life to help my people."

"Um . . ." Victor smiled, backing up a few steps as the queen stood. "You're welcome."

"And the timeline is all right with you? You'll be ready to fight tonight?"

Victor glanced at the big ornate clock standing in the corner of the negotiation room. It was nearly noon. "I'll be ready, my Queen, but a craftsman is waiting at the palace. Do you mind if we hurry back?"

"A craftsman? I'd hoped to have lunch with you. You've been here a handful of days, and we've hardly had a chance to talk."

"Well, I mean, you were busy at the feast, and before that . . ." Victor shrugged—there was no need to recount all the hectic activity since his arrival. "Anyway, I'm sorry about missing lunch, but when I invited this guy to the palace, I didn't realize we'd be meeting with Xan so soon. I guess I could reschedule—"

"No." The queen waved her hand and walked to the door leading to the portal room. "We'll have more time after this duel." She paused to look at him again, her brows drawing down as her expression became more serious. "You *will* win, won't you?"

Victor grinned. "That's my plan."

"Qi Pot is well-respected—not as feared as Obert, but that's largely because he's younger and has fought fewer duels."

"I have a plan for him." Victor tried to smile reassuringly, hoping the queen wouldn't ask for details. He doubted she'd feel encouraged if she heard the outline of his strategy.

"Good. Very well, then, Victor. Go to your appointment. I'll see you before the duel."

Victor bowed. "Your Majesty." Before she had time to second-guess his release, Victor hurried out, and a few moments later, he was stepping out of the portal, back at the palace in Gloria. Bryn awaited him, and he smiled and nodded when he recognized her posture and scowling eyes through the gap in her visor.

She saluted and stepped away from the other guards in the chamber. "Where to, sir?"

"Where's my guest waiting?"

"The eastern parlor, sir."

Victor nodded and looked at the group of four guards at their posts on either side of the door. "Can one of you fetch Artificer Trobban from the eastern parlor and bring him up to my suite?" They all saluted, but one junior member— Victor could tell because he only had one yellow rose embossed on the gorget of his breastplate—hurried through the door. Victor gestured toward the door. "Let's go, Bryn."

He followed her back to his quarters, though he probably could have led the way. He had a decent mental image of the palace layout, at least the parts he'd frequented over the last few days. Still, it was customary for his "escort" to take the lead, so he humored her. Along the way, she asked, her voice echoing hollowly from the inside of her helmet, "How did the negotiation go?"

"Pretty good, I think. The queen seemed happy. I have to fight at sundown."

Bryn's steps faltered, and she looked over her shoulder. "Are you prepared?"

"I better be!"

"Must you always jest?" A moment after speaking, she hastily added, "Sir."

"I'm not really joking. There's not a lot I can do between now and sundown. I came to this world to fight duels, so, yeah, I think it's fair to say I better be ready." Bryn was silent after that, and when they reached his quarters, she took up a guard position beside the door. "When's the last time you had a break?"

"During your negotiations, sir."

"Oh. Yeah, I guess that makes sense. So you're good?"

Her helmet inclined marginally. "I'm good."

"Let me know when Trobban gets here." Victor let himself into the room and smiled at the scent of fresh flowers and clean air; the housekeepers had flung the windows wide and tidied up while he was gone. The central room in the suite was dominated by a long, darkly stained wooden table, and he walked over to it, pulling out a chair that afforded him a clear view of the door. Then he rummaged through his storage ring, taking out Arona's phylactery.

Almost before he had time to set the dark rune-etched bone on the table, a cold blue mist began to gather in the shadows under the table. A moment later, they swirled up, coalescing into the shape of a slender woman in dark layered robes. "Hello again, Victor." She looked around, squinting at the light streaming through the tall windows. "Your quarters are quite fine." She'd only seen the sitting room with the curtains drawn the night before.

"Yeah, I'm not complaining." Victor smiled, leaning back. "The artificer I told you about should be here in a minute or two."

"Wonderful! I'm excited to hear what he thinks of my predicament. And how are you? When we last spoke, you mentioned negotiations?"

"I'm good. Everything went fine—I have to fight tonight."

Arona's ghostly figure moved to hover near the chair on Victor's left. "Are you as nervous as the first time?"

Victor took the hint and pulled the chair out for her. "No. Partly because Kynna's negotiations went so well. Even if I lose, she and her people are going to come out all right. At least for a while."

Arona nodded, sliding her ethereal figure into the seat. "So you don't feel the same pressure. That should help you relax and do what you do best."

"I hope so. I'll find out how effective my new class refinement will be."

Her dark lips spread into a sly grin. "A new class? Now that you hold my very existence in your hands, are you willing to tell me what tier you've reached? If I were guessing, I'd say the eighth."

Victor chuckled and leaned back in his chair. "Really? Only Level Eighty?"

"Oh, am I so far off? Have you reached the ninth tier?"

Before Victor could answer, a knock sounded on the door, and Bryn called out, "Sir Victor, your guest has arrived."

Victor looked into Arona's dark ethereal eyes. "Ready?" She nodded, and he called, "Send him in." He watched as the door swung wide, and Trobban came through, dressed much the same as he'd been in his shop, though with a fancy red silken cloak thrown over his shoulders. "Hello, Trobban." Victor stood and gestured to the chair across from Arona. "Please sit down."

Trobban approached, and when he saw Arona's ghostly figure, he paused and retrieved some spectacles from his pocket. He put them on, adjusting a tiny dial next to the hexagonal blue-tinted right lens. "My, my. Hello there, Champion Victor, and what should I call you, lovely lady?"

Arona smiled and waved a ghostly hand. "Flattering phrases won't win you favors with me. Call me Arona, for I've no pride in my many titles and feats."

"Very well. It's my pleasure to meet you." Trobban sat at the table, and his gaze drifted to the rune-etched bone. "Is this your work, Lady Arona?"

"It is, though I must confess I finished it in haste."

Trobban stared at the bone through his strange spectacles, slowly nodding. "Hasty you may have been, but here you sit—a spirit whole, a mind intact. You've done fine work here."

"Have you thought about Arona's situation, Trobban?" Victor wasn't in a big hurry, but he also didn't want to sit and listen to Trobban flattering Arona all afternoon.

"First, I'd like to confirm a few things with your charge, Sir Victor." Trobban focused his gaze on Arona. "Is it truly your wish to alter your primary Energy affinity?"

"It is."

"Have you considered the potential for a loss in potency? I mean, should your Core be so fundamentally changed?"

Arona's ghostly hood moved up and down. "I've read about the topic at great length. There are records of people changing their Core and primary affinity without a significant loss of power. There are a handful of complementary attunements, and if I could awaken one—"

Trobban nodded. "Awaken or gain. I've thought long on your situation. Are you set on inhabiting a vessel born by natural means?"

Victor frowned and interjected, "You mean a person's body?"

"Yes. Typically, a lich will have a corpse prepared to receive their spirit. Usually, it would be a stronger vessel than they gave up. The process involves replacing certain organs and enriching the flesh with Energy, rituals, and artifacts. Obviously, whatever caused the vessel's original death must be repaired, and—"

"I don't wish to be a lich, Artificer Trobban."

Trobban nodded. "There are other means of inhabiting a living vessel. There are ways to preserve the life of a body while the spirit is removed." He looked at Victor. "You should be familiar with that possibility, being a Spirit Caster. Once the spirit is out, we can—"

"I won't steal another person's body!" Arona's ghostly fists clenched.

"Then we must consider my original question. Are you willing to look into vessels not born by natural means?"

Arona frowned. "A construct?"

Trobban nodded. "Just so."

"They're so limited, though. I'd never have the potential of a true Core or a proper bloodline. Racial advancement treasures wouldn't work, and—"

"Ah, pardon me, Lady Arona, but I believe your knowledge about constructs is lacking in some departments. There are ways to create vessels every bit as potent as an epic-tier natural species. It's all a matter of preparation, Energy infusion, and of course the acquisition of appropriately powerful artifacts—a heart, a mind, a Core, the materials for the flesh and bones, and other special organs like eyes, sexual—"

Arona's frown had fallen away as the man spoke, but she waved a hand, cutting him off. "To make a living construct equivalent to an epic-tier species would be an enormous undertaking with expenses rivaling even my former master's greatest projects. I refer to a man who is a veil walker and has been for thousands of years. I don't have access to those sorts of resources."

Victor frowned, contemplating everything he'd heard. He could offer to help, but he understood Arona's objection; he had a few million beads, but that likely wouldn't come close to scratching the surface of what Trobban was proposing. Before he could think of a comment that wouldn't sound inane, Trobban spoke again, "There are other options. There are ways to create living vessels that do not require the sacrifice of another soul. Certain trees have the potential—if we could graft a branch from the Er'va'leigh oak, I could encourage it to grow into an approximate replication of your former body—I'm assuming that's what your spiritual projection is based upon?"

Arona nodded. "It is. Will it be able to accept my full Energy level?"

"I believe so, though it may take some time to mature to that potential." Trobban frowned. "Speaking of growing, how do you feel about embryonic spiritual implantation?"

"You mean for me to inhabit the body of an unborn being?" She frowned. "My old master spoke of it. I'd have to supplant the nascent spirit of the being, and then I'd also be forced to grow at a natural pace. I don't relish the thought of another childhood."

"So, that brings us back round to the idea of a properly prepared undead vessel. With enough time and the right affinity, it's possible that you could spark life within such a body. If we could convert your death-attuned Energy into a new Core—"

"How much are we talking?" Victor interrupted. "I mean to build her a proper vessel from natural artifacts and whatnot."

Trobban smiled and shrugged. "Each treasure would be a monumental expense, and we'd need many."

Victor rubbed his chin, stroking the stubble along his jawline. "Trobban, will you please step out? I'd like to speak to Arona alone for a moment."

"Of course!" His chair scraped noisily on the tile as he slid it back. Arona stared at Victor as Trobban's heels clicked on the same tile, hurrying toward the door. "Shall I wait without?"

"Yeah, don't go far," Victor called.

When the door clicked shut, Arona said, "It's too great an expense. This is something a veil walker might attempt, someone who's gathered treasures for millennia."

"Listen, I didn't want to say this in front of Trobban because no one knows yet, but Dar didn't just send me here to fight off a couple of champions who are threatening Kynna. He wants me to help her conquer this world. We're talking nearly a hundred nations. I'll have to fight a shitload of champions, but there will also be many nations who won't want to fight, who will take a knee, offering tribute and swearing fealty to Kynna. I get a piece of all that tribute. I can *demand* certain things. It's customary."

"And you'd squander part of your well-earned treasure to help me build a body? I won't allow it. I'd rather create a proper undead vessel, and then I can seek my own solution." As Victor's countenance grew increasingly stormy, she asked, "Why, Victor? Why would you offer so much to someone who, really, hasn't done anything for you? To someone whom you hardly know?"

He shrugged and spoke his mind, tired of games and duplicity. "Mainly because I like you. I don't know why, but every time we've been thrown together, I thought you were pretty cool. Then there's the fact that I don't like Death Casters, and I can't stand the idea of you being forced to be one. Once you're properly undead, tell me, do you think you'll lose some of that yearning you feel to get away from death-attuned magic?"

Arona's raspy voice grew quiet and small, and Victor could hear the fear in it. "I don't know. It *would* change me, but I don't know how much."

"Right. Besides all that, you should know it's worth a lot to me to hold up a middle finger to a guy like Vesavo. The guy gave me the creeps and reminded me of all the assholes I dealt with from Dark Ember, especially Hector. You know, there are a ton of high-tier assholes on that world, and I still feel like I need to pay them a visit. They treat humans like cattle there!" Victor growled and shook his head. "I'm getting off track, but my point is that if I can help you, a person I think of as a friend, escape the curse of being like those *pinché* mother—eh, you get the idea. I want to do it."

Arona stared at him for a long minute, but she slowly nodded. "If you can help me build an epic-tier vessel, and Trobban can convert my Death Core into something else in the process, then I will swear fealty to you, Victor. I will serve you until such time that we both feel I've earned what you've given me. I will go with you to crush the Death Casters on Dark Ember. With an epic-tier vessel, I can reach veil walker status! I can grow to be a proper companion to someone as mighty as you. I will dedicate my—"

"Easy!" Victor laughed. "Let's not get ahead of ourselves, all right? First, we need to get all the shit together. Now, don't mention the succession war to Trobban, all right?" When she nodded, he called out, "Trobban, get in here."

The door opened, and Trobban veritably ran back to the table. He seemed eager, as though he had an idea of what Victor was about to tell him. "Yes, Sir Victor?"

"Sit down, please." Trobban nodded and dropped into the chair, leaning an elbow on the table as he stared intently at Victor. "Okay, we're going to do an epic-tier vessel. Are you capable of craft—"

"Yes! Yes! I can do it, Lord Victor! With the proper materials, we can create the perfect vessel for you, Lady Arona! Why, I can—"

"Hold on, man!" Victor chuckled. "Listen, you need to talk with Arona. You need to consider every possibility. It's imperative that she comes out of this without losing any potency but also with a new Core and, at least, a new primary affinity. You should know that I have a potent Spirit Core, and if I can be of any help, I'll be willing."

"I will endeavor to meet your demands, milord." He ducked his head, and Victor sighed. It wasn't lost on him that the guy had gone from calling him "sir" to "lord" now that he thought he was about to bankroll an extravagant project.

He thumped his thumbs on the table, thinking. After a moment, he nodded. "Listen, Trobban, it might take us some time to gather everything we need, but you need to make a list, and I'll work on it. More importantly, you need to understand that you and I are the only people on this entire planet who know about Arona. If word gets out, I'll know who to blame. Understood?"

"Absolutely, sir! My lips are sealed. I'll do *nothing* to jeopardize a project like this; I stand to gain too much!"

Victor nodded. He hadn't considered that. For an Artificer, crafting an epic-tier body for Arona would probably be the equivalent of . . . Victor couldn't think of a proper comparison. Maybe it would be like killing a legendary beast, like a great ancient wyrm, all alone. "All right," he said after a moment. "I'll leave you two to talk and consider all the options. I have a duel to fight soon, and I'm damn hungry."

# 18

## FURIOUS MOMENTUM

Victor could feel the rage building. He could feel it streaming into the special pathways that ran parallel to the more robust ones he'd built up along with his Core. Each time Qi Pot struck a painful blow with that deadly, slippery, shadow-clad rapier, another surge of the potent heat rushed out of Victor's Core and into his body. Despite his awareness of it, despite knowing how it affected him, Victor couldn't keep the fury from creeping into his mind, clouding his vision with a red lust for vengeance and slaughter.

He gnashed his teeth and growled, grunting as he fought, jabbing his great heavy spear more and more deftly. His defensive battle had slowly shifted to the offense as he cared less and less for his health and slowly stopped trying to avoid Qi Pot's slashes and stabs. He'd known this would happen. He'd planned on it. When he first saw Qi Pot in the negotiation, taken in his lengthy, wiry fencer's build and seen his long slender rapier, Victor had known how this fight would go.

Qi Pot's strategy was clear: He saw Victor as a brutish, barbaric berserker who relied on his overwhelming strength and ferocity to win fights. In that case, Qi Pot intended to wear him down much as a matador bleeds out the great bull, so much stronger and fiercer than himself. His speed and grace were remarkable; at the start of the fight, he'd deftly maneuvered around Victor's spear, scoring gashes on his hands and arms, stabbing the tip of that lightning-fast weapon into his ribs, stomach, chest, and back. He stabbed it into his thighs, his glutes—everywhere.

Victor was crimson with his blood, and if the arena's sands weren't black and red, they'd be painted, too. Even so, the dark wet streaks were plain for all to see. Victor had lost gallons of blood. The problem for Qi Pot was that Victor was more than enormously resilient. A man like Qi Pot could cope with resilience. Despite his great vitality and the durability of his Quinametzin flesh and bone, Victor bled, and if something could bleed, it would eventually grow weak and slow. With the accumulation of hundreds or thousands of wounds, Victor would be vanquished. Unfortunately, Victor was more than resilient.

Victor had the regenerative capabilities of a monstrous behemoth; as Qi Pot lashed that wickedly fast, wickedly sharp rapier in and out, Victor bled, his wounds closed, and his body regenerated the lost blood. Before the rage began to overtake his mind, Victor wondered where his new blood and flesh came from. Was it manifested from Energy? Was it pulling molecules out of the air and altering them? Was he somehow splitting and multiplying his cells? His mind didn't linger on the question long; each cut added to the other half of the equation that summed up Qi Pot's doom: his rage.

Victor's ability to heal and stay fresh despite his mounting wound tally was one thing, but every cut and stab also added to his Furious Battle Momentum. As rage filled Victor's extra pathway and began to infuse his flesh, he healed even more rapidly, and, worse for Qi Pot, he became stronger and faster. And so, after dragging the fight out for nearly twenty minutes—a short time in the grand scheme of things but a very long time in a life-and-death contest—Victor's fury became unbearable, and he lost all sense of strategy.

He lashed out with the spear, and the rage fueled his movements. The great, weighty weapon was like a feather in his hands, and it ripped the air with whistling shrieks as he stabbed and hacked the double-edged spear blade about. For the first time, he fought as if he meant it, and despite his blind fury, he used the weapon's length to his advantage, bullying the rapier-wielding Qi Pot into a full-blown retreat.

Qi Pot wasn't just a fighter, though; he was a man who'd achieved great heights as a cultivator of Energy. He gathered shadows and fire, making himself momentarily ghostly, flickering with dark flames as he streaked around the arena, seeking to find Victor's flank again. Victor was so fast, so strong, so utterly dominant that Qi Pot had to burn more and more Energy to move outside the arc of the berserker's enormous reach. He became a specter of black flames, and his rapier thrusts shot forth like arcs of molten metallic fire that splashed against Victor, charring his bloody clothes but hardly marring the titanic warrior's flesh.

Victor began to laugh—a maniacal, madness-tinged sound that echoed hoarsely through the arena, silencing the crowd as they watched him glide over the sand, a predator closing in for the kill. His eyes blazed with molten fire, smoke drifted from his nostrils, and though Qi Pot continued to score magical blows, burning enormous torrents of Energy to stay ahead of Victor's lightning pursuit, he only empowered the berserker further.

The onlookers had been raucous at first, cheering for both warriors at the start of the fight. As Qi Pot bled Victor bit by bit, skillfully dancing in and out, leaving a bloody mark on Victor's flesh or plain yellow tunic with each attack, the crowd had cheered. They'd grown wild with adoration for Qi Pot's flourishes, and he'd put on quite a show for them, whipping his rapier through the air as he performed mocking bows, his face full of contempt. Now, though, Qi Pot's confident smile was gone; his movements were precise and lacked extraneous flourishes.

Victor couldn't savor the destruction of Qi Pot's morale. He was too busy fantasizing about dismembering him. Red visions of bloody destruction ran through his mind as he pursued the smaller man, and each time those dark, fiery shadows lashed out, the red filter on his vision grew darker, and his muscles surged with renewed strength and speed. He hacked his spear like a club or sword—or axe—and it shrieked through the air, never intended by its maker to be used in such a manner. Still, the force of those hacks was undeniable; the weapon's length and the absurd power behind the blows made it harder and harder for Qi Pot to avoid, even in his dark shadowy fire form. Eventually, it hit home.

The first hacking blow of Victor's spear caught Qi Pot at the knee and snipped through his flesh and bone like a cleaver through a carrot. The man could barely scream before a follow-up, a backhanded upward slash, brought the side of the spear blade into Qi Pot's armpit, severing his rapier-wielding right arm. After that, Victor dropped the spear and pounced, preferring the feel of flesh and bone crunching under his knuckles, savoring the hot sprays of blood and the coppery taste of victory.

When the veil walker, Grand Judicator Lohanse, gripped his arm and tried to pull him off, Victor instinctively rolled his wrist, grappling with the man out of pure muscle memory. He wrapped his powerful fingers around the veil walker's wrist and, to the stunned gasps of thousands of spectators, threw Lohanse to the side so he could resume his bloody destruction of Qi Pot's corpse. Of course, Lohanse wasn't a child or a mere mortal to be so easily dismissed. He gathered his aura and let it loose indiscriminately, bringing most of the people in the stands to their knees.

Victor felt the aura. It was thick and hot like molten iron, with depthless chasms of pride and mountains of knowledge. It pulled and pressed on him as if it might fold his molecules into one another and erase him from existence. Even so, a small part of Victor's mind, a tiny piece of his rational self, recognized that he'd felt worse. With that little kernel of thought in his barely lucid mind, he growled and stood up from the ruined corpse, his fists dripping blood as he looked with furious, bloodshot eyes into the stunned countenance of the veil walker.

"You will *kneel!*" the Grand Judicator growled and clenched his fist. Searing bands of lightning-charged Energy wrapped around Victor and hurled him face-first onto the sand. Even influenced by his Furious Battle Momentum, he couldn't move his arms inside those straps of burning Energy, and as the lightning crackled, he felt the veil walker's probing Energy in his pathways, grasping the rage-attuned Energy there and ripping it out. As the fury left Victor, his tense, rigid body relaxed, and Lohanse released his bonds of electrical force.

Victor struggled to his hands and knees and was acutely aware of the quiet. The only sounds coming down to him from the stands were those of people groaning and grumbling as they returned to their seats and recovered from the veil walker's show of force. Murmurs turned into hushed whispers as they looked down to the sands where Victor knelt beside the ruined corpse of Qi Pot with Lohanse standing tall over him, arms folded.

To Victor's relief, it seemed the veil walker wasn't one to hold a grudge. "Stand up then, warrior. You've won." With a grunt, Victor clambered to his feet. Lohanse raised his voice, holding his arms outstretched. "I give you Victor, Champion of Gloria, the winner of today's contest!" The crowd's reaction at first was tepid—some cheers and claps sounded from the stands near Queen Kynna's boxed section. After a few seconds, though, people began to feel encouraged, and fear of the veil walker's wrath subsided.

More and more cheers resounded, and then Lohanse spoke to Victor, his voice easy to hear despite the din. "Well? What prize will you claim?" He glanced at the bloody mass of flesh and bone that used to be Qi Pot soaking into the sands. Victor frowned, suddenly unwilling to claim the heart of his demolished foe. His anger was gone, and, it seemed, much of his pride and lust for glory were, too. Glancing inward, he saw that this Core was dim. Lohanse had relieved him of more than his rage. Still, he was Quinametzin, and he'd not be so easily cowed.

"I will have my enemy's heart."

Lohanse sighed, *tsk*ing. "As you wish." He raised an arm and announced, his voice booming through the arena, "As his prize, Victor will claim the heart of his foe." To Victor's surprise, the crowd's cheers surged with the announcement, and he felt the adulation tickling his Core, lifting his levels of glory-attuned Energy. He laughed and raised his hands, making bloody fists as he turned in a slow circle. He saw Kynna leaning forward in her throne-like chair, her hands grasping the arms. Her eyes were bright, and when those eyes locked on Victor's, she inclined her head slightly, dipping her tall crystal crown.

That was when the Energy hit him. As he'd been basking in the roars of the crowd, it had gathered around Qi Pot's corpse, and the System didn't care if he was ready or not. It struck him like a poleaxe, knocking the sense from his mind and lifting him off the sands as it poured into his pathways, refilling his Core and then spilling into his flesh as it pushed him toward the next level. It felt like a lot, and Victor wasn't disappointed when he opened his eyes to a System message:

***Congratulations! You have achieved Level 71 Berserker of Unstoppable Momentum and gained 9 strength, 14 vitality, 9 agility, and 9 dexterity.***

"Claim your grisly trophy, warrior," Lohanse said. "I've the nobility of Xan to deal with, but I'd rather you were clear of my arena before I left."

"I'm okay now, Grand Judicator." Victor glanced at him and quickly added, "Thanks for helping me cool off." He knelt by the body of his former adversary, summoning a knife from his ring.

"You aren't the first rage-attuned fighter I've dealt with. Even so, I'll wait for you to finish. You're quite impressive, Victor, and I can see you play a long game with these fools, hopefully with the good of Gloria in mind. Even so, don't become so enamored with yourself that you fail to realize you aren't the only special fig on the tree. As your queen works to negotiate further duels, your contests will become more difficult. Have you fought a steel seeker yet?"

He waited until Victor yanked the heart out of the body and looked up to nod before continuing, "I suspected as much. Your will is powerful, and for an iron-ranker, your aura is prodigious. You'll be formidable when you break through to the steel ranks, but only if you live that long. There are those who will recognize the threat you pose. I'm sure many already have. This window, when you are still fighting your way up to the first ceiling—this is when they'll strike. Be wary of 'new' champions in your coming battles."

Victor peered up from where he knelt, locking eyes with the enigmatic veil walker, but the man only nodded once, and then he was gone, like ashes in a stiff breeze. Victor stood, held his bloody prize aloft, smiling fiercely as the crowd roared their approval, then walked out of the arena, his mind more troubled by the veil walker's words than he wanted to admit. He'd gone further than he'd wanted during the fight; no one would see the way he absolutely dominated Qi Pot and think he wasn't a threat. Worse, he'd stood up to a veil walker, brushing off his aura as if it was a minor discomfort.

"*Pinché* rage," he sighed as he stepped into the ready room and found Bryn already waiting.

"You lost control of your affinity?"

"Did it seem that way?"

"I could only imagine that was the case. Why else would you risk death with the Judicator?" She chuckled. "Besides, I just heard you cursing your rage."

"True," Victor laughed. "Was Kynna angry?"

"*Queen* Kynna was pleased to have her aggressors dealt with! She asked me to see that you are 'well treated' this evening so that you're 'fresh and relaxed' for tomorrow's award ceremony." Her inflection made it clear that she was quoting Queen Kynna.

"Award ceremony? I didn't have one for the first duel."

"She's aware and asked me to thank you for your patience. Between the celebratory feast and the rapid acceptance of Xan's duel, there wasn't time."

Victor frowned, looking toward the closed door behind Bryn. "She sent my escort to tell me all this? I feel a little snubbed, if I'm being honest."

Bryn stared at him for a long moment, then reached up and lifted her helmet off, cradling it in the crook of her left elbow. To Victor's horror, she fell to her knees and bowed her head. "My apologies, Lord Champion. I have failed to convey our nation's gratitude properly. I did my best, but surely Chamberlain Thorn or Queen Kynna, her exalted self, would have been better suited to deliver you home to the palace. I will convey news of my failure to my superior officer, Guard Captain Wash."

"Damn, Bryn!" Victor chuckled nervously. "Will you please get up? I didn't mean that—I was just curious why they sent you alone this time."

"In truth, milord," Bryn said, head still bowed, "the queen was eager to hurry back to the palace ahead of you. She has much to prepare for your celebration tomorrow, which will be difficult to orchestrate considering the city is in the midst of a week-long debauchery-laced festival. When news of this victory reaches the populace, it will be difficult to get anything done." She cleared her throat and glanced up at him. "And, with a plea for your discretion, I will venture to say that Chamberlain Thorn was afraid to come here after seeing your performance in the arena."

"All right, all right. Get up, will you?" Victor walked over to the counter where refreshments were on display and used the wash basin there to clean the blood from his hands and arms. Bryn approached and, while he was scrubbing, poured a glass of chilled wine.

"You must be parched."

"Yeah. Have a glass. We'll head out after I wash my face."

"I was going to suggest that; it's caked with dried blood."

"I can feel it." Victor stoppered the drain and let the ornate faucet, cast in the shape of a swan neck, fill it with cool water. While the water ran, he said, "So, what's on the agenda tonight? How will you see that I'm, uh, what was it? 'Fresh and relaxed' tomorrow?" He glanced at Bryn and saw that his attempt at humor had struck a little too close to home; her cheeks were flushed, and she was trying not to look at him. Hastily, he said, "I think a big dinner and some good booze will suit me just fine. Maybe you could invite the old champion. What was his name? Foster? I wouldn't mind having someone to shoot the breeze with before I hit the sack."

Bryn's relief was palpable. Victor could only imagine what she feared he'd ask for. "I think that should be easy enough to arrange! I thought perhaps you'd enjoy a bath and massage—we have a very skilled Elemental Therapist at the palace. I was awarded a session when I was promoted, and it was the most wonderful experience I've ever had."

"Sec." Victor dunked his head in the basin and scrubbed his hair and face vigorously for several seconds before lifting it out. The water was deep red. "I think a bath would be great, and shit, yes, I'd like a massage." He grabbed a towel, dried his face, and gestured to the door. "Shall we?"

"Yes!" Bryn lifted her helmet to her head, then led the way down the corridor to the portal room. "I enjoyed watching your fight tonight, Victor. I could tell some of the others were worried at the start, but I could see you weren't bothered much by the wounds Qi Pot delivered. He chose the wrong sort of weapon to face one such as you."

"Yeah." Victor looked sideways at her. "What kind of weapon do you think would be better?"

"Ideally? Something that would be harder to heal from. A projectile weapon, perhaps. A powerful bow—an artifact that could generate its ammunition, for instance. If the bolts or arrows were driven deeply and difficult to remove, surely they'd take a toll, even against someone with your constitution."

"Hmm. Yeah, I don't love arrows. What other ideas do you have?"

"Anything other than a dagger or rapier!" She snorted. "Perhaps a great blade, though everyone saw how you dealt with Obert's sword. If not a weapon, then perhaps devastating Energy attacks. I think you'd need to take great damage quickly—I can't see how anyone could win by trying to wear you down inch by inch." She sounded excited to be given leave to discuss strategy, and Victor nodded, encouraging her. "Can you tell me, Victor, how you could bleed so much and still fight? Is it your bloodline?"

"I'll share some secrets with you, Bryn, but not yet. Let's get through the next couple of days, find out who I'm fighting next, and then maybe we can talk strategy. Would you like that?"

"Very much, sir! I think you'll like Foster, too. He knows a great deal about the empire and the many men and women who fight as champions."

Victor clapped her shoulder as they entered the portal room. "That's great, Bryn. You'll join us, of course. Bring a friend, if you want. I mean, you can put that together while I'm getting that massage, yeah?"

She stared at him with wide eyes. "I, um, of course, I'll be on duty, sir. I'll be glad to watch over you during your dinner with—"

"Nah, I'll protect myself tonight, Bryn. Seriously, bring a friend or two. Heck, are you married? Bring your, uh, significant other—whoever you want.

We'll have the meal in my quarters, then sit around and talk about fighting. Yeah, I guess whoever you invite should be interested in that." Victor nodded, gave her shoulder another slap, then stepped through the portal.

She joined him on the other side of the portal and, as though they hadn't just traveled thousands of miles, said, "I'll have the Elemental Therapist sent to your rooms, sir. In the meantime, I'll begin making the arrangements for the dinner." After a moment, she added, "Thank you for the invitation."

Victor smiled, ignoring the other guards in the chamber as he regarded her. "That wasn't so hard, was it? Go ahead and get started on all that. I can make it to my quarters." She bowed, and Victor left, grinning stupidly. In a way, he was messing with her; he had a good time putting people off balance, and he thought Bryn was kind of funny when she got flustered. Still, he wanted to make some new friends, and he thought she was pretty cool.

As he strode through the palace, heading for his rooms, he couldn't help but feel good, despite a distant, niggling worry about the veil walker's words. It only made sense that powerful people were watching the duels. There were tens of thousands of people in those stands; Gloria's upset victories were sure to draw attention. When he talked Kynna into challenging some neighbors, life was going to get . . . *dangerous*. He was ready for it, and as far as scheming steel seekers might go, Victor figured he'd just have to stay a step ahead.

# 19

## THE ROAD AHEAD

**V**ictor walked through the remnants of his impromptu celebratory get-together, idly counting the empty liquor bottles on his way to the balcony doors. He stopped at thirteen, shaking his head and chuckling. Foster, Bryn, and her two friends from the palace guard were all above Tier Eight, and they hadn't struggled in the least to clean out Victor's liquor cabinet. He pulled the doors wide, letting in the fresh late-morning air, then stepped out, turning his face to the sun, soaking it up. He felt remarkably good.

Bryn hadn't been lying about the Elemental Therapist. The fellow had used water and fire affinities to do incredible things to Victor's muscles. Besides his ability to chill and warm his tendons and muscles from the inside out, the man had been a skilled masseur, something Victor couldn't remember ever experiencing, at least not for a long, dedicated session like that.

He stretched, arching his back, then patted his stomach, not surprised to find it still satisfied after the food and drink he'd consumed late into the night. Bryn had arranged quite a feast, and though Victor could recall enjoying the company of her friends, he honestly couldn't remember much about the conversations they'd had. "Now, though, it's time to get to work." With a sigh, he turned away from the sun and walked to his door. When he opened it, he didn't find Bryn but one of her comrades.

"Good morning, sir."

"Good morning. Will you advise the queen that I'd like to meet with her at her earliest convenience?"

"Right away, sir!" The young man slammed his fist to his chest and took off at a jog, his plate armor clanking with each stride. Victor closed the door and spent the next few minutes getting ready for the day—showering, shaving, cleaning his teeth, and putting on the perfectly clean clothes that he wore almost every day.

While he waited for word from the queen, Victor pulled some of his study materials out of his storage ring and stacked them on the small round table in the central parlor of his suite. He planned to do a little more research into elder magic, and along with it, he intended to mess around with one or two of his older, less utilized spells. It had been many months—years?—since he'd figured out how to create weaves of his affinities that produced justice-attuned Energy. He'd even discovered a powerful spell to use with it, The Inevitable Huntsman, but he'd so rarely had occasion to invoke the magic that he wondered if he couldn't improve or alter it somehow.

He had beautiful large, thick sheets of paper that he'd gotten from Dar for writing out spell patterns, and he'd just taken one out and begun to delicately sketch the pattern for the Huntsman spell when there was a tap on his door. "Come in," he called.

He had his back to the door, but he heard it open, gliding near silently on its well-oiled hinges, and then a strident voice startled him into nearly dropping his pen. "Her Majesty, Queen Kynna Dar!"

Victor spun in his chair to see Kynna gliding into his quarters, the jewels sewn into her dazzling pale gray and blue gown glittering in the light from the floor-to-ceiling windows. Her crown nearly brushed the lintel, but the palace had been designed with massive statures in mind, and it missed it by an inch or so. Mortified by the state of his quarters and ill-prepared state, Victor jumped to his feet and sketched out a hasty bow.

The queen smiled at him, then turned to the man holding the door. "Thank you, Seneschal Lovalle. Please wait without." The slender, neatly coiffed man stooped into a low bow and swept out of the room, closing the door behind him. "Good morning, Champion."

"Um, good morning, my Queen." Victor straightened and gestured to the empty seat to the right of his own. "Would you care to sit?" The truth was, he was trying to get her to look his way before her gaze lingered on the mess in the sitting area near the windows.

It seemed it was too late, in any case. As she glided into the suite and approached the table where Victor was working, the queen said, "I'll have Thorn speak to your housekeeping staff. This is no fit state for a Royal Champion's chambers."

"Um, no, Your Majesty, please don't. I asked them to come back later. I, uh, didn't know I'd have a guest."

Kynna froze halfway to the table, staring at him with a blank expression. Her eyes weren't particularly bright, generally, not like Dar's, but at that moment, they were hardly glowing—almost as if they were veiled by mist. It made Victor wonder about the nature of the eyes themselves. Were there actual fires burning in the sockets? Were the flames inside a transparent shell of something . . . keratin? "Did you not summon me?"

"I, uh, sent my guard to let you know that I wanted *you* to summon *me* whenever it was convenient."

Kynna started forward again, shaking her head and *tsk*ing. "Perhaps the young man was overzealous. No matter. I'm here. What can I help you with, Victor?" She sat down, gracefully folding one leg over the other as she turned the chair to look at him more easily.

"Um, do you want a refreshment?" Victor prayed she'd say no. He had no idea what was appropriate to serve a queen.

"No, thank you."

"Right, well, I wanted to talk to you about our strategy moving forward. I mean, now that your immediate threat has been dealt with, we'll need to start implementing Dar's plans."

"Ranish Dar? What further plans are there? I assumed you'd linger here a while, ensuring no further encroachments, but I have a new cadre of champions now that we've conquered Xan and Frostmarch; I don't think you should feel bound to further service." She spoke plainly and seemed so oblivious that Victor had to lean back in his chair and think for a moment. Hadn't he said he was there to help Gloria rise to . . . glory? He strained his brain, trying to think of his words when he'd first met the queen.

"My Queen, has Ranish Dar not conveyed his further wishes for my, uh, service to you? Didn't I make it clear why I was here when I presented you with my spear?"

"You said that the time had come for my house to ascend to its rightful place of prominence on Ruhn." She spread her hands and gave a slight, elegant shrug. "Both Xan and Frostmarch had recently conquered one of our other neighbors. With your two victories, we now sit at the head of a five-kingdom hegemony—more power than Gloria has held in twelve centuries."

"Yes." Victor nodded. "It's a good start."

"Start?" Kynna raised a delicately feathered black brow, and Victor thought he saw the fire in her eyes grow brighter.

"Yeah. Ranish Dar believes it's time for a new empire to rule Ruhn, and naturally, he wants his descendants to be in charge."

Both of Kynna's brows shot up, and her eyes widened further as she leaned forward and hissed, "He wants me to initiate a war of succession?"

"Yeah—initiate and win."

She reached up to her crown and tapped a nail against the crystal. A chime rang out, reverberating as a pale blue dome of Energy surrounded Victor, Kynna, and the table where they sat. "Such words will bring imperial assassins!"

"You think spies are listening?" Victor scowled and looked around his room.

"When such words are spoken, one must always assume! Victor, what you suggest is insanity. Do you understand what such an action entails?"

"I have some idea, yeah. Your ancestor schooled me a bit before he sent me here. Still, let's review. What do *you* think it entails?"

"Even at the head of five nations, Gloria amounts to less than a tenth of the power of one of the great houses, of which there are seven. They all rule hegemonies of at least five major nations on the eastern continent. Consider that Khaliday, the imperial seat, is equal to any three of the great houses. Now, consider that, in order to challenge Khaliday, we'd need to conquer one of the great houses, and to challenge a great house, we'd need to fight our way through dozens of lesser kingdoms here, on the western continent."

"Hmm, actually, that sounds a little better than I'd feared. So, we'd snap up five or more nations by beating a great house? On top of that, once you rule a great house, you can challenge the emperor directly?"

Kynna stared at him as though he'd grown a second head. "Victor, the champions of Frostmarch and Xan were formidable by the standards of far-flung western kingdoms, but they were children compared to the veritable demigods who fight for the great houses."

Victor nodded slowly. "I know. I know we've got a ways to go before we challenge a great house, too, but we need to start making moves that way. We need to start strategizing about which kingdoms here, on the western continent, will most easily be bullied or tricked into a duel. Which kingdoms will bend the knee? We need to build momentum quickly to make it harder for the great houses to prepare and to minimize the time they have to try things like assassination."

The queen stared at him for a long time, and he could only imagine the wheels turning in her head. If Victor left, she'd have a very real chance to spend centuries in peace, ruler of a powerful mini-empire. If she went along with Dar's idea that she should try to conquer the entire planet, in her mind, she would be walking a path where defeat wasn't just possible but *likely*, especially considering what she thought she knew of Victor's capabilities. "Are you in contact with my ancestor?"

"I am."

"Then I must choose my words carefully, mustn't I?" She shook her head; whether it was at Victor or her own words, he couldn't tell. "I didn't bargain for this when I appealed to Ranish Dar for help. You speak blithely, but there will be no peaceful resolution for a nation that instigates a succession war—either we win, or the emperor will wipe out my bloodline. Of course, you bear the same risk as a champion, at least personally, but tell me, are you also putting your loved ones at risk?"

Victor had to admit she made a good point. It was one thing to risk yourself, but to risk your entire family, from your children to your distant cousins, was another matter. "I understand your concern."

"I must think on this. I know I risk my ancestor's wrath, but . . ." She trailed off, shaking her head. "I must seek the counsel of people I trust, Victor. Tell me one thing: Did you truly hold back so much against Obert and Qi Pot, or are you mad? I do not lie when I say that Obert would never dream of challenging one of the champions of the great houses."

"I might be crazy, Queen Kynna, but I'm not here for any reason other than I need some tough *pendejos* to fight. If Dar just wanted to beat the guys putting pressure on your family, he could have found someone in Sojourn to do the job. I'm here for the guys no one else wants to fight." Victor shrugged as if that was all he had to say.

She *tsk*ed. "Such pride! Do you not fear death?"

Victor sighed and leaned back, drumming his fingers on the arms of his chair while he thought about how to answer the question. "I have a Spirit Core. You know that, right?"

"Yes, I can discern that much."

"Well, I've seen the other side. I've seen spirits and even spoken to a loved one after she passed. I've had my ancestors talk to me while I fight. They've even offered me boons. I don't view death as the end anymore. I might once have worried about dying, worried I'd leave things unfinished in this world, but that worry has changed. Now, I worry I won't do enough in this life to earn a proper place among my ancestors.

"I'm a fighter, Queen Kynna—it's pretty much the only damn thing I have a hope of being *excellent* at. I won't earn glory for my ancestors by choosing easy battles." Victor leaned forward, his eyes intense beneath the glower of his dark, heavy brow. "I *need* you to start this war because I don't see another easy way to get a fight with those *pendejos* on the eastern continent." For the first time, Victor let his aura slip a little in the queen's presence, giving her a taste of the heat and weight of it, the bloody taste and sharp edge, the hunger for glory tinged with the stomach-turning scent of fear and the blood-boiling fury of the mountain.

She leaned back, and her pale gray skin paled further as she visibly swallowed. She glanced toward the door as though weighing her odds at making a hasty retreat. Victor only let his aura ripple out for a second, though, and when it passed, it was as if the room grew brighter. Kynna cleared her throat and nodded. "I have much to think on. Please delay your next message to my ancestor until we've spoken again."

"I will." As she stood and started for the door, Victor stood. "My Queen?" When she turned, he held his massive black spear in his hands. To her credit,

Kynna didn't flinch. "I promised you this spear and swore to use it to vanquish the hounds on your borders. Will you take it now?" Victor fell to a knee and held the spear out.

Kynna took a quick breath, and he could tell she'd had words on her tongue that she halted just before they escaped. After a moment's consideration, she reached out, rested her fingertips on the sturdy weapon, and nodded. "I will. My thanks, Champion of Gloria." As she finished the words, the spear disappeared, summoned into a storage container, no doubt. "I look forward to your award ceremony this evening, Victor. Will you wear a proper uniform if I have one sent here?"

"Sure." Victor nodded as he stood, then walked over to the door, pulling it open for her. "Thank you for coming to see me so quickly. I didn't expect such a courtesy."

Kynna seemed to appreciate the chance to retake the upper hand. She smiled crookedly and glanced toward the mess in the sitting area. "I can see that." Victor wanted to deny having drunk all those bottles of alcohol, but he just nodded with a slightly chagrined smile. And Kynna stepped through the door. Over her shoulder, as her entourage formed around her, she said, "I'll have that uniform sent over soon. See you tonight, Champion Victor."

"Tonight, Your Majesty." Victor watched the group of guards, ladies-in-waiting, and officials make their way down the hallway, wondering what they all did while they waited outside a door for their queen. Returning to his chambers, he retrieved Arona's phylactery from his storage ring.

Her spirit rapidly materialized as he moved over to his sitting area to gather up the many empty bottles, dirty plates, and soiled linen napkins. He stacked them on the oversized ottoman that ran the length of the central couch, and Arona drifted over. "I see you survived your duel."

"Yeah. Sorry I didn't summon you right away, but I had to . . . *entertain* last night." He gestured to the mess. "I was just going to leave it for the cleaning staff, but now I feel guilty; I had a pop-in visit from the queen."

"Oh?" Arona moved to "sit" on the couch, even though she didn't really touch it.

"Yeah. She was slightly more clueless about Dar's plans for Gloria than I expected. I suppose I should be irritated with Dar for leaving me to break the news, but I guess it's on me, too, for assuming. Anyway, how'd it go with Trobban? When I got back, your phylactery was on the table, but I didn't see any notes or anything."

"I'm sorry I missed you. I was exhausted—keeping myself outside the phylactery takes much effort. As for Trobban, he's quite knowledgeable, but for each idea he has, he insists he's seen another dozen in texts he's read, so he wanted to do some research before devising a final plan for the components of my vessel."

"And you? I didn't get to speak to you without him listening. How do you feel about everything?" Victor couldn't help imagining a robot or a Frankenstein's monster when he thought of a "vessel" being created for her. He hoped it wouldn't be like that, but what did he know?

"I'm excited but apprehensive. Trobban believes there are natural treasures that can be used to form a Core, one that will absorb the Energy I've built up in this phylactery so that it will gain ranks nearly equivalent to what I had in life. He insists that he's read accounts of people's affinities changing when they adopted such a Core. In his opinion, it won't be difficult to change my affinity, but rather a byproduct that would be more difficult to avoid."

Victor plopped down on the couch. "I mean, that's good news, right?"

Arona's ghostly face brightened as she smiled, and her raspy voice smoothed out slightly as she replied, "It's wonderful news. Wouldn't it be grand to grow strong enough to face the likes of Vesavo? I'd so love to confront him about the torture he put me through—about the horrors he's committed on various worlds."

Victor nodded, smiling grimly. He could relate to the sentiment. "I know what it's like to want to force powerful people to confront their bullshit, but let's not get ahead of ourselves. Even Dar is leery of insulting Vesavo."

"True. Still, if I could drink, I'd toast to our future goals. I'm glad I met you, Victor. I wonder where I'd be right now if I hadn't—serving Ronkerz? No, I don't think that foolish mission into the Iron Prison would have happened if you weren't around. I'd be slaving away on some horrid project for Vesavo, likely dreading his next summons." She surprised him by visibly shuddering. It made Victor chuckle as he tilted his head, looking at her sideways.

"It's crazy how your spirit form mimics how you were in life. Even your voice—raspy and low. Do you think your new body will change you much?"

She smiled, exposing her sharp canines. "It depends on how talented Trobban is. I've seen constructs that looked just like living, breathing people. The artifacts and natural treasures he's researching will play a part. I'm *excited*, Victor!" She leaned forward as the truth of her emotions came out.

Victor laughed and nodded, smacking his fist into his hand. "Me too, Arona. I mean for you, but also me. When I look down the road ahead, the various crossroads and one-way turns, I see some that lead to victory and some that lead to death, but almost all of them lead to glory."

# 20

## A GILDED CHAIN

Victor stood in the wings of the stage, waiting for his name to be called. He shifted, strangely nervous about being the center of attention in such a stolid, formal ceremony. Victor *liked* attention, but he was far more at ease giving an impromptu speech or, if truth be told, fighting in front of a large crowd. He didn't like the idea that he was expected to dress and act a certain way. In his mind, it was almost like a wedding ceremony or, more to his experience, a confirmation.

He was dressed in his new official uniform—similar to the guards' uniforms, only fancier, made of some kind of silky Energy-rich material with a subtle inner luster. Even the dark gray pants, boot-cut to accommodate his polished, shiny black boots, seemed to gleam in the darkness of the shadows where he stood. Tucked into the pants was a gray form-fitting long-sleeved shirt, over which he wore a royal-blue uniform coat emblazoned with a brilliant yellow rose on the breast. The jacket was festooned with gilt embroidery along the sleeves and on the edges of the high collar. He felt he looked all right but really wasn't a fan of the getup.

He fidgeted, Kynna's voice echoing back to him as it was projected out to the audience—thousands of nobles and ten times as many commoners who'd won a "lottery" for tickets. Kynna was going on about the tribulations they all had suffered through together, about how the foes of Gloria had been given justice for their crimes, and how Gloria was rising as a nation of import on the western continent of Ruhn. Overall, she was whipping up the people's pride, invoking past greatness and hinting at future growth and influence.

Only about half a day had passed since he'd spoken to the queen, so Victor didn't view it as strange that he hadn't heard from her one way or the other about proceeding with Dar's plans for a succession war. He figured she had a lot of thinking to do and would probably want to speak in seclusion with a few people she trusted. The prospect of war was a big deal, and he could see why she wouldn't want to do it, but he also understood the implied threat—Dar had sent him, and if Victor returned early, what might a powerful deity-like ancestor do? Despite everything he knew about Dar, Victor still wasn't sure about the man's motivations. He didn't *think* he'd punish Kynna, but what if he pressed the issue?

As Kynna's speech rose to a crescendo and the audience's reactions grew louder, he contemplated helping Kynna get out of the situation. All he had to do was claim that he felt victory wasn't likely and didn't want to risk his life to challenge further champions. Dar had given him that out; he'd said something along the lines of this "campaign" lasting only as long as Victor thought it should—that he could withdraw when he felt victory wasn't achievable. If Victor left now, Kynna's people would be safe for a long while—decades or centuries—and he'd have done something great. Why did he feel that wasn't enough?

He supposed part of it was that he knew he'd be lying and that Dar would see through it. Victor was not worried about his next fight, regardless of who it would be against. He and Kynna had a lot of work to do before they could challenge a great house, at which time Victor might feel his first genuine fear of defeat. Was he being cocky? Sure, he was, but that was his nature. He'd been that way before he'd woken up his Quinametzin bloodline, before he'd walked with the righteous fury of an awakened mountain, and before he'd embraced his affinity for glory. Now, the idea of backing down from a challenge such as the one posed by a succession war felt almost as unnatural as trying to breathe water.

"That's your cue, milord," the retainer holding the dark wing curtains aside said, startling Victor out of his ruminations.

"She announced me?" How had he missed that?

"Aye, milord," the young man said, smiling and ducking his head. Victor cleared his throat, straightened his shoulders, and marched through the gap in the curtain. The stage was bright, illuminated by brilliant glow lamps high above, and the audience was thrown into shadows as a result. Still, with his Quinametzin eyes, he could see them—thousands and thousands of faces staring, silent in their rapt attention. He shifted his gaze to the center of the stage where Queen Kynna stood, glorious in her jeweled gown, her crown glittering with the inner fire of whatever great magic it contained.

She beckoned him to come forward, and he did. When he stood before her, she looked to the audience and, in a voice that carried as though amplified by a hundred hidden speakers, she said, "People of Gloria, I present to you our champion, Victor of Tucson."

The applause and cheers were thunderous, and Victor felt his heartbeat quicken under the focus of so many cheering folks. His Core surged with glory-attuned Energy, which leaked into his pathways. Unable to restrain himself, he lifted a fist high, and the crowd redoubled their cheers. It was deafening.

Queen Kynna delicately raised her right hand, and the assembly hall grew silent almost instantly. "Champion, for your victory over Obert and the Kingdom of Frostmarch, I present to you one of the most valuable treasures recovered from the vaults of our foe." She held out both hands, cupped together, and a glittering, gem-studded, gold-foil package appeared there, about the size and shape of a large orange. Victor could hear the collective intake of breath as the gems picked up the lights and sparkled, creating a dazzling display that seemed almost like illusory fireworks around Kynna and Victor.

"This beautiful package contains the egg of a creature of myth here on Ruhn, a Coldwater Sea Wyrm." Again, the audience collectively gasped, and a single strident voice cried out, sounding more dismayed than excited. "You can hear from our citizens' reaction, Victor, that this is a treasure dear to the people of Ruhn, for Coldwater Sea Wyrms have not been seen in our seas for nearly a thousand years. You see, their eggs are known to wake the secrets in a person's blood, sometimes bringing forth latent attributes but always advancing a person's racial status."

Kynna paused for a moment, then turned and held the egg high, greatly expanding the size of the mystical light show it projected. "Do any of the fine people of Gloria begrudge our champion this prize? Is there any more worthy?" The response was silence, though Victor swore he heard people weeping. Kynna turned back to Victor and proffered the egg. "Will you accept this gift, Champion?"

Despite a small surge of guilt, a tiny voice in his mind that couldn't believe he was going to receive something so treasured by these people after only being there a few days, Victor saw the egg for what it was: the whole reason he'd come to Ruhn—advancement. "I will." He held out a broad palm, and the queen gently placed the egg in the center of it. Victor held the egg carefully but lifted it high, turning to face the enormous crowd. "Thank you, people of Ruhn!" His voice carried, just as the queen's had, and the crowd once again erupted in cheers.

The queen allowed the cheers to go on for a moment, smiling at Victor with her hands delicately folded before herself. "Nicely done, Victor. Please store away your prize, and then, if you would, please kneel before me." Her voice didn't carry this time, but Victor heard it clearly. He sent the egg into his storage ring, then looked at the queen.

"Kneel?"

"Please, Champion. I will award you your second prize."

Victor hated to kneel, especially with an audience, but he'd already done so to Kynna several times, so it seemed strange to balk. He nodded, then, smooth as a panther might crouch in the tall grass, he lowered himself to one knee. Queen Kynna held up her hand again, and the audience grew so silent that Victor could hear her quick, shallow breaths. Was she nervous?

"People of Gloria, today we stand free, our chains shattered and thrown to the side, and our future bright with the potential for true glory—a virtue for which our great nation was named! This turn of events is thanks to the valor of one man, a man who, until now, had no ties to our world. He served my ancestor, the great Ranish Dar, but he was a stranger to us, a visitor. Nevertheless, he came and fought not only the champion of Frostmarch but that of Xan. In the face of overwhelming odds, he struck down our enemies and lifted the grip of their cruel blockades. Today, Gloria breathes again, thanks to his courage."

Kynna paused, allowing the audience to absorb the impact of her words, then turned and faced Victor fully. "For such heroism, words are not enough. Treasures are not enough. Deeds of such magnitude deserve deeds in return. Thus, Victor of Tucson, I bestow upon you not only our nation's eternal gratitude but also something far greater."

The queen turned back to the audience, spreading her arms for effect. "From this day forward, Victor shall be named Duke of Gloria, a title that carries with it the rights, privileges, and responsibilities that few have known. With that title, he shall take possession of the richest lands in all of Xan—the Duchy of Iron Mountain." For the first time, the crowd wasn't silent or cheering deafeningly; they murmured, a buzz of surprised reactions to the proclamation.

Kynna turned to look Victor in the eyes again. "The estate and all its wealth are now yours, including the stewardship of its people. As Duke, you shall oversee the noble Haveshi family, Qi Pot's surviving kin, and see to their well-being and livelihood as a testament to your honor." Her tone grew soft, though her words were still carried out to the audience. "These lands will prosper under your care, just as our nation has thrived under your strength. Let this be a bond between us, Victor—a stake in the future of Gloria and a reminder that the freedom you fought for is now tied to you. The people you are responsible for will flourish or fail depending on our great nation's course in the coming years."

As the crowd buzzed and Victor frowned, absorbing the import of the queen's words, one man's voice cried out, rising above the general clamor, "Who will be champion?"

The queen smiled and turned. Again, she spread her arms gracefully. "Rest assured, dear people, that Victor, Duke of Gloria, will remain our champion as long as he so desires. The offices of Duke and that of Royal Champion are not mutually exclusive." She turned back to Victor. "Rise, Victor, Duke of Iron Mountain, Champion of Gloria. Rise and greet the people of your nation."

Still frowning, well aware of the snare Kynna had just tightened around his ankle, Victor stood and turned to face the crowd. When he didn't speak, and the crowd's murmurs turned into a hush, Kynna cleared her throat. "Fear not the glower on our champion's face—he's a fearsome man; how else would he defend us? Now, feed his lust for glory, Gloria! Cheer your new duke! Cheer your *champion*!"

Once again, the crowd erupted in thunderous applause, and Victor, ever the slave to his pride and hunger for glory, couldn't help grinning fiercely as he held his hands above his head. He wanted to summon Lifedrinker, to let her bask in the glorious attention, but he knew better; his axe was still a secret on that world. Still, he pumped his fists in the air, pacing back and forth. After the crowd's enthusiasm refused to wane for several long seconds, he began to shout, bellowing into the air, roaring as his Core swelled with the glory-attuned Energy that found its way into his pathways.

After nearly a minute of that, Kynna used whatever uncanny ability she had to silence the crowd, and Victor calmed himself, lowering his fists and heaving for breath as he turned to regard the queen. "I'm pleased that our champion is so fierce and that you love him so, Gloria. Now, please follow your ushers' instructions as you safely exit the hall—it's time for you to return to the festivities! I'm extending the national holiday for another week!"

Victor was saved from further bouts of cheering as the heavy midnight-blue curtain dropped from the rigging in the loft to conceal the stage. Alone on the stage with the queen, Victor glowered at her. "I know what you're doing."

"Of course you do, Champion. You're an intelligent man." She looked like she'd say more, but a dozen attendants had rushed the stage, and they were no longer alone. "Let us speak soon? I'm sure you're curious about your new holdings and how they might affect the . . . course of our diplomacy."

Victor stepped close and spoke as plainly as he could without providing fodder to the many spies, no doubt listening to them. "I know how I want things to go. You know how Dar wants them to go. I don't think my new connections to your world will change much. Still, yes, my Queen, let us speak soon. I'd like to review how my role will play out now that I have a great duchy to manage."

"Excellent. Tomorrow?"

Victor forced a smile. "If it pleases you."

She shooed away a lady trying to help her doff the long jeweled gloves she'd worn for the ceremony. "Unless you intend to consume the egg, that is. The literature all says that a person who eats one is likely to be incapacitated for upwards of a week."

"I'll wait until we've spoken."

"Very well. Congratulations, Duke Victor . . . what was your surname? I know I've been told—"

"Sandoval."

"Duke Sandoval, then. It has a nice ring. Until tomorrow." With that, she allowed her attendants to sweep her off the stage, and Victor was left standing in the gloom behind the dark curtains.

He pulled off the fancy jacket, sent it to storage, then stomped out of the enormous assembly hall, using the side exit where he'd been let in a couple of hours earlier. Of course, Bryn saw him as soon as he came through the door into the cool night air and hurried forward. "Your coach is ready, sir."

"Too much to ask that we walk?"

"The streets are crowded, especially around the hall—they're still releasing the audience." She hesitated a moment, then added, "I heard the news. Congratulations on your elevation."

"Elevation?"

"To the noble class. The Duchy of Iron Mountain is well known, even here in Gloria. There are stories about those lands—your wealth, in property alone, is now second only to the royal family."

"A pretty trap," Victor sighed, walking toward the bulbous, living-wood coach that had earlier delivered him.

"A trap?"

Victor ignored her until they were inside the plush leather interior of the coach, and he felt it gently lifting into the air. "Kynna wants me to have something more to lose than just my life." He frowned, and Bryn stared into space, perhaps trying to make sense of the statement. "What's the deal with the Haveshi family? Why am I in charge of Qi Pot's kin?"

"Because he was a duke, and there was no clause in the terms of the duel requiring his family to be slain or banished with his death. Queen Kynna is now the de facto ruler of Xan, so she can grant the various holdings of that kingdom to people she views as loyal. Now that you have been given Iron Mountain, Qi Pot's heirs will be stripped of their inheritance and most of their wealth. She's making you the honorary patron to their clan."

"Was his full name Qi Pot Haveshi, then?"

"I'm unsure." Bryn shrugged, making her armor clank. "I've only ever heard him called Qi Pot. Perhaps it's an assumed name or a title he earned with one exploit or another."

"Goddamn it," Victor sighed, viciously scratching the sides of his head with his nails.

"What's—"

"That's the second time I've been given responsibility for the survivors of someone I've killed in a duel. It's bullshit. The first time was just a single girl—now I have a whole clan to look after? And how many will try to kill me in my sleep? I doubt they're all children, right?"

"That would be suicide for them. Their futures are now tied to yours. With your demise, they will be at the queen's mercy, or should you die in a duel, whatever ruler seizes the queen's power and lands."

"And?"

"And most rulers would simply banish them to avoid trouble." She shrugged. "Banish or kill."

"So, are they expecting that now?"

"Possibly. Queen Kynna is known to be kind, so they likely aren't afraid they'll be executed. However, banishment is surely on their minds. Keep in mind that while you are irritated by this turn of events, the Haveshi are only one noble family the queen has to sort out among dozens—nay, hundreds. She will have a very busy few months consolidating her grasp of the political landscape in her new hegemony."

Victor's stomach rumbled, and he frowned, leaning back and thinking. He was irritated, but Bryn had made a good point; Queen Kynna had a big headache on her hands, and if Victor and Dar got their way, things would only get more complicated for her. He was complaining about being responsible for the fate of a single family and a single—albeit apparently large—duchy. At first, he thought she was just trying to tie him to something on Ruhn, and he felt that was still true, but he also thought she might be trying to give him a glimpse into the complexity of taking on the rulership of an entire empire.

There were millions of people living on Ruhn. Millions of lives would be impacted by a succession war. Just because the nations of Ruhn didn't fight openly with armies didn't mean people wouldn't die. It didn't mean that people wouldn't be forced from their homes. It was a lot to think about. His stomach rumbled again, and Bryn cleared her throat.

"Dinner, sir?"

Victor shook his head. "I have something I've been wanting to eat back in my quarters. I need to do some thinking—let's head straight to the palace." She nodded, and Victor smiled. He wondered what she'd say if he told her the thing he was hungry for was Qi Pot's heart.

# 21

##### ❈

# A MEETING WITH THE QUEEN

Victor sat, sipping a cup of spiced coffee, heavy with cream, looking out over his balcony as he contemplated the changes Qi Pot's heart had wrought in him. The heart had been potent, though nothing more than Obert's. It had been different, though; Victor had felt Qi Pot's strange, hot, shadowy Energy coursing through his pathways. He'd felt it trying to do *something*, but it hadn't taken; either his body had resisted it, or the heart hadn't been potent enough. Whatever the case, Victor hadn't gained any new feats, affinities, bloodline alterations, or anything of that sort. However, he'd earned a rank to his Core and advanced to Level Seventy-Two.

He hadn't been too surprised by the level; he felt he'd been close to Seventy-One before killing Qi Pot, so the additional Energy infusion from the heart had pushed him over the edge to the next. With a sip of hot cinnamon-flavored coffee, he sighed and looked at his status sheet:

| Status | | | |
|---|---|---|---|
| Name: | Victor Sandoval | | |
| Race: | Quinametzin Bloodline: Epic 2 | | |
| Class: | Berserker of Unstoppable Momentum, Legendary | | |
| Level: | 72 | | |
| Breath Core: | Elder Class: Improved 6 | | |
| Core: | Spirit Class: Epic 3 | | |
| Breath Core Affinity: | Magma: 9 | Breath Core Energy: | 2500/2500 |

| Energy Affinity: | Fear 9.4, Rage 9.1, Glory 8.6, Inspiration 7.4, Unattuned 3.1 | Energy: | 36871/36871 |
|---|---|---|---|
| Strength: | 508 | Vitality: | 673 (740) |
| Dexterity: | 208 | Agility: | 231 |
| Intelligence: | 172 | Will: | 673 |
| Points Available: | 0 | | |
| Titles & Feats: | Titanic Rage, Ancestral Bond, Flame-Touched, Greater Titanic Constitution, Titanic Presence, Desperate Grace, Challenger, Elder Magic, Born of Terror, Battlefield Awareness, Battlefield Presence, Aura of Command, Epic Quinametzin, Mountain's Resilience, Behemoth's Regeneration, Blood Supremacy, Furious Battle Momentum | | |

For the first time, will wasn't his highest attribute. His vitality had caught up to it, and with the bonus from his wyrm-scale vest, it had cleanly outstripped it. When he added his Sovereign Will boost, his vitality nearly hit one thousand. He knew from talking to his friends and loved ones that such a number was unheard of on Fanwath. However, he supposed there were some folks on Sojourn and Ruhn with stats that were that high. "Well, I'm not done yet." Victor chuckled.

Looking at his status sheet again, he frowned at his Breath Core rank. He needed to work on that, and it seemed as if he might have to do old-fashioned slow and steady cultivation. Maybe if he could kill some more wyrms or other creatures with Breath Cores and eat their hearts, he'd see a boost, but so far, that hadn't been on the menu. He had the egg to eat, which apparently had come from a wyrm, and was eager to see what would come of it, but first, he had his meeting with Queen Kynna to attend.

He sighed, tossed the remainder of his coffee over the balcony railing, and went inside to finish getting ready. Ten minutes later, Bryn guided him through the palace toward the expansive royal gardens on the back acreage. The palace grounds took up several square miles, and the queen's gardens were supposedly quite something. Victor hadn't yet checked them out.

"Does it feel different, milord?"

"What's that?"

"Being a grand and fine duke, sir." Bryn looked at him sideways, and Victor saw a glint of humor in her eyes.

"Very clever."

"I notice you aren't wearing your uniform, milord."

Victor snorted. "Nah, too shiny for me. I'll wear it only upon royal decree."

Bryn chuckled. "Such a rebellious champion, er, excuse me, duke."

"All right, all right, that's enough of that shit." Victor watched her walk for a moment, then added, "You've got quite a spring in your step today. Did you get some good news?"

"Actually, I did, sir! I've been informed by Captain Wash that I'll be accompanying you as you travel to your new duchy."

Victor's eyebrows shot up. "Oh? Ha! No one told *me*. Well, I'm glad to have you, Bryn. You're sure that's what you want? I'll probably be there most of the time. Don't you have family—"

"I'm happy, milord. I find my duty as your guard and guide quite entertaining."

Victor nodded. "Good."

They passed through a resort-like rear patio complete with pools, fountains, and rose hedges—all yellow. Then they walked through a tall archway in a red-brick wall, and Victor had to pause to take in the many sweet smells and the gorgeous hedgerows. They were comprised of flowering shrubs laid out in a meandering pattern down a gentle slope toward a lush green copse of woods in the distance. He could see the queen's entourage about halfway down the hill. "Looks like we're heading the right way."

"Yes, sir. I was told she'd be in the garden."

Victor nodded and followed Bryn through the maze-like hedges, and when he came to the broad central path, lined with weird, fantastical marble sculptures and flower-filled planters, the queen turned toward the two of them and waved. "Might as well wait here, Bryn. She'll want privacy."

"Aye, milord, her retainers are moving off." It was true—Queen Kynna's cadre of eight Queen's Guards and her ladies-in-waiting were separating themselves from the monarch. The ladies moved off in clusters of two and three, murmuring and giggling. The guards took up a star-shaped pattern a reasonable distance from the queen, leaving her alone as Victor approached.

"Hello, Duke Sandoval." She smiled, performing an almost mocking curtsy, lifting her silky, pale-blue skirts.

Victor bowed. "My Queen."

She held a finger to her crown and tapped her nail against it, producing her weird blue static Energy bubble around them. "For our privacy."

Victor nodded, folding his arms over his chest and inhaling deeply. "At least it doesn't block the smells. This garden is something else."

"It's beautiful, isn't it? My favorite part is the grove." She nodded down the slope toward the trees at the base of the hill. "There are special tree gardens and living sculptures in there. My great-grandmother had a powerful affinity for plants." While Victor followed her gaze, the queen seemed to gather herself, building the impetus to broach the topic of their meeting. "Do you feel I've tried to entrap you?"

"In a way, I guess so. I was irritated at first. I mean, I still am. I didn't come here looking to manage an estate or to have people follow me." Victor held up a hand to forestall her objections. "I know it's an honor. I know you've given me a piece of coveted property. I also know why you did it. I mean, it doesn't take a genius. You hope I'll grow fond of the place and the people there. You hope that I'll feel a connection to them, and, being so connected, you hope that I'll understand the risks of a succession war better."

She nodded, her high crystal crown glittering with a dazzling reflection of the morning sun. "It's more than that, though, Victor. I *do* want you to understand the risks, but I also want you to share in them. Now that you're a titled noble, should you lose in a duel—"

"My lands and people will be at the mercy of the winning king. I get it. Right now, it doesn't mean much, but I suppose your plan is to have me spend time at Iron Mountain, growing to care about the folks there, huh?"

"Am I so transparent?" She smiled and waved a hand. "Don't answer that. I've had a long heart-to-heart discussion with Thorn, my most trusted advisor, as you've no doubt guessed. I believe I have come up with a compromise for you and Dar to consider." Victor nodded, perhaps a little absently. He'd seen people moving around on the next tier of the garden, further down the hillside. Were they Kynna's retainers?

"Thorn brought up a grudge my father had with the ruling family of the Kingdom of Ardent. They lie to the east, removed by nearly a thousand miles and two other smaller kingdoms. Thorn believes we could make a believable argument for pursuing vengeance against Ardent. In order to challenge them, per the rules of the Empire, we'd need to share a border."

Victor nodded. He hadn't seen the movement again and decided it might have been a songbird or something. "Which gives you an excuse to attack the two kingdoms separating you, I guess?"

"That's right. I believe—" Kynna gasped, squeezing her eyes tight as she reached up to grasp her head in both hands.

"Are you all right—" She fell toward Victor, and he caught her in his arms, and that's when he felt it, too—a potent, draining vortex, sucking the Energy out of his Core. As the blue static Energy shield faded around them, Victor looked inward and saw that his rage-attuned Energy was being drawn out of him. It was unpleasant and left him feeling weaker, but it was *only* his rage. His other attunements roiled and swelled with power.

He looked around, saw Kynna's guards jogging toward them, and shouted, "Something's wrong!"

Kynna was a dead weight in his arms, completely unconscious. Victor held her close, turning in a circle, and that's when the shrubs exploded as a dozen crackling magenta portals spun into existence, out of which dozens of soldiers poured. Victor saw figures wielding large weapons and wearing heavy armor and, along with them, just as many lithe fighters in sleek leather or silky garb. They immediately began to channel Energy as they clashed with Kynna's guards.

Victor saw Bryn and a couple of other royal guards surrounded by at least ten attackers and wanted to run to help, but he was stuck with Kynna; a dozen of the strange soldiers had already broken past Kynna's other guards and were charging him. Alarm bells clanged from the palace, and he hoped help was on the way as he shifted Kynna, planning to set her on the ground so he could summon a weapon.

Victor wasn't often caught unawares, but one of the attackers was absurdly nimble and quick, and he felt a stab in his shoulder as a knife drove through his clothes. He took a stumbling step, finding combat with no rage in his Core strange and foreign. He felt like he was outside himself, that his body was slow and clumsy. He'd been admiring the garden, talking to Kynna, and now—another blow, this time from a mace, caught him above the ear, and Victor felt the stab of split skin and the concussion of his skull being rattled. He stumbled to a knee, hunkering over Kynna, trying to shield her from a flurry of attacks.

As more attackers swarmed him with stabs, slashes, and thudding blows, he tried to recover his wits and remember what he should do. A voice—his own—roared in his mind, "Channel Energy into your armor, fool!" but something was making him dull and slow. Something was still pulling at his rage-attuned Energy. Then, as a rapier gashed his forehead, sheeting blood into his eyes, he saw it—a pulsing, throbbing, purple-glowing rod impaled in the ground a dozen yards away where a hedge used to be.

"A trap," he grunted, then, as Kynna and he received more stabs and Energy-infused attacks, he bunched his legs and *leaped* out of there. The Titanic Leap was his most clumsy ever, but it was enough—he soared some twenty feet into the air, then nearly five times that far ahead, just past where Bryn and the other guards were being overwhelmed. Victor crashed onto the cobble path and fell, sliding on his knees in his efforts to keep Kynna from tumbling free of his arms.

Victor immediately felt his head clear, and his fury began to stoke. As his eyes blazed with molten fire, he surged to his feet, still holding Kynna, and turned to glare at the dozens of attackers. The Queen's Guard were formidable combatants, and they were putting up a desperate defense to keep the attackers who badly outnumbered them at bay. Victor could see Energy spells of all sorts—fireballs, glowing shields, ghostly translucent weapons, and even showers of mystical bolts.

He caught a glimpse of Bryn, utterly surrounded, bleeding, her weapon gone from her hand, but a large shield held before her as she stood back-to-back with a Queen's Guard. She'd tell him to leave. She'd tell him to take the queen and run. Wouldn't she? Shouldn't he?

Victor looked at Kynna and saw her face was bloody from a broad, bone-deep gash on her brow and that arrows and stab wounds covered her body. Was she even alive? Her crown had been knocked off, and her hands hung limp, but in that second of hesitation, while he contemplated the "right" thing to do, he heard Bryn cry out, and he knew that she and the Queen's Guard would soon be killed. He glanced up the hill but didn't see any help mobilizing. What was going on? A coup?

A huge warrior wielding a massive, two-handed mace with a spiked ball on the end waded into the fight where Bryn and the Queen's Guard held something like fifteen attackers at bay. Victor wasn't sure how, but it had to do with some enormous surge of Energy the Queen's Guard had unleashed—a rippling curtain of weird pink clouds that seemed to obscure spine-tipped tentacles. They grasped and stabbed at the attackers, pulling them off, and for a moment, Bryn was clear, and her desperate dark-gray eyes locked onto his.

"Fuck this," Victor growled, and he reached into his repertoire of spells and cast one he'd let languish for far too long—Guard Ally. A shield of brilliant golden, glory-attuned Energy surrounded Bryn, and suddenly, Victor felt the jostling of the enemies around her. He felt the stabs of spears and the slashes of swords, the burning of fireballs, the jolts of lightning. He felt everything intended for her, only doubly so.

Grunting with the effort, he lowered Kynna to the ground, and then, as cuts and burns and gaping wounds appeared on his body, then rapidly healed, he stepped over Kynna's insensate form and summoned Lifedrinker to his hands. She thudded onto the pavers before him, her heavy axe-head driving them into the soft earth as he grasped her handle. Victor, buffeted by more and more blows, felt his mind slipping away, lost in the torrent of rage that slid into its own special pathway created by his Furious Battle Momentum.

Before he lost himself, he channeled Energy into his armor, and his disguise of soft, bloodstained clothes was replaced by the fierce black-and-red shell of his wyrm-scale and lava king hide armor. The blows intended for Bryn continued to rain down on him, but now they were mostly rebuffed. Still, Victor's rage had clouded his vision red, and he'd had *enough*. He cast Iron Berserk, knowing his epic-tier Core could substitute any of his affinities for rage to keep it going.

For the first time on Ruhn, Victor took on his proper titanic aspect. He surged from ten to more than twenty feet in height. Lifedrinker was no longer an unwieldy burden as his strength soared and his massive bones stabilized his form. He lifted her high, and as she sang with furious bloodlust, bursting into molten flames, he *roared*. As the blows aimed at Bryn pounded into him, he focused on the giant warrior with the two-handed mace and cast Energy Charge, fueling it with fear-attuned Energy.

In a cloud of black smoke and shadows, he ripped the garden path to shreds and then slammed into the warrior, sending him flying, bouncing, and careening off other warriors. His head caught the edge of a stone bench, and Victor saw his skull come apart, and then he was wading into the fools surrounding his friend. Lifedrinker split bodies in twain, like a cleaver quartering chickens. No armor stood before her. No bones or spells of shielding could stop her smoldering, depthless obsidian edge from rending the bodies of Victor's foes.

As blood and viscera sprayed, he roared and laughed. His Iron Berserk didn't add to his madness, and the blows had stopped falling on Bryn, so his Furious Battle Momentum had not yet driven him beyond reason. With a bit of sanity still providing clarity, Victor looked over the ten corpses near his feet and roared at the Queen's Guard and Bryn, "Protect the queen!" and then he charged another pack of attackers.

The Queen's Guard he rescued fell back, knowing well their duty to the monarch. Victor's great body filled the gap as he wove into the attackers, cleaving and hacking with the precision of a master. Lifedrinker felt light in his hands, but her blade was like a razor-edged wrecking ball. Hundreds of attacks hit him, but the assassins were like children fighting a madman in heavy armor. For every five stabs or cuts or spell-blasts, Victor demolished another attacker. His strength was at levels he'd never experienced as his Furious Battle Momentum began to stack with his Iron Berserk.

Lifedrinker's great wedged blade caught an armored warrior on the shoulder plate, split through it, cleaved through his arm, then his torso, and then his other arm at the elbow. His top half was thrown to the side by the swing, but his legs stood there before Victor kicked them aside and focused on the last group of attackers still battling a desperate pair of Queen's Guards. He strode forward, too mad to use his Energy Charge, and on his third stride, Lifedrinker *whooshed* through the air and split three of the assassins to pieces. In a shower of blood, Victor bore down and *screamed* his fury.

The roar was enough to stun the remaining fighters. Even the Queen's Guards were awestruck, stumbling back as Victor fell on the last of the attackers, feeding his blood-hungry axe as he slaughtered them. Before long, he stood over the last of the black-clad assailants, their guts and blood steaming in the cool air, his chest heaving, his throat gurgling with a low, maniacal laugh. The surviving guards, including Bryn, still glowing with a shimmering shell of Victor's Glory-attuned Energy, rushed the queen up the path toward the palace.

Enough of Victor's mentality was intact that he knew he didn't need to chase them. He'd hardly taken a wound as he slaughtered the assassins, so his Furious Battle Momentum wasn't built up enough to overcome his prodigious will. Instead, he stood in the gore-strewn garden, massive axe in his hands, staring at the ruined corpses of his foes.

As his blood slowly cooled, bit by bit, he began to take note of the strange rods, now tipped over and inert. He sent Lifedrinker into storage with a quick, "We'll talk soon, *chica*," and then he walked over and picked up one of the rods. His frown deepened when he saw the pale green ribbon around the device. He'd seen ribbons like that, hadn't he? With a great effort of will, he pulled the rest of his rage back to his Core and canceled his Iron Berserk.

His head cooler and clearer, he stared at the ribbon and searched his memory—the queen's ladies. He'd seen several of them wearing ribbons like that. Victor glanced up the hill and saw the Queen's Guard ushering Kynna into the palace—she was walking. Victor looked around the battlefield again, moving to collect the other rods; there were nine, and they each bore the pale green ribbon.

He studied the ruined corpses of his foes and the handful of dead Queen's Guard. Where were the queen's ladies? Not a single one was dead on the field, and none had escaped with the queen. Had they disappeared before the ambush? Could they all be traitorous? It seemed so improbable, but he couldn't think of another explanation. Someone had planted the rods, and somehow, all the ladies had slipped away before the ambush. Scowling, Victor sent the rods into his storage container and then started toward the palace. That's when the Energy hit him.

# 22

## FIRE AND ICE

The fact that Victor didn't gain a level from his slaughter of the would-be assassins told him a great deal about them; they weren't steel seekers, and they likely weren't even Tier Eight or Nine iron rankers. Still, the surge of Energy was enough to distract him for a moment, refill his Core, and speed up his body's natural regeneration. When it was over, he stooped to pick up the queen's fallen crown, then jogged out of the garden, pounding up the inclined pathway to the palace, intently scanning every doorway, every window as he approached the central portico where he'd seen the Queen's Guards ushering her inside.

Soldiers were forming up near the tall glass double doors, and when they saw him running their way, Victor wasn't surprised to see some panic enter their eyes; he was still clad in his armor, and though he'd returned to his standard giant size and sent Lifedrinker back into her storage container, he presented a fearsome sight. Captain Wash was there, though; he calmed his troops and shouted them out of his way. "She's inside, Champion."

Victor nodded and slowed his jog to a walk as he pushed the enormous glass door open. There, he saw the queen, still surrounded by her Queen's Guard, while all around her attendants, soldiers, noble folk, and officials scurried about. They shouted instructions, questions, and generally alarmed-sounding statements while the queen ignored them and locked eyes on Victor. Bryn stood beside her, a battered shield still on her arm, but Victor's magical aegis was gone, dispelled by the influx of Energy he'd received from the dead assassins.

As he stepped close, Victor held out the queen's crown and knelt before her, perhaps to reassure everyone whose nervous fear hung palpably in the air. Kynna took the crown in bloodstained fingers and, with trembling, halting movements, lifted it to her head. Victor could see the evidence of recent healing all over her; pale, new skin marred her forehead where she'd been gashed, similar freshly healed wounds covered her arms, and despite its heroic attempts to repair itself, her gown was gashed, torn, and stained with the queen's blood.

"Thank you, Champion. Thank you, Victor. My guards tell me the assassins are all slain. I owe you much, but I fear we have snakes among us. I fear—"

"It was your ladies." Victor produced one of the ribboned rods he'd pulled from the garden's soil. "Where are they?" He looked around the big marble-decked hallway at the clusters of panic-stricken faces and the frantic, rushing servants. He saw none of the queen's ladies-in-waiting.

Queen Kynna took the rod, hefted it, and delicately held the pale ribbon between her fingers. "They mock me."

"Who?"

"Come, Victor. We must move to my private wing. There, I'll explain." She turned, and the guards formed around her as she marched purposefully down one of the broad arched hallways.

Victor followed and found Bryn striding beside him. He looked down at her, taking in the dents and puncture marks in her once-shiny armor and the wide, almost haunted look in her eyes. He gestured to her helmet. "Take that off. You're done fighting for now. Let yourself breathe."

"I . . ."

"Consider it an order."

"Yes, Champion." Bryn touched her helmet and exposed her strong, tanned face, crusted with dried blood. He saw her breathe deeply as they marched, and Victor knew what she was thinking: Everything had happened so quickly, she'd thought she was going to die, and now life was moving on as usual. It was a strange feeling the first time it happened.

"You've never fought in a battle you thought you were going to lose before, have you?"

"I . . . No. I suppose I haven't."

"Well, you didn't die, so don't be afraid to look into the face of death and laugh later today."

She spoke softly, eyeing the guards and the queen ahead of them. "Because of you." She cleared her throat and said it more clearly. "I'm alive because of you. That . . . spell. I've never been shielded so fully. Are you a Paladin Class?"

Victor chuckled. "Not even close." He reached over and clapped her on the shoulder. "Don't give me all the credit. You and the Queen's Guard gave me a chance to break the queen free, and then, when I saw how valiantly you were fighting, it convinced me that I had to do the stupid thing—something I'm quite used to, by the way—and not run away with the queen. I'm glad for that."

"How did you kill so many so easily? How—Your *axe*! What a weapon! I—"

"*Shh!*" Victor jostled her again. "Let's not spread the word until we're sure the cat's out of the bag. I don't know how many witnessed my fight, but I'm still kind of hoping it was just us." Victor nodded to the queen and her guards. He turned his head, looking over his shoulder to see at least two dozen nobles and retainers following behind, keeping a "polite" distance. "The queen," he said, more loudly, "should tell these people to get lost for now." He knew Kynna could hear him, and he hoped she'd act without him having to insist.

They'd just turned toward the broad spiral staircase that would lead up to the queen's second-story wing when the clamor of stomping, metal-clad boots came from an adjoining passage. Victor turned to see Chamberlain Thorn charging at the head of fifty or so royal guards; they flooded into the main hallway, putting themselves between Kynna and all the retainers following behind. The chamberlain looked panicked, his face drenched in a sheen of sweat and his breath coming in harsh gasps. "My Queen! I was seeing to your instructions in Frostmarch when I heard of the attack!"

Kynna stopped at the foot of the staircase, her guards, Bryn and Victor, between herself and Thorn. She turned and seemed about to speak but hesitated. Victor frowned, looking again at the chamberlain. What was going on? If he'd been in Frostmarch, wouldn't he have come from the same direction as the queen and all the nobles bunched up in that hallway? He stared at the man, looking at the sweat and panic in a different light; what if he was worried about something other than the queen being attacked? What if he was worried about her surviving?

Kynna's voice rang out, forcing Victor's mind out of its speculations, "Thorn, I wonder, why do you suppose Guard Captain Wash was having trouble mustering his soldiers? Why do you think he could only find a handful on duty and was delayed in responding to the threat?"

"My Queen, I shall immediately have the man investigated!" Thorn turned to one of the soldiers beside him and began to bark an order, but the queen interrupted him.

"Where are the Rochan sisters, my dear Chamberlain?"

He looked at her, eyes wide. "I . . . I don't know, Your Majesty! Were they slain in the attack?"

Victor watched Kynna's face, noting how she shook her head slightly, not a negation of the question but a gesture of dismay—disappointment. "Wasn't it unusual for you to request such a favor? I don't believe I ever received such a request in all the years you've served my family." Her voice became a mocking parody of Thorn's, "*Please*, my Queen. It would mean *so much* to my wife. Her cousins would be eternally grateful!' Oh, Thorn! How *could* you? I want you to know that after Victor has taken your head, I'll root out your entire bloodline for this. Those women will be merely the start!"

Hearing those words and his name snapped Victor's mind into focused clarity. Thorn had asked the queen to allow those women to be her ladies-in-waiting for the day. They'd set up the formation, allowed for the portals to open, and weakened Victor and the queen. They'd escaped before the attack, and Thorn had kept the royal guards away. Were they all loyal to him or just this fifty?

While his mind raced, putting the connections together, a clamor arose from behind Thorn's troops; the retainers and noble folk were fleeing. Victor summoned Lifedrinker and pushed Bryn back. "Get the queen and her guards out of here."

"You think I'll surrender?" Thorn bellowed, suddenly clad in dark blue plate-mail armor that instantly rimed over with frost. "*You* are the one who should be begging forgiveness, my *Queen*! *You* are the one who threatens to destroy all that we hold dear! You are the one who—" A deep *thum* sounded behind Victor, echoing in the corridor and rattling his heart in his chest. His brain had only just realized it was the sound of a bow being shot when Thorn fell to his knees, a meter-long feathered shaft protruding from his chest.

The royal guards he'd brought with him drew their weapons, and Thorn fumbled with a flask, but Kynna wasn't done. *Thum, thum, thum* sang her bow. Arrows that imploded with weird crackling Energy slammed into their ranks, drawing soldiers into them, smashing them together, and turning them into metal-clad hunks of gelid, bloody flesh. She killed at least twenty of the soldiers with her attack. He might have hoped she had more shots like that ready, but she gasped, "Victor! Finish them! That's all of my Energy!"

Victor shoved Bryn. "I said get her out of here!" Then Lifedrinker was in his hands, and he could feel the rage coursing into his pathways. Victor cast two spells nearly simultaneously: Iron Berserk and Energy Charge. He streaked over the marble floor on wings of purple-black shadow, rapidly surging in strength and stature. Lifedrinker led the charge, her gleaming obsidian edge singing for blood as Victor aimed her at the chamberlain.

Thorn had poured something over his wound that dissolved the arrow and mended his flesh. He saw Victor coming, and though a frosty metal visor masked his face, Victor could see the panic in his movements as he summoned a shield and braced. The impact from his charge was cacophonous. Lifedrinker wouldn't be defeated easily, and she screamed like a vengeful spirit as she ripped into Thorn's mighty bulwark. Whatever metal the shield was crafted from wasn't easily split, but split it she did. The sound was horrific and only the tip of the iceberg as Victor's Core poured Energy out to defend him from the cataclysmic crash.

Somehow, Thorn stood against the impact. Victor reasoned he must have had a defensive class, and he wasn't a low-tier iron ranker. Waves of displaced Energy rolled off around him, sending the soldiers and corpses nearby flying, bouncing down the hallway like caricatures of people in a video game. The white marble turned black as hot Energy rolled over it, cracking the walls and splitting the tiles with flame-filled crevices.

Lifedrinker's massive, heavy axe-head bit through the shield, inch by inch, and then her top edge began to dig into Thorn's metallic breastplate. Her edge found the armor a much softer barrier than the shield, and Thorn gave up his resistance as she drew blood. He wailed and flung his shield to the side, rolling away from Victor's irresistible charge. "You *fool*!" he screamed, and then Victor felt a wave of power as he summoned a frosty scepter topped with a potent, ice-like jewel.

Victor's rage was stoked; he was berserk, and his Quinametzin blood was hot, but the waves of cold coming off that jewel were like nothing he'd ever felt. Frost coated his hot flesh instantly. The marble around him froze and split with thunderous *pops* and *cracks*. Bits of stone and mortar fell from the ceiling, and the already damaged floor shattered in an ever-widening radius with Thorn at the center. The chamberlain screamed, "I am no piddling iron-ranker! No back-water champion for you to toil against! Because I choose a life of service does not a weakling make *me, boy*! I don't care *who* sent you!"

Victor scowled and lifted Lifedrinker. Her mighty edge, rimed with frost, scraped the crumbling ceiling, and a huge chunk of marble fell to shatter against his shoulder. He hardly felt it. Thorn looked up at him with icy blue eyes, and a surge of frigid Energy radiated out of his scepter, so chilling that the moisture in the air fell to the ground as snow, and Victor felt his tough, titanic flesh growing numb and stiff, his fingers and muscles unresponsive. The red fled his vision, and, to his horror, his eyes began to ice over.

Behind Thorn, in his frozen, blurry vision, he saw the remaining soldiers fall to the ground, shattering like blood sculptures. The marble was covered in a sheet of dense ice by then. Victor could hardly move, and though Thorn stared at him, oozing with smug victory, he felt no panic. His body was freezing over, and his rage was halted in his pathways, but something in his chest was still roiling with angry heat—his Breath Core and its potent, furious, magma-attuned Energy.

Thorn might be a steel seeker, and his Energy was a well with depths that stretched beyond what Victor could grasp, but Victor held the fury of a sleeping god in his chest. He held the rage and heat of the earth awakened, and all he had to do to grasp it was weave a bit of magma-attuned Energy with his rage into the pattern for Volcanic Fury. Though he stood frozen, and Thorn began to relax, sensing his victory was complete, Victor found that his magma-attuned Energy flowed easily out of his Breath Core and into his central pathway, thawing it along the way.

As he warmed his pathway and tricked some rage-attuned Energy into it, Thorn spoke into the air, perhaps using some device or spell to communicate with a distant ally. "I have him and will finish the job. Once he's out of the picture, I'll try to reason with her but keep the boy in hand; we may need to go ahead with our original plan."

Bryn stood before the queen's doors with two of the Queen's Guard—a man and woman she didn't know well. "You reckon he'll stop 'em all?" She glanced away from the stairwell to the man on her right. He was tall, his armor streaked with soot and blood; he'd been one of the first Victor had rescued after saving her.

"You saw him destroy the assassins." She didn't need to say more; how could he lose? She'd never seen anything like it.

"But Thorn and them royal guards . . . I mean to say, Thorn might not be a champion, but he's been around a long time. I've felt his aura in negotiations. I've heard him talk before *he* came, saying he could probably kill Obert if things got bad enough."

Bryn scowled. "Well, he didn't, did he? If he wanted to be champion, he had plenty of time to step up! He's a coward and a snake! The queen shot him, didn't she?"

The other Queen's Guard spoke up. "Too right, she did! Duke Victor will finish 'em off! He probably already has; you all heard the crash!" It was true. Shortly after they'd climbed the stairs and run to the queen's quarters, the whole palace had shaken. Marble tiles had split even in the hallway where they now stood.

Bryn realized she could see the other woman's breath as she spoke, and she tested it herself, huffing some air out before her in a white cloud. Wasn't Thorn an Ice Elementalist? "Something's wrong. It's too cold."

"Look!" the first guard said, pointing toward the stairwell. Sure enough, frost was gathering on the marble and slowly spreading toward them, climbing the walls and creeping over the marble.

"It's too quiet," the second guard said. Bryn couldn't argue; Victor wasn't a quiet fighter. Was he defeated? Should they retreat? "Bryn, you're his guard. You need to go and look. If we don't hear back, we've got to move the queen to the escape portal."

"I—" Bryn didn't want to say what was in her heart; she was afraid. Was her duty worth her life? Growling, she remembered Victor's words; she'd already fought once today, thinking she was going to die. She was different now. Death didn't own her anymore. "I'll go look. I'll try to signal if you should flee." With that, she crept forward with trembling knees, glad it wasn't apparent through her heavy armor. She still wore her battered shield on her left arm; if she couldn't repair it, and if she didn't die, it had earned an honored spot on her family's hearth.

When she stepped onto the frosty marble, she had to use her Balance of the Wipperlash spell, magically enhancing her agility to the point where she could daintily tiptoe through the slippery, icy mess to the steps. Once there, she crept down, crouching, ever peering ahead, alert for the smallest sound. When she rounded the last turn, she could hear a familiar voice speaking.

". . . keep the boy in hand; we may need to go ahead with our original plan." The voice paused and a moment later said, "Yes. Yes, have the women keep him in the summer tower."

It was Thorn, and he didn't sound defeated or, frankly, even wounded. He sounded smug and confident. Was he talking about Prince Tomorran? Was Victor dead? Bryn crept forward to peek around the central column, affording herself a clear view of the hallway. The scene that unfolded was one of nightmares. Ice hung in thick sheets from the broken walls and ceiling. On the floor were the fractured bodies of every soldier Thorn had brought with him, and in the center of all those horrific, frozen sculptures stood Victor and Thorn.

Victor was, again, twice his usual size, looming large over Thorn, his great deadly axe high over his head, frozen near the thirty-foot-high arched ceiling. Victor was coated in ice, his flesh blue, his red-black armor dim, obscured by the frosty stuff. He wasn't moving, and no breath plumed from his mighty lungs. Thorn stood before him, holding a potent, ice-attuned Energy focus, and he seemed to be preoccupied, muttering as he summoned a book and began to leaf through it.

Bryn frowned. Could Victor be dead? Defeated by ice? As she formed the thought, a sheet of the stuff fell off Victor's torso to crash at Thorn's feet, and the chamberlain jumped back, startled. He lifted his focus, and a pulse of potent frigid Energy rolled out of it, eliciting deep cracks from the depths of the palace as more and more marble was flash-frozen. Thorn lowered his focus and growled at Victor's frozen figure, "Give it up, fool. Just die before I have to waste the effort on—"

He danced back, interrupting himself as the ground around Victor began to hiss with steam, and the ice instantly thawed. Great sheets fell from Victor, the ceiling, and the walls, and then Victor's magnificent gleaming black axe fell like a guillotine, nearly splitting Thorn in two. Somehow, the chamberlain *slid* back, gliding over the wet ice-littered ground in his frosty blue armor. Victor's entire body was steaming, but apparently he was just getting warmed up.

As Bryn watched, Victor lifted his axe, and it burst into flames. *He* burst into flames—red fire limned his body, and he began to exude black smoke like a man made of living brimstone. Bryn couldn't see his face, but most of the smoke came from his deep, heaving exhalations. Rather than swing that massive axe again, he leaned toward Chamberlain Thorn and screamed. The roar had a different quality to it than the battle cries he'd let loose in the garden.

The sound was like thunder, like an avalanche, like the world waking up and announcing its fury. The walls and ceiling came apart, crumbling before Victor's voice. Great sheets of marble fell, smashing into Thorn, forcing the chamberlain to expend more and more Energy shielding himself. Still, Victor wasn't done. As his body smoldered and the palace fell apart around him, he lifted his foot and *stomped*.

Bryn had never felt an earthquake before, but she'd heard tales of them—this was what she'd imagined. When the stairs bucked and cracked beneath her, she leaped, using every ounce of magically enhanced agility she could muster, fleeing the fight, rushing upward ahead of the crumbling steps. When she pounded onto the rapidly thawing marble of the queen's hallway, she screamed, "Run! The palace isn't safe!"

The Queen's Guard didn't have to be told twice; the hallway rippled as if it were alive, marble tiles popping loose, the walls cracking and falling apart, and of course plaster and tile falling from the heights. Bryn held her shield over her head and charged through the open door behind the guards. When the queen saw her, she shoved past her guards as they tried to rush her into her study and the secret passage beyond. "Does he yet live?"

Bryn knew she didn't mean Thorn. She wanted to know if her champion would survive the day. "He lives, but he's gone mad with fiery rage! Thorn tried to freeze him—he has Tomorran, but I know where! We must flee; Victor will bring the palace down!"

# 23

## SCHEMERS

When Victor's blood ignited with the hot, boiling fury of the volcano, rationality fled his mind. He vaguely remembered screaming at Chamberlain Thorn with a voice powerful enough to shatter marble, but he had no memory of casting Wake the Earth. Unfortunately, when his mind was enraged by Volcanic Fury, it seemed to fixate on that one ability among all his others. It was almost as if the spirits of the great, sleeping gods of the earth wanted to use him as a conduit for their depthless, frustrated malice.

There was no telling how much destruction he might have wrought if he'd finished with Thorn and turned his madness against the city. Luckily, or perhaps unluckily, depending on whom you asked, he'd been in the middle of an enormous marble and granite structure, standing on the ground floor, with a vast edifice over his head and half a dozen subterranean levels below. As he pummeled Thorn, and the world shook, the ground gave way, and even for a burgeoning titan engorged on the fury of the mountain, thousands of tons of stone was enough to dampen his rampage.

When he came back to himself, Victor was in the dark, and his hand was clenched around the cold, dead flesh of Thorn's neck. Dust and soot were thick in the air, and, bit by bit, he began to notice small details—jumbles of broken stone, the hiss of gasses venting from subterranean outlets, and the soft, almost comforting glow of magma, burbling as it cooled. Victor's first panicked thought was of Lifedrinker, but she was there, close at hand, with her dark edge buried in a massive granite slab.

With a grunt, he stood to retrieve her, and that was when he realized he had a System message waiting for him:

*****Congratulations! You have achieved Level 73 Berserker of Unstoppable Momentum and gained 9 strength, 14 vitality, 9 agility, and 9 dexterity.*****

Had he already claimed his Energy from Thorn, then? Was that what had, ultimately, broken him out of his rage? Victor looked around the dim space and saw that above his head was nothing but broken, jumbled stone slabs and that another such slab pinned Thorn's legs to the ground. Piles of broken stone were everywhere, and he had vague, foggy memories of throwing them off himself. He wondered if he'd been buried or injured by the collapse. He supposed he'd never know; he healed too quickly while enraged, and if the influx of Energy from Thorn had been enough to level him, then it would have healed any lingering wounds, too.

His little chamber beneath the rubble was only about a dozen giant-sized paces across, and he figured he'd need to start digging if he was going to get out of there. Victor touched Lifedrinker's haft, sending her into storage, and then he summoned a sharp knife into his hand, turning to Thorn's corpse. "If you're going to cause this much damn trouble, I'm taking your *pinché* heart."

While he worked, Victor's mind wandered to worrisome topics. Had he killed any innocents in his rampage? Had the damage he'd done to the palace killed anyone? He hoped not—people on Ruhn were generally well into their iron ranks, and the folks in the palace were usually higher than average. Surely, most of them could get away while the ground shook. Surely, there were enough guards and high-level nobles around to help any children.

"Right?" he asked the sticky, cold organ as he pulled it from Thorn's chest. The heart wasn't able to reassure him, so Victor sent it into storage. Looking around, he saw other, partially buried corpses, but they were members of the royal guard, no doubt the men and women who'd come with Thorn and died before the collapse.

He was looking up, contemplating his best route of egress, when, with a faint tinkling of chimes, he heard Queen Kynna's voice as though she stood close by, pitching her voice for just his ears, *"Victor, my scryers have located you in the wreckage. Soon, the Earth Elementalists will have you free. Thank you for slaying Thorn, my champion. Thanks to you and the brave efforts of Guardswoman Bryn, my son is safe, and a coup has been thwarted. Please stay safe where you are; it will be more than an hour before the Elementalists have cleared the way."*

Victor tried speaking back to her, "Um, okay. Was anyone hurt in the, uh, battle?" Could he play the destruction off as simply the side effects of his struggle with Thorn? Whether he could or not, it didn't seem the queen could hear him. No further message was forthcoming. He found a relatively flat hunk of marble and sat down, contemplating his situation.

His thoughts started with how he felt; he didn't like it. Objectively, he supposed he should feel good. He'd saved Kynna and Bryn in the garden and stopped and killed Thorn. He'd even gained a level in the process. Wasn't that *good?* Why, then, did he feel like he'd gotten too drunk and done something terrible? Why did he feel *guilty?* He knew the answer; he'd lost himself to the rage again, and, as good as it felt in the moment when he was smashing and destroying and killing, it felt awful in retrospect.

What it boiled down to was that Victor didn't like having control taken from him, even if it was his own magic doing it. He hadn't liked it when his original Berserk made him that way, and he didn't like it when Volcanic Fury did it. "Why then, *pendejo*, did you choose a new class that gives you yet another way to lose control?" He chuckled, shaking his head as he gathered saliva in his mouth to spit, trying to rid himself of some of the dust that had caked his airways.

He could hear distant rumbling and scraping and figured it was the queen's Elementalists working to move the wreckage of the palace. He wondered how far up they were. How many underground passages and galleries had he and Thorn fallen through? Thinking of Thorn reminded him of the man's heart, and Victor decided he might as well do something productive while he waited. He dug the cold, sticky organ from his storage ring and contemplated it.

Thorn had been a steel seeker. A cowardly one, but a steel seeker, nonetheless. He'd had a powerful affinity for ice or something similar; would that hinder Victor's ability to absorb the Energy? He was anything but cold, after all. "*Pendejo*," he cursed again, gathering more spit. "That loser could have beaten Obert or Qi Pot. Why didn't he?"

He supposed there were a few good explanations. Thorn might have been a coward, only willing to fight when he'd been caught in the act of orchestrating a coup. Maybe he'd been afraid that after beating one of the "backwater champions," as he'd labeled them, a more powerful kingdom would come calling. "Or maybe the piece of shit was working for someone else." Victor wondered about that—would it be so strange for the great houses to have agents spread out through the lesser kingdoms?

The heart didn't appeal to him in its cold, clotted state, and Victor was tempted to summon his camp stove and cook it up. Something in his gut said that would be wrong, though; perhaps part of his "ritual" was to eat the hearts raw. So, holding his breath and trying not to think about what he was doing, Victor tore a massive hunk of the heart off with his teeth and began to chomp it down.

The meat was cold. At first, he thought it was just that Thorn's body had cooled, and the heart had lost its vibrant heat. He soon realized it was more than that; it wasn't that the heart wasn't warm—it was *cold*, like meat taken from a freezer and barely out of the rock-hard stage. What was more, as Victor swallowed his first bite, he could feel the coldness spread through his belly and into the surrounding flesh. As he chomped off another bite, he wondered if he was making a mistake.

Victor didn't take small bites, but Thorn had been a giant—a man of nearly the same stature as himself when he wasn't enraged. Despite its coldness, the heart didn't taste bad once Victor's saliva loosened up the blood. That fact encouraged Victor that he, hopefully, wasn't making a foolish mistake by consuming flesh that was clearly attuned to an affinity he didn't share. The frigid feeling spread through his body as he ate, and he could feel the tendrils of that icy Energy seeping into his Core space. When he gazed inward, he saw those tendrils of blue, frosty Energy rebuffed by the heat of his Spirit core.

He wasn't left guessing about what would happen to him for long. As the Energy infused his flesh to the point where he passed beyond cold to numb, System messages began to scroll into his field of view:

*****Congratulations! You have gained a new affinity: Blue Ice.*****

*****Warning! Incompatible Core: Spirit Cores cannot have an elemental affinity.*****

*****Compatible Breath Core Found: Elder Class. Reapplying acquired affinity.*****

*****Congratulations! You have gained a new Breath Core affinity: Blue Ice.*****

*****Applying Energy gains to Breath Core.*****

*****Congratulations! Your Breath Core has gained three ranks: Improved 9.*****

Victor read the messages and felt a swelling of frigid Energy in his chest. He nearly panicked, fearing his magma-attuned Energy would be overwhelmed, but the spike in "blue ice" Energy reached a crescendo and then faded, leaving him feeling almost normal, if not a little . . . cooler. He turned his gaze inward, studying the space where his Breath Core lay.

Swirling, almost lazily, his ball of angry, magma-attuned Energy traversed the space in direct opposition to a ball of frigid-looking, deep blue icy Energy. Victor knew from the System messages that it was called "blue ice," but he had no idea what that meant other than it was cold even to look at. The two orbs of opposing power circled his Breath Core space, almost like they were squaring off, sizing each other up. It was amusing to watch, but Victor hoped he hadn't created something untenable in his Breath Core.

As the sounds of stone grinding and shifting grew closer, he decided to experiment a little. Standing and facing toward the center of his little cave of crushed marble, he opened the pathways to his Breath Core, inhaled deeply, and, just as he'd learned to do so many months ago back in the Untamed Marches, he exhaled a plume of fiery, magma-attuned Energy. It wasn't nearly as impressive as when he was under the influence of his Volcanic Fury spell, but the stream of liquid fire was significantly broader and stretched further than when he'd first acquired his Breath Core.

As the hot molten rock smoked and sizzled, he looked into his Breath Core again and saw that both Energy orbs were reduced. Was his Energy cap the same for both attunements? Looking at his status sheet to confirm, he saw:

**Breath Core Energy: 1780/2800**

He'd gained three hundred maximum Energy from his Core's new ranks, but his total was a singular value; he didn't have different tallies for the two Energy types. "So, how do I breathe blue ice?"

He opened his pathways again, took a deep breath, and this time, instead of firing off his breath by reflex, he looked inward to his Breath Core space, and using his will, he pulled a strand of the icy blue Energy into his pathway before exhaling. Just as he'd hoped, a plume of frosty, crackling air erupted from his mouth, coating the sheet of still-smoldering magma and freezing it over. More than that, he could hear the stones beneath the sheet of frosty ice cracking as the frigid substance bit deeply into them.

"Now *that's* badass!" Victor slapped his hands together, then looked at his Breath Core Energy levels again:

**Breath Core Energy: 770/2800**

He was rather happy to see that his Breath Core's Energy wasn't being split by the two affinities but rather that he had a total sum of Energy that he could use as he wished, much the way his epic-tier Spirit Core worked. The thought made him wonder if that meant his Breath Core was well-constructed and wouldn't need tweaking before he advanced to epic tier and beyond. He also wondered if he'd be able to enhance his Breath Core cultivation by adding a source for the strange "blue ice" Energy.

He must have spent more time thinking and experimenting than he thought, because a great clatter of crashing stone interrupted him, and a stream of light shone down into his dusty, smoky space. "Duke Sandoval?" a strident woman's voice called, and he shielded his eyes to peer upward where a large woman wearing honest-to-God brown corduroy overalls stood in the hazy opening, peering back at him.

"That's me!"

"Are you well?"

Victor chuckled and began hopping up the broken stones toward the opening. "That's likely a matter of opinion. Some would say no."

The woman peered up at him and took in the clean, undamaged appearance of his clothes—Victor had long since sent his armor into hiding. "Ancient Gods! How'd you survive this catastrophe?"

Victor brushed his hands together, wishing his skin could similarly clean itself, and shrugged. "I'm tough and lucky, I guess." He wasn't sure he should claim responsibility for the "catastrophe." Was the queen spinning a different tale? Still, his guilt tweaked his guts, and he blurted, "Was anyone else hurt?"

"Aye, plenty! Still, the gods must favor Gloria, for none are reported dead save those traitors what caused this disaster! Her Majesty says you had a hand in that, milord, so you have the thanks of me and mine. Imagine! Trying to kill such a wonderful woman as Queen Kynna Dar! And her poor *son*! Such an innocent lad! I'm beside myself!" She shook her head and sighed, then pointed further upward toward another, brighter light. "I should stop my rambling, sir. Head on up—I've made steps there in the larger stones. Take your time; we've folks waiting to tend to you."

"And you?"

"I'll clean this mess up as much as I can. Her Majesty is eager to have Thorn's body so's she can search for evidence of his accomplices. You, um, didn't take his rings or—"

"Nah. They're all there." Victor waved and started climbing. It was true; the woman had basically built a staircase out of the rubble with comfortable grooved steps seemingly molded into the marble. He wasn't sure how he felt about Kynna blaming Thorn for the destruction, but he supposed a person *could* make the argument that this was all the traitor's fault. If Thorn hadn't attacked Kynna, Victor wouldn't have had to fight him. It wasn't as though Victor had *wanted* to use his Volcanic Fury; he'd needed it to break the former chamberlain's ice spell.

The cheers of guards and more Elementalists broke him from his introspection, and he smiled as he emerged from a massive pit into the dusty, broken remnants of the central portion of Kynna's palace. He was glad to see that the four wings were mostly intact, visible over the rubble, and that the grounds and gardens seemed relatively whole. For once, he was happy that his power wasn't truly the equivalent of a great volcano.

He waved to the folks hard at work clearing away the mess, then caught sight of Kynna, still surrounded by her Queen's Guard. She was waving him over from atop a partially broken staircase. Victor jogged over, nodding and waving to every soldier and worker he passed; all stared at him with a mixture of adoration and awe. Some cheered, some shouted his name, and some simply stared, dumbstruck by his presence.

When he mounted the steps and stood before Kynna, he knelt, biting back a quip about how easy it was to impress her people. Before he could speak, asking something inane like how she was or saying something lame like he was glad her son was all right, she grasped his shoulder and pulled him to his feet. "You've saved our nation, Victor. I'll not have you kneel this day."

Victor looked around at the dusty, bloody faces of the Queen's Guard and asked, "Is Bryn—"

"She's well. I insisted she see a physician. She suffered a head wound while rescuing my son, but Leyna here says that she'll be fine." The queen glanced at one of her guardians. "Yes?"

Standing there in a battered silvery breastplate tooled with enameled yellow roses, the woman nodded quickly and, in a hoarse, breathy voice, responded, "Aye, my Queen. The physician said she'd be right as rain in no time."

Queen Kynna, her hand still on Victor's shoulder, smiled and gently squeezed. "You see, Champion? Your loyal guardswoman is well, my betrayer is dead, and my son is safe." She gestured to the wreckage of her palace. "This will be made whole again, given time. In the meantime, I'd like to travel with you to Iron Mountain." She reached up to tap her crown, encompassing herself, Victor, and all of her remaining Queen's Guard in her blue dome of privacy.

"Something more?" Victor prompted.

"I'm quite sure Thorn wasn't acting alone. I believe he was . . . prodded to act. I've reconsidered my ancestor's proposal, Victor, and I believe it's time that we speak in earnest about the next steps. If the nations of Ruhn want to scheme against me, plot my demise, and threaten my child, then I believe it's high time we gave them a reason to fear us."

"Us?"

"Well, Victor, after hearing the tale of your performance in the garden and seeing how you stood up to Thorn, I must admit that I've gained a . . . new perspective with regard to you challenging more dangerous champions." She turned back to the wreckage. "Still, it's a pity Thorn's schemes brought down the palace, don't you think? The word going around the city is that my new champion was nearly killed by the man. He might have emerged victorious if he hadn't brought the palace down on himself."

As she turned back to him and winked, Victor grinned and nodded. "Yeah, he was a real mean bastard, that Thorn. Lucky for me, a giant chunk of granite fell on his head."

# 24

## THE WEIGHT OF RULE

The vast teleportation network on Ruhn made traveling between cities and larger towns painless, but it took something away from the scale of the world, at least in Victor's mind. When he and the queen's entourage traveled from Gloria to Iron Mountain, nearly five hundred miles distant, it only took a few seconds. His first view of his duchy was a dim, stone-walled room where rune-inscribed metallic inlays made intricate patterns on the floor—the portal chamber.

A guard wearing gray and black livery and wielding a lightning-tipped spear immediately took a knee. The queen's emissaries had already prepared the duchy for their change in rulership. "Your Grace," the tall, narrow-faced man said. "I am Gand, your guard captain."

"It's good to meet you, Gand. I'd tell you to stand, but the queen will be here any second." A flash of light heralded more arrivals, and soon, the room was filled with nobles, ladies-in-waiting, Queen's Guards, and, of course, Kynna and her son Tomorran. As the party, some thirty people, filled the portal chamber a little uncomfortably, Victor turned to Gand. "Where's my chamberlain? Have rooms been made ready for the queen and her people?"

"Duke Sandoval," Kynna said, coming to stand beside him. "My Queen's Guards are interviewing and vetting your household staff. I'm sorry, I meant to tell you, but the preparations for our departure got away from me."

Gand looked up from where he knelt. "I was about to say the same, milord. Most everyone's in the great hall with Her Majesty's people."

"I have people in place, Victor." Kynna turned to Gand. "Please rise, Captain. Tell me, where are the Ladies Davas and Loray?"

Gand stood and nodded to the door. "Without, my Queen."

"Very good. Please give Duke Sandoval a tour of his estate, and my people will see to us."

"As you say, Your Majesty." Gand bowed low, then turned to Victor. "Shall we, milord?"

Victor turned to scan the throng of people, ignoring the murmured conversations. When his eyes settled on Bryn, he nodded. "Let's go, Bryn." He turned to Kynna and bowed. "I'll speak to you soon, Your Majesty?"

"Yes. I'll be in touch."

Victor nodded, then followed Gand out the door and past another row of royal dignitaries he vaguely recognized from Kynna's palace. With Gand leading the way, Victor and Bryn were given a lengthy tour of an estate that rivaled Kynna's royal palace in grandeur. Victor was, frankly, struck dumb, a little numb and withdrawn as he realized that the entire place was, technically, his. So long as Gloria wasn't conquered and he wasn't killed, the enormous structure with hundreds of rooms, including vast ballrooms, a great hall, kitchens, parlors, a library, a martial hall, barracks, and three different wings of bedrooms and suites, was his.

The estate put his home on Fanwath to shame. It put Rellia's *palace* to shame. The tower where Victor's suite was located had twenty floors and a magical elevator that used spatial magic to deposit him at his desired level nearly instantaneously. More than the structure itself, the estate was loaded with valuable furnishings, art, and every little thing that Victor would never think of—curtains, dishes, glassware, linens, pantry items, and a million other tiny objects he took for granted.

The tour took more than two hours, and Victor was feeling overwhelmed enough, but when they finished in his master suite and stepped out onto the balcony, he got his first clear view of the *real* value of the Duchy of Iron Mountain—the land. The first thing he saw was the mountain. His palace, for there was no denying that was what it was, was situated on a massive hilltop, but if he looked to his left, down the slopes of the hill and overtop miles and miles of orchards, he saw the mountain for which the duchy was named, and it made him feel tiny. It also woke something in his chest—the Iron Mountain was a slumbering volcano.

The peak stood alone. A few rolling hills drifted away from its shoulders, but otherwise, the great conical, steel-gray slopes rose up starkly to form an enormous mountain, the top of which was slightly concave, draped in white snow, and obscured by clouds. It was like a thing from a fantasy book cover—a mountain that seemed impossibly huge and out of place, rising from thousands of square miles of green forests and cultivated land.

Victor stared at it for a long time, listening to the song in his chest as his magma-attuned Energy echoed the deep, soundless voice that rippled, unnoticed by most, through the land. The mountain made the one where he'd battled Hector look like a hillock. Its presence rumbled in his bones, and he began to truly understand why the System called such beings "sleeping gods."

"Um, milord, if you look to the right, you can see the town, well, more of a city these days, really."

Victor blinked, finding his eyes dry, and wondered how long he'd stood staring at the volcano. He glanced at Bryn and Gand, offering a quick, reassuring smile. "That's a hell of a mountain."

Gand nodded. "Aye, milord. The greatest peak on the western continent." He gestured to the right. "The town, though, sir. I can point out a few of the more prominent locales."

Victor nodded and turned to look where Gand pointed. His palace had high walls, but they were far below his tower. Looking past them, Victor traced his eyes over perhaps a mile of manicured garden-like lawns, and then, at the demarcation of a much smaller, more decorative wall, the town began. It wasn't nearly as large as Gloria, but as Gand had indicated, Iron Mountain was more of a city than a town. Gand pointed out a famous inn, the market square, the city administration hall, the guard barracks, and, on the banks of a broad, slow-moving river, the warehouses where the wealth of the duchy was made.

Iron Mountain's lower slopes were peppered with mines, and all manner of metals, precious and otherwise, were mined from its enormous slopes. They were brought on rails to the town, shipped off on barges, and taken to other towns and cities where they were processed. "It's by design, milord. The original Duke of Iron Mountain hated the smell of industry; he insisted on selling the ore raw, despite the value he gave up by foregoing smelters and forges. He argued that the duchy was rich enough, especially when you considered the orchards. We feed half the continent."

Gand sounded proud, and Victor, looking out at the beautiful countryside and the neat, orderly little city, could understand why. It was a lovely place. He said as much, "It's a beautiful place, Gand. I'm assuming you're able to give me this tour because you were cleared by the queen's people?"

"Yes, milord. I was among the first to go through their vetting process. They were thorough, but I can understand why. Terrible what happened in Gloria!"

"Yes. The queen's being careful for a reason. On that topic, tell me, where are the Haveshi?" Victor knew that Kynna had sent her agents to gather up the former ruling family of Iron Mountain, but he didn't know where she'd put them.

"They're awaiting you in the Hunting Hall, milord."

"The Hunting Hall? Was that on the tour?"

"I pointed it out, milord, but we didn't go inside. It's a large parlor where one of the earlier dukes, Avard, I believe, liked to keep his trophies and artwork with a, well, a hunting theme."

"And all the Haveshi clan is there?"

"Yes, milord."

Victor sighed, dreading what came next. "All right. Let's go get this over with. I can't imagine they enjoy being left in the dark."

Gand's gray eyebrows twitched as though he wasn't sure if he should smile or frown or agree or disagree. After a moment's hesitation, though, he nodded. "Aye, milord."

As they walked, Victor asked, "Are they . . ." He wanted to say 'popular,' but considering he was a duke now, he tried to elevate his vocabulary slightly. "Well-loved?"

"For the most part, aye, milord. The people were proud of Duke Qi Pot, and while he was away doing his duties for the king, his brother ruled Iron Mountain with an easy hand."

"And his brother's name?"

"That would be Lord Draj, milord. I beg your pardon; I suppose he's no longer a lord."

"Draj Haveshi? Is he the head of the family, then?"

"There's also his mother, Lady Tyla, milord, but she's softer spoken than Draj."

Victor nodded, and they walked in silence for a while as he thought about the situation. He didn't like having the former ruling family of the duchy living under his roof, and he intended to remedy that situation, but he had to be delicate. He tried to imagine someone he cared about in their situation; this was their home, and it was a beautiful place where he was sure they'd built many memories. Kynna had told him he could do as he pleased—even banish them. The thought made him sick to his stomach, though, and he knew she'd already guessed he wouldn't do either.

Despite the discomfort of the situation, he hoped to find some kind of middle ground. He'd seen dozens of beautiful estates on the edges of the city as he'd scanned it from his tower. Surely, these people could be made happy and whole without having to share a roof with the man who'd killed their former head of household. What a fall, though—to go from this palace, ruling over these beautiful lands, to mere citizens. Victor felt like he wouldn't be able to stomach it. He'd leave.

"How many people live in the duchy?"

"Upwards of eight hundred thousand, milord."

"And the coffers? How do they stand?" Victor wouldn't be surprised to find the duchy's wealth drained and mysteriously missing.

"That I don't know, milord. Sir Draj would have an idea, but your treasurer will no doubt finish her vetting soon, too."

As they turned down a wide arched hallway with paintings of forest scenes lining the walls, Victor turned to Bryn. "Did you get ahold of the Artificer?"

Her helmeted head nodded. "Yes, milord. Trobban will settle his affairs and arrange to travel here within the week."

"Good."

At the end of the hall, eight guards wearing the yellow rose of Gloria on their breastplates stood guarding a pair of wooden doors carved with hounds, birds, trees, and the like. Gand stopped and said, "The Haveshi are within. Would you like me to announce you, milord?"

"No. You and Bryn can wait here." He moved between the guards and stood before the door, gathering himself. He was his natural size—something close to eleven feet tall—and he'd shifted his Sovereign Will bonuses to agility and dexterity; he didn't think he'd need strength or vitality and figured a little boost in his motor skills might help him avoid making awkward movements, tripping on a rug, or something equally embarrassing.

Before he opened the door, he cast Inspiration of the Quinametzin and grinned as the shadows lifted from the hallway, and the soldiers nearby shifted and inhaled sharply. He tugged the doors wide and stepped through.

Victor didn't mean to glare as he scanned the room, but his natural expression was rather predatory; his dark brows were constantly angled downward, and his eyes were sharp and hawkish, accentuated by his long, straight nose. For that reason, when he saw some of the folks who looked up at his entrance flinch back, he forced himself to smile as he reached back and pulled the doors closed behind him.

The Hunting Hall was large with high, vaulted ceilings, and though one wall was dominated by floor-to-ceiling windows, gauzy gray-green curtains hung over most of them, giving the lighting a calm, peaceful effect. The décor was interesting; just as Gand had said, there were many trophies from hunts on the walls and stands—the horns, claws, and teeth of fantastic beasts mounted on plaques, as well as a great many taxidermied heads. Victor saw bears, stags, great serpents, and dozens of creatures he couldn't name.

Couches set in conversation groups were scattered about, and on them, Victor counted at least twenty people with a strong familial resemblance to Qi Pot. Another dozen or two folks with wildly disparate appearances were undoubtedly children or in-laws. It was a good-sized clan, by Victor's standards, but he knew there were other families on worlds like Ruhn and Sojourn with thousands of members. As people realized he'd entered, their conversations died, and everyone, even the children, stood and turned to face him.

He looked around, his inspiration helping him to read the expressions— fear, anxiety, and anger were common, but he also saw curiosity and, in some of the younger faces, hope and perhaps a bit of admiration. What tales had they heard about him, he wondered. The room was silent, and in that silence,

Victor's ears picked out their nervous breaths and the tapping at the window as a soft breeze jostled the branches of a fruit tree grown a bit too close to the building.

Victor didn't know what Draj or Tyla looked like, but he supposed he didn't care. His words were for the entire clan. "Hello, everyone. I'm Victor Sandoval, and, by right of conquest and royal decree, I'm the new duke of these lands." He let his gaze traverse the group, settling on many sets of eyes, waiting patiently to see if anyone would be foolish enough to object or declare their animosity.

No one spoke, but many men and women began to take their knees. Victor held up a hand. "I'll not demand you kneel here. What would be the point of such a show between us? If I wanted to teach you a lesson in humility and force you to demonstrate your obeisance, I'd be sure to arrange an audience first." He chuckled, ever amused by his ability to pull words he barely understood from the depths of his mind thanks to all the reading he'd done at Dar's behest.

As those who'd begun to kneel returned to their feet, Victor focused on a woman with three small children clutching her skirts. The kids, two boys and a girl, regarded him with big, fearful eyes, making him want to lighten the mood. "My goodness," he said, scanning the other children in the room, "what well-behaved children! I know it can't be easy keeping still and quiet, and I want you to know that I appreciate it. I'll be sure to reward your good manners.

"As I said, I'm the lord of these lands now, and I understand how that must be difficult to hear. I understand that many of you may wish for my demise. I'm sure many of you also wonder what fate is in store for you. Surely there are rumors, though, yes? I haven't spoken publicly, and I know Her Majesty, Queen Kynna Dar, hasn't made any proclamation, so you must be feeling some dread."

"Ancient Gods, just tell us!" a young man wailed, and Victor chuckled as a taller teenage girl clamped her hand over his mouth.

"Fair enough. Well, you should put most of your fears to rest; I've no intention to punish you for being related to a man who, by all accounts, was simply serving his king—" He was forced to stop as gasping sobs escaped many of the men and women. More than one collapsed onto the couches, unable to stand on shaky legs. Victor smiled and gestured to one older woman struggling to stand again. "Stay seated, please. In fact, everyone, take a seat. I should have started with that."

He stepped farther into the room and waited while almost everyone sat, especially those with children. Some didn't sit, however. Some stood with arms folded, glowering. Victor marked those faces, intent on learning if it was simply pride that kept them on their feet or if they harbored dangerous ideas about vengeance. Looking at those folks, wondering if he should be ready to fight, his sharp Quinametzin eyes picked out some interesting details; these people wore no jewelry, nor did they have weapons. Had Queen Kynna's people stripped them of their belongings?

"I've heard good things about your family, and I intend to see that you have every opportunity to maintain some status in the duchy, but I'll also see to it that other options are available. I can't imagine it would be easy to live in the shadow of this palace after having once ruled from it."

A woman with dark hair and eyes, dressed in an elegant silken blue gown, spoke up. "We must leave the palace?"

Victor turned to regard her. She sat on a pale leather couch, with her legs crossed, and held the hand of a blond-haired boy who couldn't have been more than six years old. "Pardon me for asking; I've yet to put faces to names. Might I have yours?"

"I am Tyla Haveshi." The answer surprised Victor, and he fought to hold his face neutral. The woman didn't look more than thirty years old, but she was the matriarch of this clan. He should have expected as much, but it was hard to escape his old notions. He'd imagined she would look more like his *abuela*.

"I'm pleased to meet you, Tyla." He knew better than to address her as "milady." Kynna had made that clear to him; he was the lord of these lands, and these people, in particular, would need to be reminded of that fact. Even so, some of the men and women gathered there gasped and looked stricken by what they viewed as blatant disrespect.

"I'll be glad to meet with each of you regarding the prospect of continuing to serve the duchy, and, in some cases, it might make sense for those people and their immediate family members to live in the palace. However, most of you will be expected to live elsewhere. I intend to provide your family with a sizeable estate and lands in the duchy."

"You'd throw us from our home, then?" This time, it was a man who spoke up, one of those who hadn't sat down when he'd asked them to. He was tall, with dark curly hair and golden eyes, and looked very much like Qi Pot.

"Draj, I presume?"

The man folded his arms over his chest and nodded. "That's right."

Victor didn't press him about not addressing him respectfully. Not yet. He'd anticipated an objection like the one Draj had voiced. "I know I'm new to these lands, but I've read a history or two. The Haveshi held power in Iron Mountain for just over seventy-four years, shortly after Qi Pot won his first duel for King Groff. Is that right?"

"That's correct."

"Well, what was the name of the duke before that?"

"I—"

"If you don't remember, don't feel bad; over the last twenty-four hundred years, there have been no less than eighty different families, under the rule of twenty-nine different royal bloodlines, to hold the claim to these lands. Qi Pot was Duke of Iron Mountain for far longer than some of those other dukes, but not the longest—not even close." Victor allowed his voice to grow deep, speaking from his gut as he let his aura slip its bonds. "In short, Haveshi Clan, your claim on these lands is nothing unique, nothing *special*."

As people gasped and shrank back from the weight of his aura, Victor glared at Draj and growled, "Sit down." The man fell back onto the couch behind him, and everyone else who still stood quickly followed suit. Victor walked toward the windows, reeling in his aura; he'd tried hard to focus its weight in Draj's direction, but some of it had pressed down on the children, and he already felt guilty, hearing sobs as they struggled to breathe.

When he had it in check and silence once more reigned in the room, he pointed out the window to the massive mountain near the horizon. "This duchy is called Iron Mountain because of that mighty peak, not because of any family in this palace. One day, I'll leave, too. One way or another, someone else will rule these lands. It's just the way it goes. This duchy is part of Gloria now, and if you play your cards right, every single member of your family might gain lands and titles that make you look back fondly at the times you spent here, thinking them quaint and small."

"Does Gloria have so much to offer? Duchies greater than Iron Mountain?" someone asked. Victor didn't see who; he was still staring at the mountain.

"Not yet." He turned and clapped his hands, startling almost everyone. "I'll have one of the queen's stewards begin interviews. If any of you want to serve the duchy or the crown, I'll help arrange it. As for the rest of you, I'll have the details regarding your land grant and estate ready for you in a day or two. In the meantime—"

"Milord!" Tyla stood, still clutching the hand of the little boy. "If you're done . . . impressing my family, I would like a chance to speak. Even before you arrived, we all came to an agreement. In the event that you decided to show mercy and if we weren't banished, we all agreed that we wanted to continue to serve the people of Iron Mountain. We wish to swear fealty, Lord Victor. We all wish to serve your household."

Victor folded his arms, frowning at the woman, wondering why nothing could ever be simple. Couldn't they all just move out? Couldn't he just get back to training and planning the next duel with Kynna? He had a *magical egg* to eat! For a brief moment, he wondered if he could return to Kynna and refuse these lands. Was that an option? Instead, he nodded, forced a smile, and gestured to a couch. "Let's sit down, Tyla. I'd like to hear more about your family."

# 25

## SCHEMES

When Victor finally returned to his chambers atop the central tower in his palace, he was exhausted. Tyla Haveshi had kept him talking to her, her son, Draj, and half a dozen elder cousins—the decision-makers in the clan—for nearly four hours. In the end, Victor concluded that the people of the Haveshi family were more afraid of fading into obscurity than they were upset about the loss of Qi Pot and their status as the de facto rulers of Iron Mountain.

It wasn't that he trusted Tyla or the many people in that room, but after four hours in which he'd been introduced to children and been regaled with tales of the honors so many of them had won, Victor couldn't detect an ounce of animosity. He couldn't believe that so many people with such varied experiences could hide hatred or lust for vengeance so smoothly. Of course, he was smart enough to know that he was projecting his own mentality and morals onto those people, so he knew better than to grant everything they wanted carte blanche.

He'd still insisted that they take up residence in the city, but he'd been very open to the idea that many of them would continue to serve the duchy and, as they'd all requested, his household. It was almost as if they wanted him to be their surrogate patron. After listening to Tyla talk about tradition for over an hour, Victor was beginning to understand that it wasn't all that uncommon for a lord of an estate to do so. Somehow, that wily, young-looking old woman had made him come around to the idea that he was, for all intents and purposes, responsible for them now.

Tyla had let one little revelation slip during their hours-long talk; she was close friends with Queen Kynna and had been since long before Xan had been aggressive to Gloria. When Victor learned that much, a lot of pieces fell into place. Kynna had known that Tyla would behave this way, that she would cling to him and want to make her family indispensable to him—dependent on him. The most annoying thing about knowing that was that it had still worked;

Victor *liked* Tyla, and even Draj had begun to grow on him, offering advice and information freely, putting his knowledge of the duchy on exhibition.

Victor shook his head, sighing, looking out over his balcony toward the enormous Iron Mountain. Its slopes were painted orange by the impending sunset, making Victor think of fire and magma. He wondered just how long it had been since the monstrous volcano had last blown its top. It had to be thousands of years. A knock sounded, and he turned away from the view, striding across the richly appointed sitting room to the foyer and the door that led to the guardroom outside his elevator.

When he opened the door, Bryn stood there, and just behind her was Queen Kynna. "Her Majesty is here to see you, milord."

"Thanks, Bryn." Victor pulled the door wide and gestured for the queen to enter, bowing slightly. "Hello, Your Majesty."

"Good evening, Victor. I hope you don't mind me coming by for an evening meeting. I took the liberty of ordering us dinner so you won't be starved while we work."

Victor pushed the door closed and gestured to the large dining table. "Please have a seat. As for starving, I *am* hungry but had something else in mind."

"Your egg?" She chuckled and sat down, surprising him by not taking the seat at the head of the table but rather the one to its right.

"Yeah. Don't worry, though, it'll wait."

"You won't have to wait long. Once we go over a few things, I'll have much to occupy me as I prepare for the next challenge."

Victor thought it would be weird to choose a seat other than the head of the table, but he hoped he wasn't sending the wrong message. He hoped it wasn't a trap. He chuckled under his breath at that thought—how strange politics were! Before he'd been summoned to Fanwath, could he ever have imagined that he'd be worrying about the implications of taking the wrong seat at a table?

Kynna lifted her crown off and set it on the table to her left, but she tapped a nail against it, creating her privacy barrier before she turned to Victor. "It grows heavier and heavier throughout the day."

Again, Victor wondered at the double meaning of her words. Was she being literal, or was she demonstrating that she understood the weight of ruling over people? He decided to play it neutrally. "I can imagine."

"Do you want to talk about your time with the Haveshi family?"

"Well, I learned that you happen to be good friends with their matriarch."

"I am—I *was*. We haven't spoken much in recent years. Still, I don't believe she or her sons were pleased with how King Groff was treating Gloria."

"They're very eager to continue their service to the duchy. I was intent on removing them from the palace and their official duties, at least at first, but after our meeting, I'm starting to think I could use their help and loyalty. How do you feel about it?" Victor didn't want to ask for advice openly, but he supposed a little humility might serve him well.

"Tyla knows that the star of her family has fallen. They could be stripped and banished, forced to start over in a new world. If we sent them to another high-tier world, they'd be paupers, and if we sent them to a frontier world, they'd have to fight for their position, and then, if they rose to power, they'd be ruling over a backwater. I believe that Tyla is grateful we're not doing that to them. My agents took their dimensional containers when they rounded them up, but we have them set aside. If you agree, I believe you could win much favor with them if you return all or most of their personal belongings."

"Do I need to earn favor with them?"

"Perhaps that's the wrong term—loyalty might fit better. As for whether or not you need them . . ." Kynna paused and stroked her sharp, elegant jawline for a moment. "Iron Mountain is not a trivial duchy to rule. It's enormously rich and influential, and there are a million moving parts to the industries here. You could find commoners familiar with the workings of the mines, the orchards, and the ports, but their loyalty will be just as questionable as you might find the Haveshi's."

"So, you think I should just trust Draj and let him continue to operate things?"

"I wouldn't precisely trust him, but you could certainly *use* him. Your problem, Victor, is that you're alone on Ruhn." She held up a hand and shook her head. "No, I don't mean that you don't have me or your loyal guardian outside that door, but you don't have a network of people you know and trust. You have to put some faith in people; sometimes, it will bite you, and sometimes, it will reveal new allies."

"Yeah, but is it smart to trust the people whom I've displaced?"

"Again, I caution you not to think in those terms. These people are *alive* at our mercy. They're still allowed to live here at *yours*. Many rulers of the kingdoms of Ruhn would have had every one of them relieved of their heads by now."

Victor sighed and waved a hand. "All right. I understand your point. Let me ask you something else, though. If the veil walkers ensure that people follow the laws of warfare on Ruhn, why are assassins sanctioned? Why didn't they intervene when Thorn tried to take your life and captured your son?"

"The veil walkers who remain on Ruhn are concerned with the small folk. The rules for warfare and the resulting duels are meant to protect the commoners of Ruhn from the whims, schemes, and ambitions of the nobility. They care not if my rivals slay me and mine in our sleep."

"Yeah," Victor sighed, "I guess Dar kind of touched on that with me. It's wild to see it in action, though." Victor pointed to the blue dome surrounding his dining table. "You think you're safe here?"

"No, not safe, but safer. My coming here will throw any traitors' schemes into disarray."

"Traitors meaning people in Gloria." Victor nodded, understanding how moving her court away from the capital in the wake of his destruction might thwart other immediate plots to dethrone her.

"Yes. As for schemes, Victor, we have our own to consider." She smiled wryly, shifting in her seat to look at him more directly. "I believe I can create a plausible connection between Thorn and the Kingdom of Bandia."

Victor frowned, trying to picture the complex map of Ruhn in his mind. "Can you remind me—"

"Bandia is a coastal kingdom on this continent, and if we conquer it, we'll be within our rights to challenge one of the kingdoms on the eastern continent."

"So does that mean we can skip the kingdoms between here and, uh, Bandia?"

"No! The rules on warfare are clear; we must share a border or body of water with the kingdom we challenge. The beauty of my strategy is that we can begin to work our way toward Bandia, and we can do it without declaring a succession war; with Thorn's 'connection' and the attempted coup, we have a plausible reason for wanting to conquer Bandia, and thereby, the kingdoms between us."

"So, Thorn's betrayal provided you an excuse to start the succession war in secret, huh? I'm assuming that will result in fewer assassination attempts than if you openly declared it?"

"Precisely. Thorn's relation to the Queen of Bandia—she's his second cousin—and their recent communications cloud the waters just enough for us to justify action."

She seemed excited and hungry, and Victor wondered what had changed. It didn't sound as though Thorn's "connection" to Bandia was really what was motivating her. "You don't *know* that the Queen of Bandia was involved in the coup, though?"

"I believe she's been whispering in Thorn's ear for years—decades, even. Looking back with a critical eye, I can see how her kingdom benefited from diplomatic overtures Thorn argued were best for Gloria. Well, you saw the state of my nation when you arrived. I believe the man has been undermining me since the moment I took the throne. My father loved him dearly and thought he was a brilliant strategist, so I never suspected him."

"Are we going to stop there? I know you said we'll be within our rights to challenge a great house once we conquer Bandia, but are you going to? Are we taking this all the way?"

"My brush with death and my son's capture drove something home for me, Victor. So long as there are divisions in society, such as the one between the great houses and the lower kingdoms of Ruhn, then it's never safe to be on the ladder's lower rungs. It's far easier to throw someone off if they're below you. Don't you agree?"

"Yeah, for sure. They call it 'king of the hill' for a reason."

"So, I tire of being at the bottom of the hill. I thought a calm, quiet life was what I wanted, but that coup attempt woke something in me. I believe I have a bit of my ancestor's desire for glory in me, Victor, and I'll not sit down here and allow my 'betters' to decide my fate." She sneered as she said "betters," and Victor grinned fiercely.

"That's what I like to hear! Hell yes! When's my next duel?"

Kynna smiled and reached over the table to clasp his wrist in her long slender fingers. Her eyes widened, and Victor knew why—her fingers felt like ice cubes on his hot flesh. "Your skin is so hot!"

"Heh. It was worse before I—" Victor almost said "before I ate Thorn's heart," but he caught himself just in time. He chuckled and shook his head. "Before I learned to control my Energy."

"I'm pleased you're eager to fight, Champion, but this will be a careful process. We must go through the motions of investigation and accusation. We must feign diplomacy, and when that falls through, we'll need to pressure our eastern neighbor, Lovania, into a duel. It will take time—months, likely. In the meantime, you must make yourself as strong as possible."

As she drew her hand back, Victor nodded and turned to look at the evening sky outside his balcony. "I want to visit that mountain."

"The mines?"

"No, the mountain. I can feel it. Its spirit calls to mine, and I think it will be worth my time to explore its depths . . . or its heights. I'm not sure."

"I—" Kynna frowned and glanced at her crown. "I want to object, but I just asked you to make yourself strong. I cannot stand in your path if you feel something in that mighty mountain that calls to you. However, I'll send a Spatial Magus with you. Florent is a good man, and he'll be able to craft a portal that will bring you back here should the need arise."

Victor thought about it for a moment, and though he didn't like having strangers looking over his shoulder, he didn't see a real downside. "I'll bring Bryn, too, and I suppose that means I'll probably put some trust into the Haveshi family to run things around here. I mean, you'll be here, too, right?"

"Yes, Victor. I will keep a keen eye on Tyla and her son, but I believe you're making a wise decision. Now," she said, smiling and gesturing toward the door, "I received notice that our dinner is here. Shall we eat?"

"Sure." Victor leaned back, suddenly feeling a little better about everything. He felt like he had a path before him, and though it was convoluted, with many stops along the way, it *felt* right. He'd build his strength, and when the times were right, he'd fight some duels. He was beginning to feel a little flutter in his gut, something he hadn't noticed in a long time—he was excited.

He was eager to face off against the champions of the "great houses" and to show them what *he* was made of, especially after hearing Kynna talk about how they viewed themselves as better than the rest of the people on Ruhn. He supposed that it was rather apparent in how they labeled themselves, but that didn't make him dislike them any less. More than that, he was eager to visit that mountain. When he looked at that great peak, he felt a small echo of what he'd felt when he'd visited the ivid hive world. It was a sense of wonder and awe, and he wanted a closer look.

He and the queen ate a meal her personal chef and attendants served, and Victor savored every delectable bite. They made small talk, and, for the first time, Victor felt he was beginning to get to know the queen as a person and not just as a ruler or Dar's distant granddaughter. He asked her about Tyla Haveshi and how they knew each other, and that's when Victor learned that Queen Kynna was a lot older than he'd thought.

"We hunted together often when I was younger," she said breezily, sipping her wine while Victor stuffed a large forkful of dense chocolate cake into his mouth. "I'd say the first time we went out was something close to sixty years ago. Coincidentally, we stalked the slopes of the Iron Mountain; she was teaching me to track the great cats that lurk in the heights."

Victor tried hard to keep his face straight when she said "sixty." When his eyes betrayed his surprise, he feigned difficulty swallowing and, with a chagrined smile, cleared his throat and said, "My eyes were bigger than my mouth."

"I hope you left room for your treasure. Will you consume it tonight?"

"I figure I'll be out a few days. Is that all right?"

"I'll manage things around here while you recover. Would you like me to speak to Tyla and Draj on your behalf? I can assign them each an assistant who will report back to me."

"And then you'll report to me?"

"Of course! I'll share everything I learn with you, Victor. Our fates are entwined now."

Victor sighed and leaned on the arm of his chair, making it creak and complain. He rested a hand on his distended belly. "That was delicious." Kynna's eyes narrowed, and he wondered if she was irritated that he hadn't echoed her overture of partnership.

He didn't have to wonder long. "What motivates you, Victor?"

He decided to be straight with her for once. "It's funny you ask, 'cause I reflected on that earlier while we ate." Kynna's eyebrows arched, and she leaned forward but didn't speak, so Victor continued. "I feel excited at the prospect of fighting these champions of the great houses. I love the energy of a crowd, and I love to fight, but I also love to beat the shit out of *pendejos* who think they're better than everyone else. Yeah"—he nodded and smiled—"I'd say that motivates me pretty well."

"I think I'm beginning to understand why my ancestor sent you to us. The members of my Queen's Guard were impressed by you—enough to speak about you in hushed voices, afraid they'd incite your wrath. Your loyal protector, Guardswoman Bryn, refuses to speak about what she saw when you and Thorn brought the palace down around you. Such loyalty given so quickly isn't something I've ever seen before. I know the people I brought here are loyal to me, but that's after decades of building relationships. She must see something great in you, and I must confess that I'm starting to see it, too."

"Ahem." Victor shifted uncomfortably. "Look, Queen Kynna—"

"You may call me Kynna when we're alone, Victor." Again, she reached over the table to grasp his wrist, her touch tender, and Victor wondered if he was receiving mixed signals or if she was coming on to him. He didn't know how to react, but one thing was sure—he wasn't looking for that kind of relationship just then, especially not with a queen he was supposed to be working for. He held still, though, and didn't pull away, waiting to see if he was overreacting or reading the situation wrong.

"Okay, well, Kynna, I don't try to build loyalty with people. I'm just myself, and if that inspires loyalty, then I'm not going to complain. Bryn's a smart, capable woman, and I think we shared a moment there in the garden when she almost died. I think she knows I witnessed her coming face to face with death, and that created a connection between us. That's all it is."

Kynna smiled, gently squeezing his wrist before letting go. "You're an interesting man, Victor. I looked into death's eyes in that garden, too, you know. I'm very grateful that you were there. Tell me, how many times have you stared into the abyss?"

Victor exhaled slowly, feeling his heart begin to beat normally again as she leaned away from him and folded her napkin, placing it on the table. "A few times, I guess."

She nodded, staring at him for another long, awkward moment before saying, "This was a lovely evening, and I think a productive one, too. I'll speak to you after you consume your treasure, yes?"

"Yeah, of course."

"In the meantime, we'll get things in order here in the duchy, and I'll prepare Florent for his new assignment with you."

As she stood, Victor followed suit, escorting her to the door. "Thank you, Kynna. It was nice to get to know you a little."

"I feel the same." She smiled, and then, as he opened the door, she stepped into the guardroom, where her attendants waited to follow her into the elevator.

When she was gone, Victor looked at Bryn and exhaled noisily. "Sheesh! That was a stressful dinner."

"The food looked good."

"You saw that?"

"Well, they had to bring it through the door . . ."

"All right, get in there. There are plenty of leftovers. Let's have a drink and look out over my dominion from the balcony. What do you say?"

"Well, I'm on duty . . ." She laughed and turned to push Victor's door open. "I think one drink will be fine, considering you're the duke."

"Yeah, just one, though, 'cause I have an egg to eat."

Bryn laughed and lifted her helmet off, walking over to the table where the platters of food waited. "I can't believe you haven't eaten that thing yet. I wouldn't have made it two steps off the stage before stuffing it into my mouth."

"Oh yeah?" Victor chuckled as he walked over to the fully stocked bar in his parlor. "Remind me to keep my treasures hidden from you."

"Of course, milord." Bryn grinned, slicing a thick cut of something like a roasted duck.

Victor poured their drinks and carried them out to the balcony, where he did just as he'd said he would—observed his domain. The countryside was dark, but up on the mountain, he saw the faint amber lights of the mines—tiny glowing dots on the vast dark slopes. Looking the other way, he saw the city's lights. He contemplated the thousands and thousands of people living there. How strange to think that he was responsible for them all! "Strange and sobering," he sighed, sipping his dark, spiced liquor.

"Does it weigh on you?" Bryn asked, coming to stand beside him with her plate of food.

He passed her the drink he'd poured for her and shrugged. "Yeah. It does, but I know what I'm good at, and I'll keep working on that. There are people here who can help with all this." He nodded toward the city.

"It's a wise leader who knows when to delegate."

Victor snorted, taking another sip. "That a lesson one of your captains taught you?"

She laughed and elbowed him. "How'd you know?"

"Eh, it reminded me of something a friend of mine would say; she was always quoting things from her time in the military. You'd like her, I think." Victor sighed happily, pleased with how the night went and even more pleased with how the future was shaping up. He and Bryn stood together, enjoying each other's company but not needing to speak much. Victor mulled over thoughts of old friends and watched the city, and she ate, often grunting in pleasure as she sampled something particularly tasty.

When she was done eating, and they'd finished their drink, Victor walked her to the door and said, "I'll probably be out for a while. Don't let anyone in here."

"I won't, milord."

"Good night, then." He pressed the door closed with a solid click. He threw the bolt home, locking it solidly, then went around the apartment, locking all the windows and the balcony doors—it was time to consume his treasure.

# 26

⁂

# TENECOALT

Victor stood in the central room of his chambers, half of which was taken up by the dining table and half by a sitting area with a few built-in curio cabinets and bookshelves. He'd locked all the windows and doors, but considering the recent assassination attempt and the fact that he only had a couple of allies in the entire world, he decided a bit more safeguarding was in order. He didn't want to lie helpless for days when there were plenty of folks on Ruhn who wanted him dead.

With that thought in mind, he touched most of the furniture—the dining table and chairs, a couch, and a couple of end tables—sending them into the enormous storage ring he'd taken from Loyle after their duel. Standing in the center of the now empty space, he took the vault pendant from around his neck and turned the key, quickly setting the clicking, ticking, steaming device at his feet.

The little marble-sized ball rapidly expanded until an eight-foot globe sat before him, clicking softly as the heat generated by the weird spatial magic faded. As a credit to the solid construction of his palace, the hardwood slats beneath the rug didn't creak or sag. Victor stuck the key in the vault's complex circular lock, and as it *thunked* into place, he turned it until the round vault door opened with a hiss of cool misty air.

Victor cast Alter Self, reducing his height to step into the vault. Out of habit, he knelt beside the satchel containing the ivid royal jelly. His lips spread in a smile, and his eyes shone with delight as he beheld and *felt* its seemingly depthless potential. He didn't know when he'd use it, but he knew the time wasn't yet upon him. It was just a feeling, an intuition, but the idea of consuming that potent stuff made him think it would take him apart, atom by atom. He closed the satchel and turned to the vault door, removing the key from the outside before pulling it closed and locking it from the key slot on the inside.

Victor didn't know how hard it would be for a high-level iron ranker or a steel seeker to break into the vault, but he knew it wouldn't be easy. In his estimation, anyone trying to smash into the magical metallic orb would destroy the entire palace before they managed to dent the thing. He figured Kynna and her allies would come to his aid long before his little sanctum was breached. He moved to the center of the space and sat down, summoning the gilded, jewel-studded egg from his storage ring.

He held it in his lap, feeling its weight, wondering at the strange idea of coating a natural treasure like an *egg* with gold. He hoped whatever artisan had done so had worked some magic into the shell, keeping the morsel inside fresh, or at least edible. He took a deep breath, preparing to try to crack the ornamental shell, when another thought came to him. *Breath.* Was there enough air in his vault to support him while he lay insensate from the egg? With a chuckle, Victor consciously stopped breathing, giving himself a visceral reminder about how *little* he needed to.

He'd learned as much back at Dar's lake house—swimming beneath the surface for dozens of minutes on a single breath. His epic-tier bloodline and racial status meant that his body's cells were saturated with Energy. They fed off it far more than they did more natural things like food, water, and air. That thought sent his mind spiraling down another rabbit hole—why did he assume Energy wasn't natural? Was it just prejudice—a product of his youth spent in a world devoid of it?

Victor gave his head a quick shake, forcing his focus back on the egg. His wandering mind made him wonder if he was procrastinating, and if that was the case, he was determined to put an end to it. With little hesitation, he pressed his thick thumbnail through the golden shell of the Coldwater Sea Wyrm's egg. A heady scent tickled his nose almost immediately—like a mixture of honey and blood. He'd wanted just to pierce the golden shell, but his nail had gone through into the meat of the egg that was, apparently, soft-shelled.

Victor licked his thumb, where some of the gelid material had clung, and his mouth exploded with flavors—a bit like any other egg, but intensely magnified in flavor and somehow sweet. He could taste hints of minerals but was also so overwhelmed by the flood of Energy that came out of it that he nearly lost his ability to focus. His eyes became blurry, and tears streamed from the corners as though he'd eaten something intensely sour, even though it wasn't. With trembling fingers, Victor carefully peeled away the gem-encrusted golden shell, and then, before too many wisps of that potent Energy drifted away from the egg, he put it into his mouth whole.

As he chomped the egg into mush, gulping it down, Victor's mind exploded with dopamine, and waves of euphoria washed over him, sending shivers and tingles over his entire epidermis. He collapsed backward, his vision utterly blasted by exploding lights, and lost all track of his conscious thoughts.

He drifted, insensate for a long while, and though he couldn't form coherent thoughts as the egg did something to his body and mind, later he might look back and wonder at the odd, dreamlike memories of that time—glimpses of explosions in space, matter coming together, stars pulling apart. Great, tumultuous sounds like standing at the base of a thousand-foot waterfall, like mountains coming down, rumbling and roaring as their stony slopes smashed themselves into rubble, then pebbles, then silt as they sluiced away into nothing. These were just impressions, nothing concrete, and yet, that drifting exposure to those gigantic sights and sounds would shape his dreams for months and years.

When he had the presence of mind to recognize himself—his thoughts and feelings—he was in a much calmer place. A dark void where he drifted, bodiless. When he began to put his thoughts into order, remembering what he'd been doing, he had the wherewithal to peer into that darkness, wondering if he was meant to see something. It was an odd sensation, looking with no eyes. Even stranger was how he could *feel* the lack of air and matter, even though he seemed to have no body.

Almost as though that realization was the key, a pinpoint of light appeared in the void. Seeing it, Victor focused his attention that way, and then the pinpoint exploded, encompassing him in its brilliant shades of verdant green and hazy blue. Along with the light came feeling, and hot, humid air wrapped him in an embrace that felt like home. He saw his bare feet standing on lush warm grass. Looking around, he saw ferns, dense jungle trees, vines and thorns, and all the little creatures that made that foliage their home.

The trickle of a nearby stream brought his attention to the space behind him, and there, sitting on a large moist boulder, was a man who looked both strange and familiar. He was a big, brooding figure wrapped in colorful green and yellow-scaled leather. He wore a tooth-adorned necklace and clutched a massive macuahuitl—Victor recognized the weapon type from previous visions into his bloodline. He focused on the man's face—darkly tanned skin, golden-brown eyes, a hawkish nose, and a dark brooding brow. Suddenly, the familiarity became clear: He resembled Victor.

"Strange," Victor said, stepping toward the man. "Usually, when I have a bloodline vision, I feel like I'm walking in my ancestors' shoes, not staring at them."

The brooding figure broke his stony expression by grinning, exposing straight white teeth. "You've eaten something potent. Your bloodline was already nearly pure, and now I'd say you've woken so much of me that my memories are boiling in your blood, eager to expose themselves to you."

"So," Victor said, sitting on a rock across from his ancestor, "you're not real? I'm not speaking to your spirit?"

"Ha! I'm as real as you are! As real as your blood. When I had my children, some of me was built into them. Those bits of me went down and down and down through the generations, buried deeper and deeper, but you've been working to bring them out, haven't you?"

"Yeah, I—"

"No need to respond, Victor. I know what you know!" He laughed. "I've always been a part of you, as have your other ancestors, even your dear, sweet *abuelita*. We're all in here." He reached forward to tap Victor's chest with a thick, powerful finger.

"But you're somewhere else, too . . . your spirits—"

"Of course! We leave some of us in our children, but our *selves* carry on. I wonder what I'm doing now? Do you think I found a new life? I know you've listened to your ancestors. Chantico has spoken to you more than once. I wonder if I'm out there somewhere." Victor didn't think he expected an answer, so he just nodded. "Are you wondering why I'm here? Why the magic of that egg you consumed has awoken me and granted you this strange vision?"

"Don't you know?" Victor arched an eyebrow.

"Ha! Of course! You're burning with curiosity!" He chuckled, then reached down to the little stream and scooped up a little crystalline water, flicking droplets off his fingertips at Victor. It felt good in the sweltering heat, and his ancestor chuckled. "I'm Tenecoalt, Victor, the most prominent progenitor in your blood. You're alone, trying to embrace a bloodline you only partially understand. I will provide some guidance."

Victor's heart began to race. Was he finally going to have some answers? Something more than the cryptic hints Ranish Dar doled out? "I'm eager—"

"I know you are! Listen, Victor, we have some time, but as you no doubt know, time moves strangely when the world you inhabit is inside your mind. One task before us is to make proper use of the Energy and clever nature of that natural treasure you consumed. I see you've managed to awaken a Breath Core. That's a feat worthy of praise; in my time, only a few of our kin managed as much. I know you played a large part in the battle against a tremendous elder wyrm. Even I would have struggled to slay such a beast! Alone, I mean"—he chuckled—"not with the aid of an army of hunters."

"I—"

Tenecoalt held up his hand. "Allow me to speak for a while, brave descendent. The wyrm reminds me of something important, and I think we have the time. You've done well to learn a great secret of us Quinametzin—well, of us and others with similar titanic ancestry. Our flesh is potent—resilient and malleable,

able to adapt and overcome almost any adversity. You've already awakened many secrets of our blood. For instance, not every species can gain regenerative abilities like those you boast. Not every species can awaken a Breath Core.

"When you consume a vanquished foe's heart, you consume a piece of their spirit, and as your mighty Quinametzin gut absorbs their flesh, your blood sifts through the tiny building blocks, delving it for secrets to incorporate. You must know that not every heart is worthy of your attention, and even if you come upon a mighty heart, if you feel undeserving, the ritual will fail."

Victor nodded. "I understand."

"You begin to reach true heights of power. I know from your experiences that there's a new entity in the universe, a faceless 'System' that guides you, though I'm sure it takes its toll from your successes. Soon, you must shrug off the shackles of that nebulous master if you intend to grasp the true meaning of your bloodline. No doubt it will feel scorned and retaliate, likely sending tribulations and challengers your way. In that case, you should learn as much as possible, gain as much power as possible, and ensure you are ready to face dire threats before you do."

"How—"

"Gleaning what I can from your memories, I believe the 'System' will put you on the road to your own liberty. When you pass beyond this 'Level One Hundred' and begin to construct your own 'class,' you will touch upon the truth. When you taste it, when you see the trail of blood, hunt it down, Victor. Do not be quieted and made docile by the promises of the System and its minions."

Tenecoalt dragged his hand through the water again, flicking more cool water at Victor and then himself. "Do you enjoy this heat?"

Victor nodded, turning to gaze up at the hazy yellow sun. "I do."

"Good. This is what the world was like when we walked the Earth. Hot and green, a threat around every corner. The world was full of Energy, and we learned to use it for ourselves. We were among the best at it, infusing our bodies with it to great effect. I feared nothing, Victor—no creature, no man, no monster, no demon. With my macuahuitl, crafted from the metal of fallen stars, I killed giants, dragons, wyrms, and great, undying fiends that poisoned the land where they walked. Embrace that heritage, Victor! Don't bend to this System! Not for a moment longer than you must.

"A final admonishment before I help you with the natural treasure that threatens to dissolve your flesh: Your people are gone from the Earth, whether by choice or vanquishment, I do not know, for in my memory, the Quinametzin were numerous. Make the worlds you tread upon remember us! Do great deeds, and just as you must move out of the System's shadow, you should bow to no one—no prince, no king, no emperor, and Victor, no queen. If fate conspires against you and someone capable of slaying you demands you kneel, then you must be willing to die on your feet with a weapon in your hand. You're strong enough now to make that choice."

His words hit Victor hard. How many times had he knelt to Kynna? Was it so wrong to show respect? Before he could argue or ask why, Tenecoalt answered his thoughts, "Regardless of your justification, Victor, your spirit wanes when you submit. If you find my words too harsh, if you wish to be a shadow of your progenitors, then that is your choice."

"I don't want that. I want to be strong and true, but I want to be respected and loved, too."

"Then find a balance without compromising yourself. The Quinametzin do *not* kneel." Tenecoalt sighed and shook his mane of long black hair. "We waste precious time. I advise pushing the Energy from your natural treasure into your Breath Core. The contents of that ancient egg are potent and fierce, and I believe it will benefit you far more used that way than if you spend it on your already well-advanced Energy Core.

"As for your bloodline, I have further good news. You've awakened much of me, and so have you awakened my memories and experiences in your blood. You won't know it, but those memories will speak to you. Listen to your instincts! Let them guide you with the wisdom of our people. When you face a difficult decision, think about how you *feel*. When you hear a warning in the back of your mind, *listen*. Though it seems innocuous and may feel like nothing when you sit alone in the safety of your fortress, this is the greatest boon you've yet received from your bloodline."

When the fierce warrior paused, Victor knew what he was expecting. "Thank you, Tenecoalt."

"So, you agree, then? About your Breath Core?" Before Victor could form his mouth around the word "yes," he felt something. It was a stirring in his chest as though a great blockage had been cleared, and cold, roiling Energy began to course through him. Rather than unpleasant or numbing as such dense, powerful Energy ought to feel, it was refreshing and seemed to balance the heat of his other Energies.

"There. As I feared, using the Energy is bringing our time together to a close. I'll surely see you again, Victor, my brave descendant. Heed well the lessons I planted in your mind this day."

"I will," Victor said, but he'd barely said the words before his vision faded, and blackness once more claimed sight. The world became silent again, and he drifted in that dark, endless abyss for what seemed like a very long time. He drifted for so long that he lost track of it, and when dreams began to seep into the nothingness, he didn't even realize it. He dreamed of wild rides on the backs of stallions, swimming in deep icy waters, and laughing with friends and loved ones.

When his eyes fluttered open, he was fresh from the throes of one of those latter dreams, and upon seeing the domed ceiling of his vault chamber and remembering where he was, the smile on his face rapidly faded. Blinking, feeling a hollowness in his gut where some nebulous family or friends had been while he dreamed, he realized System messages were waiting for him. As he read them, his melancholy receded as a broad, bright-toothed grin split his lips.

*****Congratulations! You have advanced your bloodline: Epic 5.*****

*****Congratulations! Your Breath Core has gained six ranks: Advanced 5.*****

*****Congratulations! You have gained a new feat: Wisdom of the Quinametzin.*****

*****Wisdom of the Quinametzin: Your bloodline is rich with mighty ancestors, and they live on in the history written in your blood and bones. Your instincts are supernaturally accurate, and your feelings about a person, thing, or place are the echoes of your progenitor's memories.*****

"Well," Victor said, his cheeks beginning to hurt from the smile on his face, "that's pretty badass."

He was curious about his Breath Core's Energy, so he looked at his Energy status:

| Breath Core: | Elder Class: Advanced 5 | | |
|---|---|---|---|
| Core: | Spirit Class: Epic 3 | | |
| Breath Core Affinity: | Magma: 9, Blue Ice: 9 | Breath Core Energy: | 5900/5900 |
| Energy Affinity: | Fear 9.4, Rage 9.1, Glory 8.6, Inspiration 7.4, Unattuned 3.1 | Energy: | 36871/36871 |

If he remembered correctly, he'd had 2800 Breath Core Energy prior to his advancement, so he'd more than doubled it. It still looked like a small number compared to his Spirit Core's Energy, but it was a hell of a lot more than one hundred, which he'd started with when he'd first eaten the wyrm's heart. With a satisfied grunt, he clambered to his feet and smashed his head and shoulders into the top of his vault. "What the . . ."

He looked down at his legs and torso, holding out his arms and hands as he stooped over in the chamber. He'd made himself smaller when he went into the vault, but even considering his Alter Self had been canceled by his time under the effects of the egg, he'd grown a great deal. If he were guessing, he'd say he was now more than fourteen feet tall. "*Chingado,*" he sighed, then reached into his pathways and built the pattern for Alter Self.

When he reduced himself, it felt easy—effortless, even. His body responded to the magic far more rapidly with less Energy input than before. Did that mean he could alter himself even further? Was he becoming more like Tes in that regard? Was it thanks to his now mid-epic-tier bloodline? "What the fuck comes after epic?" He laughed as he turned the key in the vault door, ready to see what he'd missed while sitting around chatting with his hundred-thousand-year-old ancestor.

# 27

## MEETINGS

As the heavy, rune-inscribed door to his vault *thunked* open and air hissed out, Victor inhaled deeply, suddenly aware of how stale the vault's atmosphere had become. He had a moment to wonder if there'd been any oxygen left in it at all and whether bad air could affect his epic Quinametzin constitution before he heard a startled gasp and the clatter of something falling to the ground. He shoved the door open in a heartbeat and leaped out, only to find a wide-eyed Bryn stooping to pick up a toppled wooden chair. "Hey," he grunted.

"Lord Victor! Thank the elder gods!" She seemed annoyed by her own outburst and scowled as if to compensate for her enthusiasm. "Apologies, I was startled by the door opening."

Victor looked past her and her chair to the door leading out of his suite. "Why are you inside?"

"After you'd been . . . out for a week, the queen investigated your chambers to ensure you were well. When she found this metallic . . . chamber, she grew worried and instructed me to have a guard watch it. We'd hoped you put it here and that you were within, but we couldn't be sure. She's had more than one master Artificer examine the runic script, but none determined a way to open it without causing great harm."

Victor nodded while she spoke, turning to retrieve his key and then seal up the vault. When he turned the lock fully to the left, it began to vibrate and hiss with steam, slowly shrinking in on itself. "Yeah," he said, and gestured to the now waist-high metal globe, pulsing with glowing runes. "It's mine." He grinned at Bryn. "Didn't want people peeking at me while I was unconscious."

"A wise precaution. However, I wish you'd told me . . . milord." She looked at him more closely, staring up into his eyes. "You seem different. Your eyes are so clear—luminous, really, and you seem to have more . . . presence? I can't put it into words, but I suspect you had some racial advancement?"

"Yeah. My bloodline gained three ranks." Victor smiled and stepped forward, clapping her on the shoulder. "It was a hell of a trip, Bryn. How long was I out? I mean, how much longer than a week?"

"Ten days altogether, milord."

"Shit! Really? Any emergencies?"

"Nothing serious. The queen has been busy with negotiations, but her people, along with some help from the Haveshi, have been managing the duchy. The Artificer Trobban has come up to see you four times, more and more exasperated as I sent him away."

"Have you been here the entire time?"

"I've taken on a squire, milord. His name is Feist—a promising young prospect of the Queen's Guard. Her Majesty was pleased to allow me to take him on."

"And you trust him? He's not a spy?"

"You mean for the queen?" When Victor nodded, Bryn smiled and shook her head. "No, milord. I don't think so. I've known Feist since before we both began working for the crown; we adventured together."

"All right. Well, that's good, 'cause I don't want you working twenty-four hours a day. Well, let's see here. What first?" Victor rubbed his chin as he stooped to pick up his marble-sized vault, hanging it around his neck. He badly needed a shave. "I'll get cleaned up. I need you to set up a few meetings—the queen, Trobban, and Draj Haveshi. I assume he's the one who's mostly been running things?"

"I believe so, milord."

"All right, and you can cut that shit out while we're alone—the 'milords,' I mean. Come on, Bryn. You're like my number two on this planet; you can call me Victor."

She nodded sharply, her well-tanned, scarred cheeks coloring just a little. "Understood."

Victor grinned. "You weren't worried, were you? Did you think some schemers managed to lock me up in that vault?"

"Not exactly worried, mil—Victor, but a bit anxious." She smiled and nodded again. "I'm pleased to see you're well."

"More than well, Bryn! Now, let's get going!" Victor clapped his hands, chuckling as she practically jumped toward the door. "I'll be ready in fifteen minutes." As she hurried out, Victor took a minute to replace the furniture he'd stored away, then took a long, luxurious shower. He soaked in the hot steamy water that fell from a vaulted twenty-foot ceiling, scrubbing with woodsy soap. He shaved with a blade that felt sharp enough to split atoms and lemon-scented cream that he found sitting ready for him before a magically fog-free mirror.

Once he'd dressed and stepped out of his bedroom, he found the first of his appointments—Trobban, the Artificer—sitting at his table. "At long last! Lord Victor!" The man jumped to his feet, bowing deeply at the waist.

"Sorry to keep you waiting, Trobban. I hope you kept yourself busy while I was . . . occupied."

"I have, milord! At great expense to myself, I've completed the skeletal structure of Lady Arona's new vessel. While she and I agreed on the optimal components, I haven't the means to acquire them all, so I've been eager to meet with you again."

Victor nodded, gesturing to the table. "Please, retake your seat." Once they were both sitting, he said, "Tell me about the skeleton."

"The skeleton? Oh, for the vessel! Yes, yes! I've been painstakingly growing the bones from a crystal lattice. It's a costly process, both in terms of Energy and materials, but when I had the Golemancer class, I learned many tricks to perfect the process. I've completed the structure, matching Arona's exacting specifications for size and shape."

"Um, about that—what did she decide as far as her . . . appearance goes?"

"She wants to maintain a similar aspect to the vessel she lost—her natural one. I convinced her to increase her size slightly, insisting it would make her more formidable and durable, though adding to the cost."

Victor nodded slowly. "And the bones? They're crystal?"

"A living crystal lattice, milord. It's wonderfully versatile stuff and more than capable of housing epic-tier pathways and supporting a similarly powerful body." He frowned and began to wring his hands as he added, "It's just a matter of the cost. I'm out of pocket—"

"How much?"

"Nearly five million standard beads, milord."

Victor tried to hide his reaction, shifting in his seat as he frowned. "For the skeleton?"

"Yes, milord. The reason I'm eager for reimbursement is that I've got a line on a perfect heart for the vessel, but the fellow who's selling it isn't willing to take installments—"

Victor abruptly stood, shoving his chair back noisily. "Hang on." He walked over to the door and opened it, finding Bryn standing near the gilt black-enameled elevator doors. "Hey, Bryn, did you get ahold of Draj?"

"Yes, milord, he's due at the top of the hour." When Victor raised an eyebrow, she added, "In about thirty minutes."

"Tell him I need him now. I need some information about the duchy's treasury."

"Yes, milord!" Bryn turned and pressed the elevator call button, and Victor rejoined Trobban at the table.

"We'll have some funding information soon. Tell me about some of the items you need to acquire."

"Yes, of course, milord. As I said, there's a fellow selling a heart crafted from the heartwood of a Mowpanian elder tree. A steel-seeking Animancer constructed it as part of her journey of enlightenment, and though she never used it, I believe it would be the perfect source of vitality for Arona's new vessel."

"And the man selling it? What does he want?"

"He's seeking similarly powerful artifacts of dense Energy suitable for the crafting of an epic-tier automaton Core—or ten million beads."

"Won't Arona's new body need an object like that?"

"Yes, milord, but I haven't a line on anything suitable yet."

Victor frowned and leaned back in his seat, drumming his fingers on the arms of his chair. "I mean, you must have some ideas for Cores. Is there anything on this planet that would work, or are we forced to trade for it from people who've been collecting artifacts all over the universe?"

"For a Core?" Victor saw Trobban's eyes dart toward the windows to his balcony. "There are indeed treasures on Ruhn that would be suitable. In fact, there's a source rather nearby . . ."

"Don't hesitate, man! What is it?"

"Well, Iron Mountain, milord. A crystal recovered from one of the mines nearly thirty years ago was of suitable Energy density. I believe the King of Xan gifted it to one of the great houses—"

"Only one?"

"Only one so far, aye. At least, as far as public knowledge goes—" He cut his words short as a knock sounded at the door.

"Come," Victor called.

A moment later, Draj Haveshi was striding toward the table. He bowed deeply as he walked, and then, when he was just a few feet from Victor, he lowered himself to his knees. "I am at your service, Your Grace. My family is eternally grateful to serve. When the queen delivered your pardons and requests for temporary service, it was like a reprieve from the heavens. We—"

"Draj, stand up and have a seat with us, please. I don't need you to profess your loyalty any further." On the surface, Victor thought Draj sounded fake. He almost seemed like an actor performing on stage, but something deeper, something that spoke from the depths of his bones, told him this man wasn't a threat. Victor wondered if it was the wisdom of his ancestors helping him to prioritize his focus.

"As you say, milord." Draj, wearing a fine gray and white suit with the yellow rose of Gloria stitched beside the gray, snow-capped peak of Iron Mountain's coat of arms, stood, bowed again, and sat across from Trobban.

"Have you met Trobban, Draj? He's a master Artificer and happens to be working on some very important projects for me."

"No, milord." Draj stood and stretched out his hand. Trobban nearly knocked his chair over in his haste to stand and take the man's hand, clearly unused to being in such vaunted company.

"Pleased to make your acquaintance, um, Lord Haveshi."

"A pleasure to meet you, fine sir. I am, however, no longer a lord." Draj shrugged and chuckled. "Might I inquire as to the nature of the, ah, projects?"

Victor answered for Trobban. "No. Sorry, Draj, but they're of a personal nature. Even so, I believe the duchy and Gloria as a whole will benefit greatly from their completion. Eventually." Victor felt that he was being at least mostly honest—Arona was a powerful entity, and if she found herself indebted to the people of Iron Mountain, he knew she'd feel obligated to even the scales.

Draj didn't argue. "Of course, milord! What aids you aids the duchy. How might I be of service?"

"Well, I was going to meet with you about the duchy's economic standing. I keep hearing about the wealth, and it's apparent everywhere I look, but I'd like to wrap my head around the big picture. Before you give me all the details, however, let's deal with the small part that might impact Trobban."

"Of course, milord. Only ask, and I will provide the answer."

Victor nodded, thumping a heavy hand on the table as he looked from Trobban to Draj. "First, there's the matter of Trobban's operating fund. While I was . . . indisposed, he was forced to fund my projects from his own pockets. He's owed nearly five million standard beads. Can you arrange a disbursement for him?"

"Ahem." Draj held a fist to his mouth, perhaps trying to cover his reaction. After only a slight hesitation, though, he nodded. "Of course, milord. There are sufficient discretionary funds for such a payment; however, I would greatly appreciate some advance notice if you believe you'll need continued payments of such . . . magnitude. You see, there are ongoing projects in the duchy, and many departments clamoring for increases in their budgets, and unplanned expenses can greatly impact those sorts of—"

Victor waved a hand. "Draj, I completely understand. I'll do my best to give you more warning in the future." Victor looked at Trobban. "That goes for you, too, Trobban. Give me a chance to prepare before you incur such expenses going forward."

"Yes, milord!" Trobban bent forward, trying to bow in his chair, nearly placing his forehead on the tabletop.

"Draj, what do you know of—" Victor turned to Trobban. "What was that crystal called?"

"I believe the King of Xan named it the Azurite Star, sir."

Draj nodded, looking from Trobban to Victor. "That's right. It was pulled from Iron Mountain close to half a century ago. Duke Qi Pot gave it to King Groff, who gifted it to the Queen of Kuria, seeking her favor and financial aid to break Lovania's blockade, cutting Xan off from trading across the Horizon Sea."

Victor nodded, waving his hand. "I get that. Basically, it's out of our reach, right? Over on the eastern continent?"

"Yes, milord. I'm not sure what Queen Livessa has done with it, but she wouldn't part with it easily."

"Right, but it *came* from Iron Mountain, yeah?"

"Indeed, Your Grace, but that shaft was closed when the mountain expressed its displeasure."

Victor's eyebrows shot up. "Come again?"

"It's quite well documented, milord. The Argonthall Shaft, named after the baron who founded it, was one of the deeper mining operations, dug to follow a shaft of heart iron. It operated for nearly four decades and provided tremendous wealth and treasure to the duchy. When they took the Azurite Star from those depths, the mountain rumbled, collapsing part of the shaft and threatening an eruption that would destroy most of Xan. The Earth and Fire Elementalists from across the kingdom, along with several from neighboring nations, had to work for more than a year to calm its fury."

Victor nodded, grinning. "So, the mountain isn't as deeply asleep as it seems. Are there Elementalists currently working to keep it docile?"

Again, Draj nodded. "The Order of the Mountain, Your Grace. They maintain their hermitage midway up the slopes in a great cave they've built into a temple of sorts."

Victor looked at Trobban. "I'll work on the issue we discussed. In the meantime, is there anything you can do to move the project forward?"

Trobban nodded emphatically. "Yes, milord! Once I've been reimbursed, I'll be able to acquire some of the lesser artifacts I'll need for the, um . . ." He glanced at Draj, then shrugged and simply said, "Project."

"Good. Leave us for now—Draj and I need to speak about the duchy. I'll call for you before I leave."

"Leave?" both men asked. Draj looked at Trobban, a slight scowl of irritation marring his usual diplomatic poise. Trobban simply looked down, stammering an apology.

"Yeah, leave. I have things to do, men. Don't worry, I'll be in touch, and the queen has given me one of her, uh, portal magicians."

Trobban's eyes widened. "Ah, a Spatial Magus?"

"Is that their official title?"

Draj replied before Trobban could. "It's their class, Your Grace. It's a well-kept secret of the royal families—the path to that class."

"Not that other classes cannot create portals or teleport . . ."

Draj spoke over Trobban, "But none quite so well as the Spatial Magi."

Victor didn't want another rabbit-hole discussion. "All right. Speak to you soon, Trobban." He watched the man scurry out of his seat, bowing low, then hurrying out the door. He looked at Draj. "How much money does this duchy make every month?"

"Well, sir, that's a rather complicated question, and there are many variables—"

"Ballpark." Victor groaned at himself. "I mean, give me a general idea—a rough average."

Draj frowned, clearly uneasy with Victor's bluntness, but he closed his eyes briefly and then began to rattle off an answer, "Profits from the mine leases come close to twenty million most months. Tax revenue from land grants and agricultural goods easily amount to another ten million. Market taxes from the city vary but range between three and seven million. Port and passage fees on the Green River are usually nearly a million beads per month." Draj frowned, rubbing his chin as he thought. "There are the hunting permits and dungeon licenses, building permits . . ." He sighed and shook his head. "I'd need to get my books, milord, if you want more details. Roughly, though, I'd say, altogether, close to forty million beads per month."

"And how much goes to the crown?"

"Queen Dar has lowered our tribute from nine percent to seven."

"Oh? Good." Victor nodded and gestured expansively. "Look, I know all of this is expensive. But you have to level with me. How much will that five million to Trobban impact the treasury?"

"Sir, per the policy set by Qi Pot, we maintain a treasury capable of paying the duchy's expenses for three years. Beyond that, we have a discretionary fund of nearly ten million beads. I know it sounds like a great sum, milord, but there are many petitions for many projects, and there are never enough beads to go around. For instance, the duchy maintains not only this palace but also dozens of other governmental buildings, which are in constant need of maintenance and updating. Roads and riverways require—"

"Relax, Draj." Victor tried to smile reassuringly. "I'm not planning to drain the treasury dry. I just want to know what I'm working with." Victor's heart wasn't in the conversation. He desperately wanted to finish his meetings to make his way up to the mountain. More than ever, he felt it was calling him, almost as though his duels and the succession war—his reason for coming to Ruhn—had just been a thread of fate drawing him to the real purpose. Iron

Mountain had something for him. He wasn't sure what, but he could *feel* it, and again, he wondered if his ancestors were guiding him.

"Milord, might I inquire as to your intention for me and mine? From the queen, I understand that you saw purpose in us, a way to employ our talents for the duchy, but nothing has been formalized. I am made a common, landless citizen for the first time in nearly eight decades. I—"

"Draj, what would you suggest if you were in my shoes?"

Draj straightened in his chair, his eyes narrowing slightly as he considered his words. "Milord, if I were in your position, I would recognize the value of trusted, capable hands to manage the duchy's more . . . delicate affairs. Your recent ascension has created opportunities, and with them comes the need to solidify control, ensure stability, and foster the duchy's prosperity. As you and Queen Kynna have noted, a man in your position can hardly afford to oversee every aspect personally."

He paused, leaning slightly forward, his voice becoming more deliberate. "As for my family and me, we have decades of experience running estates, managing trade, overseeing mining operations. Though I lack formal holdings now, I have not lost my knowledge or my connections. If you were to grant me a formal title—for Qi Pot, I was seneschal, and I would gladly fill that position for your court—my family could once again serve not just the duchy but you personally, milord."

He glanced up at Victor, gauging his reaction before continuing. "Iron Mountain is vast, and its wealth even more so. It will require skilled management. My talents lie in turning wealth into opportunity, ensuring the duchy's success. And, of course, our loyalty would be undivided, as it has always been."

"A title doesn't make you a landholder, Draj."

"True, milord, but you've offered us an estate in the city—"

"I'll do better than that." Victor paused, thinking. For once, he was happy that he'd sat with Ranish Dar for hours discussing courts, titles, and all the little things he thought he'd never have to deal with as a champion—basically, a glorified gladiator. "I want you to write up a proposal, one that grants the Haveshi family a reasonable portion of the ducal demesne—nothing absurd, but enough to ensure you're respected at court. Provided the proposal is reasonable, and Queen Kynna agrees, I'll grant your mother the title of viscountess, and I will formally reinstate you as seneschal."

Draj leaped to his feet, his chair skittering over the hardwood floors. As soon as he was up, he fell to his knees, pressing his forehead to the ground. "Lord Sandoval, you honor me and my house. What you propose is beyond what we deserve, and I am humbled by your generosity. I swear, if thy words be true, then we will be true to thee."

He stayed that way, head on the floor, while Victor mulled over his words. Why had he switched to archaic-sounding language? Had he really said "thy" and "thee"? Had he used some old-fashioned words that the System simply translated that way? Victor got so distracted by the tangential thought that it took Draj clearing his throat and swallowing nervously to remind him where he was. "You may stand, Draj. Go now and discuss things with your family. I'll review your proposal when you're ready."

Draj thanked him at least five more times before he slipped through the door. Meanwhile, Victor contemplated the mountain. He could feel it pulling him as if it were a magnet, and he was an iron filing. It couldn't be a simple coincidence that something Arona needed was deep in the mountain's guts. He knew the pull was more than that, however. There was a connection there, and it was personal—not just a piece of treasure for a friend.

He sat there at the head of his table, staring out the window at the distant blue-gray peak for a long time, so lost in thought that he hardly noticed the shifting of the shadows as the sun moved through the sky. When Bryn knocked on the door, and he was startled out of his self-imposed glamour, he almost felt he'd been asleep. "Come," he barked, his voice rough in his dry throat.

The door swung open, and Bryn announced, "Her Majesty, Queen Kynna Dar, is here to see you, milord."

# 28

✦

# PLACING TRUST

nd so, with another few weeks of pressure, I'm confident we can force a duel. I don't know how the rumors are spreading, but the fact that you've been sequestered for the better part of two weeks is working in our favor. Even in Gloria, there are whispers that Thorn badly injured you, and my agents in Lovania seem to think that Queen Fabaj is overconfident in her champion's abilities; I'm hopeful that she'll accept a duel so long as the terms are even slightly favorable for her." Lovania was Xan's—Gloria's now—eastern neighbor.

Victor nodded, mulling over his thoughts. Kynna had spent close to an hour bringing him up to speed on all that had occurred while he was processing the wyrm egg. The information was interesting on an academic level, but he'd had a hard time staying focused, his mind constantly drifting toward the mountain. Was it worse than before he'd eaten the egg? Back then, he'd certainly found the mountain intriguing, even felt some kind of kinship with it, but he hadn't felt such a *pull*. Was it his bloodline feat? Maybe it wasn't a pull; maybe the instincts of his ancestors were *pushing* him.

"Victor?"

"I'm sorry, Queen Kynna. My mind is swollen with thoughts after my experience with the egg. To your point, would it be helpful if I remained . . . absent?"

She arched an eyebrow, lifting a polished, violet nail to her lower lip, gently stroking the plump pink flesh. Not for the first time, Victor felt she was being seductive, and he shifted, clearing his throat and forcing his eyes to stare into hers. "Did you have something in mind?"

"As I mentioned before, I need to visit that mountain." He tilted his head toward the window. "My . . . *experience* has left me even more sure of it. I feel it pulling, and unless there's some objection, I'd like to leave as soon as possible."

Kynna clasped her hands atop the table, fidgeting with her thumbs as she closed her eyes briefly, clearly considering her words. "Victor, I hope you understand the far-reaching repercussions to Gloria and its citizens should you fail to return."

"I won't abandon you, Kynna. Your magus is coming, right? The guy who can make portals?"

She nodded, unclasping her hands and turning her gaze toward the window. "Yes. Florent has been briefed and stands ready."

"Well, that's good, then—"

"What is it, do you think? What draws you to that peak? Are there creatures you wish to slay in its depths? I've had my historians look into the mountain and this duchy, and there have been times when it was seen as a destination for adventurers more than a source of mineral wealth."

"I . . ." Victor stopped, considering his words, and then, more carefully, started again. "I've had a connection to a volcano before. A kinship with the rage that can cling to the fiery magma. You've seen me fight; you know I can . . . *lose* myself." He sighed, shaking his head. "I'm just speculating now, but maybe this mountain senses me and the kinship I've shared with that other volcano." He didn't want to mention his former class—Dar had drilled into him all too well the benefits of being an unknown quantity when it came to politics.

"Is it true then? Does the mountain have a spirit? Is it alive?"

"I don't know. I only know that at least one *other* mountain was. When I felt its spirit and made that connection, it was like—well, imagine I was a candle flame, and the mountain was the sun. I had a lot to learn from the depths of its wrath."

"Why was it angry?"

Victor chuckled, shrugging. "Maybe it's because it became a volcano—all that magma flowing through it. Or maybe it became a volcano *because* it was angry." Again, he barked a laugh. "Maybe I'll get a chance to ask this one."

"You think it's angry, too? Victor, if this mountain were to erupt, most of Gloria would be made into a wasteland. The Elementalists in their temple keep it calm; you mustn't—"

Victor held up his hands, shaking his head. "Don't worry about that! I have no intention to go in there and rile things up. I'm going to see where my instincts lead me and then go from there."

"Following your instincts? That's your argument for why I should trust you?"

"No, my Queen, you should trust me because I've put my life on the line for you a few times now, and your ancestor, Ranish Dar, sent me here to help you."

Kynna nodded, her crystal crown tilting precariously. "Very well, Victor. I shall trust you. Please stay in touch, and please return in the event I need you. If you are delving deep and the need arises, rest assured that Florent will be able to mark your location, allowing him to create a portal through which you can return to your explorations."

"Seriously? That's pretty damn awesome."

"Florent is a steel seeker, though his talents lie well outside the realm of combat. If things grow violent, his first instinct will be flight. Please, Victor, do not let him be slain; he's a good, kind man and a boon to our nation."

Her voice softened as she spoke about Florent, and a certain light entered her eyes, making Victor wonder if his suspicions about her intentions toward him had been misplaced. He decided to press the conversation into more personal territory, if only to satisfy a question that had been itching to be asked since he first met the queen. "Kynna, may I ask a personal question?"

"I wish you would! I tire of these matters of state."

"What happened to Tomorran's father?"

"Ah!" She smiled and chuckled softly. "It's not as personal as you thought, Victor. Anyone in Gloria could tell you that my former husband passed through his test of steel shortly after Tomorran was born. As you know, the council of veil walkers who watch over Ruhn do not allow members of that tier of society to live among us. Galentine was given a choice: join the council of veil walkers as an apprentice or leave the world. He'd already decided before we became lovers, fully intending to leave and continue his journey of enlightenment, so no one was surprised when he moved on."

"And you're good with that?"

"Ah, now it becomes a bit more personal!" She shook her head, smiling as she leaned a little closer. "Do I wish he'd put off his ascension for a decade or three and spent some time with Tomorran? I'd be a liar if I denied it. He made himself very clear, though, when we became entwined. It was a condition of our love—his desire to chase his breakthroughs would not be diminished."

"He must have been quite a guy." Victor left the other half of his opinion unspoken—that he thought Galentine sounded like an asshole. Of course, part of him acknowledged some parallels between himself and Valla, only that she'd been the one to make the decision for him, whereas Galentine had simply been honest about his pursuits.

"He is a fascinating and impressive individual, a peerless artisan, and a kind, gentle soul. I thought that Tomorran's birth would change him, make him want to work less and spend more time with us, but I was wrong. As he puts it, his passion for creation isn't something he can control; he's driven by his muses, unable to live without pursuing their demands." She reached up and gently ran her fingers along the crystalline surface of her crown. "He created this for me as a parting gift."

Victor could hear some genuine sorrow tinging her words, and, of course, those words evoked more comparisons to himself and Valla in his mind. "It's beautiful, Kynna. I want to call him a fool for leaving you both, but I've had my own troubles of a . . . similar nature, and I'm no one to judge."

"Driven, are you?" She chuckled as he shrugged and nodded. "Well, your pursuits certainly seem different from Galentine's. Still, I wish you luck and hope you find something to help you in your quest for advancement in yonder mountain. When shall I have Florent report for duty?"

"If it's okay with you, immediately."

"Yes, that'll be fine. I'll maintain close communication with him. Meanwhile, I have much to do. To start, I have meetings with my cousins for the next three days. Everyone's still quite upset about the coup attempt and my sudden relocation. I'm rather enjoying keeping people at arm's length! It's driving the nobles of Gloria mad that I'm only allowing five visitors through the portal chamber daily. More than that, I'm only giving them day passes!"

"Ha! I guess that keeps security easy."

"Indeed!" Kynna stood, smiling, and turned toward the door. "It was nice to get to know you a little more, Victor. I hope we'll sit together again when you return from the mountain."

"Yeah." Victor also stood and, feeling awkward, reached up to scratch his fingers through his short, stiff hair. "I feel the same way."

"Travel safely. I'll look forward to our next meeting."

"Um, yes, my Queen. Until next time." She stood by the door, hesitating, and Victor's mind raced with possible reasons. Was she expecting some show of affection? They'd never hugged or anything like that. When she glanced at the door and cleared her throat, Victor's mind stopped racing, and he slapped himself on the head. "I'm sorry!" He hurried over and opened it for her, holding it wide. "Thank you for your time, Your Majesty."

She smiled a little crookedly, her eyes amused, as she passed through. When her guards and retainers formed around her, Victor heard her say, "Larassa, find Magus Florent and have him report to Victor's chambers immediately." Then they were in the elevator, and Victor couldn't hear anything more.

He looked at Bryn. "Anyone else?"

"No, sir."

"Okay, get your shit together; we're heading up the mountain. Don't mention that to anyone."

Bryn jerked upright, her armor clanking as she turned to stare at him. "My shit, sir?"

"Get all your stuff! I mean anything you want to bring. We'll be hiking around the mountain and probably going deep into the mines or tunnels or whatever's up there."

"Should I bring Feist?"

"Oh, yeah. I forgot about him. Yeah, I need to meet him, and you might as well have some help."

She gestured to the elevator. There were no stairs to his suite, which likely wouldn't pass any safety regulations, but Victor didn't think there *were* any regulations, especially when the duke's palace was the building in question. "Is it all right to leave for a few minutes? I need to go wake him."

"Yeah, go for it. I'll be alert." While she waited for the elevator, Victor went back into his quarters and took Arona's phylactery from his container. As soon as it touched the open air, foggy mist began to seep from the bone, slowly coalescing into the translucent likeness of Arona's long-gone physical form.

In her usual raspy, deadpan tone, she said, "I was beginning to think I'd been forgotten."

"Nah, not forgotten." Victor smiled and gestured toward the sitting area near the balcony. "Let me fill you in on what's happening." She followed him over and "sat" on a couch near him while Victor reviewed everything Trobban had told him. He also spent some time going over the events of the previous days, including a vague summary of his experience with the egg and his intention to visit Iron Mountain.

"Did you gain much from the natural treasure?" She eyed him speculatively, and Victor shrugged.

"I got a few ranks to my bloodline and learned a lot more about it."

"Ever so mysterious, Victor. Some sort of titan, yes?"

"I told you that?"

"Come! You were shouting it in the challenge dungeon." She frowned, shaking her head. "Or maybe it was afterward, at your party? In any event, either you or someone else mentioned to me that you had a titanic bloodline."

"Yeah, that's true." Victor looked at her, watching the realistic expressions traverse her ghostly face, wondering why a spirit would need to look like a person's dead body. He knew that he could alter his appearance on the spirit plane. Could Arona alter hers on this one?

Her thoughts weren't in line with his, it seemed. "Some cultures believe that the spirits of mountains are closely related to titans. Some cultures believe that mountains *were* titans."

Victor's eyes bulged at the idea. He peered out the window at the darkening slopes of the enormous mountain on the horizon. "That would be a big, *pinché* titan!" He looked back at Arona. "If that were the case, wouldn't people know? I mean, if their spirits are in there, couldn't they communicate?"

"They certainly *could*, but they're called 'sleeping' gods or giants or titans for a reason. The ones who speak are mad with rage—volcanos." She made a dry, raspy sigh and shrugged. "I speak only of legends and myths, but Victor, there are people on my homeworld who think titans themselves are naught but myth. I think you'd take exception to that."

"So you think the pull I feel might have more to do with my bloodline than my, uh, rage affinity?" Victor wanted to tell her about his Herald of the Mountain's Wrath class but wasn't sure it was relevant, seeing as he'd already taken a different one.

"I don't know. Perhaps the pull is strong because they're both a factor."

"I had a, uh, experience with another volcano."

"Oh?"

Victor nodded, then related some of the story about his encounter with Hector atop his then-dormant volcano. When he finished, Arona looked pensive. "What is it?"

"What if this volcano seeks your aid in freeing it—waking it? You mentioned Elementalist monks, yes? What if the volcano doesn't like being calmed? What if it has fury it wants to vent?"

"I don't think a volcano that damn big and powerful would be held down by a handful of iron rankers. I don't care what class or affinity they have. If that thing wanted to blow its top, it would. I mean, maybe those guys are good at soothing it, but it's definitely not captive."

"I appreciate your respect for the mountain's power, but Victor, how do you know it's only a handful of iron rankers? What if it's a hundred? What if some of them are steel seekers?"

Victor shook his head. "Arona, I felt the power of a volcano a tenth of Iron Mountain's size. It was a *force*—something that made Ronkerz feel puny."

"Well." Arona pressed her dark lips together, shaking her head in defeat. "I hope you're right, and I hope you'd do the right thing in any case. You wouldn't trade a great spirit's freedom for the lives of countless people, would you? You wouldn't destroy the nation you're supposed to be championing." Her words were statements, but Victor could feel the questions behind them.

"I'm not a monster, Arona. I'm not like Vesavo."

She leaned toward him, and Victor felt the air around him noticeably drop in temperature. "I believe you, Victor. Still, what if the mountain *is* a sleeping titan? What if it *does* want your help to free it? What if it promises you secrets and artifacts and natural treasures? What if—"

"Arona!" Victor stood, feeling agitated. He couldn't help but raise his voice as he gesticulated, pacing toward the window and back. "You're panicking about fucking *ideas*. You're also worried because you've never had to depend on someone who wasn't a power-mad nutcase. Listen to me: I'm not going to help that volcano explode. If it wants help with something, I'll find a way to do it that won't kill everyone and ruin Dar's kingdom." Victor laughed, shaking his head, but Arona didn't seem to share his amusement. She looked chastened, and it made Victor feel guilty. How often had Vesavo cussed her out? How often had he yelled at her?

"Understood."

"Oh, don't do that now! Come on, Arona. You know what? I *appreciate* you mentioning all this. I appreciate you looking out for me. Because of what you said, I'm going to be a lot more careful when I go in there. If that *pinché* mountain used to be a titan or maybe only part of that myth is true and it's somehow *related* to titans, then I need to be careful, but I also need to listen to my instincts, okay? There's a reason I feel this pull, and it doesn't *feel* bad."

"Will you bring my phylactery or leave it here?"

Victor had intended to bring it, but did she not want him to? "What would you prefer?"

"Bring it! I may be able to offer you advice at a pivotal moment."

"And if the volcano erupts and I'm killed? You'll be trapped under a billion tons of rock and lava."

"Do you think that will happen?"

"No." Victor smiled.

"Then I will trust you." As if on cue, a knock sounded at his door, and Arona began to disperse. "I hope we speak again soon, Victor."

"We will." Victor watched her flow into her phylactery, picked up the bone, and sent it into storage. "Come in," he called.

Bryn opened the door, and she and two men entered. She and one of the men wore dark leather armor with metallic breastplates, both embossed with golden roses. The other fellow wore black robes and carried a smooth black staff shod in rune-inscribed silver. Both men were young-looking, though Feist, the soldier—or squire, as Bryn had styled him—was far swarthier in appearance. His brown hair was long, his skin well-tanned, and his light-brown eyes peered about with curiosity. The other man, Florent, was pale with strange yellow eyes and bore a strained expression as though simply walking into the room was a chore.

"Your Grace, might I introduce my squire, Feist, and the esteemed Spatial Magus, Florent." Bryn bowed, swooping her arm to indicate the two men. They bowed in turn, Feist far more gracefully than Florent.

"Good to meet you, men." Victor turned to the window, pointing to the mountain in the distance. "Florent, can you make us a portal to that mountain, or do we need to travel there?"

"Milord, last week the queen bade me travel to the foothills of that mountain to learn a portal site. I did so, and now, if you wish, I can open one at your command."

Victor's eyes widened. He'd expected the man to say no. "She did that? That was pretty damn thoughtful, wasn't it?"

"It was, Your Grace," Bryn chimed in.

"I'd say so, milord." Feist grinned, putting his fists on his hips.

"Well, it was *I* who made the journey . . ." Florent sighed, letting his protestation die on his lips. He stepped farther into the room. "Shall I commence?"

Victor nodded. "Commence."

## 29

## INTO THE MOUNTAIN

When Victor stepped out of Florent's strange, crackling black portal, he felt the mountain before he saw it. It was like being a little kid and standing in the shadow of a giant. The presence was heavy, though Iron Mountain was just passively *being*; it wasn't trying to crush him with the weight of its aura, nor was it filled with any palpable rage like the volcano under Hector's base had been. Still, Victor hadn't felt that sense of insignificance since he'd been to the ivid world to meet their queen.

As he adjusted to the weight of the mountain's presence, he looked around and got his bearings. His palace and the town of Iron Mountain were north of the mountain's slopes, and, turning to look that way, he could see a long, wide road leading away into the thick forest canopy; he wasn't high enough on the slope to see beyond the trees. Victor turned to see the road continue into the mountain's foothills, branching off to the east and west several times before winding out of sight behind craggy ridges.

The mountain rose into the sky, farther than he could see, the peak lost to the hazy mists of the upper atmosphere. From his palace, he hadn't realized how the foothills of Iron Mountain were, in reality, mountains themselves. Even standing among them, well aware of their size, they seemed tiny simply because of the enormous craggy gray peak that loomed over them. Still, now that they were close, Victor realized they had a good deal of hiking to do if they wanted to get onto the mountain proper.

"Gods!" Feist said, taking his helmet off to get a better view. "Never seen the place up close. That's a hell of a mountain!"

"Calm yourself, Feist." Bryn sighed. She looked at Victor and shrugged sheepishly. "Apologies for my squire's boisterous nature, milord."

"You kidding me? I don't mind; he's right!"

With a crackling *woosh*, Florent stepped through his portal, and it snapped shut, disappearing in a wave of sizzling silver sparks. He looked at Victor and then gestured to the cobbled roadway. "I chose this location because, according to my guide at the time, the branching roads lead to different mine entrances, but if you stay on this main path, you'll eventually come to the Temple of the Elements."

"That's where the Fire and Earth Elementalists live?" Bryn asked, saving Victor the trouble.

"Yes, ma'am."

"It's Bryn. No need for formality."

"Does that go for me, too?" Feist asked, and Bryn cuffed him on the back of the head.

"Don't embarrass yourself!"

Victor chuckled but didn't comment. He turned up the road and started hiking. The grade was steep, but his long Quinametzin strides devoured it. As he went, he reached into his pathways and severed the connection to his Alter Self spell, expanding to his true height. It took Bryn a few minutes before she gave him a double take. "Did you grow?"

"Yeah," Victor chuckled. "The egg brought out more of my bloodline." He glanced up and down the quiet road, watching Feist and Florent bring up the rear. When they were close, he asked, "Where's the railway?"

Florent responded, "For the ore? A dozen tracks meander through these canyons and up the slopes to the various mines. They converge near the base and take a parallel course to this road farther down near the forest."

Bryn looked at Victor, and he could tell she was wondering about his plan. "Should we stop at one of the outposts and get a guide?"

Victor shook his head. "I know it seems strange, but I'm, uh, following a feeling. I can tell the mountain wants something from me."

"I imagined we'd go to the temple and ask the Order for guidance."

Victor shook his head. "I don't think they can help me." He turned and started walking again.

Bryn kept pace beside him, her armor clanking as she walked. "Why?"

"It's just a feeling." Victor laughed at her frustrated scowl. "I know, it's irritating. I don't know how to explain it. I'm just going to follow my instincts 'cause something is pulling or pushing me toward . . . *something* in this mountain."

Bryn just nodded and put her head down, digging into the steep upward climb. Victor could hear Florent and Feist behind him, and though Florent wasn't the sturdiest-looking man he'd ever seen, Victor knew there was no way a guy past Level One Hundred could possibly struggle with any sort of hike. As the minutes ticked by and they climbed hundreds of feet in elevation, Victor often thought about summoning Guapo and making quick work of the ascent, at least until they came to trails or tunnels that made it impractical. Something about having the mountain under his feet was satisfying, though, and he rather enjoyed the vigorous exercise in the mountain air.

He didn't doubt that the others could summon mounts or other means of quick travel, but they didn't mention it, which gave Victor another sort of satisfaction—these three were following his lead and doing so without any real question or objection. It was something he'd taken for granted lately, likely ever since the campaign for the Untamed Marches. He'd become accustomed to leading to the point where it didn't faze him.

They passed many iron signposts denoting different shafts or other locales on the mountain, from outposts to an occasional homestead. After passing a sign next to a rocky trail that read *Yarrow Keep*, Bryn commented, "I didn't know anyone lived up here."

"Nor I," Florent huffed from behind them.

Victor shrugged. "I'll ask about it back at the palace, but I imagine there have been land grants up here over the years. We're talking a hell of a lot of acreage surrounding this peak."

After a few grunts of agreement, they walked in silence for a while, their huffing breaths accompanied by the sounds of nature—birds singing, canines yipping in the distance, and the occasional yowl of a big cat. When they came to a crossroad on the main trail with a narrow path leading off to the right at a downward slope and another to the left that seemed to climb a sheer cliff face carved into the stone by some Elementalist in the distant past, Victor felt a change in the mountain's pull.

When he stopped, Bryn took a few steps and then turned back to face him. "Resting?"

"No. I think we need to go that way." Victor pointed to the trail that climbed the rocky face to the left.

"Narrow," Florent grunted, leaning on his slender black staff. He scanned the cliff and pointed, directing Victor's gaze upward. "It switchbacks a dozen times before it curves out of sight up there. I could shorten our climb by portaling us to the top."

Victor's eyes widened. "You can do that?"

"Of course! If I can see it, I can make a portal to it. It's a costly spell with a long cooldown, but it's different from the one that I used to bring us to the mountain. That one requires me to create an anchor, meaning I have to physically be at the location before I can create a portal to it in the future."

"Well, shit. I don't see why we can't cheat a little; there's nowhere to get off that trail, so I don't think we'll miss anything."

Florent nodded, then, gazing up toward the distant, faint track of the cliffside trail, he thumped his staff on the hard, cobbled roadway. Victor felt a surge of potent Energy, and then, with a sizzling, tearing sound, a black portal opened in the air before him. "Go," Florent grunted.

Victor stepped through first, and just as when he'd taken the portal from his palace to the mountain, he felt a brief sensation of coldness. Then he stepped out onto the narrow, stony pathway. He took a few steps, making room for the others, then took a moment to look down at his ant-like companions on the roadway below. "That saved some time," he muttered as Bryn emerged from the portal and hurried toward him.

Everyone was on the new path a few seconds later, and Victor led the way around the stony escarpment. The drop to his left was dizzying, but it didn't bother him much; Victor figured he'd probably be able to land on his feet by activating Titanic Leap, and even if he couldn't, he didn't think a fall would kill him, even thousands of feet down onto rough, jagged boulders. There was a lot to be said for having an epic-tier vitality and a titanic constitution.

The trail, carved out of the stone of the cliffside, continued deep into a narrow canyon between the side of Iron Mountain and a nearby "foothill," which was larger than any of the mountains Victor had visited around Tucson. They followed it for hours, steadily climbing higher, and when it wound around again, heading straight up a new canyon—a natural split in Iron Mountain's shoulder—the sky had grown dark, and the sun was a distant memory.

Before climbing into the new canyon, Victor gestured to the relatively flat stony area on which they stood and asked, "Does anyone need to rest?"

Florent stepped forward, his face a little flushed but his breathing regular and unstrained. "Unless you intend to make camp, I would rather press on. No sense delaying the inevitable."

"I'm fine," Feist added.

Victor looked at Bryn, and she simply gestured with her hand, pointing toward the trail. He nodded, grinning, and continued to hike. The moon and stars provided plenty of light for Victor's eyes, and he led them deep into the canyon, always following the ever-present tug at his Core or his heart or his spirit—he didn't know exactly what part of him was being pulled, but he felt it. By midnight, they'd passed two forks in the path, climbed another thousand feet, and traversed two rocky ridgelines.

When they crossed the second one, Victor stood and looked back to the north, over the vast, dark sea of the forest, and sure enough, he could see the distant lights of the town. Bryn stood beside him and sighed, wiping some sweat from her brow. "We're pretty damn high, Your Grace."

Victor clapped her on the shoulder. "I like the way you talk, Bryn."

"Thank you for not insisting I be polite."

Victor had to laugh at the idea and, shaking his head, turned and continued to climb. Two hours later, Florent called out, "I see a cave!"

Victor had a habit of watching the trail in front of his feet, looking for stones to step on and ensuring he didn't slip on loose scree. When Florent called out, he looked back to see where the man pointed, and sure enough, about a mile up the canyon and on the other side, he saw the oblong crescent of pitch-black darkness that stood out among the starlit boulders. When his eyes settled on the opening, Victor felt the pull with renewed intensity, and he simply *knew* that was where he was meant to go. "That's it," he grunted.

"Shall I create a portal, or would you like to progress on this trail?"

Victor let his gaze drift back to the stony path, following it up the canyon with his eyes. He could see that it probably wrapped around the canyon to the far side farther up, but if they could skip that hike, it would save them hours. "Portal," he grunted.

Florent nodded, then moved past Victor so he had more open space before him. He slammed his staff on the ground, and Victor felt a surge of Energy, and once again, Florent's dark, crackling portal appeared. "After you, Your Grace."

Victor brushed past him and stepped into the void hanging in the air. His foot came down on gray stone, and he stepped into the opening of a dark, dusty cave. While he waited for the others, he peered into the deep shadows, his Quinametzin eyes straining to pierce the dark. It looked as if it went deep and descended rapidly. Standing there in the cave opening, he could feel something calling to him even more intensely.

There weren't words or coherent thoughts associated with the call, but Victor was more and more sure that it was the mountain and not some other being. Perhaps his ancestors were aiding the call, allowing it to affect him more profoundly, but Victor felt it was something in his blood—a kinship the mountain recognized. He couldn't get any sense of emotion from the pull; it didn't seem desperate or angry or hopeful. It was just a pull that said *come*, and something in Victor wanted to answer.

The sizzling crackle of Florent's portal fading brought Victor's mind back to the present, and he looked at his companions. "Anyone need rest?"

"Not I, Your Grace." Feist thumped his breastplate with his gloved fist.

Victor chuckled at his enthusiasm but looked at Florent. "You're good?"

"Fine, if a bit bored."

"Well, maybe things will get more interesting in this cave." Victor gathered some inspiration-attuned Energy and summoned his coyotes. As the shimmering silvery mist gathered on the cave floor and his five companions sprang into existence with yips and yowls, Victor laughed to see Bryn take a step back, her hand reaching for her sword. As he squatted to pet the cheerful canines, they swarmed him, licking and slobbering all over his face and neck. "All right, all right!"

"You're a summoner?" Bryn asked, eyes wide. "You never used your pets in battle—"

Victor stood, and his cheerful demeanor turned into a glower as he stared at Bryn, Florent, and Feist. "You might see me do a few things in here that I'd rather the rest of Ruhn wasn't aware of. Consider this mission and anything you witness to be a secret between us. Agreed?"

"Yes, milord!" Again Feist slammed his fist to his chest, and this time Bryn joined him, nodding and saluting.

Florent chuckled and nodded. "I've no one to share such things with, milord, but rest assured, you'll have my secrecy."

Victor nodded, then turned to his coyotes and clicked his tongue, jerking his thumb toward the tunnel. They cried and yowled in excitement as they took off, eager to be the first to discover something interesting for him. "They'll scout," he explained. As he started after the coyotes, Victor summoned a Globe of Insight, charging it until it blazed like a star in the air over his head. With that brilliant illumination, his eyes pierced the depths of the tunnel for a hundred feet or more, and he could see that it wound slightly to the right.

"Were those wolves, Lord Victor?" Feist asked from behind Bryn as they walked. "I've never heard such funny cries. It almost seems they were trying to talk."

"Coyotes. They're related to wolves but usually smaller. Mine are quite a bit bigger than natural ones. Coyotes are clever and brave, and they rely on one another to survive." Victor could feel his companion spirits deep below them, racing ahead. He couldn't see through their eyes but could get general sensations and emotions from them. It seemed they were still together; the tunnel hadn't branched yet.

As they descended, the cave grew larger rather than smaller, and Victor found himself able to stand upright and take comfortable strides. He imagined that the people who'd carved the trail into the stony cliffs leading to the cave had probably been prospecting—looking for mineral deposits and whatnot— but this cave seemed natural, and Victor didn't see any evidence of mining. "There wasn't a sign by the trailhead leading here, was there?"

"No, milord," Feist replied. Victor was starting to like the guy; he was quick-witted and eager.

"Doesn't seem like any mining operation reached this tunnel, does it?" He looked over his shoulder, addressing the question to all three of his companions.

Florent shook his head. "I think not, milord."

"Strange, don't you think? That trail in the cliff face couldn't have been easy to make."

"On the contrary, milord," Florent replied again, "for a powerful Earth Elementalist, it would be a few days' work at most. I'd say it's likely a noble in times past wanted to explore this cave and sought an easier route for his hired hands."

"Hmm." Victor stopped, pausing to better concentrate on his coyotes. They were fast when they had room to run, and it felt as though they were very distant, as if they'd covered miles. "My coyotes are way ahead of us. They haven't run into anything—" Victor gasped, choking off his words, as he felt a surge of panic mingled with excitement. His coyotes had come upon something. He got an impression of a vast space, heat, and the undeniable *danger* sensation from all five of them. Then, they were gone.

"Are you all right?" Bryn grabbed his shoulder, and Victor shook his head, trying to banish the startled panic and fear his companions had sent his way.

"Something just killed my coyotes."

"Gods!" Feist cried. "I'm sorry, milord!"

Florent saved Victor the trouble of explaining. "Those were spirit totems, Feist. They aren't dead forever." He looked at Victor. "Isn't that correct, milord?"

"Yeah, that's right. Still, something killed them in about two seconds flat." He glared at the three of them. "Maybe you all should wait here."

Florent shook his head. "I have strict orders to accompany you, milord."

"I'm not letting you go down there alone!" Bryn looked horrified at the thought.

"I'm with you, Your Grace!" Feist announced.

Victor smiled at Feist, nodding as he locked eyes with the young man. "I appreciate your bravery." He turned to Florent. "But if I tell you to run, you better have a portal ready."

"I always have an escape portal ready, milord! How else do you think I can feign such bravery?" He grinned lopsidedly and winked, getting a few hearty chuckles out of Feist.

"Fair enough." Victor looked up at his Globe of Insight, then canceled it, reclaiming his Energy. As the tunnel was thrown into darkness, Florent's black staff began to glow with silvery light.

"Shall I extinguish this, milord?"

"Up to you," Victor said, casting Banner of the Champion, blasting the tunnel with its blazing golden light.

"Gods! I feel that!" Feist cheered, pounding his chest with his fist. Even Florent stood taller, the wan pallor of his flesh perking up with some color.

Bryn was beaming ear to ear as she peered up at the bloody sun on Victor's floating, magical standard. "I'm learning a lot about you today, Your Grace."

"C'mon." Victor started down the tunnel, his lengthy strides forcing the others to half jog to keep up. "You're probably going to learn a lot more."

# 30

## BARRIER

With his banner blazing, Victor led the way deeper into the vast, steeply descending tunnel. Loose boulders here and there, dust, and rubble marked their progress, but other than that, the tunnel was empty. Such a sizeable subterranean space in a wild System-controlled world seemed as if it ought to be home to many creatures, but neither Victor nor his companions spotted so much as a mouse or even cobwebs. The air was dry, and though it started out cool, it became progressively warmer as they descended.

After walking for more than ten minutes, Victor stopped and turned to his companions. "The area where I lost track of my coyotes isn't far, perhaps a hundred or two hundred yards around that bend." He gestured to where the steeply descending tunnel rounded a wide corner to the right.

"Shall I scout?" Bryn asked, stepping forward.

Victor chuckled and shook his head. "No. I'll go ahead, and if you hear the sounds of battle, you can come and see what it is and whether you'd like to get involved. Keep yourselves safe, though—I'm sturdier than I might seem."

"Oh, I don't know, milord," Florent whispered, his voice carrying a note of droll humor, "you seem quite sturdy to me."

Victor chuckled, gave his companions a solemn nod, then turned and loped down the hallway. With his banner blazing behind him, it wasn't easy to notice, but when he began to round the corner, he thought the shadows ahead were lighter. A dozen more steps revealed why. The great tunnel opened into an even greater subterranean hall. It was a space that could hold a thousand titans Victor's size. The space had a ceiling that had to be five hundred feet high with a glowering ball of orange-red fire hanging from black chains mounted to its stony surface.

Stepping into the space, Victor saw that the distant opposite wall looked to be made of dense-looking, yellow-gray metal that shone softly in the light of the globe of fire. Something massive shifted in the shadows to his right, and he whirled to see a humanoid figure, though one that made him feel small. He might have said it was an iron automaton if he didn't know about magical alloys and rare, Energy-dense elements. It was about fifty yards from him, and even at that distance, he could see it was much larger than any giant he'd faced—certainly taller than he was in his berserk, titan form.

The figure's round metallic head shifted toward him, its baleful red eyes staring his way as it slowly, with surprisingly limber joints, lifted a titanic black great sword. Victor had the distinct impression that it was giving him a fair warning and that violence would ensue if he moved farther into the chamber. Was that what happened to his coyotes? How could something so enormous and seemingly cumbersome kill five of his quick, clever companions so suddenly?

Rather than be caught by surprise, Victor channeled Energy into his armor, cladding himself in his wyrm-scales and lava king hide. His Sojourn set enchantments gave his armor a fiery orange glow that seemed to intensify when Victor readied for a fight, and readying himself he was. He reached into his storage compartment and summoned Lifedrinker into his hands, grinning fiercely when he realized his latest size boost meant he could handle her almost comfortably, even without casting one of his berserking abilities.

*"At last! Will we fight, my love? Will we spill the blood of your foes?"*

"Maybe, *chica*. God, it feels good to hold you, though. Stay ready!"

*"Always!"*

Lifedrinker's gleaming black axe-head began to glow with a fiery inner light, and Victor could see the air around her shimmering with heat waves. He took a step, and the great black-metal golem or automaton or whatever he was supposed to call it took a single step and swung its sword in a flat arc. At first, Victor thought it was malfunctioning and trying to cut him even though he was still nearly half a football field distant, but then the air that the tip of the sword cleaved and crackled with red, lightning-filled Energy, and a wall of destructive force rolled toward him like a deadly tidal wave.

Victor had about two seconds to react and, without thinking, activated his Flight of the Lava King armor enchantment. Enormous fiery wings sprouted from his back, and when he looked into the air above that wall of deadly Energy, he exploded upward, leaving billowing clouds of black smoke in his wake. He soared over the metallic man's attack, and as he streaked toward his enemy, Victor cast Iron Berserk.

His body surged in power and size, and Lifedrinker became comfortable in his hands. He lifted her high and directed his flight downward, streaking like a fiery comet toward the metal giant. The golem—Victor had mentally settled on that label—moved far more fluidly than anything that size made of metal had any right to do. It stepped to the side and raised its thirty-foot sword, aiming to swat Victor out of the air. Victor didn't shrink away from the blow, even as that black blade exploded with crackling red-lightning Energy.

As he came down, Lifedrinker's brilliant, gleaming, incredibly dense edge met the sword in a cataclysmic crash. Focusing on his movement, unable to stare at her impact, Victor knew she won the contest because she didn't stop. She didn't even jerk in his hands much. She continued to fall toward the golem's chest, and her enormous, wedge-shaped axe-head punched through a foot of dense metal to sink into the cavity beyond. As Victor leaped back, leaving Life-drinker to do her work, he saw the top half of the golem's enormous sword still sliding over the stony ground.

"Yeah! *Drink!*" he roared, laughing madly as the golem thrashed its truncated sword, stomping toward Victor. For his part, Victor kept backpedaling, enjoying the show as red currents of Energy coursed into the dense, mirror-like black surface of his axe. The golem tried to cleave the air with its shortened weapon, and Victor could see red lightning sparking in the air, but it wasn't enough to ignite another wave of deadly destruction. He laughed, taunting the golem as it stumbled toward him, its movements slowing by the second as Life-drinker tore torrents of its vital power away.

When the golem's steps looked almost like a slow-motion movie, he darted forward and flanked the thing, slamming a shoulder into its side. He grunted with the impact, driving with his powerful legs until the enormous construct began to teeter. It tried to swing its broken sword at him again, but Victor slipped behind it, and while it rocked unsteadily, he gave it another shove. This time, as it rocked forward, he squatted down, hooked his hands around its tree-sized ankle, and, with all his might, *heaved.*

The golem toppled, futilely trying to break its fall with too-slow arms, and when it impacted the cavern floor, it split the stone and shook the ground like a building falling. Victor looked up to see dust and small hunks of stone falling from the ceiling. He almost sprinted for the tunnel, sure the whole place would come down, but the tremor of the impact was short-lived. Whatever had created the tremendous stony hall had built it sturdily.

The golem wasn't yet dead, but its movements were slow and weak, and it seemed stuck, its arms pinned beneath it. Steam and smoke poured from the seams of its joints, and every so often, an arc of red electric Energy would lash out with a crackling *zap.* Victor moved around the side of it, grasped the rough black metal of its shoulder, and heaved, trying to turn it onto its side; he didn't want to leave Lifedrinker pinned beneath it. The thing was heavy, but since it wasn't quite dead, it actually helped Victor in his efforts, pushing with its damaged, grinding arms, trying to right itself.

By the time Victor managed to complete his deadlift, screaming and red-faced from the effort, the automaton was nearly still, and white steam veritably billowed out of the enormous rupture in its chest where Lifedrinker had buried herself to the haft. He grabbed her and yanked, pulling her forth with a massive arc of red-tinged lightning. Before the mechanical giant could find a way to repair itself, Victor lifted Lifedrinker and walked around its twitching arms to smash her into its passenger-car-sized head, over and over.

With each upswing of Lifedrinker's flaming obsidian blade, gears, crystals, and electricity-charged motes of Energy flew through the air. Heaving from the workout, sweating through the red heat of his rage, Victor dismantled the automaton, and Lifedrinker continued to drink the bright red Energy that leaked from its shell. He wasn't sure how long he toiled, but it had to have been five or ten minutes before he looked up from the wreckage to see his companions standing nearby, watching in various states of disbelief.

"I think it's dead, Your Grace!" Feist called.

Victor regarded him through his red haze of fury, and as the squire's words slowly registered, he began to laugh. It was a deep belly laugh, and the mirth chased the rage from his pathways, ending his Iron Berserk. As he returned to his normal size, leaning against one of the titanic construct's mangled legs, he realized he was standing in a sea of pulsating orbs of shimmering Energy. They were hazy but bright, filled with the potent Energy of a high-level conquest.

Considering the ease with which he'd dispatched the construct, Victor was a little surprised by the volume of Energy that surged toward him, but the thought was dashed from his mind as he was overwhelmed. The influx lifted him from his feet and sent his mind reeling down rainbow-hued passages of kaleido-scopic confusion. He caught glimpses of things that only served to confuse him further—waterfalls, flaming comets, erupting peaks, slender reeds blown by pink-hued winds, and a tree with branches that scraped the firmament.

When he came back to himself, he sat on the cavern floor, back to the ruined golem, and he could hear the sound of movement and soft conversation nearby. ". . . think the innards are largely intact, at least in the torso." It took his disoriented mind a moment to recognize Florent's voice, but Bryn's reply was easier to place.

"Don't touch anything until Victor awakens."

"Naturally! I'll keep my fingers intact, thank you very much."

Before he spoke or moved, Victor focused on the System message floating before his eyes:

*****Congratulations! You have achieved Level 74 Berserker of Unstoppable Momentum and gained 9 strength, 14 vitality, 9 agility, and 9 dexterity.*****

"Really?" he grunted. It seemed to him the golem had been far too easy to slay to grant him an entire level, but he supposed it wasn't something he'd complain about.

"Your Grace?" Bryn called from somewhere above and behind him. He grunted again, pushing himself to his feet, and looked to see Bryn and Feist standing atop the golem's chest. Florent was *inside*, peering out through one of the rips Lifedrinker had made. Thinking of his axe, Victor whirled around but relaxed when he saw her resting where he'd left her, blade half-buried in the stone of the cavern's floor.

"How long was I out?"

"Just about ten minutes or so, milord. This monstrosity certainly spilled a great amount of Energy for you."

"Yeah." Victor frowned, moving to look past the golem at the rest of the cavern. The enormous metal wall drew his eye. More pointedly, the gigantic vault-style door at its center seemed to call his name; whatever was in the mountain, whatever had been reaching out to him through his instincts or his blood or his spirit—it was beyond that wall.

"Your Grace," Florent's voice came to him, echoing oddly from inside the golem's chest, "there are quite a few likely valuable components inside this automaton."

"We'll talk about that in a minute. Did any of you examine that door?"

Victor pulled Lifedrinker from the stone with a grunt, hefting her over his shoulder, wincing as her enormous weight pressed down on his scale armor. As he strode toward the door—easily five hundred yards distant, he heard his companions scurrying down from the golem's corpse. Bryn called out, "No! We didn't want to leave you, and it didn't seem like anything was urgent about it."

Victor heard her, but he didn't respond. He was too focused on a shiny square of silver-colored metal beside the enormous vault door. His eyes were good, not quite good enough to read them, but good enough to see letters etched into the metal. Bryn jogged to catch up to him, and when she was beside him, she asked, "I saw you fight in the garden and against Thorn, but Victor, I didn't realize you were that *big*. Did your bloodline advancement increase your, um, giant size?"

"Titan," Victor rumbled absently, but her words cut through his focus, and he paused, turning to look back toward the ruined metal golem. "How big do you figure that thing is?"

Feist and Florent were jogging toward them, and the Spatial Magus answered, "Approximately forty feet tall and hundreds of tons in weight, milord."

Victor looked down at Bryn. "How tall was I compared to that thing?"

"Maybe three-fourths." She glanced to Florent and Feist for confirmation.

"That's right, milord," Feist said, nodding. "I'd say your fearsome helmet was about midway between the thing's head and its waist."

Victor nodded, scratching his chin. "Yeah, Bryn, I guess so. It's weird, 'cause I thought when I took that form, I was already at my, uh, bloodline's potential. I guess I was wrong."

"I can't claim to have ever seen a titan, Your Grace," Florent said, slowing to a stop as he reached Victor's position, "but there are many myths likening them to mountains, so . . ." He trailed off, allowing his words to build their own implications in everyone's mind. Victor only nodded. Was it a coincidence that Florent was the second person in as many days to talk to him about mountains in relation to titans?

"Let's see what that plaque says." Victor turned and started walking again, his long strides forcing the others to hurry.

"Plaque?" They'd already covered half the distance, but still, Bryn had to squint at the vault door for several seconds before she said, "Oh! I see it."

When they stood before the door, it dwarfed even Victor. It was easily twenty feet in diameter, though the keyhole in the spinning locking lever was sized for a normal—giant-sized—key. Victor looked at the plaque and read aloud, "By decree of His Majesty, Longar Fray, Sovereign of Iron Mountain, this passage is sealed for all eternity. Let none dare trespass beyond this point. To linger here is death, for the full measure of our king's wrath shall fall upon any who violate this sacred order."

Victor turned back to the enormous, broken form of the metal golem. "You figure that thing was the guardian?"

"I see nothing else that it could be, milord," Florent agreed.

"Um, who was Longar Fray?" Bryn asked.

"Sounds like he was calling himself a king, doesn't it?" Feist asked.

Victor ignored them as they continued to speculate, leaning close to peer into the keyhole. It looked very complex—grooves arranged in a half-moon for multiple key tines seemed to go very deep. Compulsively, he reached up and tried to turn the wheel, but it didn't budge. "I need to get past this door."

Florent cleared his throat. "Milord, if the man who made this door was the lord of Iron Mountain, perhaps the key is in the palace."

Victor backed up several paces, looking up and down the metal wall. "It must have cost a fortune to build a wall like this. That metal *feels* dense. Can you guys feel that Energy in it?"

Florent nodded. "I certainly can, milord, and you're not wrong—that metal is amber ore."

"*Holy shit!*" Victor smacked his head, remembering the treasure he and Thayla had stumbled upon when they were thralls in the Greatbone Mine. They'd found crates of ore like this—maybe a ten-thousandth of what was represented by the wall before them—and it had made a fortune for Lam. "So, if I need to smash my way through, I'll probably have to break the stone and tunnel under it."

"I wouldn't advise such measures, milord." Florent moved past him to point at the runes etched into the metallic barrier. "This wall is fortified with dense enchantments. I believe it likely has deep footings. Even if it doesn't, I can't imagine the crafters of such a formidable barrier wouldn't think of the possibility you suggested. If I were intent on keeping people out, I'd enchant the wall to collapse the surrounding stone rather than allow a breach."

Victor turned and scanned the cavern again, ensuring he hadn't missed anything. After a long, fruitless perusal, he looked at Florent. "Can you make a portal here? I mean to and from?"

"Yes, milord. I can create an anchor here."

"All right. Bryn, Feist, you two will wait here. I'm going back to the palace to see if we can find a key. If not, I'll bring some Elementalists, and we'll try crafting a tunnel under this wall. We can start farther back and go deep, hopefully avoiding any traps."

Bryn nodded. "A clever plan, Your Grace." He thought it was funny how she reverted to formal language when Fest and Florent were close, but he supposed it was for the best; she was trying to set an example for her squire.

"Your Grace, that may work, but it's a rather remote possibility, and such a tunnel would take some time to construct—"

Victor waved a hand, cutting Florent off. "I don't care what it takes, my friend; I'm going through that wall. If I have to bring the fucking mountain down around it, I will." Victor didn't mean to speak so vehemently, but the call was getting very strong, the urgency eating at him like a constantly overfull bladder. He nodded to Florent. "Go ahead. Make your portal."

"Milord," Bryn said as Florent gathered his strange, potent Energy, "might I suggest you bring that craftsman working for you? In our small conversations, he mentioned that he specializes in crafting constructs. It seems to me he might be very intrigued by yonder automaton."

Victor grinned and held out a massive fist. "That's a damn good idea."

Bryn smiled, her brown eyes glinting brightly in the fiery light of the cavern as she wound up and gave Victor's much larger fist a solid punch. Victor's middle knuckle popped, making the impact even louder, and he laughed. "Hell yeah, Bryn!" He nodded to her and then Feist. "Keep in touch. If all goes well, we'll be back really soon." The portal flared to life behind him as he spoke, sizzling and popping with Florent's black-tinted Energy.

"It's ready, Your Grace!"

Victor nodded, then stepped into the void.

# 31

## THE KEY

Yes, Your Grace, according to the historical documents, Longar Fray was King of Iron Mountain some three thousand and twenty years ago. It was his son, Cadman, who first took the oath and joined the Empire."

Victor nodded and gave the young man another appraising look. He was another Haveshi—Draj's fourth son, Sonland, the senior archivist for the duchy. "But I thought Iron Mountain was part of Xan. Was that not the case?"

"Not initially, Your Grace. Iron Mountain was a kingdom in its own right when the Empire was first formed. The kingdom fell to Xan seventy-four years later. Originally, the two nations signed a one-hundred-year treaty, but Fray's bloodline died out following the war, and when Toradan, King of Xan, sought to make the merger permanent, no one from Iron Mountain stood against him." Sonland spoke with a clipped precision and often paused to adjust his strange crystalline spectacles. As he completed his sentences, he had a habit of nodding as though he were confirming his words to himself.

"If Cadman was King of Iron Mountain when the empire was formed, what happened to Longar?"

"Records from that time are limited, Your Grace, but I found no indication that he died. A few archived correspondences indicate that he was 'seeking enlightenment' when he passed the rule on to his son. At that time, Ruhn did not have open trade routes with Sojourn, so some of their language was archaic. Still, I believe that the 'enlightenment' he sought was related to him being a steel seeker."

Victor rubbed the back of his neck, shifting in his seat. He wasn't tired, not physically; his body felt limber and rested after the massive Energy infusion he'd taken in upon slaying the guardian golem. However, he'd been waiting around for hours and was ready to get back to his quest. "So, he became a veil walker and left? That's your opinion?"

"I believe so, milord. I've not found any record of him reappearing on Ruhn."

"Okay, this is all very interesting, Sonland, but can you tell me if Longar Fray lived here? In this palace?"

The young man nodded, reaching up to adjust his glasses again. "Yes, milord, this has been the seat of Iron Mountain's ruling house for nearly four thousand years."

Victor looked around the library with renewed respect; it was hard for him to fathom four thousand years, let alone a palace that was that old. He'd never been much of a scholar in school, but he could remember learning about ancient Greece and thinking about how impossibly old those structures pictured in his textbook seemed. If he recalled correctly, they were more like two thousand years old. How could this palace, in seemingly perfect condition, be twice that age? He had to chalk it up to people living a lot longer and to magic—two factors that certainly could change the course of civilizations.

When Victor had come to the library and requested information about Longar Fray, he'd been a little vague about what he wanted. He wasn't sure he wanted people in the palace to know about the vault-like door he'd found in the mountain. He still didn't know whom he could trust. "Was there anything else about Longar? Anything to do with the mountain?"

"The histories are ancient, Your Grace, and not very detailed. He was an adventurer king, though, and it's said that he spent many years on the mountain. He's credited with locating many of the richest veins of ore and slaying many ancient and powerful creatures that dwelled on Iron Mountain's slopes and in the depths of its caves."

"Any, um, warnings?" Sonland's expression told Victor that he knew he was fishing, but the historian played along.

"Warnings from Longar Fray, milord?"

"Yeah, concerning the mountain?"

"No, Your Grace, nothing comes to mind."

Victor fidgeted, feeling antsy. "Right, well, who do I talk to about finding a big key with multiple prongs from Longar's era?"

"A key, milord?"

"Yep. A key that wasn't made to open any locks in this palace." He held his fingers about eight inches apart. "It'll be about this long and have three tines, two of which will be pointed to the sides. I'm ninety percent sure it'll be made of amber ore."

"If it was meant to safeguard valuables, it's likely somewhere in the ducal treasury vault, Your Grace."

Victor snapped his fingers. "*Now* we're getting somewhere. Where's my treasury?"

"I believe it lies beneath your residential tower, milord. My father and Treasurer Evelda Gladston have access. I'm sure either will gladly show you to—"

Victor shoved his chair back noisily and stood; he'd remembered the gilded portcullis on the basement level as soon as the man mentioned his tower. Guard Captain Gand had shown it to him on his first day in Iron Mountain. "Thank you, Sonland. It was nice to meet you, and I'll be sure to let your father know that I approve of your appointment here."

Victor strode to the door where his escort—two household guards and a page named Reva—awaited him. Sonland sputtered his thanks and promised to be of service if Victor needed more information, but Victor just waved absently as he exited the library; he couldn't stop thinking about that door and his need to open it. "Reva, fetch Lord Draj and have him meet me at the treasury immediately."

"At once, Your Grace!" She snapped a sharp salute and sprinted toward the nearby stairs, her polished black shoes clicking loudly on the marble.

Victor looked at the two guards. They'd been waiting outside his chambers, stationed there by Queen Kynna to watch for his arrival, and he'd commandeered them for his own purposes. "You two don't need to follow me around if you don't want to. I'm heading back to my tower."

One of the guards, a tall, lanky fellow whom Victor had seen fighting in the queen's garden, answered, "Your Grace, we've orders to keep sharp about your whereabouts so long as you're in the palace. Queen Kynna—"

Victor waved his hand, cutting him off. "It's fine."

With renewed purpose, he led the way back to his tower. When they'd first arrived through Florent's portal, he'd sent another page to fetch Trobban, the Artificer, and Florent had gone to brief the queen on his exploits. They were supposed to meet back at his quarters as soon as possible, so it wasn't just his usual giant strides that spurred his quick pace through the palace; Victor was eager to get back to the mountain, eager to see what was beyond that enormous enchanted metal wall.

The library was in the northern palace annex, so it wasn't too much of a surprise to find Draj and Reva, the page, already waiting at the stairwell leading to the lower levels of his tower. Despite the very early morning hour, Draj was dressed sharply in a gray-and-black suit and looked alert as he bowed. "Greetings, Your Grace. I'm told you wish to inspect the treasury. I'd anticipated such, and I assure you that you'll find all is in order."

Victor looked at him for a long moment, realization dawning on him. Draj thought he was conducting a surprise inspection of the duchy's stored wealth. He supposed it made sense; it was probably something he *should* have done during the first day or two of his arrival. Wouldn't most new dukes want to confirm with their own eyes that their treasurer hadn't run away with the duchy's riches during the changeover?

He nodded and gestured to the stairs. "After you, then." Draj turned and hurried down the steps, and Victor followed. The treasury was on the first lower level, and when they got off the stairs and approached the gold-plated metal portcullis, Victor was surprised to find the treasurer, a mousy little woman dressed in layered crimson robes, already there, working to disarm the many wards.

"I sent Evelda ahead, milord," Draj said, looking over his shoulder. Victor had only met the woman once when he'd been introduced to most of the palace staff, and she hadn't made much of an impression. Still, she seemed pleasant enough, and as the portcullis began to clatter up into its recess, she turned and bowed low. Draj nodded to her. "Very good, Evelda. You may wait here."

"Just a moment, Draj." Victor turned to the little woman, noting that she'd kept her gaze down, avoiding eye contact. "Evelda, do you have a good accounting of the contents of this vault?"

"Every bead, coin, gem, and bauble, Your Grace." Though she answered quickly and with a sure voice, she still didn't look up.

"Draj, can you say the same?"

"No, milord. I have a general sense of the value and know where the beads are kept, but I—"

"Then I think I'd like Evelda to provide my tour."

"I—" Draj frowned, glancing back at the small woman, but then he nodded and stepped aside. "Very well, Your Grace."

Victor smiled at him and, as he walked past, gave him a clap on the shoulder. "It's nothing personal, Draj, but I'm curious about some of the older . . . trinkets in here."

Victor stepped through the opening into a short metallic tunnel. He could feel the thrumming Energy contained in the runes carved into the metal— runes that would no doubt erupt with deadly traps if Evelda hadn't disarmed them when she opened the metal gate. As he stepped into the expansive metallic chamber beyond, he could hear Evelda's shuffling steps behind him.

To his surprise, the duchy's treasury wasn't crowded. It wasn't piled with gold and gems and sacks of beads. It didn't have racks of gilded armor and weapons or stacks of antique paintings, vases, and statues. It was a rectangular, metallic room lined with similarly metallic chests in neat rows. Victor turned to Evelda. "Dimensional containers?"

"That's correct, Your Grace. All of the wealth is stored in them, save a few items that can't be housed in such a manner. You'll find them through yonder door." She pointed to a square metal door set into the left-hand wall. "A few conscious baubles left by former members of the ruling household, milord."

Victor moved deeper into the vault and motioned for Evelda to approach. He hadn't altered his size, and she only stood a few inches higher than his waist, so he had to lean down when he spoke in a low voice. "I'm looking for a special key. It'll be one of the oldest items in the treasury. It should have three prongs and be about—"

"I know what it is you seek, Your Grace!" Evelda scurried toward the far right-hand corner of the room and rested her hand atop the chest there. "When I was an apprentice here, I was drilled regularly on the contents of each chest. The objects in this one are the oldest, and I struggled with the many strange items. Still, old Undrona taught me well, and I remember the key quite fondly; it's been a mystery to the treasurers of Iron Mountain, you see. There's not a lock in the entire duchy that it fits."

"That's what I wanted to hear. I should've come to you first."

At his words, Evelda turned to him, and, for the first time, Victor noted that her eyes were like little blazing suns in her gray-skinned face. "Thank you, Your Grace!"

Victor couldn't help himself and asked, "Do you have Igniant ancestry?"

"Um . . ." She looked away again, turning back to the chest. "Yes, milord—from my paternal grandmother."

"You're familiar with the queen's ancestry, right? Ranish Dar?"

"Oh, yes, milord. I believe my grandmother was a cousin to the Dars." She hummed softly, and then, as a gleaming yellow-tinted metallic object appeared in her hand, she crowed, "Found it!" She turned to Victor and held it up. A foot-long key with three distinct prongs, two of which were angled to the sides. It was lengthier than Victor had envisioned, but a good bit of that length was taken up by the knob on the end, set with a golf-ball-sized ruby. "Milord, am I permitted to ask if you found the matching lock?"

Victor stepped forward and took the key. He turned it left and right, then slowly nodded. "I think so. I can't divulge what it's for just yet, but if all goes well, I'll put the mystery to rest for you." He glanced around the treasury and then, leaning close to Evelda, quietly asked, "Can I trust Lord Draj when it comes to the contents of this treasury?"

"You're asking me, Your Grace?" For the second time, the woman looked up with those blazing eyes of hers.

"I am. Call it an instinct, but I think you'll be honest."

"And honest I shall be, milord. Lord Draj submits a quarterly report on the Duchy's finances, and each time, he has me double-check his figures for the treasury. Never once has he asked me to alter the numbers to match a more convenient fiction. I cannot say the same for his predecessor."

"You've been here longer than Draj?"

"I've been here three hundred and fourteen years, Your Grace."

Victor smiled and nodded. "I'm glad we met, Evelda."

Still looking up at him with those bright eyes, she smiled, and her plump cheeks dimpled at the corners of her mouth. "I'm very pleased to have met you more personally, as well, milord."

Clutching the key, Victor nodded and then turned to stride out of the vault. Draj stood in the antechamber, his hands clasped before him. As his little entourage formed around him, Victor nodded to his seneschal. "Draj, I want to congratulate you on maintaining such a well-accounted treasury. Everything looks to be in order."

As he strode up the stairs, his guards and page in tow, Draj called after him, "Thank you, Your Grace!"

A few minutes later, after a short ride in his magical elevator, Victor entered his quarters and found Trobban and Florent awaiting him in the parlor; he'd left the door unlocked for them. As soon as he bid the guards and Reva farewell and closed the door behind him, Florent called out, "Any luck, Your Grace?"

Victor held aloft his prize, glinting brightly in the light thrown by the recessed Energy lamps. "Hell yes, I had some luck. Can you cast your portal again yet?"

"Nearly, milord. I can sense the cooldown winding away."

Trobban stood and walked toward him. "What's this about a gigantic iron automaton, Your Grace?"

"First of all, it's not iron. It's black metal, but it's a hell of a lot tougher than iron. I wrecked it pretty badly, but I think you might find some valuable components inside—maybe even something you could use for our project."

"I'm always eager to examine the work of other artisans. It sounds like this one might be quite old, yes?"

"Yeah, if my theory is right, it's over three thousand years old. I think an ancient king put it there to guard his secret. What the secret is"—Victor thumped the heavy ruby-topped key in his palm—"we're going to find out."

Florent cleared his throat and added, "The construct used a devastating Energy attack—more Energy than I've ever seen released at once. Luckily, Duke Sandoval was able to avoid it."

Victor arched an eyebrow at him. "You talking about that wave of red lightning?"

"Yes, milord. Your guards and I stood well back until you split the golem's focus with your axe. I believe it was unable to replicate the tremendous release of Energy without that gigantic sword."

"A focus, you say?" Trobban rubbed his chin.

Florent nodded. "Yes, it was severed in the battle but remains largely intact. I'm sure you could learn much from studying it."

Victor had begun to pace back and forth, unable to contain his eagerness to get back to the cavern and the locked door. To distract himself, he asked, "You spoke to Queen Kynna?"

"I tried, Your Grace," Florent replied, "but she wasn't here. She traveled early this morning to Gloria—meetings with her family or some such." As he finished speaking, he leaped to his feet and snapped his fingers. "Portal's ready, milord."

Victor nodded and pointed to the empty area in the center of the room. "Let's do it."

Florent lifted his staff, gathered some Energy, and released it in a torrent of crackling black sparks that seemed to rip a hole in the universe. As the gap expanded, Victor tried to watch, peering at that weird dark Energy as it sizzled and stretched the void at its center. He couldn't find anything to focus on, though, and soon the portal was large enough to step through. When Florent nodded, Victor used it.

He emerged to a new scene in the gigantic cavern. Bryn and her squire had set up a camp of sorts. They'd put up a sizeable pavilion-style tent about fifty yards from the amber-ore wall, and a wide area around it was fortified with spiked barriers—sections of metallic fence adorned with dozens of three-meter metallic spears. Another smaller pavilion was set up like a kitchen with a table, counters, and a cooktop. In a gap in the fortifications, Bryn and Feist stood, stripped down to their gambesons, sparring with swords.

When they saw and heard Victor emerge from the crackling portal, Bryn shoved Feist away and jogged over to him, red-faced and sweating. "You made good time, milord. Does that mean you were success—" She cut her words short as Victor held up the key.

"Nice little camp." Victor nodded toward the fortifications. "You had all that shit in a storage ring?"

"Yes, sir! I figured we might need to make camp during your explorations of the mountain and prepared accordingly."

Victor smiled. "You're pretty damn good, Bryn. Remind me to give you some sort of accolade when we return." While he spoke, he heard the others come through the portal behind him, and he turned to Trobban, who was standing, mouth agape, staring at the enormous amber-ore wall.

"Incredible!"

"The golem is over there." Victor gripped his shoulder and turned him so he could point out the black semi-truck-sized figure on the far side of the cavern. Victor looked to Florent, then back to Bryn. "Listen up, folks. I'm going through that door if this key works, and I think it will. You all might as well continue to fortify this position and hold it. I know you're all curious about what's on the other side, and you can look through, of course, but I'll be going alone. If there are more things like that"—he jerked his thumb toward the destroyed construct—"then I'd rather only have me to worry about. Understood?"

"Yes," Florent was quick to respond.

"Yes, Your Grace." Bryn snapped a salute.

Victor looked at Trobban, but the Artificer was already drifting toward the broken golem. "Okay, my earlier orders still stand: Only Queen Kynna can know about this place for now. Don't travel back and forth to the palace bringing everyone and their mother here."

Feist, who'd just jogged over, busy fastening the straps to his breastplate, muttered, "Why would we want everyone's mother here, Your Grace?"

"Exactly my point, bud." As always, the urge to go deeper, the pull on his blood, was nagging at Victor, and he couldn't stand still any longer. He nodded and turned toward the enormous circular door. "I'm going. I guess, if there's some kind of sleeping evil god or something in there, be ready to run."

"Do you think . . ." Bryn's words trailed off, and Victor glanced at her, seeing real fear in her eyes as she appraised the gigantic amber-ore wall in a new light.

"Listen," Victor said, turning to face them all, "I was mostly joking about that, but this kind of barrier wasn't made for anything small. Either Longar Fray was trying to keep something in, or he was trying to keep everyone out. We don't know why, so we need to be careful. Florent, do you have that escape portal ready?"

"Always, Your Grace."

"Then stand back here with the others." With that, Victor turned and strode the fifty yards or so to the door. He could feel the call, the pull, the push, and he knew, no matter what, he was going through this wall, whether the key worked or not.

"Your Grace." Bryn's voice was right behind him, and he turned to her, frowning.

"What, Bryn?"

"Um, if—if, um . . ."

Victor groaned. He was so *close*. He wanted to snap at her, to yell at her to back off, but he gathered his will and took a deep breath, pushing his impatience and the mighty *pull* aside. "What is it, Bryn? You can say it."

"If there is something awful, milord, some ancient dead god that wants to kill us all, should—should we close the door?"

Victor grinned. "So *that's* all you wanted? Hell, Bryn, if something like that happens, then do it. Yeah, I wouldn't want to unleash something like that on a bunch of innocent people." He nodded again, then held out a fist, and she half-heartedly punched his knuckles.

"I hope it's not something like that, Your Grace. Victor."

"Me too. Now get the fuck outta here, will you?" He laughed to lighten his words, and she grinned as she turned to jog back to the others. Victor turned back to the door.

His hand was steady as he held the key up to the lock, turning it until the tines lined up with the correctly shaped slots. When he began to push it in, he worried he'd done it wrong or that the key wasn't quite right because it got stuck about three inches in. He tapped it, twisting lightly left and right, and then it began to sink again, perhaps having cleared some ancient corrosion or grime.

The entire vault door vibrated almost imperceptibly when the key was half-way inserted. When it was three-quarters in, the amber ore began to glow with faint luminosity. When it was fully inserted, the key clicked, and the ruby shone with brilliant red light. Licking his lips in anticipation, Victor turned the key, and it smoothly rotated with a rapid series of clicks. He kept turning until it stopped after three complete rotations, and then he heard the workings of gigantic gears as the enormous bolts holding the door shut slid open.

When the noise ended, and the door ceased its glowing and humming, Victor pulled on the handle and, on noiseless gigantic hinges, it swung wide. The door was thick—at least eight feet wide—but it swung open with the lightest of touches. Beyond, a twenty-foot tunnel of solid amber ore stretched toward a circle of darkness. Victor turned back to his companions, watching him with weapons in their hands, and nodded. Then he stepped into the tunnel.

He'd taken three or four steps when the pull on his blood, spirit, or both began to lessen, and the stress of its constant pressure faded. He rolled his neck and took a deep breath, noting the air was much cooler than on the other side of the door. That's when, like a whisper he could hear with his very bones, a voice came to him. *"Titan blood. Long have I awaited one of our kind. Come. Come and hear my tale. Come and earn your prize with a favor."*

## 32

## THE MOUNTAIN SPEAKS

Victor stopped in his tracks when he heard the voice in his head. It was deep and grating, and the depth and gravity of it alone would have been enough to give him pause, but the words—the words sent his heart hammering as if it wanted to escape his chest. Had it said one of "our" kind? His mind wanted to dispute his memory or his comprehension. Maybe the word had been "your." Gritting his teeth, steeling himself for whatever might come, be it a fight, a revelation, or simply disappointment, Victor continued to the end of the amber-ore tunnel.

On the other side of the enormous metallic wall, the cavern continued, but this half wasn't lit by an artificial fiery sun. Enough light seeped in from behind for his Quinametzin eyes to pierce the shadows, allowing Victor to see what awaited him: a dusty cavern littered with broken stones that seemed to have fallen from the soaring stony ceiling over the years or centuries. Scanning the irregular cavern walls in the distance, he thought he saw a passage that continued farther, so he began walking that way.

As he went, the deep, rumbling voice reverberated through his bones again, *"Long have I slumbered, and long will I yet."*

Tired of guessing, Victor began to voice his questions aloud, "If you're sleeping, how are you talking to me?"

*"An . . . irritant has disturbed my rest these past few millennia. A . . . sliver of my consciousness stirs."*

"Are you a titan?"

*"World breaker—world maker! They cry out their names for us, but deeds speak louder than names."*

Victor reached the tunnel opening and saw that it descended steeply. He could feel something down there, like a pulsating, radiating heat.

As he stared into the darkness, the voice spoke again, *"Continue, child of titans. Let my voice guide you in your task."*

"Task?"

*"The irritant—a dungeon spawned of the Energy rich in the roots of my resting place. Once a distraction, a bit of noise to blot out the memories, now a thorn in my ribs, infected by something . . . other, an entity with rules and laws foreign to my nature."*

Victor had begun walking at the voice's urging, but now he paused again, staring down the slope, noting how a faint red-orange glow radiated in the depths. "What can I do about a dungeon?"

*"Once, another came here. A mortal warrior who hunted in the depths. He was greedy and guarded his discovery with metal he dug from my vaults. I didn't mind—a simple distraction, something to help me pass the eons. He stopped coming, but then the . . . other came. It hid the dungeon from my view. Bit by bit, it steals the treasures from the depths and pulls them away. It uses my own dungeon as a gateway! Bit by bit, it leeches the Energy from my veins—some for the dungeon, but most drawn . . . elsewhere. As my kin, you must deliver justice. Destroy the dungeon if it is no longer mine!"*

A sinking feeling in the pit of his stomach forced Victor to reach out and lean against the warm stone wall. Warm? When had the stone stopped being cool to the touch? He shook his head, refocusing on his disturbing realization. "Are you talking about the System?"

The voice came to him again, ponderous and heavy, each word slow to follow the one before. *"System? Do not speak in riddles, child of titans. Enter the dungeon. Destroy it, and if the Other dwells within, slay it as well! Earn my gratitude and honor the blood of your ancestors!"*

Victor turned to lean his back against the stone wall and, after a moment, found himself sliding down to sit on the tunnel floor. So many thoughts fought for his attention that he couldn't focus on any one of them. Part of him wanted to marvel at the idea that an ancient titan was speaking to him—a being big and powerful enough to claim Iron Mountain was his . . . resting place? Was he still alive, or was Victor talking to a spirit? Before he could focus on the question, another part of his mind clamored for attention: Was he really considering trying to help the being?

Victor was no "world breaker." He wasn't someone who could lay down to rest and have a mountain grow over him. If this ancient, powerful being had a beef with the System, then why didn't he just handle it? Why was he asking Victor to risk everything—to challenge the System's authority long before he was ready to do so? Worse, he felt as if his ancestors were in league with the titan. How else could he explain the call in his blood? The urging to move forward that had seemed to harmonize with the mountain's pull? Hadn't it grown in strength tenfold after he'd spoken to his ancestor in his bloodline vision?

Could Victor even defy the mountain's—titan's—request if he wanted to? The pull seemed to have relaxed as soon as he'd stepped through the amber-ore wall, but would it come again with renewed urgency if he turned to leave? Did he *want* to leave? This was the first being who claimed real kinship with him, and he was a . . . Victor didn't know how to describe a being so vast.

Frowning, he shook his head. He was wrong to say the mountain was the first titanic being he'd encountered. The Degh giants on Zaafor were supposedly descended from titans. According to Khul Bach, they'd been far more titan-like before fracturing their ancestor stone. How pitiful they seemed now, though! They were little more than overgrown humans!

Nevertheless, the being speaking to Victor was the real deal. Victor could *feel* it. He could sense the awesome power behind those words and all around him. Somehow, Iron Mountain *was* the titan and vice versa. Despite his uncertainty, despite his righteous fear of angering the System, Victor knew he wouldn't back away. He had too many questions and too many answers to gain by cooperating with the mountain. Hadn't Tenecoalt told him to start preparing to go against the System? Well, maybe he could do so without overtly declaring war. Hadn't he almost broken one dungeon already? The System hadn't punished him for that, only kicked him out.

"How," he asked, still sitting on the floor, "how do I break a dungeon when the System will remove me and repair any damage I do?"

*"Why do you tarry, titan-blood? Do you fear the Other so much? Master your fear, as all great titans do! Slay the beast that claims lordship over the dungeon. Its lair will be the heart of the place. Find the dungeon Core and shatter it. There will be no repairing such damage."*

Victor stood, brushing his pants off as he contemplated. The only dungeon "boss" he'd killed had been in the dungeon near Greatbone Mine, and he hadn't exactly hung around looking for a dungeon Core. Would it be so easy? Kill a boss and break some object, and then he'd be done? Would the System be angry? Despite his questions and qualms, Victor's feet began to move almost of their own accord. He didn't walk away but farther down the tunnel.

"How old are you?" he asked the dry, warm air.

*"Ancient, child. I've slept for longer than I can recall. I've watched the seasons change millions of times."*

"How do you sound so . . . normal? How do you stay sane for millions of years?"

*"I sleep, and I dream. You speak to only a tiny part of me, child. Remove this thorn, and this fraction will sleep a while, too."*

Victor wanted to ask how that was possible. How could a person fragment their consciousness, leaving most of it to slumber while a piece awoke to deal with an irritant? Did various parts of the titan's mind wake at different times? Hadn't it said it watched Longar Fray as he delved into the dungeon before the System took it over? Was Victor filling in too many blanks, or did that make sense? He realized he didn't know when the System had come to Ruhn. A thousand years to him seemed like ancient history, but it was, apparently, a blink of an eye to the mountain.

Just as he couldn't fathom existing for millions of years, he realized he couldn't properly grasp the mind of an entity like the one speaking to him. They might be—distantly—related, but that didn't mean Victor could properly comprehend the motivations of a being so . . . vast. "I could tell you about the 'other,' if you'd like," he offered, trying to see if he could get a bit more out of the sleeping titan.

*"A thorn. A nuisance."*

Victor continued to descend, and while he did so, he spoke, hoping the System was too busy to listen to his every word as most people under its dominion assumed. "Everyone calls the 'other' the System. I don't know how it got that name, but it controls Energy in a huge part of the universe. It rules over millions of worlds. It rarely speaks directly to people, but it inserts itself into everyone's lives by controlling their Energy, their attributes, their skills, spells, levels, classes—everything. It controls every dungeon on the worlds it rules over, and if you dare to go against it, it does what it can to see you destroyed. It—" Victor stopped speaking as he felt a faint vibration under his feet. The mountain had shifted.

*"Child, I am not ready to wake, but you stir my wrath. Shall I rise? Shall I bring ruin to this world and challenge the Other? Shall I ravage world after world? I feel my blood begin to quicken! Is this fury, is this rage? Do I feel again? Shall I return to the waking world? Shall the lesser beings scream my name in their lamentations and prayers once more?"*

The ground rumbled again, this time more violently, and dust fell from the ceiling as tiny cracks appeared. Victor felt his heart hammer as the furious magma in his Breath Core began to roil, responding to the mountain's waking ire. "No!" he screamed. "No, brother!" he shouted. "Let me be your axe. Let me be the one who strikes a blow for our kind and reminds the System of your power!"

Victor stood stock still, afraid he'd doomed Ruhn and perhaps other worlds with his loose tongue. He should have thought things through a little more—of course a titan like the one under Iron Mountain would have an insurmountably massive pride. How else would he respond to Victor telling him the System was ruling over him? As dust continued to trickle down, Victor held his breath, fearing another, larger tremor, and he slowly became aware of a different sound, a distant rhythmic, rumbling susurration. Was the mountain breathing?

*"I would slumber yet. You are young and tiny, but you have the blood. Yes, a small brother, but a hardy one. You will suffice, and I will grant you guidance and a boon, but first, you must do as I ask and remove this thorn from my side. Should you fail and die, my fury will spark alight my blood, and vengeance will be exacted in your name, young titan."*

It seemed a cliché, but Victor gulped—the first time he could remember doing so in light of disturbing news or events. His "favor" for the sleeping titan had just taken on a new level of gravity. If he failed to help the titan—if he died—it wouldn't only be him that paid the price. All of Ruhn would suffer. "At least," Victor sighed, imagining the ancient, powerful being going on a rampage against the System.

While the sleeping titan had spoken, Victor's feet had carried him forward, and now he stood in a great dome-shaped cavern. The warmth and red-orange light came from a pool of bubbling magma at the center. Caustic gases hung in the air, but Victor's feats and bloodline protected him from the poisons and the heat. He stepped forward, eyes focused on the pool because he saw something on the far side—a pedestal of stone cut in perfect right angles.

Because the mountain seemed to have calmed, Victor asked, "Can I know your name, *hermano?*"

*"Speak it not lightly, little brother: my name is Azforath."*

As he walked around the bubbling, stinking pit of magma, Victor said, "My name is Victor."

*"Victor. Yes. This is a suitable name."*

Victor grinned, pleased by the mountain's approval, and stepped close to the pedestal. It was about eight feet high, its top a perfect square of black stone about a yard on a side. As he drew near, the smooth surface shifted, and golden runes far too reminiscent of those in System City Stones moved just out of reach. Standing before the pedestal, Victor waited for Azforath to tell him what to do, but the titan was silent. With a shrug, he reached forward and pressed his palm to the smooth surface.

*****Congratulations! You have discovered the Crucible of Fire! Enter? Yes/No*****

The System message danced in his vision, almost mockingly. "So this is the entrance to the dungeon," Victor grunted. He felt a tiny echo of the outrage Azforath had hinted at. What bullshit! The System showed up on worlds like Ruhn after beings like Azforath had already conquered—created?—them and gone to rest, and had the gall to take over as though it were responsible for everything they'd done? It controlled everyone's lives, putting training wheels on every aspect of Energy-based advancement, and for that simplification, it took a tithe in Energy, freedom, and . . . glory.

That realization hit Victor like a hammer. Living, advancing, and thriving under the System's dominance meant nothing truly belonged to anyone. Everything everyone gained was done with the System snooping over their shoulder: every spell and skill, every level and class—all curated and approved by the System. If someone strayed outside the lines, it would offer a quest to someone else to come and kill them. Victor knew he was being watched. He knew Lesh's abandonment of his quest didn't mean the System had pardoned him. The System was biding its time, waiting for him to stray outside the lines again. Would this be that time?

"Do you have any words for me before I enter?" he asked the hot, smoky air.

*"Go boldly, child—brother. Take what you will and destroy the Core. I will be here to guide you further upon your exit."*

"And my prize?"

*"Ha! Spoken like a true titan. I will have your prize as well, little brother."*

Victor nodded, focused on the System message before him, and selected the "yes" option. Energy, pure and golden, pulsed out of the pedestal, washing over the stone, the magma, and Victor. As it passed, Victor's reality shifted, and rather than the lava-lit cavern, he found himself standing at the mouth of a canyon with high red-toned rock walls.

A roadway of sorts, paved in crumbled, sharp, obsidian-hued gravel, led into the canyon, where, perhaps a quarter of a mile distant, a high black stone wall stood. At its center was an enormous metal portcullis, and five rows of ten armored figures were arrayed before it. The figures were huge and monstrous—some with two heads, some with four arms, some with bat-like wings, and many with claws and scales and fangs. All wore rusty iron plate armor and carried oversized weapons—axes, spiked clubs, spears, and hammers.

Victor took a single step, and a System message appeared:

*****You have entered the Crucible of Fire! Fight your way past the seven gates to challenge the Lord of the Crucible.*****

"All right." Victor channeled Energy into his armor, cladding himself in wyrm scales and thick, tough hide. He glared out of the lava king's maw, summoning Lifedrinker to his hands.

*"Do we fight?"*

"Hell yeah, *chica*. We're gonna kick some ass." As he strode down the road, his boots crunching on the sharp stones, Victor cast Iron Berserk and summoned his banner. He exploded with power, his vision tinted toward crimson, and he reveled in the idea that he was about to strike his first deliberate blow against the System. He might not be ready to challenge the System directly, but destroying a dungeon it was using to siphon Energy away from an ancient titan seemed like an excellent way to dip his toes in the "disruptor" pool.

He'd be lying if he claimed his nervousness about the prospect had wholly left him. He wasn't sure the System would take his actions as a deliberate affront, but he knew he'd have to contend with some consequences if it did. In his mind, though, it was a moot point: he was Quinametzin. He was a titan. His ancestors told him that, ultimately, his path couldn't be contained by the System's rules. They'd told him to listen to his instincts, and everything in him said he couldn't say no to Azforath. What good, then, would it do for him to worry about the System's reaction? It would be what it would be.

The thought was so liberating that Victor lifted his head to the black sky and howled, invigorated by the freedom of a mind unshackled from fear. What was the point of fearing choices already made? The monstrous figures heard his howl and, though they'd been waiting, ready to play out some predetermined System-designed drama, they began to bark, howl, roar, and yip. Some of them broke ranks and charged toward him, and Victor felt the giddy anticipation for a fight that always made him grin.

He channeled his Sovereign Will into his strength and vitality, lifted Life-drinker, and cast Energy Charge, ripping up the gravel road as he tore down the slope to the lead figure—a massive two-headed giant wielding a gnarled, spike-studded club. As he drew near and had to look down to see his foe, he realized they were giants, but they weren't nearly titan-sized. Lifedrinker ripped the first enemy in half before he could even crash into the creature.

His charge carried him past the massacred foe to slam into a cluster of three, and then the fight was on. Victor waded into the mass of monstrous figures, swinging Lifedrinker like a baseball bat. She whistled through the air, and as her multi-ton axe-head impacted the monsters, she ripped them to pieces. Their armor was like cardboard, their flesh and bones like gelatin. The hot, dry air became humid with blood as it exploded in sprays and mists for hundreds of feet with each impact.

Victor was a machine of destruction, and Lifedrinker was his wrecking ball. The monsters were numerous—fifty, all told—but they might as well have been wheat trying to stand before a master harvester with the world's sharpest scythe. In less than five minutes, Victor stood over a mound of broken, gory bodies, the dark ground slick with viscera and blood. He looked toward the gate, expecting it to open, but then a System message appeared:

*****Congratulations! You have overcome the first of ten waves guarding the gate. Brace yourself—wave two approaches. Each wave will be fiercer than the last. Flee now, if you must!*****

Victor looked back the way he'd come and saw a glowing yellow portal shaped like a doorway back at the mouth of the canyon. He wondered if he'd be offered a chance to leave after each wave. Growling, he twisted his hands on Lifedrinker's haft and turned to face the gate. "Come on then, *pinché* assholes. Let's get to work."

# 33

## THE CRUCIBLE OF FIRE

Victor stood, chest heaving, atop the latest pile of bodies, the remains of the final wave of attackers sent to defend the first gate of the dungeon's "crucible." Gore dripped from his axe and from himself—every inch of his armor was soaked with it, dripping into the widening pool at his feet as the armor's self-cleaning enchantments worked to sluice it away. Grunting, he hefted Lifedrinker to his shoulder and stepped around the broken, torn remnants of his foes, glaring left and right, hunting for further targets for his rage, hoping that some still lurked among the charnel mounds.

His Iron Berserk had worn off during that last wave, and his fight had grown a bit more desperate, contending with the much stronger foes. Even so, he'd never contemplated failure; his Furious Battle Momentum had never let up, and as the blows of his enemies mounted, Victor's strength, speed, and ferocity had risen to incredible levels. Even now, as he glared around, seeking something more to fight, the world was tinted in deep shades of crimson, and his hunger for battle was unslaked.

Even without his active berserk ability, his natural regeneration continued to knit the cuts in his flesh and smooth out the lumps of countless contusions. He was distantly aware of System messages floating in front of his face, and though they irritated him, a tiny part of his mind knew they were important. With nothing left to fight, he stood amid the corpses, viscera, pools of blood, and gore and simply breathed, waiting—at first for something more to kill and then, as his rage slowly cooled, for his mind to come back to him.

The process was accelerated as a great mist of Energy rose from the corpses of his foes and poured into him. The waves of euphoria washed away his fury, recharged his Core, and finished the renewal of his flesh. His consciousness wasn't aware of any of that, though, as it drifted through strange, disjointed visions—oceans churning, geysers erupting, strange shadow figures climbing insurmountable slopes, planets colliding, breaking apart, and reforming as great beings traversed their broken landscapes.

When his mind returned to his body, and he saw that he knelt before the open gate amid the wreckage of his foes, Victor smiled, almost lazily rising to his feet as he scanned through the System's messages:

*****Congratulations! You have cleared the first gate of the Crucible of Fire! Collect your reward inside the gatehouse!*****

*****Congratulations! You have cleared the first wave of a group-rated challenge as a solo adventurer, earning a bonus to the value of your reward!*****

*****Congratulations! You have achieved Level 75 Berserker of Unstoppable Momentum and gained 9 strength, 14 vitality, 9 agility, and 9 dexterity.*****

*****Congratulations! You have increased the rank of your Sovereign Will ability: Epic.*****

*****Sovereign Will, Epic: As an act of concentration, you can apply up to 50% of your total will attribute to any two of your physical attributes.*****

"Holy shit." Victor's eyes were focused on the last two messages—he'd nearly given up on improving Sovereign Will. He ran it *all* the time, and the only guidance he'd gotten from Dar about the ability was to keep using it. It looked like his persistence had finally paid off in a big way. Before, he'd been able to apply a third of his will to two of his physical attributes. At this point, a third of his will was about 224 points. Now, he could apply *half*, or roughly 336 points. In other words, this upgrade had granted him another 112 attribute points times *two*.

"Two hundred and twenty-four extra stat points for free, *chica!*" he crowed, hefting his enormously heavy axe above his head.

*"We have bathed in the blood of your foes, and now we reap the glory!"*

Victor laughed, pleased by Lifedrinker's outlook. After a moment to savor their bond, he regarded the other messages again. Another level, which didn't surprise him, even though levels were supposed to be getting slow now that he was mid–Tier Seven. After all, he'd just killed five hundred foes, and the last few waves hadn't been pushovers. More intriguing was the fact that the System had just rewarded him for completing "group" content by himself. What did that portend for the rest of the crucible?

Victor walked through the squelching, blood-soaked gravel to the gate and looked inside. Sure enough, a black stone chest sat to the left of the pathway, flickering with golden System-style runes. The messages and the chest helped him confirm his suspicion that the System wasn't always listening and watching what he did. If it knew he was in the dungeon with the intent to destroy it, to help a sleeping ancient being strike a blow against it, would the System reward him? Would it be increasing his rewards for the difficulty of the challenge? Wouldn't it, instead, make things harder for him?

Of course, the thought brought to mind a dozen other questions. *Could* the System listen to him and watch him all the time? It certainly seemed able to send him messages whenever he leveled or did something with one of his skills or spells. Victor couldn't help imagining it was like a complicated network—constantly monitoring on a base level but only really paying attention when something specific happened. It *chafed*—feeling as if he was always being watched—but the idea that it wasn't consciously watching all the time gave him a little comfort; there was some wiggle room, an opportunity for . . . *rebellion*.

Victor had to face the facts; his current trajectory was leading that way. He might not be able to do anything significant yet, but if his ancestors and the very nature of his blood were steering him in that direction, would he fight it? Would he turn aside? Would he turn his back on that part of his nature? And if he didn't? What price would he pay to try to throw the System off, to operate outside it? How might an entity capable of conquering *galaxies* respond?

The mountain, the sleeping ancient titan, had grumbled about rising from his slumber and battling against the System's imposed control, but how far could even such a mighty being take his war? He'd spoken about breaking the world and others besides, but would the System even care? It controlled *millions* of worlds. If the System couldn't oppose a titan like Azforath directly, couldn't it simply isolate him or wait for him to wear himself out and go back to sleep? What would the System care if a few billion lives were lost in the process?

Victor sighed, pushing the thoughts from his mind; he had work to do and couldn't solve the riddles that plagued his mind by standing there in the gateway. He walked to the chest and unceremoniously lifted the lid, waving away the glittering golden steam that poured forth so he could look within. Two objects lay inside the chest—a brilliant, glittering, sapphire-colored gemstone the size of a baseball, and a brick of lustrous silver-hued ore.

The ore was dense, heavier than gold as Victor lifted it out, but there wasn't any clue about its nature other than the deep well of Energy he could feel within it. As for the gemstone, it was a similar situation. It felt incredibly potent and rich with Energy, but there wasn't any sort of identifying label tucked away inside the chest, and the System didn't provide any further enlightenment. Victor tucked both treasures away, intent on asking Trobban about them.

Part of him hoped the gem was what he'd come to the mountain hoping to find: an "Azurite Star." It matched Trobban's description, but Victor couldn't believe he'd already found one. It seemed too easy. Before moving on, he sat on the now empty chest and took out the Far Scribe book he shared with Bryn. He figured he'd delayed giving her an update long enough.

*Bryn,*

*Don't go any deeper than where I left you. Everything should be fine, though. There aren't hordes of demons or anything on their way up. Haha. Guard that door, and I should be back before too long. I'll update you if anything delays me too much.*

*Your Boss*

He chuckled at his lame attempts at humor and almost scratched out the "Your Boss" part, not sure Bryn knew him well enough to realize he was being stupid. He shrugged, though, and left it. He knew, if he were being truly conscientious, he'd warn her about the sleeping godlike being on whose resting site they were treading and probably about the dungeon he'd entered, but some lingering paranoia kept him from doing so. As far as he was concerned, the fewer people who knew exactly what he was up to, the better. Shrugging, he walked the rest of the way through the gatehouse and laid his eyes on the second part of the "crucible."

The sharp black gravel road continued for a hundred yards and ended at the edge of a lake of bubbling lava. Victor could feel the deep well of magma-attuned Energy out there and briefly contemplated pausing to cultivate it for his Breath Core. The oxygen in the air was thin, and Victor knew if he weren't Quinametzin and if he didn't have a magma affinity and the feats that made him resistant to poisons, he'd be suffering from the gasses that hung above the burbling, hissing, smoldering semi-liquid. As it was, he simply breathed shallowly and narrowed his eyes as the caustic blend made them water.

Stepping closer to the edge of the lake, he saw solid stone platforms or pedestals dotting its surface, leading away to the distant shore where, another hundred yards farther on, he could see the next gate. "So, I need to cross, huh?" He almost laughed. The lake was maybe a quarter-mile across, and he figured he could cover the distance in a few Titanic Leaps. Even easier, he knew he could use his armor's enchantment, Flight of the Lava King, to clear the distance in a matter of seconds. He wouldn't need to hop from platform to platform.

Nodding with a grin spreading over his face, he held Lifedrinker before himself, channeled some Energy into his armor, and activated the Flight of the Lava King. With a crackling *woosh*, his fiery wings sprouted from the air near the center of his back and cracked down, sending black smoke and ash whirling behind him as he sprang into the air, streaking across the lake of lava just as he'd envisioned it. He moved his gaze toward the far rocky shore and descended, ripping through the air with no resistance.

When his feet set down and he jogged toward the gate, gradually slowing his momentum with each step, he wondered if he'd cheated somehow, breaking the gauntlet by trivializing a crossing that was supposed to be a challenge. When his fiery wings faded, and he stood a dozen yards from the gate, he stared at it, waiting. He wondered if something would come through that he'd have to fight, or if the entire point of the second gate was to see if he could cross the lava.

The gate didn't move, but after two or three minutes, he heard a noise behind him—a squelching, hissing, burbling sound. At first, it had blended in with the usual sounds of the hissing magma as its surface broke with giant swollen gas bubbles. Victor whirled, lifting Lifedrinker high, only to see dozens of dark lumps of cooling magma forging through the barely liquid surface of the lava lake. They looked like stones being pulled by invisible lines through the thick liquid, moving quickly enough to leave short wakes.

Victor narrowed his eyes, watching as the first of the dark lumps reached the shore, and then, with a squelching surge, it exploded out of the lava to land on two lumpy magma-coated legs. "What the fuck?" Victor readied Lifedrinker and pulled a rope of furious rage-attuned Energy into his pathways, preparing to cast Iron Berserk. As he did so, more and more of the magma-covered humanoids lurched onto the shore, dripping molten rock around them that hissed and sizzled.

They weren't huge—somewhere between a human and a giant in size—but they were bulky, and their very nature sent a shiver of doubt down Victor's spine. How could you kill something made of lava? "One way to find out," he grunted, striding toward the nearest one. It didn't seem to have eyes or ears, but somehow, it knew he was coming. It squared off with him, spreading broad hands with glowing-hot fingers. Victor grunted, hacking Lifedrinker down in an overhead chop, aiming her massive, gleaming axe-head at the monster's crown.

To Victor's amazement, the thing reached up and grasped the sides of Lifedrinker's blade, halting her momentum cold. Victor's eyes grew wide with shock as the creature pulled, nearly yanking his axe from his hands. "Hell no!" Victor roared and cast Iron Berserk. Victor gave in to his rage as his muscles exploded with unnatural growth, and his figure stretched, towering over the monster. How *dare* this thing try to strip Lifedrinker from him?

He ripped the axe back, viciously raking her blade over the creature's fingers. They fell to the stone ground with little plops, but by the time Victor turned, lifting the axe high, ready to hack into the monster, he saw that they'd regrown. Worse, five more of the monsters were closing in on him. In his titanic form, they were like children to him—stocky, fiery, faceless, extremely strong children. Victor, his vision clouded with crimson, stepped forward and heaved Lifedrinker in a broad, flat cleave. Her impossibly sharp obsidian edge split the magma creature like a cleaver through taffy.

As the top half flew to the side and the bottom staggered and fell, Victor bore down and *roared* at the other approaching magma-men, activating Voice of the Angry Earth. The roar echoed through the vast canyon, shaking the ground, sending waves of magma over the lake, toward the far shore, and, nearer to hand, the magma-men fell to their knees or toppled backward, stunned by the force of his voice. Victor gleefully, *madly*, strode among them, ripping Lifedrinker left and right, sending chunks of semi-liquid magma sliding over the ground on steaming, hissing skid marks like monstrous versions of a snail's trail.

All told, he slaughtered thirty of the magma *things*, killing them before they could even muster an attack, thanks to the stunning effect of his furious sonic attack. When he stood on the shore, and no further creatures approached, he whirled to face the gate, only to see that the magma-men he'd first slain were climbing to their feet—new, bubbling magma-meat growing to replace the parts he'd cleaved away. Worse, the pieces he'd cut off were growing new parts! As Victor stared, his enemies recovered and more than *doubled* in number.

*****Congratulations! You have reached the second gate of the Crucible of Fire! Survive the magma sprite onslaught!*****

Despite his rage, Victor's will and the magic of Iron Berserk allowed him to regain his senses. Enough so, that he realized he might be working against himself if he went on another rampage. Would they continue to multiply? Victor bolted down the shore of the lake, breaking out of their midst and taking advantage of their plodding movement to give himself time to think.

"Let's try something, Beautiful," he grunted, lifting Lifedrinker high. He darted forward and brought her down, just hard enough to cleave into one of the sprite's shoulders but not split it in half. Once she'd gotten a good, deep bite, he let go, allowing her to do her thing. "Drink!" he screamed, kicking another sprite away and then jogging off. When he turned to see how Lifedrinker's ability to drain Energy was progressing, he was horrified to see another of the sprites grab her handle and yank her out of his comrade.

As the little *pendejo* lifted her high, looking almost comical with the over-sized weapon, Victor growled and ran toward him, channeling his Energy Charge spell. He slammed into his enemy, leading with his shoulder, and when he made impact, it felt as if he'd tried to tackle a brick mailbox—back when he was an ordinary human. The crash was thunderous, the shockwave enough to knock all the nearest magma sprites onto their asses, and Victor felt his Core pouring Energy into the shield to protect him from the forces generated.

The sprite was a sturdy, heavy, *strong* creature, but it wasn't powerful enough to withstand those torrential forces. As the creature exploded, hunks of magma flying in every direction, Lifedrinker fell to the ground with a tremendous *thud*, splitting the stone like a ball bearing hitting glass. Victor yanked her up immediately, feeling relief and pride vibrate through her and into his hand. "Sorry, *chica!*" he cried, mortified that an enemy had held her against her will.

*"Let us slay!"*

Victor grinned madly despite his lack of a plan. He turned and jogged ahead of the small horde of magma sprites, racking his brain for a new idea. He'd killed one, hadn't he? Could he just whittle them down with Energy Charge? As he turned to assess the field, he had a rapid change of heart. The magma sprite he'd "killed" was coming back to life—a hundred times! Each chunk that had resulted from Victor's explosive impact was growing into a new sprite.

*"Chingado!"* Victor spat, then jogged closer to the wall, running parallel to it to give himself more space as the much larger horde of magma sprites inexorably advanced. Mentally, he ran through his abilities, trying to think of one that could kill a sprite without splitting it. His gauntlet's lava lash would be useless, likewise his berserking abilities; what good would it do to make himself more deadly with an axe that could only increase the count of his foes?

He could switch weapons, but to what? A spear, a sword, a hammer? What difference would any of them make? If he hammered one hard enough to kill it, would that not splatter the magma? He could pull them apart—same problem. He could throw them into the lava, but that would only delay them. He could summon coyotes or his bear, but again, they couldn't harm the sprites without increasing their numbers. In the end, Victor figured he had two possible strategies.

His nightmare alter ego, Terror, could probably kill the creatures, draining them of Energy, but only if they were capable of feeling fear. Victor wasn't sure about that, and he wanted to keep his wits about him as much as possible, so he decided to go with his other idea. He sent Lifedrinker into her storage container, and then he began to pace back and forth, waiting for the horde of magma sprites to get closer. While he paced, he breathed in and out, deeper and deeper, gathering his breath, channeling the Energy that hung thick in the air.

As the front row of the magma-men closed the distance to twenty yards, Victor grinned at them. "Okay, assholes. You like fire, huh? How do you like *ice?*"

# 34

## ELEMENTAL LESSONS

Victor exhaled, infusing his breath with frigid Energy. A plume of frosty air exploded from his lips, instantly dropping the ambient temperature and bathing the front line of the magma sprites in its icy embrace. Victor's affinity wasn't with water or even simple ice—it was with something called "blue ice," and though it might be related to a typical water affinity, it was different, always frozen. He'd tried to manipulate the output, but just like his magma, it was what it was; there was no liquid component.

He'd even experimented, spraying his frozen breath with its flecks of brutally cold ice onto the ground, watching as it took ages to dissipate, never leaving any water behind. So, while his Breath Core's capacity wasn't nearly as robust as his Spirit Core, the Energies inside were exceptionally potent. Like his magma, his blue ice went a long way, and when that foggy, bitterly cold air hit the sprites, it bit into the molten material of their flesh and froze it on the spot. There was no eruption of steam; that would imply the sprite's heat was sufficient to alter the state of Victor's breath. It wasn't.

Victor's breath weapon wrapped its glacial embrace around the leading sprites and almost instantaneously extinguished the heat radiating from within them. They shrank in on themselves, contracting as their molten flesh turned to solid stone in a series of rapid gunshot-like *cracks* that rang through the cavern. Their glowing, fiery bodies turned dark, and as Victor backed away, peering through the icy fog to see the results of his efforts, he found that nearly a dozen of the sprites had slumped down, looking more like inert basalt boulders than monstrous humanoids.

"*Hell* yeah!" he grunted, backpedaling, giving himself a little more room for his next blast. He moved to his right, angling for the edge of the oncoming horde, and unleashed another gout of frozen air. As his breath stole the vital force from the sprites, he worked his way around his slow, trudging foes, jogging along the shore of the molten lake. When he'd reached their back line, he blew forth another great plume of frozen air, catching a swath of them in its icy embrace.

Victor turned his gaze inward, weighing the Energy left in his Breath Core, and saw that it was low, just tiny globes of magma and blue ice swirling in the space, languidly chasing one another's tails. "All right." Victor began to pump his lungs like a bellows, drawing the magma-thick air into his chest, siphoning off the rich Energy, and exhaling plumes of black smoke. Quietly, he thanked whatever magic in his Breath Core allowed him to use one Energy type to fuel both his attunements as he stoked his ball of magma-attuned Energy into a massive blazing orb.

As soon as his Breath Core felt full to bursting, he pulled a strand of the blue ice Energy into his lungs and blew out another plume of frozen air, this time only catching half a dozen of the sprites in its cone. Even so, he'd whittled their numbers down significantly. Where before, he'd faced more than a hundred and fifty of the things, he thought he was down to something closer to a hundred. Their formation was shaped like a teardrop—thick where they drew near to him and tapered where the stragglers got hung up on the inert forms of their frozen brethren. Victor continued to lead them in a circular chase as he, once again, drew magma-attuned Energy from the air.

It seemed that as long as he had even a tiny bit of blue ice Energy in his Breath Core, if he started a breath attack with it, his Core would convert his magma-attuned Energy on the fly, bolstering his attack. Unfortunately, it didn't seem to be a one-to-one conversion. Fueling his icy breath with mostly magma-attuned Energy drained his Core rapidly. It didn't matter; Victor had everything he needed to keep recharging his Core, and the creatures were incredibly easy to lead on a merry chase.

As he worked, he contemplated the challenge of the second gate; it was a good trap, he supposed. The magma sprites were tough, and killing them with anything other than ice seemed nearly impossible. Still, if this dungeon had been designed for "groups," what would the odds be that at least one member couldn't produce a similar attack? He honestly didn't know—would regular ice work? Was his attack only so effective because of the extreme coldness of his blue ice?

On the other hand, if the sprites were faster or had ranged attacks, it would have been a lot more difficult, even for Victor. As it was, he took his time, circling his growing garden of inert, seemingly dead sprites, dragging the living ones through it, getting them hung up, and blasting them with frozen breath whenever he had enough Energy. It took him nearly an hour, most of that time spent building up his Breath Core's Energy, but he did it, whittling them down until, with a final blast of frigid air, he leeched the smoldering, life-giving Energy from the final cluster of magma sprites.

He'd breathed his icy breath so many times that the ground was white with it. The temperature had plummeted on that side of the lava lake so much that the surface of the bubbling, roiling body of molten stone had solidified for nearly a dozen paces out from the shore. Victor stood, hands on knees, regaining his breath as the System confirmed his victory—thousands of motes of Energy began to gather around the basalt garden of dead, inert sprites. The Energy gathered into a great pool of shimmering white, luminescent liquid-like pools and then, in a rush, flowed toward Victor.

As before, he was struck dumb—blinded and deafened by the euphoria that sent his mind tripping through now-familiar scenes. Later, as his conscious thoughts began to reform, he thought he understood something about the visions, a sort of pattern. They all had to do with growth or strife or creation—great challenges overcome by tremendous forces or effort. It was the inkling of an idea, but it was there, tickling the back of his mind as his subconscious worked on it. When he opened his eyes, he found more System messages awaiting his attention:

*****Congratulations! You have achieved Level 76 Berserker of Unstoppable Momentum and gained 9 strength, 14 vitality, 9 agility, and 9 dexterity.*****

*****Congratulations! You have increased your Breath Core's Rank: Advanced 6.*****

*****Congratulations! You have learned the Breath Weapon Mastery skill: Basic.*****

*****Congratulations! You have cleared the second gate of the Crucible of Fire! Collect your reward inside the gatehouse!*****

*****Congratulations! You have cleared the second wave of a group-rated challenge as a solo adventurer, earning a bonus to the value of your reward!*****

Victor initially celebrated another rapid level gain, but when he read the line about "breath weapon mastery," he stood, dumbstruck for several seconds, trying to wrap his head around the idea. How had he only *just now* gained such a skill? Thinking about it, he realized that, despite knowing how to breathe magma for a good long while, he'd only done it a handful of times. He never used it during sparring because who would want to be bathed in magma? Even Lesh wasn't fireproof.

In this battle, he'd crossed some invisible threshold of understanding, and the System had recognized his efforts. Searching the contents of his mind, thinking about "breath attacks," he found new thoughts—things he'd "learned" via the System's instantaneous delivery of knowledge. He understood better how to posture his chest, how to control his airflow, and how to properly feed the Energy in his Breath Core into the wind he exhaled. He understood that his natural form of "breath attack" was a cone but that there were other variants available if he'd only practice them.

"Holy shit." He laughed, surprised by the sudden windfall of knowledge. Of course, his celebrations made him reconsider his dark musings about the System only hours earlier. Was it overbearing? Was it a leech? Or did it provide an opportunity for people to wield power that might have otherwise been hoarded by beings like titans, dragons, and the Fae, to name just a few of the "elder" races Victor had heard of? If nothing else, the reward reminded him that the System and its designs weren't a simple matter of black and white.

As he walked toward the now open gate, his thoughts of dragons brought his mind around to Tes. Had she been "against" the System? It didn't feel like it to Victor. She'd mentioned that her homeworld, Aradnue, had driven the System away when it tried to insert itself into their affairs, but the dragons weren't exactly at war with the System, were they? Wasn't Tes working within the rules? Wasn't she, in fact, a member of some group called the Celestial Envoys? She'd been careful to warn Victor about elder magic, insisting he not share it, hadn't she?

Maybe that would be the path for him, too—apart from the System, but still working within it. Was it right to try to destroy something that benefited other people? Again, the questions only reminded Victor that he had a long way to go and a lot to learn before he declared war on the System. His actions in this dungeon, whatever they turned out to be, were a favor to an ancient, powerful being—nothing more. He chuckled as he lifted the lid to his second chest. "Yeah, keep telling yourself that, *pendejo*."

Inside, he saw something that made him frown and nervously press a hand to the wyrm-scale hauberk Tes had crafted for him—put her *own* blood into. It was a breastplate, a piece of armor obviously finely made and practically humming with the Energy that thrummed through its dense material. Victor tentatively stretched out his left hand, touching the cool, deep blue-black surface. It was smooth and slick, reminding him of the paint on a fancy sports car; though it was clear the metal wasn't painted or enameled, the luxurious sheen was due to the material itself.

Gorget plates rose up on either side of the neckhole, and around them and down the sides, the armor was lined with engraved and faintly glowing silver runes. Victor's studies with Dar—the many books the master had assigned him to read—finally paid off, allowing him to discern the import of those magical letters: They were enchantments for resizing, repair, and Energy absorption. It wasn't until Victor reached down to lift the breastplate out of the chest that its potency really sank home. He couldn't lift it with one arm.

Grunting with stubborn effort, he grasped the neck, sinking his fingers into the supple black leather of the lining, and pulled, only managing to tilt it up against the side of the chest. "What the hell?" The thing was heavier than

Lifedrinker. Victor brushed his hands together and then grasped it by the arm-holes with both hands, heaving in a proper deadlift posture, and managed to pull the absurdly heavy armor out of the chest, staggering backward with the weight.

He had a feeling that, if he bonded with the thing, it would get easier for him to carry, but he'd stubbornly wanted to see if he could lift it. Thus, having proven himself, he sent a trickle of Energy into the shiny blue-black metal, and a System message crowded into his vision:

*****Aegis of Charyssor: Crafted from the discarded shell of Charyssor, an abyssal leviathan found in the depths of the Umbral Sea of Maersh, this armor has been painstakingly cut from one of the densest, most Energy-rich natural substances in the known universe. Originally designed for the Behemoth King Dotra the Ever-Hungry, it was stolen by the master thief Lonagan Heart and discarded into the Endless Pit of the Vas'ra Wasteland during the Entorridian Uprising. With Dotra's demise, the armor is free to be bonded by a new bearer. It is a living artifact, capable of growth, healing, and the consumption and dispersal of tremendous amounts of Energy.*****

Victor read the paragraph, still staggering from the weight in his arms, his eyebrows arching in surprise. He'd never read a System item description like it, and it was clear that the artifact he held in his arms was special. What wasn't clear was whether he was even capable of wearing it. He *knew* he was strong, especially for his level, but even with Sovereign Will pumping his strength close to a *thousand*, he was struggling to hold the armor. It would be easier if he cast Iron Berserk, but he still doubted it would be bearable for more than a few minutes. He shook his head in dismay. Was he honestly going to have to set this thing aside until he got *stronger*?

Even as he contemplated it, he'd had to set the armor at his feet, unable to hold it even waist high any longer. If he somehow managed to wear it, he wasn't sure how long he could stand under its enormous downward pull—even berserk. "Well," he grunted, "at least I have something to look forward to." He reached down and sent the armor into his largest high-quality dimensional container ring, the one he'd taken from Fak Loyle. Almost immediately, the ring grew hot on his finger, going from an elegant silver-colored band to red to orange to white-hot in seconds.

In a panic, Victor reached in and summoned the armor out, dropping it to the stone floor with a thunderous crash that dislodged stones from the gate-house ceiling. *"Chingado!"* Victor punched his fist into his palm, then shook his hand as the ring rapidly cooled. He'd almost destroyed it! He stared at the armor where it sat on the crumbled stone pavers. There was no way he was going to leave it behind; it seemed that it was more than just a magic item;

it was a *legendary* item. He reached to his chest, where the vault sat under his armor. "If it can hold the ivid royal jelly, then it can hold this armor. Right?"

When the empty air didn't provide an answer, Victor lifted the vault off his neck and backed out of the gatehouse. He set it on the field where he'd killed the magma sprites and twisted the key, allowing the vault to expand with its usual show of sparks, steam, and clacking, clicking hops. He'd never put something too powerful into a storage ring before, and, in a way, he was glad to see what would happen; at least he'd had a little warning before the ring blew up or collapsed or whatever it would do if it actually failed.

With that in mind, he comforted himself as he dragged the armor into the vault; he figured he'd have a few seconds to get it out if things went badly. With the armor leaned against the vault wall, opposite his satchel with the royal jelly, he stepped out and closed the door. He stood for several long minutes, watching the vault, his hand held against the side, waiting to see if it would warn him in any way that the contents were too potent to contain in its miniaturized state. Nothing happened, though, and Victor, holding his breath, turned the key, activating the vault's shrinking magic.

It seemed to contract at its usual rate, and Victor didn't notice any more steam or sparks than usual. When it stopped, and he picked up the marble-sized vault, it wasn't hot. Still, he held it for several minutes, and when nothing happened, he expanded it again, looking inside to reassure himself that his two most valuable treasures were still intact. After he'd shrunk it again and hung the marble and key back around his neck, Victor quietly thanked the invaders from Dark Ember for the powerful Fae-crafted vault.

With that handled, Victor touched his hand to his wyrm-scale armor again, almost glad that he hadn't had to choose his new treasure over Tes's gift just yet. He strode through the gatehouse into the third section of the "crucible" and stopped in his tracks, feeling as if he was being watched despite the empty black gravel road that stretched ahead, meandering through the strange canyon walls to the distant third gate. He narrowed his eyes, scanning the walls of the canyon and peering up into the impenetrable darkness of the dungeon's "sky." Nothing moved.

He continued forward, his boots crunching on the sharp obsidian gravel, and summoned Lifedrinker to his hands. It was almost funny to feel her weight, in comparison to the breastplate, and find her easy to wield. "Okay, *chica*, something's out there. You ready for—"

Victor's words were cut short as the road a dozen yards ahead of him exploded in a shower of stinging, razor-sharp, stony projectiles. He leaped backward, ducking his chin to protect his eyes as the shower continued. He heard his enemy before he saw it, a rough susurration, as scales slid over stone and then great hissing screeches as it tore out of the ground and slithered toward him. It was a wyrm—a big red-scaled one with a crown of smoldering horns.

Victor didn't need to think about it; he cast Iron Berserk instantly as he lifted Lifedrinker and got ready for the assault. The creature didn't charge him, though; it didn't try to clamp down on him with its jaws that could probably bite through a small passenger car. It reared up, trying to match Victor's enormous height, and belched forth a massive cloud of black smoke followed by a hissing, crackling gout of fire. The flames hit Victor full in the chest, washing over him in a wave that felt oddly like standing in a hot shower.

In his fury, Victor laughed cruelly, baring his teeth and roaring into the wyrm's fire. The poor creature couldn't have known how ineffective its flame attack would be. How could it know that Victor had a magma-attuned Breath Core? How could it know that his titan bloodline was resistant to the elements? How could it know about his brush with fiery death and his acquisition of the Flame-Touched feat? How could it know that his armor was incredibly resistant to fire?

As the thing continued to belch forth a truly prodigious jet of flames, Victor lifted Lifedrinker high and cast Energy Charge, streaking into those flames and bringing the axe down with unimaginable force, splitting the wyrm's horn-covered crown to tear through scaly hide and bone, to bury her blade into its enormous skull. Victor wasn't sure if that was a wound a wyrm could normally live through, but Lifedrinker didn't give it any chance to regenerate. She drew torrents of fiery Energy into herself as the wyrm collapsed, falling like a smoking, smoldering giant serpent from a King Kong movie.

Victor watched as the great corpse twitched and the light faded from its saucer-sized yellow eyes. It was dead. Before he could even wonder if there were more enemies en route, he saw the Energy gathering around the serpent's body, and he knew he'd passed another obstacle. The System might not announce it yet, but it wouldn't grant him Energy unless the fighting was over. "That was quick," he commented as the surge of Energy slammed into him.

# 35

❧❦❧

# WYRM DREAMS

When Victor recovered from his Energy infusion, he was almost surprised by the scant couple of System messages waiting for him:

***Congratulations! You have cleared the third gate of the Crucible of Fire! Collect your reward inside the gatehouse!***

***Congratulations! You have cleared the third wave of a group-rated challenge as a solo adventurer, earning a bonus to the value of your reward!***

"No level?" He chuckled, grunting as he pushed himself to his feet. He regarded the gigantic corpse of the wyrm at his feet. It wasn't close to the size of the one he'd helped kill on Zaafor, but it was definitely no baby. He figured, from the tip of its fang-filled maw to the tapered point of its distant tail, the thing was seventy or eighty feet long. He might not have gained a level or any skill advancements from his quick battle with the thing, but that didn't mean he couldn't claim his *own* bonus reward.

Grinning, Victor summoned a sharp knife from his storage ring and ran his eyes over the lengthy corpse. "Where's your heart, eh, *hermano?*" He got to work trying to find it, slicing lengthwise along a tough ridge of thick, scaly flesh between the wyrm's under-scales and its much harder back scales. When he found the heart, something in his gut told him it was wrong, and that's when he remembered that the great ancient wyrm they'd slain on Zaafor had multiple hearts. Would it matter which one he ate? It felt as though it would. He couldn't verbalize the reason, but instinctually, he knew he had the wrong one.

So, nearly forty minutes later, Victor sat staring at not one but three bloody organs, one of which was a good deal larger than the others. "So, this was your first one, wasn't it, *hermano?*" He had a vague memory of Tes explaining that wyrms developed extra hearts as their bodies grew too large for one to circulate the blood properly. It didn't quite make sense to Victor; when he doubled in size, so did his heart, but maybe it had something to do with the *length* of a wyrm's body.

Shrugging, Victor picked up the big glistening organ and contemplated storing it away. As he hefted it, though, sticky and lukewarm in his hand, his stomach rumbled, and a slow grin spread his lips. Without further ado, he bit into it, savoring the hot, coppery tang and the surge of Energy that seeped into his blood, even as he chewed the tough meat. It took him a few minutes to chew through all the tough meat—the heart was the size of a Christmas ham. Still, it was good, at least to Victor's Quinametzin tastebuds, and when he swallowed the last bite, he could feel it churning in his gut, spreading its potent elixir of Energy, spirit, and secrets of the blood.

He took a staggering step back, his heel catching on the downed Wyrm, so he fell against it, sitting on the sharp, bloody obsidian, his back against the great creature's still-warm flesh. He tried to focus, instinctively resisting the pull of oblivion as a wave of tingling, itching, numbing sensation spread through his body, starting with his gut and working outward toward his extremities. His vision darkened, and a wave of exhaustion washed over him. Victor closed his eyes, succumbing to its embrace.

*All he knew was hunger. All he knew was the need to fill his belly with something warm and bloody. He slid through dark passages, his body undulating, speeding him along with the contractions that rippled through the muscles under his scales. When the passage ended, he continued, ripping the soil with his breaker-horn, shoving aside rocks and pushing through the dirt.*

*It was dark when he exploded into the open air, but his eyes were keen, made for a life hidden from the sun. He saw them below, hundreds of warm bodies, standing amid the tall, soft, cool grass. What a strange world! The air tickled his scales, and the lack of heat cooled his blood, but his Breath Core saw it reheated. He flicked forth his forked tongue, tasting the air, and his stomach clenched with desire when he caught a whiff of the creatures' blood.*

*He tore over the grass, sliding between tall, smooth-barked trees until he broke into the clearing where the warm creatures grazed. They caught wind of him, but too late. He spread his jaws and bit down, his great fangs sinking through hide and muscle, piercing organs and snapping bones. As the thing thrashed, bloody and broken in the grass, the wyrm—for he'd yet to earn a name—reared up and pumped the bellows of his Breath Core, sending a stream of orange and yellow flames down to cook the thing.*

*As the rest of the creatures fled, he crunched and swallowed the charred corpse, working the four-legged, stupid, but delicious thing into his throat. As he snapped his jaws back together, he turned, savoring the satisfying lump still working its way down to his stomach, and began to glide back the way he'd come; he'd seek out his lair and sleep, allowing his body to use the fuel he'd given it to build his strength.*

Victor coughed, waking with a start. He shook his head, disoriented, but not for long. He recognized his surroundings and knew what had just happened: He'd dreamed a vision of the wyrm's former life. Before he could reflect on it much, he noticed System messages and focused his bleary eyes, reading them:

*****Congratulations! You have increased the rank of your Breath Core: Advanced 7.*****

*****Congratulations! You have gained a new feat: Wyrm's Fervor.*****

*****Wyrm's Fervor: When you slay a creature and cook its meat with your breath weapon, you create a special form of sustenance that will enhance your strength and aid your growth. This is a cumulative effect and will be most pronounced after significant milestones have been reached.*****

"*Chingado!*" Victor laughed as he cussed, shaking his head. "What a fucked-up System!" He looked around for Lifedrinker and picked her up, hefting her to his shoulder. "Did you hear that, *chica*? I guess I'm not done growing."

"*Good!*"

Chuckling, he looked at the corpse and contemplated trying out his new feat, but he could see it was stone cold, and it didn't appeal to him. His *instincts* were telling him the thing wasn't fresh enough. How long had he been out? Frowning, he set Lifedrinker down and summoned forth Bryn's Far Scribe book. He flipped to the message he'd sent her and saw two replies:

*Your Grace,*

*I appreciate your update, however curt it was. I'm sure you're aware, but the mountain moved for the first time in decades, and Magus Florent and I have been fielding quite a few panicked messages from the queen's people. I've assured them that you had nothing to do with the event. Since it seems to have calmed, I'm hopeful that our operation here will go unmolested by the queen or her agents. Your man, Trobban, has been hard at work disassembling the giant automaton. He's rather thrilled with what he's found thus far, though I'd be lying if I said I could repeat any of the specifics—I tend to tune such matters out.*

*Ever your loyal retainer,*

*Bryn Tama, Unofficial Executor of His Grace's Orders*

Victor snorted at the title she'd given herself but also resolved to give her some official authority in the duchy; he was asking a lot of her, so it only made sense that she should be able to back herself up with the weight of a proper title. His eyes narrowed as he let them drift down to the next message.

*Your Grace,*

*We've not heard from you for a week now, and though the mountain is quiet and no horrors creep up from beyond the amber-ore wall, I must confess some worry. I do hope that you'll spare a moment to peruse this correspondence and deliver some small update. Thus far, the queen has only inquired about your progress once, and I fended her off with a rather clever response—that you were, indeed, progressing. I'm rather sure she's not happy with me, and I worry that her next request for information will be delivered in person.*

*With a heart ever hopeful that I shouldn't be spending my time hunting for a new employer,*

*Bryn Tama, Unofficial Executor of His (missing) Grace's Orders*

Victor laughed and summoned a pen, eager to respond:

*Bryn,*

*I'm alive, and you still have a job. I was out of it for a short while there, but I'm good now. If the queen puts pressure on you, go ahead and tell her that the mountain was stirring because it wanted me to do something and that if I don't do it, there might be a much bigger rumble, if you get my meaning. Tell Trobban I'm looking forward to hearing about his progress. As for you, Bryn, keep up your excellent work. I'll see you rewarded for your efforts.*

*By the way, how long has it been since that last message? I lost track of the time while I was . . . out.*

*Victor*

Victor put the Far Scribe book away and, while he was at it, looked guiltily at some of the others in the same container—his book with Valla, the one he shared with Olivia, the book Thayla had given him, the one for Dar, and the one he used to keep in touch with Edeya and the others on Sojourn. Those were only about *half* of the books he needed to read through, but he couldn't do it now. He had work to do. So, with a rather heavy sigh, he turned his attention away from the storage ring and picked up Lifedrinker. "Let's go look in our chest, *chica*."

*"With luck, the dungeon's ancient bounty will award us well!"*

Victor thought about her words. He was surprised she hadn't clamored for blood or battle. He voiced the other thought that came to mind: "You think maybe that's why the monsters and the treasure have been worth a lot? 'Cause the dungeon is old?"

*"I know not how I have this understanding, but yes, blood-mate—this dungeon has languished unchallenged for long and long. Its denizens grew in age and power, and its treasures multiplied and compounded."*

Lifedrinker's voice always strummed a chord in Victor's heart that somehow put him at ease, even before a fight . . . or *during* one. He loved it when she was in a talkative mood, so as he walked to the third gate, he asked, "Do you feel like you understand a lot more since your evolution?"

*"I think more. I feel more. I want more. More battle, more blood, more of your hands on me, more of your spirit mingling with mine. I want more metal and Energy! I yearn to be greater than I am. Together, we should slaughter all who stand before us, all who threaten those we love, all who dare to think of parting us!"*

"Holy shit, Lifedrinker." Victor was embarrassed to chuckle nervously at her fervor. He gripped her haft with both hands, keenly aware of her weight on his shoulder. "Listen, I want that stuff too, mostly, but there's more to life than that, right? I know, as an axe made for war, you don't really understand the concepts of things *other* than that, but maybe, well, think about what you saw me doing back when I didn't carry you in a dimensional ring. I wish . . . I wish there were a way you could experience something other than fighting—"

*"But I love to fight! I love to bathe in the blood of your foes! I love to feel your righteous fury course through me! I love our time together as we conquer fools who challenge your nature!"*

"I know, I know, *chica*. That's great, and I love you for all you've done for me, too. Let me think about this, though. I feel like there has to be more to your . . . *development*."

*"Think all you like, my gore-mate, my blood-heart. I will continue to dream of red rain and songs of terror."*

Victor didn't respond, his mind too overwhelmed by the mix of emotions coming from the axe; she was happy and content but hungry for violence, and none of those feelings seemed *wrong* to him, which was another thing for him to contemplate. He suddenly wished intelligence was his highest attribute. As he stepped into the gatehouse, he walked over to the chest, identical to the previous two, and lifted the lid, waving away the cloud of golden Energy mist that burst forth.

He almost laughed when he saw what sat within: a crown, obsidian-black and set with four hooked teeth or talons rising from the top edge, pointed slightly outward. When he reached into the chest to lift it out, it felt dangerously cold to the touch and strained his muscles with its weight. "What is it with this dungeon and heavy equipment?" Grunting with the effort, he held it up between his hands, inspecting the thing.

Its face was broad, probably the width of his giant-sized palm, and the inside was lined with supple black leather that, to Victor's memory, seemed a lot like the lining of the breastplate he'd received in the previous chest. The face of the crown was worked in an angular pattern and set with seven black gemstones. At first, he hadn't noticed them because their glossy surface matched the polished black sheen of the crown's metal. It was a beautiful thing, sturdy though it was.

With a slight frown of apprehension, Victor trickled some Energy into the metal through his hand and read the System's description:

*****Crown of the Dark Colossus: Forged in the fires of the World Heart of Tor-Bahl for the Colossus King, Brome, the metal of this crown is vestersteel tempered with dragon's blood. Set with the fangs of Angra'lovis'brakaan, the dragon-born assassin whose blood was used to temper the steel, and**

adorned with umbral opals, this crown is rumored to greatly enhance the wearer's strength, though only a mighty will can silence the whispers of Angra'lovis'brakaan's mad spirit.***

"What the *hell?*" Victor frowned, tilting the massive heavy crown in his hands. Those were dragon's teeth? It was *tempered* in dragon's blood? Part of him found the prospect thrilling, while another was revolted. How would Tes react to such an artifact? Were dragons sentimental about such things? She'd sort of made a big deal about using her blood to craft his armor, hadn't she? Or had she just said it was only fair, considering he'd given her some of his? As important as it was to him, the memory was a little foggy.

Victor wasn't an idiot; he could see how this item seemed to go with the armor he'd received from the previous chest. If it could really "greatly enhance" his strength, maybe he'd be able to wear his new armor. Was his will high enough to deal with the whispers of a "mad spirit," though? He didn't want to try to find out in the middle of a dungeon with no one to back him up. With that decided, he took a few minutes to add the crown to his growing pile of treasures in the Fae vault.

After he slipped the key and vault back around his neck, Victor picked up Lifedrinker and proceeded through the gate into the fourth section of the crucible. Again, caustic gas and smoke filled the steamy air, and he saw another lake of magma stretching away into the dungeon's strange midnight canyon. This time, rather than tiny islands dotting the magma intended for someone to leapfrog across, the road continued, though it became a stone bridge where it met the lake.

The canyon had a bend about half a mile from where he stood, making it impossible for Victor to see the next gate, nor could he see any defenders. Remembering how the magma sprites had climbed out of the last lake and how the fire wyrm had exploded out of the ground, he readied himself just the same. He summoned his banner, ensured he was still bolstering his strength and vitality with Sovereign Will, and hefted Lifedrinker, holding her ready as he stalked toward the lakeshore.

Nothing attacked him on his way to the bridge, and when he stepped onto it, out of the rough sharp gravel and onto dark basalt stones, nothing exploded out of the semi-solid surface of the magma lake. Victor chuckled—he'd expected to be swarmed when crossing the lake. With a deep breath of less-than-pleasant air, he started forward, crossing the molten surface under a haze of gasses and vapors. He idly wondered what the temperature was in that canyon and how bad the air would have been for a normal person.

Could he have even walked in this dungeon when he was new to Fanwath—a human with no Core? How different he was! How different his *life* was! Could he ever have imagined that he'd be striding over a bridge crossing a lake of magma, carrying an axe that a pickup truck would struggle to haul? He laughed, and his voice echoed oddly over the molten lake. If he saw himself now, bigger than any NFL linebacker could ever dream, wearing armor that bullets couldn't touch, flickering with flames like some kind of hell-born warrior, his old self would have shit himself.

As he walked, the rest of the canyon, up to the next gate, slowly revealed itself, and Victor saw that an expansive open area stretched out from the lake shore, and an army stood there, arrayed for battle. They weren't monstrous humanoids like at the first gate. No, these beings looked far more formidable. They were humanoid in shape, but they weren't misshapen or stricken with seemingly random mutations. These figures were lithe and graceful in their movements—tall, angular, and dark, their flesh glinting like polished black glass.

He figured they were all between ten and fifteen feet in height, but their arms and legs were long and lean, their hooked fingers resting on the ground as they stood ready. A thousand smoldering red eyes stared at him as he stopped and took in the sight of the army. They wore no equipment, but it didn't look as if they'd need any; their hook-like fingers looked as though they could rend steel, and their skin looked harder than metal.

As he stood there, wondering if he should lure them onto the bridge so he wouldn't have to face so many at once, he heard something behind him, the click of stone on stone, and whirled to see, halfway between him and the far shore, another army of the dark figures advancing. As he watched, slowly nodding, his mind grappling with the challenge before him, stone rumbled, and a hundred cave openings appeared in the canyon walls. Glowering red eyes tracked him from their depths. "Shit," he breathed.

*****Congratulations! You have reached the fourth gate of the Crucible of Fire! Survive the obsidian lurker ambush!*****

# 36

### LIFEDRINKER'S BITE

Victor existed in a haze of mad fury and a blind need for destruction. His consciousness had narrowed to a pinpoint focus on the world in front of him and the target of his axe. Besides rage, the only other emotion that brushed the surface of his waking mind was wild, cruel glee as he slaughtered one foe after another. If he could step outside himself and watch the destruction he wrought, he might have been stunned by the carnage. He moved like a piece of construction equipment—a backhoe or bulldozer or excavator—ponderous and unstoppable as he waded through the hordes of obsidian lurkers.

Lifedrinker's razored, glass-smooth blade glowed white-hot with her matching fury and battle lust, and as she bit through each gemstone-hard lurker carapace, the sound of her rending echoed through the canyon like the screams of dying angels. The lurkers felt no pain. They didn't cry out or stop fighting as Lifedrinker took their limbs—they pressed the fight, scrambling over one another for a chance to stab their diamond-hard hooked talons into Victor.

When the battle started, Victor wasn't so incensed, so incapable of strategy. He'd cast Iron Berserk and gotten to work on the hordes of monstrous creatures, using his Energy Charge and Flight of the Lava King whenever they were off cooldown to keep from being swarmed. Even so, each engagement resulted in stabs and gashes, and with the very first wound, his Furious Battle Momentum began the countdown to his unshackled, mindless fury.

And so it went, for minutes and minutes, Victor battled, and inch by inch, he lost his mind. With each hard claw that punched through his wyrm-scale vest, more rage surged into the special pathway that ran parallel to his other one, mingling with his blood, his bones, and his very cells, driving him wild with anger. His thick hide leggings could slow the piercing, grabbing claws, but not enough to keep his flesh whole. Blood flowed, and Victor screamed, and the battle raged on.

Despite his madness, Victor kept to the bridge. They came to him, a never-ending tide of heaving, thrashing, clawing, long-limbed, silently menacing foes. His blows were wild and powerful, his axe like a bladed wrecking ball as he stood and cleaved, throwing bodies and parts of bodies over the sides of the bridge into the barely liquid magma-filled gorge. The piles of obsidian-fleshed corpses mounted upward, macabre tributes to the destruction he wrought.

Despite his strength and speed, his wounds added up, and though his rage-fueled regeneration mended his cuts and his armor worked to repair itself, his Core drained at a steady rate. If he'd had the mind to wonder, he might have been worried about what would happen when his Core ran dry. His Furious Battle Momentum wasn't something he controlled—that tendril of rage-attuned Energy flowed into its pathway regardless of his desires—but what would happen if there was no more rage to pull?

As the count of his defeated foes climbed into the hundreds and Victor's frenzied swings became so fast that even Lifedrinker, in all her thousands of pounds of impossibly dense metal, cut the air in a blur, the Paragon of the Axe showed its first ghostly visage. Lifedrinker's blows began to land against foes lined up *behind* the front row of Victor's aggressors. As she cleaved a row of lurkers physically, the Paragon did its psychic damage to the poor wretches behind them. With each mighty, lightning-fast sweep of his great axe, Victor demolished a dozen or more of his enemies.

The press of obsidian bodies grew less intense as he swept the bridge before him clear, hacking, turning, hacking, and so on. Hunks of his foes flew through the air, their black, ichor-like blood spewing into the air to fall like a dark, tacky rain that sizzled and popped on the magma lake's surface. Steam filled the air, and Victor's maniac grin widened as he advanced along the bridge.

His armor hung in shreds, too torn to rapidly mend. His body was drenched in sweat, blood, and the steam of his foes' blood. His flesh was whole, however, and the drain on his Core had lessened now that the Paragon of the Axe was with him. That ghostly blade, echoing Lifedrinker's white-hot shape, stretched out, effortlessly slicing through the lurkers that dared to crowd closer or failed to retreat as he pushed forward. Lifedrinker's reach was enormous in his titanic grip, but the paragon added another ten feet.

As he whipped Lifedrinker in cutting arcs, he decimated the foes before him. When he felt them crowding close, he'd whirl, acting on pure battle instinct, and hack her in a great cleave that slaughtered dozens of the things. The vile, murderous lurkers had ceased their endless streams out of the caves, and, for the first time, their numbers began to dwindle as Victor pushed toward the distant gate.

If he could speak or understand the question, Victor wouldn't have an answer to why he fought toward the gate; perhaps some instinct drove him, some fighting desire to constantly press the attack. He was like a rabid panther set loose among similarly wild-eyed rats. The obsidian lurkers knew no fear and didn't hesitate in their relentless desire to rip Victor to shreds, but each time they were close enough, Victor swiped them away, torn to pieces.

The fight went on and on, and after a time, Victor reached the end of the bridge and pushed into the dwindling lines of lurkers, gaining a foothold on the solid ground before the gate. He didn't have to chase after enemies to fight; they kept coming—meat into a grinder. It wasn't until his rage began to fade and fresh-born lucidity blossomed in his mind that Victor realized he was still hacking his axe, though no further foes advanced. He turned in a slow circle and surveyed the carnage. Thousands of corpses littered the field or burned on their pyres—great heaps of the hard-fleshed creatures piled high on the semi-solid surface of the magma lake.

Some still twitched; one nearby clung to life and tried to crawl toward him, using its pointed hook fingers to drag its severed body forward. Victor stomped its hard skull, grinding it like the shell of a coconut into the stony ground. He spat, realizing some gore clung to his lips, and wiped his face on his forearm, only to smear more gore across his cheek. He looked down at himself, at his still-shredded pants and armor drenched in black filth. He hoped his armor would recover and clean itself, but his flesh beneath was hopelessly soiled.

Victor walked through the carnage until he came to a relatively clean section of the gravel road. There, he retrieved a barrel of water and some towels from his storage container and prepared to clean himself. Even as he pulled off his damaged armor, though, the System finally acknowledged his victory. A tremendous rush of Energy knocked him off his feet, lifting him into the air, driving his muscles into rigidity and his mind into senseless wandering.

He experienced a familiar cascade of visions, the kind that always flooded his mind when struck by an overwhelming surge of Energy: mountains erupting, planets forming and colliding, shadowy figures locked in titanic struggles— how he knew what each meant, he couldn't say; he simply understood. Though the scenes were like those he'd seen before, each was distinct, and this time, something new emerged toward the end. He saw a landscape of pastoral beauty, a hillside blanketed in lush, green grass. Resting there, bathed in sunlight, was a blue-tinted dragon—scales bright and metallic. Her golden eyes shifted upward to meet his, shining with a glint of recognition.

When he came to himself, it was like waking from a deep, restful slumber; he knew he'd dreamed of something meaningful but struggled to recall it. Victor traced the fragments of his memories, trying to pull the images into his conscious mind's eye, but he only saw pieces—snatches of color, feelings, and impressions. Had he dreamed of someone he knew? He thought for certain he had. He was sure it had been someone he missed, someone he wanted to see again, though he couldn't quite put his finger on who it had been. "Valla?" he wondered aloud, but it didn't feel right.

With a mental shrug, he looked to the System messages crowding his vision:

*****Congratulations! You have achieved Level 77 Berserker of Unstoppable Momentum and gained 9 strength, 14 vitality, 9 agility, and 9 dexterity.*****

*****Congratulations! Your feat, Challenger, has been upgraded! New Feat: Unyielding Challenger.*****

*****Unyielding Challenger: Time and time again, you have not only faced powerful foes but held your ground against entire armies, emerging victorious through sheer will and skill. The strength of your aura has become a force of nature, radiating defiance that breaks the spirits of those who stand against you. Effect: Enemies within range of your aura will feel the weight of inevitable defeat more keenly, further reducing their resistance to fear and causing those of lesser power to hesitate or falter when facing you alone.*****

*****Congratulations! You have cleared the fourth gate of the Crucible of Fire! Collect your reward inside the gatehouse!*****

*****Congratulations! You have cleared the fourth wave of a group-rated challenge as a solo adventurer, earning a bonus to the value of your reward!*****

Victor stood and stretched, smiling at what he'd read. After finishing what he'd started with the barrel of water, rinsing himself thoroughly, he picked up Lifedrinker and hefted her onto his shoulder. Though he wasn't berserk, she felt more manageable in his hands and didn't pain his shoulder as her tremendous weight pressed down on him. He'd gained a few levels, and each one gave him nine strength and fourteen vitality; it added up. Grinning, still feeling good thanks to his dreams and the good news from the System, he walked over to the gatehouse and approached his fourth chest.

If he'd known the battle experience and loot that awaited him in the dungeon, Victor wouldn't have needed any sort of quest from a primordial titan to enter. How could he complain about gaining levels, treasure, and feats? Chuckling, he lifted the lid and waited for the Energy mist to fade. Looking inside, he saw a single object, a bottle with dark green glass. He lifted it out, palming it, figuring it was about the size of a beer bottle. To his surprise and delight, it bore a label affixed to the cork stopper:

*Concentrated distillate of a Qo'lorian Essence Drifter: Drink to gain a permanent boost to one or more attributes.*

"Nice!" Victor almost pulled the stopper and tilted it into his mouth immediately, but he paused, rethinking the action. If it was a significant boost, and judging by his other awards in the dungeon, he figured it probably was, it might knock him out for a while—days or weeks, even. "Better save it." Wincing and ready to pull it back immediately, he carefully sent it into his storage ring. The ring immediately began to heat up, so he yanked it out.

While it was irritating to have to go through the process of putting it into his vault, the fact that his ring couldn't hold it portended good things about the "distillate." So, with a cheerful demeanor, he activated his vault, stowed his new treasure away, and then closed it up. He secured it around his neck, some deeply buried part of him thrilling at the idea of his growing hoard.

With a sigh and a stretch, he stepped toward the gate but paused to examine his armor. His pants had recovered, and so had his wyrm-scale vest. He ran his fingers over the scales, pressing and tugging on them. They seemed fine, but how many times could they regenerate? Was it an infinite process, or were they growing slightly weaker with each repair? He wished he could ask Tes about it. The thought brought to mind a faint memory—a great blue dragon in the sun—and suddenly Victor remembered his dream. "I saw her." His voice was hushed, a whisper, but Lifedrinker heard him.

*"Who, war-heart?"*

"Tes. I think I saw her when I leveled—when the Energy overwhelmed me."

*"The one who hid her teeth as she guided you through the wastes?"*

Victor snorted, smiling. "Yeah, that was her."

*"She liked me, battle-love. She said I was special—would that she could see me now!"*

"Yeah, she'd be impressed, *chica*. For sure." Victor patted Lifedrinker's haft and then stepped through the gate. The distance to the next gate was much shorter than the previous ones. He could see it across a barren plain of rocky, broken obsidian shards. Of course, he could also see its defender. The metallic warrior reminded Victor of the automaton he'd destroyed outside the amber-ore wall. There were distinct differences, however.

This being didn't strike Victor as being a construct. To Victor, it looked very much like a gigantic metal human man. It didn't have seams at its joints, nor did the expression on its shiny gray face look devoid of emotion. Its gleaming black eyes traced Victor's movements, and a scowl creased its metallic forehead, drawing its brow down as it snarled. It was titanic in size, something between twenty or thirty feet tall, and powerfully built. The giant stepped forward and stretched out an arm from which a blazing spear of light erupted, stretching to a length of twenty or thirty feet, flickering with the potent charge of its Energy.

"*Mano a mano*, eh, *pendejo?*" Victor grinned as he channeled Energy into Iron Berserk. His form exploded with size and power, and in seconds, he stood, eye to eye, facing the metal giant over the length of the battlefield. He took a single step, and the System chimed in:

*****Congratulations! You have reached the fifth gate of the Crucible of Fire! Defeat the Iron Colossus to advance!*****

Victor hoped the description was accurate. He hoped the thing was made of iron; Lifedrinker would cut it like butter. In a way, the defender reminded him of Lira, Ronkerz's Big One, who'd clad herself in a gigantic metal shell. Lifedrinker hadn't been effective against her, but that was before she'd grown, before she'd absorbed the "soul ore" and massively increased her . . . mass. "Okay, *chica.* Time to show this big metal asshole how you can bite."

"*Yes!*" she practically screamed. "*Yes, blood-heart! War-mate! Let us test my edge!*"

Grinning, Victor cast Inspiration of the Quinametzin, and as the clarity of its wonderful Energy washed over him, he crouched into a battle stance and stalked toward his enemy. The colossus moved, and it wasn't slow or ponderous. It leaped forward and to the left, significantly closing the distance between them. As Victor shifted to square off with it again, the thing pivoted and bolted into a charge, its great metal feet thunderously pounding into the hard gravel surface.

Victor lifted Lifedrinker, contemplating how to parry a spear of pure light, but even as the colossus closed to a mere fifty feet, it lunged, and the spear shot forth, lengthening to close the gap and punching into Victor's chest, just beneath his left collarbone. It had been aiming for his heart! The pain was enormous; it seared his flesh like no fire could. When the shaft of light recoiled, shortening to its regular length, the colossus raised it high, readying another blow.

The entire attack took less than a heartbeat, less than a single inhalation. The speed of the graceful metal giant combined with the lightning flash of the spear's attack was enough to confound any attempt to parry the blow, but Victor was no slouch, and he knew what he was up against now. As his titanic constitution and berserk regeneration worked to reverse the damage to his chest, he braced Lifedrinker before him and cast Energy Charge, fueling the spell with inspiration-attuned Energy.

When he streaked over the ground, closing the gap between them in a flash, Victor was confident that he'd strike his foe; had any enemy managed to dodge his charge? He was too focused to dig through his memories of countless fights, but he didn't think so. It was with some shock, then, that he realized the colossus wasn't standing where it should be, and he tore over the empty gravel-strewn field. When his charge ended, he whirled, only to be stabbed again, this time right in the center of his stomach. The pain was enormous, and he faltered for a moment, stumbling to his knees as the shaft of burning light burned through his spine.

Such a blow would have ruined most fighters; how could a man fight with his spine severed? It wouldn't be easy, certainly, but Victor didn't have to figure it out. He'd barely inhaled to roar his fury when his incredible regeneration reknit his spinal cord, and he leaped to his feet, his fury mounting by the second. This time, as he sprinted toward his foe, he watched that spear, and as it lanced out again, Lifedrinker's mirrored black blade deflected the shaft of light, and she screamed her pride and bloodlust.

The colossus drew its spear back, ready to launch another blazing attack, but Victor had closed the distance, and Lifedrinker was already arcing out in an upward-angled backswing. Her brilliant, white-hot edge met the colossus at the hip, and she tore through the fabric of his being like a hatchet through an aluminum can. Light exploded from the rend, blazing forth with burning intensity, and Victor had to use Titanic Leap to launch away from the burning plume.

As he sailed backward, he watched the colossus stagger, its Energy bursting forth like air from a balloon, and then it stopped, and Victor could see that its right leg, the one Lifedrinker had cut, had gone inert, like solid, dead iron. The rest of the colossus was still vibrant, still alive, and it took a step with its good leg, dragging the other as it rotated to put Victor in its sights. It drew back its spear, tracing Victor as he descended from his leap, and launched another lance-like stab.

Victor, mid-air, focused on the colossus's waist and activated Flight of the Lava King, streaking down beneath the arc of the spear's lance of light. He flew through the air, trailing flames and black smoke as he crashed into the colossus, his shoulder smashing into its rock-hard stomach. It might have hurt if the thing hadn't moved, but it did, toppling back like an unsecured light pole, crashing onto the ground with an earth-shaking *clang*. One thing about Victor—he wasn't one to hesitate to press an advantage in a fight. The colossus bounced once, and then Lifedrinker was buried in its chest, slamming it into the ground.

As light exploded from the massive tear, Victor leaped backward, out of the burning rays, and watched as Lifedrinker began to thrum and vibrate, drawing that explosion of Energy into herself, stifling the leak, and singing her bloody war cries as she tore the vital force from the colossal being. *"Hell yes! Get it, chica!"* Victor roared, his voice hoarse with rage, his mouth frothing as he worked to control the effects of his Furious Battle Momentum.

He still had his mind, and the fight was well and truly over, so it didn't take long for the rage to bleed from his pathways. When Lifedrinker stopped vibrating, and the entire colossus was dull, dead metal, he reached for her haft and pulled her out, widening the cut in the strange giant's metal. Lifedrinker's blade throbbed with veins of blinding light, and he knew it would be a while before she processed her massive feast.

Victor only had a moment to wonder if the fight was truly over, if there would be another defender of the gate, before he saw an enormous puddle of glittering, ghostly-white Energy orbs begin to bubble up out of the colossus's metallic form. The sight answered his question—the fight was done, and he was about to get knocked out again.

# 37

## HORDE

*****Congratulations! You have cleared the fifth gate of the Crucible of Fire! Collect your reward inside the gatehouse!*****

*****Congratulations! You have cleared the fifth wave of a group-rated challenge as a solo adventurer, earning a bonus to the value of your reward!*****

Victor blinked, reaching up to rub his eyes as he read the notifications. Was that his first victory in the dungeon that didn't result in a level? He supposed it had to slow down at some point, but he couldn't help but feel a slight twinge of disappointment. With a grunt, he pushed himself to his feet and regarded the cold iron corpse of the fifth gate's defender. It looked smaller, somehow pitiful, in its inert, lifeless state. With a shrug, Victor picked up Lifedrinker and stalked toward the open gate.

As he walked, thoughts of his most recent visions crowded his mind. He hadn't seen Tes again, had he? As always, the memories of his visions were far less vivid than he'd like, but he was left with the impression of colossal trials being overcome. Was the System responsible for the strange dreams? Were his ancestors guiding his mind as it was touched by torrents of rich Energy? Were the things he saw just random, or were they messages buried in his blood, in the fabric of his DNA?

Sometimes, he felt as if his mind was loose, ripping through the cosmos and experiencing things and places incomprehensibly distant from where he'd left his body. Sometimes, he also felt the distance was even farther—separated from his current reality by not just space but also time. Victor had heard people speak in terms of the "universe," and he'd heard people offhandedly pluralize that word, speaking as though there were multitudes. Was there more than one? Did they exist on different timelines, or were they separated by some fabric of reality he couldn't perceive? Could people move between them? Had *he*?

"The same old question." He sighed, reminding himself that he'd get nowhere down that line of thought. He'd chased it to too many dead ends when he'd learned about Olivia and the timeline of the people from First Landing, which forced him to view his *abuela* and his time on Earth as something that happened hundreds of years ago. But if they were from different timelines . . . Victor shook his head. "Focus on the now." He sighed, stepping toward his latest reward chest.

He rested Lifedrinker against the wall of the gatehouse. She'd been quiet, but he wasn't surprised; the evidence of the enormous feast she was processing still flickered in her mirrored black surface—spiderwebs of brilliant solar Energy, throbbing and flaring. Victor flipped the chest open, and when the Energy mist cleared, he frowned, initially thinking the chest was empty. When he leaned closer, though, he saw a black silken package on the bottom, blending with the shadows.

Victor tried to lift it out, but the hard rectangular object inside the silk wrapping resisted his efforts. Victor's fingers found the edge of the wrapping and pulled it away, heaving as the material beneath the object slowly slid free. Setting the silk aside, he looked again and saw a brick of red silver-veined metal sitting on the bottom of the chest. It was the second brick of ore he'd received from the dungeon, though it was far heavier than the silver-hued one he'd gotten from the first gate.

Victor refused to be bested by something so small; he wrapped his hands around it, heaving with his back to pull it out of the chest. Grunting, he shrugged and curled his arms, lifting it to his chest to look down at the metal, wondering if there were any clues to its nature or origin. No engravings or labels met his eyes, so he set it down until he could take a minute to open his vault. He had a feeling that such dense, Energy-rich ore wouldn't sit well in one of his lesser storage devices.

As he worked, Victor thought about the two bricks of ore he'd received in the dungeon. Surely, they were meant as rewards meant to be versatile to adventurers—they could be crafted into armor, weapons, jewelry, and even art. But Victor had another use in mind, and he gave it away with glances he stole at Lifedrinker, leaning against the wall. She'd feasted on Energy aplenty since her evolution, but was she still hungry for metal? What would she do with these new materials?

He wanted to find out, but a small part of him also worried that she'd become too unwieldy for him—that he wasn't ready for her to advance too much yet. This latest piece of metal was nearly as heavy as the soul ore he'd given her back on Sojourn. Would she gain so much weight, or could she shed some of her less potent material? Could she alter the nature of the materials she absorbed? He had no idea. As he hung his vault key around his neck, Victor walked over to the axe and hefted her to his shoulder. "I'll ask you about it when you're more talkative. Maybe you know more, now that you've done it once."

*"Mmm."*

"Heh," Victor chuckled and stepped outside the gate, fixing his eyes on the next section of the crucible. The dungeon's canyon walls widened before him, stretching to the point where a mile or more of space lay between them. In the distance, Victor could see the sixth wall and gate—just a thin dark band on the distant horizon, and between him and it was arrayed a vast, dark army.

The first rank was probably a quarter of a mile distant, and Victor, counting by tens, could estimate their number at two hundred. Two hundred in the first rank, and behind them were hundreds more ranks—Victor couldn't be sure because they grew tiny with the distance, but he thought there had to be four or five hundred. Adding the zeroes together, he chuckled, shaking his head. "A hundred thousand?"

He didn't fully step out of the gate; he wasn't sure he was ready for such a challenge. Instead, he dug around in his rings for the weird little scope he'd gotten during the conquest for the Untamed Marches—something he'd failed to use so many times that it was almost funny to try to think of them. The thought made him laugh, chagrined as he scolded himself. He lifted the scope to his eye. "Wouldn't it be nice to know how tough your enemies are sometimes, you *pendejo?*"

The view the scope presented to him brought more humor to his heart. The enemies in that first row of the enormous army were skeletons. Undead creatures in dark, tattered armor, with rotten flesh hanging from their bones. Their eyes glowed with baleful red light, but each was limned with a green aura; the scope was saying they were all well beneath him. Lowering the glass and sending it into storage, Victor still hesitated. A hundred thousand! Even if he killed each enemy with a single blow, could he even swing Lifedrinker that many times?

As he envisioned the battle and thought about how long it would take and how much Energy he'd have to conserve, he couldn't keep the smile from returning to his lips over and over. To say he'd fought an army of a thousand was one thing. He'd done it more than once now. To say he stood before a hundred times that many? The grin pulled at his cheeks, a hungry gleam in his eyes to match it. "So I won't cast any spells. I'll let my Battle Momentum do its work."

He figured if he reserved the Energy in his core for the rage generated by the ability, it would last a very long time. Victor was certain of one thing: He wouldn't be turning around. Accepting that fact, he lifted Lifedrinker and stepped through the gate.

*****Congratulations! You have reached the sixth gate of the Crucible of Fire! Defeat the undead horde to advance!*****

Victor heard a distant rumble and, at first, thought the dungeon would throw him a curveball, adding in some artificial storm or lightning. It took him a minute to realize the host before him was marching, a great cloud of dust lifting into the air above them. They weren't going to wait for him to come to them. "All right. Let's do this!"

He stalked forward, wondering when he'd begun to accept the inevitability of injury and pain without a second thought. He understood he'd be wounded; his strategy was banking on it. How else could he get his Furious Battle Momentum to kick in, enhancing his strength and speed to the point where he could possibly consider a battle against such overwhelming odds? Those skeletal warriors might be beneath him, but green was different from gray—they were strong enough to register.

As they grew closer, he saw them running, saw their long skeletal limbs, and realized they were all giant-sized. For the first time, a sliver of doubt entered Victor's heart—how prideful must he be to think he could face down a *hundred thousand* giant skeletons? Had he lost his mind? He glanced over his shoulder, saw the closed gate, and laughed; his chance for rational behavior was gone. "Fuck it," he growled and lifted Lifedrinker high, charging forward to meet the endless-seeming sea of foes.

As he closed the distance, the thunder of the tens of thousands of stomping feet under massive bony bodies clad in all manner of armor was enough to drown out even Victor's titanic roar as he broke his promise with himself and cast Energy Charge to start the battle. On a trail of cloudy, purple-black, smoky shadows, he streaked toward the front line of undead, and the resultant impact utterly shattered half a dozen of the fiends. Those six, exploding into bone fragments and broken, shattered gear, destroyed another twenty and knocked back a hundred, leaving Victor standing alone, chest heaving, Lifedrinker poised, for nearly five heartbeats before the horde fell on him.

The undead were big and strong and never grew tired, but they were fragile compared to Victor's titanic figure. Lifedrinker exploded them effortlessly, though the effort of swinging her was likely to take a toll on his muscles eventually. Victor's vitality was over twelve hundred with his various boosts, though, and he felt as if he could run a marathon up the slopes of Mount Olympus at a sprint and still have energy left over. Even so, could he fight a hundred thousand foes? He shook the thought aside, allowing his mind to drift and willing his fury to take over.

When he'd fought the reaver army in the Untamed Marches, Victor had used all of his abilities. He ran himself dry and would have succumbed if not for his ancestor's fire. He knew he had to be smart if he was going to fight a hundred times that many foes. He had to leave his Core full and let it slowly feed the rage into his pathways as Furious Battle Momentum called for it. His passive regeneration was enormous, thanks to his prodigious will, but even so, eventually, the ability would run him dry. He just hoped he'd finish the undead before then.

At first, the weight of the waves and waves of giant skeletons was too much. He'd cleave with Lifedrinker, but as the axe swung out, shattering five or six foes, twenty more would fill in, piling on him, pounding, stabbing, grabbing, and biting. Victor would take fifty or more wounds before he could throw them off with another enormous swing. None of the injuries were severe, nothing he couldn't recover from in a handful of seconds, but they triggered his Furious Battle Momentum, flooding him with rage.

This happened five, ten, twenty times, and then something changed. Lifedrinker began to do more than cleave or dismember the undead; she began to *explode* them. Victor's strength and speed had mounted to the point where it was a matter of simple physics—a multi-ton implement of war was impacting heavy, dense things at speeds that obliterated anything in her path. Each swing didn't just cut through bone; it reduced the undead to clouds of dust and fragments, sending shockwaves that rippled outward, staggering those further back.

The ground trembled with each impact, and the force of Victor's strikes sent shattered remnants flying through the air, piercing and scattering the ranks before they could close in. Lifedrinker was no longer just an axe in his hands— she was a force of devastation. No longer did the hordes close in before he could swing again; Victor had to stand ready, his vision lost in the blood-red insanity of his momentum, waiting for the untouched lines to climb over their staggered, broken comrades to attempt to swarm him again.

This carried on for a time, but Victor had lost all sense of strategy and didn't bother to clear his flanks. He simply drove forward, pushing himself into the surging sea of the undead until they began to close in around him. Once he couldn't destroy all his nearby foes with a single swing, they began to fly at him from the sides and rear. They drove spears into him, punched knives through his armor, and pounded heavy maces against his helmet, his back, and his shoulders.

Victor screamed an endless war cry, his eyes alight with smoldering red flames, his mouth frothing with bloody saliva, his corded muscles standing out like coiled anchor chains. Black smoke drifted from his figure as he grew ever more incensed, a mindless killing machine. Lifedrinker answered the heat building from his fury and his impossible physical activity; she blazed white-hot, further magnifying the terrible explosive impacts of her booming sweeps through the air.

Bone dust ignited in the air, filling the canyon with black smoke. When Victor staggered from a blow mid-swing, and Lifedrinker impacted the stony ground, it may as well have been a meteor strike for all the damage it did. Rock fragments erupted from the resultant crater, vaulting up and out to tumble into the horde, smashing more of the undead. All the while, Victor roared and screamed until he tore his vocal cords and blood flecked his heaving exhalations.

He fought his way through the horde once, and when they were all at his back, his madness forced him to turn and charge into them again. That first passage through the sea of undead took him hours. The second, back to the start of his mad battle, was much quicker—a few dozen minutes. Even so, Victor was constantly beset, surrounded, stabbed, hammered, and bitten, and his rage increased.

If he knew anything other than a need to kill and destroy, he might have begun to wonder if his body could take much more. He might have wondered if his Core was running low, and if it wasn't—if it kept feeding the fury that continued to build his speed and power—could he take it? How fast could he swing a weapon like Lifedrinker without ripping his arms from his torso? How much rage-attuned Energy could swell his muscles and bones before they came apart at an atomic level?

Whatever the answers to those unasked questions might be, Victor had no such worries. Most of what made him "Victor" was gone—unconscious— drifting through a dreamlike haze, unaware of the toll on his body or the cataclysmic forces roiling through it. The part of him that existed in the dungeon, that drove his body, had but one desire, one goal: destroy everything. And so he did. He waded through the horde again and again, each time more quickly and more easily.

By the end, when he swung Lifedrinker at the final cluster of undead giants, the impact of her blade exploded them into fiery showers of bone dust. Nothing remained of them. Even after they were gone, Victor fought on, his madness utter and complete. He smashed his axe into the ground and against the canyon walls. He even waded back and forth across the battlefield, pulverizing the bits of skeleton that weren't already dust. The only thing that saved him was the nature of his momentum; it wouldn't increase if he didn't take damage. As his wounds healed and he burned off the rage in his system, Victor slowly returned to himself.

When his consciousness fully returned, Victor looked around to see himself sitting atop a mound of bones and broken armor in a devastated wasteland. Craters and trenches filled the battlefield. Piles of rubble lay everywhere. The canyon walls were slumped and broken up as if there had been landslides, and the ruination of the undead horde was utter and complete. Not a single skeleton remained intact. Not a single skeleton remained *half* intact.

Lifedrinker's haft sat in his hand, her axe-head on the ground before him. She was cool to the touch, but he could see from the molten ripples on the stone where she rested that she'd been very hot indeed when he'd stopped fighting.

Victor looked at himself; his armor was mostly intact, but many large rends still struggled to close. His hands were black with soot and blood—his own—but he wasn't hurt. When he stood, his knees and hips were stiff, but only for a moment. How long had he sat, waiting for his mind to return?

"How long—" He started to ask his question aloud but stopped when he saw the System messages crowded to the side of his vision. Had he swiped them aside in his madness? He focused on them, pulling them into view:

*****Congratulations! You have achieved Level 79 Berserker of Unstoppable Momentum and gained 18 strength, 28 vitality, 18 agility, and 18 dexterity.*****

*****Congratulations! You have cleared the sixth gate of the Crucible of Fire! Collect your reward inside the gatehouse!*****

*****Congratulations! You have cleared the sixth wave of a group-rated challenge as a solo adventurer, earning a bonus to the value of your reward!*****

Victor blinked. Gaining two levels was great, but . . . was this the first time he'd been so mad with rage that an Energy infusion after a battle hadn't sobered him? How far gone had he been? He squeezed Lifedrinker's haft. "*Chica*, do you know how long I fought? How long I was out of it?"

"*Our dance of death and destruction was glorious, blood-mate! Long did we tear the life force from our foes! We fought on and on, ruining the fools who thought to overwhelm you with their numbers. Like ants into a fire, they fed us! I only wish they'd had blood, my battle-love. What glory to wade through a lake of it! Time isn't easy to mark in this strange, sunless place. But, blood-heart, I processed the metal man's Energy, which should have taken me days.*"

Victor licked his lips, a sudden cool shiver licking the back of his neck. He summoned his Far Scribe book for Bryn and flipped to the last message he'd sent. There was a new one beneath it:

*Your Grace,*

*Her Majesty, Queen Kynna Dar, has requested your presence. She's scheduled your next duel, and the meeting for terms will take place fifteen days hence. Please contact us as soon as possible to confirm your receipt of this message.*

*Your humble servant,*

*Bryn*

"Shit!" Victor summoned a pen, but when he turned the page to write a response, he saw another message from Bryn.

*Your Grace—Victor,*

*The queen's new chamberlain was watching me write that last message, so I couldn't add a few details. There are people here. The queen's people have set up a camp and brought in Elementalists to assess the situation beyond the amber-ore wall. I've been able to fend them off, warning them that you'll be furious if they interfere with your activities, but as the days pass and we don't hear from you, the queen grows increasingly impatient, and her servants here grow more and more bold. Please respond! Your duel is in four days! There are rumors among the servants that come and go—some say that Queen Kynna has reached out to her new stable of champions and is interviewing for the best candidate to face Lovania's champion.*

*I will be watching this page, Victor, until the last possible moment. Please respond!*

*Bryn*

"Shit, shit!" Victor repeated, then quickly scrawled a reply.

*Bryn, you there?*

A response immediately appeared.

*Victor? Thank the gods!*

Victor smiled, then wrote the only question that mattered:

*How much time do I have? I was out of it again.*

The response sent his mind spinning:

*Three days!*

Victor exhaled loudly, blowing his stress with the breath. He stretched his neck, popping it, then wrote:

*I'm almost done in here. Tell those fuckers to stay out, or they might bring the mountain down on us all, and I think I'm the only one who might survive that. The mountain doesn't give a shit about Elementalists. You have my permission to tell them that. Tell Kynna I'll be ready to fight for her again soon—I'll make it to her duel. I'm coming, Bryn, and I'll be bearing gifts.*

Victor slapped the book closed and hefted Lifedrinker, chuckling at how she felt almost comfortable in his hands. He broke into a jog toward the sixth gatehouse. If he understood things right, he had one more gate to get through, and then he could face the boss and, if things went well, destroy the dungeon Core. Jogging through the ruin of the battlefield he'd created, he shook his head, chuckling. His Furious Battle Momentum was formidable as hell, but it was also insane; he'd been out of it for days—at least! He didn't know how much time had passed before Bryn's first message.

At the gate, he turned to examine the destruction one more time. "A hundred goddamn thousand undead!" As he ducked into the gatehouse, Victor hoped he'd gain a level before he fought the dungeon boss; he couldn't deny the potency of the Berserker of Unstoppable Momentum, but he didn't like losing himself so much, and he certainly didn't like losing days or weeks as he recovered his senses. Was there a chance that he might not come back to himself? The System hadn't sent him any fine print. Was it possible for him to lose his mind for good? He didn't want to find out.

# 38

## DEATH TRAP

The sixth chest contained five Energy hearts—five globes of potent Energy that required a veil walker's level of power to create. Victor remembered when Dar had given him Energy hearts to cultivate his glory, inspiration, and magma attunements. His mentor had said that each heart was as potent as a hundred thousand Energy beads but that they were, potentially, far more valuable if traded to the right person—someone who needed a powerful source of a particular brand of Energy.

The five globes of potent power that the dungeon awarded him seemed exotic. So much so that Victor could only guess at their contents. One was filled with brilliant light and warm to the touch. It reminded him of sunlight, and so he guessed that was what it was—a heart of solar-attuned Energy. Another was black, but when he held it to his ear, he could hear the crackling potency of its power, and the sound triggered memories of Florent's portals. Was it a void-attuned heart?

The third heart was also warm but had a different nature than the solar heart. It radiated pink Energy and tickled Victor's skin with its delicate, gentle touch. He wondered if it had something to do with healing. The fourth pulsed with a strange cloudy Energy that reminded him of static. It numbed his hand, and when he held it to his ear, it dulled his thoughts to the point where he yanked it away, fearing it was doing some harm.

The final Energy heart was filled with a deep silver Energy that barely glowed at all. It was cool to the touch, but Victor could feel its signature tingling through his palm, reminding him of Lira's power in the Iron Prison. He had a feeling it had to do with metal and briefly contemplated trying to feed it to Lifedrinker. "Maybe when we're done in here," he muttered, slipping the orb with the others into the ring Dar had given him, the one holding his cultivation items and Arona's phylactery.

That done, and feeling some pressure to hurry thanks to the time he lost while being out of his mind with rage, Victor grunted, lifting Lifedrinker to his shoulder, and stepped into the gate opening, taking in his first view of the last stretch of the canyon before the dungeon's end. This time, he could see the next gate clearly, only a quarter of a mile distant or so. No enemies lay between him and it. His gaze met nothing but hard stony ground strewn with sharp jagged obsidian gravel.

Scanning left and right, Victor took in the steep red-brown canyon walls and frowned in suspicion as he noted dozens of small cave entrances. He couldn't be sure from his vantage, but they all looked roughly the same size—ten feet high if he were guessing. It was probably safe to say that no giants would be swarming out of those caves, but there were plenty of smaller horrors that might emerge.

He gave his armor a final once-over. The cuts and tears were repaired. His vest's missing scales had regenerated, once again leaving him to wonder how many times it could do so. Victor secured his helm, ensured he was boosting his strength and vitality with Sovereign Will, and then cast Inspiration of the Quinametzin. With the spell's influence guiding his eyes, he gave the canyon another thorough look.

Nothing new jumped out at him—figuratively or literally—so Victor gripped Lifedrinker in both hands and stepped through the gate. He took one, two, three steps before he heard a low buzzing in the distance that reminded him of cicadas but louder and deeper. As the volume mounted and multiplied, he realized it was coming from the caves, and as he scanned the cliffsides, he saw his first glimpse of the source: football-sized red and black flying insects with stingers visible from a hundred yards away as they spiraled toward him.

They exploded from the caves like billowing, buzzing smoke, circling high and then descending toward him—a red and black tsunami of promised pain. Victor watched the cloud approaching—thousands of menacing insects with dripping stingers flexed toward him. He had a hell of a constitution, and his Quinametzin ancestry made him resistant to poison, but he didn't relish having gallons and gallons of caustic poison pumped into his flesh. As the last insects cleared the caves and joined the swirling storm of murderous wasps, a flicker of a plan ran through his mind, and he began to run.

*****Congratulations! You have reached the seventh gate of the Crucible of Fire! Defeat the swarm to advance! Beware their deadly sting!*****

Victor charged toward the cliffside on the left, set his eyes on a distant cave mouth high on the sheer wall, and activated Flight of the Lava King. Great fiery wings erupted from his shoulders, and he surged into the air, throwing a cloud of smoke and heat behind. A heartbeat later, his feet impacted the stone of the cave mouth, and he squatted low, ducking inside. Moving toward the depths of the cave, he could hear the swarm behind him getting close to the cave mouth, a susurrating buzz that grew so loud that it vibrated the dust on the cave walls, sending it sheeting toward the ground.

Just as he'd figured, the dungeon was only an imitation of a real-world place; the cave wasn't very deep. After only fifty feet or so beyond the mouth, he came up to a solid stone wall. Victor turned and faced the pale circle of light that was the tunnel mouth, waiting, slowly inhaling, stoking his Breath Core. The light dimmed, then turned to blackness, and the buzzing grew unbearably loud—a sound that vibrated his bones and made his skin crawl.

Victor's Quinametzin eyes weren't blinded by the darkness the swarm tried to impose. He could see their shapes, faintly luminescent with green Energy— the faint aura of these creatures that his epic-tier eyes could suss out. They came at him like floodwaters, pouring into the cave at breakneck speeds. When they were halfway to him, Victor inhaled massively, and when he could almost reach out and grab one of the fat, throbbing, buzzing things, he blew out a gout of magma-infused breath.

In the confined space of the tunnel, it was like a bomb going off. Victor's breath weapon wasn't just fire; it was molten stone. He'd often wondered how that worked; where did the matter come from to make up the lava that poured out of his mouth like a fire hydrant of superheated liquid rock? Somehow, his mind could accept "fire breathing," but "lava breathing" was another matter. It wasn't like his lungs were full of magma. His Core was, though. His Breath Core was packed with the stuff, somehow holding it there, dense and churning and ready to flow forth in its violent, flaming, molten brilliance.

The insects in front of Victor for twenty feet were doused with the stuff, and they burst with the heat. Weighed down by the lava, their parts fell to the floor or were blown back by the continued stream as Victor charged forward, pushing through the hellish nightmare-scape of the tunnel toward the mouth of the cave. His magma Core pulsed and throbbed, releasing more and more of the superheated stuff into Victor's lung pathway, and he breathed it out, roaring as he did so, annihilating hundreds—thousands—of the bugs before he came to the ledge and leaped.

He angled his jump toward the distant canyon wall, narrowly arcing past the still-swarming cloud of bugs. He wondered how many he'd killed—what percentage of the swarm he'd dealt with—as he flew. His wings were on cooldown, but his Titanic Leap had explosive power, and he surged past the swarm, most of which were still confused by the heat and smoke he'd generated. He tried to aim for another cave mouth, but his leap was off target, and he saw he'd impact the opposite cliff a good ten feet to the left of the mark.

Victor lifted Lifedrinker and aimed for the stone wall, and she eagerly began to smolder. Her blade bit into the stone like it was made of cheese, and Victor grunted as he caught his momentum on the soles of his boots. Then, with a herculean surge of strength, he swung himself toward the cave mouth, trusting Lifedrinker to pull herself free as his outstretched arm tugged. She did, having heated her blade to white-hot intensity, melting the stone around herself.

In the new cave, Victor charged forward and found this one a good deal deeper. He glanced inward at his Breath Core and saw he still had about two-thirds of his Energy. "Good," he grumbled, hunched over, hurrying toward the back of the cave as fast as he could. Already, he heard the swarm coming. Having tested his tactic, he decided he could improve on it.

This time, when the swarm came and blotted out the light, he waited for them to get close and then annihilated them with a jet of magma, stopping the flow after a few seconds. The insects were mindless and kept coming, refilling the passage, and he did it again. The tunnel was alight with smoldering, burning insects and pools of still-glowing lava as he waited for a third wave. It was slower coming, the bugs comprising it having been outside, swarming around the cave opening.

Victor's Breath Core was down to a quarter of its power when he blasted them, and as they burned, he ran forward, cleaning out the tunnel. A small swarm still lingered near the cave mouth, and he used his Spirit Core to finish them, casting Energy Charge at one of the centermost bugs. He closed the last ten yards on a streak of rage-attuned Energy and burst through the swarm, pulverizing them to a paste as he tore over the ledge and soared out into the air, free-falling toward the distant ground.

Victor bent his knees and landed with a tremendous *thud*, sending up clouds of dust and shattering obsidian chips. He looked over his shoulder to see a much diminished swarm coming his way—the straggling insects that had been buzzing around the cave mouth and out of range of his explosive exit. He back-pedaled as he watched the approaching wasps. As far as he could tell, it was just a few hundred insects. Much better than however many thousands had first swarmed him, but Victor didn't want to feel a single one of those stings.

Something about how those stingers dripped their thick, syrupy poison and the fact that the System had mentioned their "deadly sting" told him to avoid it at all costs. He turned to jog, glancing over his shoulder as he checked his Breath Core—ten percent or so. He could feel them gaining on him, but his Flight was probably ready again. He glanced up and to the right, saw a cave entrance, much larger than most of the others, and activated his Flight. Flaming wings burst forth, and he streaked up, black smoke trailing. This time, when he landed, he reached out and gripped the stone cave mouth, stopping himself.

He turned and watched the much reduced swarm coming, ensuring they saw where he'd gone. "Come on, you little assholes!" He laughed, looking into his Breath Core again and seeing it had swelled a little. He had enough for one good blast. As the enormous wasps flew toward him, Victor turned and ran toward the back of the cave. It was only fifteen feet deep. He turned, frowning. Could he do it? Could he get them all in there before one of them stung him? He wished he had a way to bunch them up.

At that thought, he realized he did: He could summon his bear and have it fight at the entrance. Would their poison hurt a spirit totem? It wasn't that he worried about the bear dying. He knew his totem would just go back to the spirit plane, but was it right to summon one of his brave companions only to use him as a buffer, to absorb damage that might be torturous to it? Shouldn't he only summon his brothers when he thought they had a chance of winning? But why wouldn't his mighty bear have a chance? Didn't bears deal with bees all the time?

Victor began to laugh madly as he stared at the cave mouth, and just before the first wasp crossed the threshold, he cast Wild Totem with a torrent of rage-attuned Energy. His bear burst into being near the cave mouth, huge, hulking, and furious. He crowded the cave mouth despite its high ceiling. The bear could barely turn left to right, he filled the space so thoroughly. "Come on, *hermano*! Gather those little *pinché* fuckers up!"

His bear roared, and Victor watched his mottled thick hide ripple as he swiped his powerful arms, trying to bat the insects aside. He couldn't see beyond his companion, but Victor figured the swarm must be gathering close. His bear roared again, and then he was gone—vanished in a puff of red-tinted Energy steam. "What the fu—"

The swarming insects buzzed madly and surged into the cave. Had they killed—dispelled—his totem with a single sting? He felt guilty but hadn't felt anything from his bear; usually, when his totems were fighting desperately, he could feel their wounds, excitement, anger, or fear, but his bear hadn't sent a single emotion his way. Whatever had snuffed his totem had been quick and decisive—like an instantly lethal poison.

Victor focused on the swarm with renewed concentration as he gathered his breath and met them with a torrent of crackling, brilliant lava, spraying the product of his magma-attuned Energy in a cone that enveloped every one of the creatures. They exploded in ash and steam and fell burning to the ground, sizzling in the puddle of Victor's lava as it rapidly cooled. He stood ready,

Lifedrinker up, prepared to cast Energy Charge if more appeared in the cave mouth.

Nothing came, though, and after a moment, he saw the Energy gathering around the mutilated bodies in the cave. "That was it? Just a big swarm of bugs?" His hopes of gaining another level began to fade, but then, as the misty, wispy white Energy bubbles lifted into the air, they were joined by a river of the stuff spilling into the cave mouth. It hit Victor, and he arched his back, his mind fleeing the joyous rapture of his body as it embraced the flood.

Sometime later, he blinked his eyes, refreshed and reinvigorated as System messages crowded his vision. Blearily, he read through them:

*****Congratulations! You have achieved Level 80 Berserker of Unstoppable Momentum and gained 9 strength, 14 vitality, 9 agility, and 9 dexterity.*****

*****Level 80 Class refinement is available. Class refinement is permanent. Quinametzin Energy cultivators will next be offered a Class refinement selection at Level 90. To view your options and make your selection, access the menu through your status page.*****

*****Congratulations! Your Breath Weapon Mastery is now: Improved.*****

*****Congratulations! You have cleared the seventh gate of the Crucible of Fire! Collect your reward inside the gatehouse!*****

*****Congratulations! You have cleared the seventh wave of a group-rated challenge as a solo adventurer, earning a bonus to the value of your reward!*****

*****Congratulations! You have cleared a deadly encounter with flawless success, ensuring that none of your party members were slain, earning a bonus to the value of your reward!*****

*****You have cleared all seven gates of the Crucible of Fire! Make your way through the final gate to face the Lord of the Crucible.*****

Victor couldn't help a snort of laughter when he read about his bonus for not letting any "party members" be slain. "Well," he sighed, resting a hand on Lifedrinker's haft, "we did it. Eighty."

*"I wish I could have fought in that battle, heart-mate. I yearn for the taste of your enemies' blood!"*

"Heh. Soon enough, *chica*." He summoned his Far Scribe book with Bryn, turning to the last page to ensure he hadn't somehow slept for days again. Luckily, there weren't any new messages. Just to be sure, he wrote a note:

*Bryn, how much time has passed since our last message?*

He stared at the page for several seconds, and then Bryn's neat printing began to populate the following line:

*A bit more than two hours. Is something the matter?*

Victor smiled, stretching his neck until it popped.

*No. Everything's good, just checking. Talk soon.*

He closed the book and stood. Grabbing Lifedrinker's haft, he lifted her to his shoulder and walked to the edge of the cave, dropping down with a ground-shaking impact. He turned to the final gate and jogged to it, covering the distance in a few seconds. When he was inside, he turned to the little alcove where he always found his chests waiting, and this time, he was pleased to see one nearly twice the size of the previous containers. He was eager to see what was inside, but he was just as anxious to look at his Class refinements.

Victor walked over to the chest and sat atop it. He canceled his Sovereign Will boost and then pulled up his stat menu, looking at his attributes and appreciating how they'd changed during his very brief time as a Berserker of Unstoppable Momentum:

| Strength: | 580 | Vitality: | 785 (864) |
|---|---|---|---|
| Dexterity: | 280 | Agility: | 303 |
| Intelligence: | 172 | Will: | 673 |

He was pleased to see that his dexterity and agility didn't seem so anemic next to his other attributes any longer. They were certainly lower than his strength and vitality, especially with his wyrm-scale vest's boost, but they were, in his limited experience, respectable. He'd liked that about the class, that it had forced him to improve those attributes, and he hadn't had to think about where he should be putting any unassigned ones.

He'd enjoyed the power of his Furious Battle Momentum, but he didn't think he'd be sad to see it go. If it were a spell, he might have tried to alter it somehow, maybe with elder magic, but it wasn't. It was a feat, and he had no idea how he was supposed to improve or change it. Maybe with a new class. The thought made him blink, and he pulled up the class refinement menu, scanning through his options:

*****Class refinement option 1: Warlord, Legendary. Prerequisites: 1. Prior Class levels in Battlemaster, Martial Sage, or Combat Savant. 2. Sufficiently advanced bloodline. 3. Sufficiently advanced weapon skills. 4. Sufficiently advanced attributes. 5. A sufficiently advanced Core with appropriate affinities. 6. A history of leading followers into large-scale conflicts and achieving victory. Class attributes: Vitality, Intelligence.*****

*****Class refinement option 2: Colossal Spirit Champion, Legendary. Prerequisites: 1. Titan, giantkin, leviathan, behemoth, or colossus bloodline. 2. A significant portion of your total Energy earned from solo combat. 3. An affinity for glory, valor, justice, or honor. 4. Sufficiently advanced will attribute. 5. Sufficiently advanced Spirit Core. Through your many victories**

against difficult odds, you've gained the favor of your ancestors, and they see you as a living champion of their ideals. You embody titanic power, standing for glory, justice, and honor. Through your Spirit Core, your ancestors will unleash their fury on those who defy the might of their bloodline. Class attributes: Will, Vitality, Intelligence.***

***Class refinement option 3: Titan of Relentless Wrath, Legendary. Prerequisites: 1. Epic-tier titanic bloodline with a storied history of warriors or berserkers. 2. Rage, fury, or related affinity. 3. Fear, terror, or related affinity. 4. A prerequisite Class rooted in combat momentum. 5. Berserk or berserk-like ability. 6. Sufficiently advanced strength, vitality, and will attributes. So long as you hold this Class, your force of will, strength, and speed will be fueled by combat. Every wound you take and every blow you strike will drive your battle lust to new heights. The enhancements of this "battle momentum" will stack with traditional berserk-type abilities. As your wrath mounts, your aura of projected fear or terror will grow alongside it. Class attributes: Strength, Vitality, Will.***

***Class refinement option 4: No Refinement. You are pleased with the path on which you find yourself and choose to continue until your next refinement option.***

"Well." Victor reached up to rub his chin. "Isn't that pretty damn interesting?"

# 39

## LORD OF THE CRUCIBLE

Victor sat and stared at his class selections for a long while. He was, frankly, surprised that the System was still offering him Warlord. It seemed . . . *bland* compared to the other legendary classes on offer. Was it such a top-tier choice that it warranted being on offer for the last—what was it? Thirty levels? Of course, the people of Zaafor thought so; it was sought after for supposedly offering unique and powerful class abilities as one leveled through it. At one time, Victor had been desperate for it. But now he shook his head, wondering if it was truly as good as people claimed or if those people simply lacked exposure to more exotic and better classes.

Then there were the other choices—of course, he'd almost talked himself into Colossal Spirit Champion the last time he'd had the option, and he'd picked his current class with the understanding that it would serve well in a duel situation while he was trying to hide his other talents. He never would have guessed that he'd be done with Tier Seven so soon. Was it logical and right to take it now? He only had one more refinement coming his way before he had to embark on his test of steel, after all.

"And then there's you," he muttered, reading the description for Titan of Relentless Wrath again. It was clear to him that it was an upgrade from Berserker of Unstoppable Momentum. Some of the language was even the same, despite crucial differences. For instance, the language warning him of the "madness" stacking with his other berserk abilities was gone, replaced with an almost offhanded mention of an aura projecting fear or terror growing with his "wrath." More interestingly, it seemed to enhance his will alongside his strength and speed.

Victor focused on that line and then dredged his memory for the description of his current class. Hadn't it said "strength, speed, and resilience"? This new class said "force of will, strength, and speed." So, if he understood it correctly, he'd lose some boosted vitality and perhaps regeneration in exchange for a boosted will attribute. Considering he had natural regeneration and other berserking abilities that provided further regeneration, the drawback didn't bother him. Would the improvement be enough for him to control what his "aura of projected fear" did to innocent bystanders, or would he find himself terrorizing the populace every time he fought?

Victor sat and stewed for an hour or more, his inability to make a decision causing his roiling Core to flare with rage-attuned Energy as his frustration mounted. He *wanted* to choose Titan of Relentless Wrath. His rational mind told him that Colossal Spirit Champion would suit him better as long as he was being forced to fight around crowds of people and so long as he was required to behave in a way that might be contrary to his instincts. However, those very instincts were forcing his eyes back to the description of Warlord again and again. Something in his gut was telling him to take that class—that he had something to learn from it.

What finally made him pay more attention to that nagging instinct was a snippet of a memory—a conversation he'd had with Valla. Everyone on Zaafor coveted Battlemaster because it led to Warlord, but there were no records about what happened *after* Warlord. Valla and he had wondered if maybe the "Warlord" had refined his class into something better. Could it be possible that this less exotic choice would lead to something greater? Looking at the almost cryptic prerequisites, he supposed there was a risk that he wouldn't match up to whatever the next evolution required.

Again, Victor stewed. He pressed his knuckles into his chin and breathed heavily through his nose, mentally running up and down lanes of logic and faux logic. Warlord had been offered to him several times. He only had one more System-generated refinement because, at Level One Hundred, he'd be expected to create his own class. From what he understood, that self-created class would be influenced by his previous classes. What if Titan of Relentless Wrath and Colossal Spirit Champion seemed so much better because they were *evolved* classes based on Victor's previous choices? What if the one that came after Warlord would put them to shame?

"Too many speculations," he grunted. He rested his hand on Lifedrinker's haft for comfort, and her voice tingled his mind.

*"What troubles you, battle-heart?"*

"My next class choice. I don't know what to pick."

*"Will any make you weaker?"*

"Um, I don't think so, though at least one will likely make me tougher, at least for the short term." Victor's mind was on Titan of Relentless Wrath.

*"You are already tough, my blood-mate. Do you struggle because what you want doesn't feel right?"*

"Goddamn, *chica*, how can you know that? What I want doesn't match what seems smart, and my instincts are telling me to ignore both of those choices."

*"As I told you before, heart-taker, so long as you can hold me in your hands, all will be well. If you have three voices in your head, listen to the one you cannot ignore."*

"Right." Victor smiled and rubbed her haft gently for a moment before releasing it. He wanted his mind clear for this decision. The truth was that he was only speculating about why his instincts kept guiding his eyes toward Warlord. It might be that the Class abilities were worth it. It might be that he feared the System wouldn't offer it again. It might be that it would lead to a unique and powerful refinement at Level Ninety. It might be something else entirely. All he knew was that it was universally agreed that it wasn't a *bad* choice, and if his ancestor-guided instincts said to take it, he doubted it would be something he regretted.

With a final, almost mournful look at Titan of Relentless Wrath and Colossal Spirit Champion, Victor mentally selected the much more boring-sounding Warlord.

*****Congratulations! You have refined your Class: Warlord.*****

*****Your feat, Furious Battle Momentum, is no longer compatible with your Class: Removing.*****

*****Congratulations! You have earned a Class skill: Tactical Mastery, Basic.*****

*****Tactical Mastery, Basic: Your mind processes the flow of combat with inhuman precision, allowing you to anticipate and exploit openings in any situation, whether in single combat or in command of mighty hosts. Improving this skill and/or improving your intelligence attribute will enhance the effect.**

*****Congratulations! You have earned a Class feat: Warborn Mind.*****

*****Warborn Mind: Your intellect guides your response to threats. This feat permanently boosts your agility and dexterity by ten percent of your intelligence attribute.*****

Victor stared at the System messages for several long minutes, chasing the implications through his racing mind. As a wide smile spread on his face, he pulled up his attributes, wondering if the Warborn Mind feat was already in effect:

| Strength: | 580 | Vitality: | 785 (864) |
|---|---|---|---|
| Dexterity: | 280 (297) | Agility: | 303 (320) |
| Intelligence: | 172 | Will: | 673 |

He laughed when he saw the bracketed values beside Dexterity and Agility. His intelligence might be his lowest attribute, but it was already boosting his overall stats by thirty-four points! More importantly, each level of Warlord would increase his intelligence, thereby increasing his dexterity and agility. It almost felt like cheating!

Still smiling hugely, Victor tried to focus on the knowledge he'd gained from his new skill, Tactical Mastery. Whatever the System had done, though, had certainly integrated the knowledge it provided well; it was all mixed in with his other combat masteries and facts and stratagems that seemed like stuff he might have known his whole life. He hoped it would pay off, but he wasn't sure he'd ever be able to tell when he was actively using the skill. He supposed that if he started recognizing patterns and exploiting weaknesses far more quickly and efficiently than he used to, that would be all the evidence he needed.

With a light heart, pleased that it didn't *feel* as though he'd made a mistake, he stood up from the chest and turned to regard it. "Okay, let's see what we get for a flawless death trap survival." He lifted the lid and took a step back, waving away the much denser than usual fog of silvery Energy steam. When he stepped close and peered within, despite the size of the container, there were only three small items inside: two boots and a crystal gemstone radiating rich purple light.

Victor couldn't stop his hand from reaching down to grasp the gemstone. It was shaped like an egg—maybe twice the size of a chicken's. It wasn't smooth, however. It was cut into a thousand little facets that made it glitter like a miniature star in his hand. Victor stared into its depths, entranced by the lustrous, glowing, violet-shaded veins running through the crystalline core. He could feel the depths of the Energy inside but couldn't put a finger on its attunement. It wasn't anything he'd ever felt before.

Setting it aside, Victor reached in to pick up the boots. They were large—sized for a person like Victor—and crafted from supple black, finely scaled leather. Victor smelled them, savoring the heady spiced-oil scent, and rubbed the leather between his thumb and forefinger, imagining how it would feel embracing his feet. They had high uppers, and if he were still a kid from Tucson with limited world experience, he might say they looked like cowboy boots. As it was, he'd seen thousands of similarly styled boots on thousands of people from multiple worlds. On Sojourn, for instance, people would simply call them cavalry-style boots.

Victor trickled some Energy into the boots and read the System's description:

*****Terror-Scale Boots: Crafted from the scales of a living nightmare, these boots will allow the wearer to more easily slip through the veils that separate the various planes of existence. They will not grant the ability— only enhance one's existing talent. Moreover, though they may be damaged,**

**any harm they suffer will be fleeting; it is impossible to destroy that which isn't wholly real.*****

"*Qué interesante,*" Victor muttered, turning the boots in his hands. He was tempted to replace his lava king hide boots, but that would disable his Sojourn set bonuses, and he didn't want to give those up—not yet. Instead, he took a few minutes to open his vault and stow the beautiful gemstone and the boots inside with his other treasures. When he was done, he picked up Lifedrinker and approached the gateway leading to the Lord of the Crucible.

He could feel the heat radiating from the opening. When he stood inside the gateway, observing the lair of the dungeon boss, for the first time in a long while, he had to narrow his eyes and make his breathing shallow because of the temperature. The gateway marked the end of the canyon and opened into a high-ceilinged cavern with a floor nearly entirely covered with bubbling liquid lava. It wasn't the thick, almost solid stuff in the lakes he'd crossed on his way through the crucible. It was fluid, flowing, orange-hot stuff that gave off waves of vaporous heat that would've spelled doom to a natural human.

To Victor, it was just uncomfortable. Looking around the space in the baleful reddish-orange light of the bubbling lava, he saw platforms of stone here and there and, against the far wall of the cavern, maybe two hundred yards distant, a long ledge littered with bones. "No sign of the boss," he muttered, knowing full well the gate would slam shut behind him, and the dungeon would probably announce the battle when he stepped through.

He hesitated, but only for a moment; what was the point? He knew he'd keep going. He hadn't battled his way to this point only to turn back now. That didn't stop morbid thoughts from dancing through his mind. What would the System do with his stuff if he died here? Would Lifedrinker become a dungeon treasure? Would Arona's phylactery become cursed—a strange haunted bone given to some hapless adventurer in a thousand years? Perhaps the System would be kinder to her since she was a fully sentient being. Maybe Lifedrinker would get special treatment, for that matter.

Victor shook his head, banishing the idle musings, and stepped onto the narrow stone platform stretching ten yards into the lava-filled cavern. Just as he'd predicted, he only took two steps before the iron gates fell shut behind him, and the System announced:

*****You have reached the final conflict in the Crucible of Fire! Defeat the Lord of the Crucible to claim your prize!*****

Victor twisted his hands on Lifedrinker's haft, waiting and watching. He wasn't sure what the "lord of the crucible" would be, but he didn't want to step into a trap. He cast Inspiration of the Quinametzin, allowing the bright white-gold Energy to infuse his being and, with that new perspective, continued to scan the cavern. A strangely rhythmic burbling off to the left caught his attention, and Victor focused, staring at the thin line of bubbles moving through the lava. Something swimming, then? Another lava sprite, this time gigantic, perhaps?

Victor focused on a distant stone platform in the general direction and used Titanic Leap to send himself soaring through the cavern. His aim was good, and he came down with a thud, startled to feel the stone shift and wobble under his feet. It was floating! Victor lifted Lifedrinker, ready, as he watched the line of bubbles, now only fifty yards distant, turn toward him and the rocking stone platform.

With each tilt, lava burbled over the sides, but Victor wasn't thrown off balance. He was too much at home among the lava and rocks of the earth. His time as a Herald of the Mountain's Wrath had taught him to be steady on shifting stone. A droplet of lava splashed up, landing on his arm to sizzle against his flesh. Victor brushed it off, and it fell, already cooling into dark stone. A rapidly fading pink spot on his flesh was the only evidence it had hit him. His Flame-Touched and Mountain's Resilience feats made him nearly fireproof.

It was a good thing, too, because a gigantic reptilian head emerged from the lava before him and coughed an enormous gout of lava onto the platform, drenching Victor and sending him stumbling back. His boots slid over the molten rock, and he fell directly into the lava. Victor squeezed his eyes shut, and though he wanted to scream, he clamped his mouth closed, too.

While Flame-Touched made him immune to "lesser fires" and allowed him to heal from burns more easily, it didn't protect him from being bathed in lava. Mountain's Resilience protected him from *eighty percent* of fire-based damage. That meant that rather than being wholly incinerated by the super-heated liquid stone, he was simply burned viciously, over and over, as his regeneration repaired him. A single spot on his arm was one thing—something he could shrug off—but his entire body at once? Victor almost lost his mind to the pain.

His armor, resilient and immune to fire for the most part, protected him initially, but when submerged in a liquid, clothing only helps for an instant. Soon, the lava was under his armor, against his skin, burning and cooking as his regeneration battled to keep him alive. Worse, something bit his ankle, grinding down on his boot, crunching his bone, and dragging him deeper. Victor almost dropped Lifedrinker in his panicked attempts to tread lava as it burned the flesh from his bones over and over.

Something about his vitality, his Quinametzin nature, his magma-attuned Core, or his many feats must have lessened the pain somehow. How else could he have managed to avoid going mad in those seconds as his mind reeled for a response to the assault? How else could a corner of his mind have found the freedom of thought to realize he'd recognized the reptile that attacked him—it was a larger, more horn-bedecked version of the lava king helmet he was currently wearing. He was fighting an actual lava king.

No, he realized. He wasn't fighting; he was being dragged to his doom, slowly dying and soon to be made lunch by the enormous reptile. Finally, all the neurons fired in the right order, and Victor pushed aside his panic and pain long enough to know what he had to do. He gathered up his Energy from both his Breath Core and Spirit Core, and he cast Volcanic Fury.

Instantly, the pain faded as his flesh came alive with fire of its own. He opened his eyes, and through those burning orbs, he beheld the realm of the lava king. A wide, menace-filled grin spread his lips, and laughter burbled out of Victor's chest in bubbles of superheated air that slowly drifted up through the thick molten stone. With his transformation, the thing biting his boot had let go, likely finding it strange for its morsel to enlarge in its mouth.

Victor looked down, furiously searching for something to kill, but saw only the fiery orange-red liquid. He had no idea how far he was seeing—an inch or a mile, it didn't matter. Out of reflex, he began to kick and pull with his free arm, dragging himself and Lifedrinker upward. Though he felt naught but rage, a tiny fragment of his mind marveled at the warmth and comfort of the lava bath to his magma-infused body. The agony of his descent was a distant memory, and only the need to kill whatever had bitten him remained.

Some instinct kept him from breathing the lava, but Victor's body didn't need much air. He made slow progress upward, toiling hard, the frustration of his arduous journey serving to keep the rage boiling in his veins. When he noticed a lightening in the orange-red glow, his primal mind knew he was near the surface. Then something enormous bit his leg again, jerking it side to side like a terrier with a rat, and Victor screamed in pain and fury as he felt the teeth sawing through the tendons of his knee.

Instinctively, he tried to hack Lifedrinker at the aggressor, but she moved slowly in the lava despite his titanic strength, and her edge, though it hit true, was rebuffed by a great black horn. Then the pulling and thrashing ceased, and Victor kicked his way up again. He thrust Lifedrinker up, and her edge caught on a shadow. Victor pulled, heaving himself out of the lava onto a stone platform.

He was too furious to lie there and pant. He was too angry to bother examining his wounded leg. If he had, he might have balked. He might have lost the fury coursing through his veins—his leg was severed at the knee. Even so, Victor rolled to his belly and got up on his hands and knees, one fist still tight around Lifedrinker's haft. He felt no pain. He felt no fear. He knew only a blood-red mad lust to kill whatever had bitten him.

Even as his regeneration—boosted by his berserk nature—began to rebuild the lower half of his leg, stretching out naked bone inch by inch and clothing it in veins, flesh, cartilage, muscle, sinew, and flesh, he staggered up to his remaining leg, using Lifedrinker as a crutch. With blood-red, wild eyes, he faced the lake and roared his challenge, activating Voice of the Angry Mountain out of pure instinct.

The shout rippled over the surface like a gale-force wind on a placid lake. It echoed and rang from the walls, and then, like a thing from a myth, the lava king breached the surface fifty yards out. It erupted from the lava like a whale breaching the ocean waves, though this fiery whale sprouted wings of fire and soared into the air, circling the distant rocky ceiling of the cavern, banking around long, jagged stalactites as it circled its foe. It was like a stubby, muscular, meaner version of a dragon. Of course, Victor had only seen one dragon, but if he'd been sane enough to care, he might have concluded this creature was a relative.

When it swooped into a dive, aiming for Victor, he stood his ground. When it was only thirty yards above him and began to belch a torrent of fiery lava, Victor didn't flinch. When it flapped those massive, fiery wings and brought its taloned rear feet forward to snatch or impale him, Victor leaned into the attack and heaved on Lifedrinker's haft, arcing her over his shoulder in an overhead chop.

As the lava king drove its foot-long talons into his titanic shoulders, Lifedrinker buried her mirror-smooth obsidian edge into the creature's chest, splitting its tough scales and flesh under her impressive weight and Victor's enormous strength. Fire poured from the horrific gash, and the lava king roared its agony. Its forward momentum turned downward, and they fell together, a tangle of scales, blood, lava, and rolling, screaming, fighting, clawing madness as titan and lava king both refused to accept defeat.

# 40

✥

# DUNGEON CORE

Victor and the lava king grappled madly on the floating stone platform, each heave and smash of an enormous body sending the stone dipping into the magma so it splashed up and rolled over the two of them. Neither of them cared. Both were fundamentally immune to the fire. Even so, the scene of growling, cursing, clawing, biting, hacking fury was so intense that the iridescent sheen of the lava king's orange-scaled body as it writhed and thrashed against Victor's scaled armor resulted in an incomprehensible tangle of limbs, blood, fangs, and fire.

The lava king was more than a match for Victor in bulk, but Victor had the edge on strength, especially boosted by Volcanic Fury. He held Lifedrinker with one hand, a handle on his foe as she bucked and dug, screaming her frenzied hunger and pulling Energy from the mighty beast. All the while, Victor punched and grabbed, bit, and kicked while the great reptilian creature did likewise. With fangs and claws, the lava king stabbed and tore Victor's flesh, rending his armor, shredding his flesh, and cracking his bones.

Victor's regeneration was up to the task, and his fury made him immune to pain or worry, so even though the lava king was a formidable, mighty foe, it began to wane long before Victor did. After all, it was a two versus one battle at this point. Lifedrinker was taking her due, and the fire of the monstrous reptile's Core was being siphoned off and pulled away from where it was needed. The lava king tried to cough lava, but only a trickling wheeze erupted from those mighty jaws. Its flesh tried to meld back together, repairing itself from Victor's abuse, but the fire wasn't hot enough.

As he tasted the weakness in his foe, as his kill-hungry mind sensed an edge, his instincts took over, and Victor began to dominate the massive scaled body. He bent a forelimb until the scaled flesh at the joint ripped, and then Victor jerked with all his might, pulling the bone from the socket as if he were uprooting a thick tree trunk. Blood and fire sprayed out of the wound, and the lava king's thrashing became desperate. It tried to claw, three-legged, toward the edge of the platform, but Victor had tasted blood, and there was no escaping his grasp.

He clung to the creature's back, his titanic weight pressing down, driving Lifedrinker further and further into the beast's chest. He pounded his gauntleted fist into shoulder, spine, skull, and jaw. Each blow was like an anvil falling, cracking scales and bones. As the lava king's remaining foreleg slipped off the platform, futilely grasping for the presumed safety of the fiery lake, Victor grasped two of its thick black horns and cranked with all his might, turning the monster's head until something snapped like a tree branch inside its neck.

Victor dropped the now limp creature and, heaving for breath, leaped to his feet—one bare with freshly grown flesh—and glared around the eerily silent cavern. When nothing more challenged him, he lifted his face to the cavern ceiling and roared with all the smoldering breath, fury, and madness in his body. If he hadn't been on a small floating stone island amid a sea of lava, Victor might have continued his rampage, unleashing his wrath on inanimate objects. As it was, the world was a fiery hellscape, and it soothed his Volcanic Fury.

He sat on the stone, his blazing, brooding glare fixed on the burbling lava, and what thoughts danced through his mad, flame-filled mind would ever remain a mystery for, as the Energy of the lava king was awarded to him, it washed the heat from his pathways. The surge sent Victor on another psychedelic trip through space and time, an observer of worlds and people strange and wondrous.

When Victor returned to himself, he was sitting on the stone platform, his back against the smoldering scaled body of the lava king. His feet were splayed out before him, and he chuckled when he saw his bare foot. The memory of his traumatic trip under the lava was just a vague nightmare to him now. His subsequent fury and the System's infusion of mind-healing Energy had smoothed out the jagged edges of the experience, and now he could only find wry humor in the situation. "That *pinché* son of a gun bit my leg off."

Shaking his head, he looked at the System's messages:

*****Congratulations! You have achieved Level 81 Warlord and gained 24 intelligence and 17 vitality.*****

*****Congratulations! You have earned a Class spell: Locate Ally, Basic.*****

*****Locate Ally, Basic: Casting this spell will allow you to sense the location of an ally. Distance will affect the accuracy, and if the void of space or a veil of reality separates you, the most you may discern is whether or not your ally exists.*****

*****Congratulations! You have defeated the Lord of the Crucible of Fire! Search his lair to find your reward!*****

*****Congratulations! You have cleared the final encounter of a group-rated challenge as a solo adventurer, earning a bonus to the value of your reward!*****

Victor stared at the messages for a while, absorbing all of their implications, the first of which was that he'd gained a Tier Eight level, and it hadn't taken him months or years. It seemed that, yes, the curve for gaining levels grew more steep as one climbed toward Level One Hundred, but that didn't preclude quick levels if the challenge was intense enough.

The lava king had been formidable. Victor would have been killed if not for his fire resistance, his regeneration, and then his ability to negate the fire damage completely with Volcanic Fury. He could still remember a faint twinge of his panic when he'd felt, through the blinding pain of his repeatedly burning flesh, the creature pulling him deeper.

He shook his head, pushing the memory away as he read about his new spell. He supposed it was useful—certainly if he had people around him he cared about, it would be nice to be able to find them. Though, he supposed, the benefit was likely meant for a Warlord to better manage a war. Being able to track and find allies when armies and troop movements were scattered over great distances would be invaluable.

Victor stood with a grunt and looked at the enormous scaled corpse. The lava king was certainly draconian in appearance, though it seemed to lack the intellect of its greater cousins. It had fought like an animal and never spoken a word. He grabbed ahold of Lifedrinker's haft and pulled her free. She was quiet, and her glassy surface was marked with thick veins of glowing orange Energy. "You had a big drink, didn't you, *chica*?" Satisfaction radiated from her warm haft, and Victor chuckled, setting her aside and turning back to the lava king's body.

Lifedrinker had already opened its chest cavity for him, so Victor grasped the top half of the bony, scaled cut and braced his boot on the lower half as he heaved, splitting the wound wider with a sickening—or satisfying to a blood-thirsty titan—cracking, ripping sound. With its chest split wide, Victor could see the thing he wanted: the great, hot heart of the creature, still filled with blood that glowed with a fiery Energy infusion. Victor summoned a carving knife and sliced it through the massive, rubbery arteries holding the heart in place, and then he pulled the thing free, grinning as hot blood drizzled out to sizzle on the stone by his feet.

If he weren't worried about losing too much time, he would have eaten that heart then and there. His mouth filled with saliva, and his stomach rumbled its need, but Victor exercised his will and sent the heart into his storage ring before it could get the better of him.

"Okay, *hermano*," he sighed, turned his attention lower, toward the glistening innards partially revealed by the tear he'd made. "Let's see if you've still got my boot in there."

Ten minutes later, Victor set his glistening, slimy boot onto the stone platform and watched as its enchantments went to work cleaning itself. The slime slowly dissolved into steam or ran down the outside like water off a waxed piece of glass. The boot was remarkably intact—only a few teeth holes persisted, but they were slowly knitting together. Victor had pulled it from his severed leg and, not wanting to leave his poor limb to rot with the monster's corpse, he'd tossed it into the lava, where it had instantly burst into flames and sunk.

He wondered about that. Wasn't it strange that his leg had regenerated, but the flesh that was severed from him did not? He supposed he was glad about that. If it hadn't been the case, he would have found a copy of himself in the belly of the monstrous reptile. "Hell no," he snorted, shaking his head. "I can do without that." When his boot looked mostly clean, he pulled it on and then picked up Lifedrinker, sending her to rest and work on her absorbed Energy in her storage compartment.

Looking at the huge corpse, knowing that its horns and hide, at least, were worth a great deal to crafters, Victor contemplated trying to harvest it. He'd learned a bit about such processes while on Zaafor, but the thought of undertaking the task at that moment, at the end of the dungeon, felt overwhelming. Instead, he took his carving knife and, with a lot of effort and concentration, worked to cut one of the creature's thick, muscular rear legs free. He sliced the scaly flesh, tendons, and muscles until he could wrench the bone from the bloody hip joint. Then he sent the leg into storage, intending to try out his new Wyrm's Fervor feat sometime later.

He didn't want to leave the corpse to rot or be absorbed by the dungeon or whatever happened to monster corpses in such places, so instead he cast Honor the Spirits on the remains. Ghostly fire erupted around the carcass, burning it entirely, the ghostly flames reducing it to spiritual smoke that would make its way through the spirit plane and whatever veil separated that place from his ancestors. "I hope you can make good use of this great creature's remains, ancestors."

After the ghostly smoke had all evaporated, he scanned the fiery cavern, letting his eyes rest on the long, bone-covered ledge. If he were betting, he'd say his reward would be waiting there. Victor focused his gaze and activated Flight of the Lava King. On massive wings of fire, he flew over the lava to land amid the scattered, broken, charred bones. He didn't have to search long—against the rear stone of the cavern, behind a mound of bones and stinking refuse, a large

System chest sat waiting, its strange metallic runes shifting languidly beneath the surface.

Victor didn't approach the chest right away. He paused to look around the lava king's lair. Hadn't Azforath told him he'd find the "dungeon Core" there? Victor stared out over the hissing, bubbling lake of lava and hoped the damn thing wouldn't be down there, at the bottom of all that molten stone. If he cast Volcanic Rage so he could survive a dive, he'd lose his wits and forget what he was trying to do. No, he'd have to think of another plan if that was where it lay hidden.

"Cross that bridge when I come to it," he muttered, walking over to the chest to flip the lid back. It rattled and clanged against the stone wall as glittering golden steam escaped the container. When it passed, Victor looked inside and cursed softly at what he saw: black leather gauntlets with shiny obsidian metal plates on the backs of the knuckles and around the wrist portion of the armored handwear. They were undoubtedly high-quality equipment—on par with the boots and other items he'd gotten from the dungeon, but Victor cursed because he rather liked his lava king gauntlet.

Even with that thought lingering, part of his mind was lost in wonder as he studied the intricate whorls and mysterious runes worked into the dense shiny black metal. They winked with faintly pulsing silver Energy. He reached in to pick one up and had to pause to readjust his footing; they were heavy. Not as heavy as the breastplate he'd found, but he had to put his back into it when he hoisted the right-hand gauntlet out. Curiosity getting the better of him, Victor channeled some Energy into it and blinked as a densely worded System description came to him:

*****Gauntlets of the Mountain's Might: Forged in the ancient fires of a slumbering titan's hall, these gauntlets bear the indelible mark of power imbued by the colossal being's latent Energy. Crafted from voidforged steel, the gauntlets are incomparably dense, nearly indestructible, and resonate with an overwhelming sense of gravity. They will grant a tremendous boost to the wearer's physical might, providing the ability to lift, strike, and endure beyond mortal limits. Those unworthy need not attempt to wear these storied grippers—a titan's strength will ruin the physical form of a lesser being.*****

"Well, if I didn't think the System was tailoring the loot for me before, I'd have to say this is a bit too much of a coincidence." Victor pulled the right gauntlet on, sighing with pleasure as the cool leather hugged his flesh and the metal plates stretched and expanded to fit his knuckles and wrist bones perfectly. It felt good on his hand, but other than that, he didn't notice a change. He pulled off his gauntlet of Sojourn and reached into the chest to grab the other gauntlet.

When he put it on and it finished stretching to accommodate his huge fist, he felt a surge of Energy rush into his bones like a low-grade electrical shock. He felt it go up his arms and spread through his shoulders, then down, along his spine, and into his legs. It felt *good,* and he laughed at the rush of power vibrating in his bones. Glancing at his attributes, he didn't see any change to them—no new numbers in brackets—but he *felt* stronger. More than that, he felt almost as if he had an invisible shield of buzzing, humming Energy.

Victor looked at the description again and read the interesting part aloud: ". . . lift, strike, and endure . . ." Victor walked over to the stone wall beside the chest and, for lack of a better target, punched it. His right fist impacted the stone like a cannonball. Shards of stone flew in every direction, significant cracks split through the dense rock for a dozen yards like a spider's web, and, in the cloud of rock dust, Victor grinned. He felt *good* with those gauntlets on— strong and vital on a whole new level.

It was difficult to force himself to remove them, but he wanted to save them until he'd had time to fully evaluate all of his treasure and make the difficult decision about whether he was ready to give up his Sojourn set. Worse, he had to decide if he'd stop wearing Tes's wyrm-scale hauberk in order to try wearing the Aegis of Charyssor. He took a minute to open his vault and store the gauntlets away. When he stepped out, preparing to turn and lock the vault up, he spotted something strange.

Where he'd punched the stone wall, one of the cracks was wide enough to see through, and he spied a dim, pulsing red glow in the darkness beyond. Victor paused, frowning. Was it just more lava? It had a different hue, though—it was tinted more toward magenta than orange. He walked back to the chest and picked up his Sojourn gauntlet. Slipping it on, he approached the cracked stone. He picked a spot above the widest crack and punched it. The impact, while enough to split a good-sized tree trunk or fragment a cinder block, was pathetic compared to the punch he'd delivered with the other gauntlets.

Unrelenting, Victor punched the stone again and again until large chunks fell away, exposing the source of the strange reddish-pink light. It was a crystal about the size of a softball and just as round. It floated in the air above an obsidian pedestal, spinning rapidly so that the light it threw off danced on the hidden chamber's ceiling, floor, and walls. Victor ducked through the hole he'd created, and a voice, smooth and androgynous, sounded in his head.

*"Do you intend me harm, stranger?"*

"Who?" Victor asked the air.

*"I,"* the voice replied.

Victor turned around, examining the shiny, polished walls, ensuring nothing else lurked within the chamber. "The crystal?"

*"I am a dungeon Core."*

"Oh, great," Victor sighed. Of course the damn thing was alive. "Listen, I didn't know you could talk, but if I don't deal with you, the titan sleeping in this mountain is going to get pissed, and I don't know what kind of disaster that will bring about."

*"But you're a titan."*

"Not that kind of *pinché* titan, buddy."

*"What are your intentions?"* The swirling crystal—Core—had slowed and now seemed to pulse with each word.

"Afraid it's you or me, or at least some folks I care about, so . . ." Victor summoned Lifedrinker into his hands.

*"If I cannot remain, then move me; why must I be destroyed?"*

"Oh. I can do that?" Victor frowned and took a step closer to the pulsing Core.

*"Yes. The vessel you opened near the final chest will suffice to hold me. Take me out of this dungeon, and it will cease to be. Place me elsewhere, and I will create a new dungeon."*

"And you won't be . . . *upset?*"

*"On the contrary, if you can place me where more adventurers will gain entry, I will be grateful. I have languished alone here for millennia. You were the first entrant in a very long while."*

Victor tapped his chin for a moment, thinking, then shrugged. "I don't have a problem with that. How do I . . ." He trailed off. Stepping closer to the glowing orb, he sent Lifedrinker back into her ring and stretched out his hand.

*"Yes. Simply grasp my Core, but be prepared for a backlash of Energy. I believe you are sturdy enough to weather the storm. Why do you not make use of the treasures I toiled to bring to you?"*

"You picked those?"

*"Yes! I wanted to reward you greatly for your visit and your travails. I hoped you would speak of me to your comrades and kin, and more people would find their way to my dungeon."*

Gritting his teeth and bracing his feet, Victor stretched out his hand to grasp the orb. Wild, potent Energy arced out, striking him like a lightning bolt, but it carried through him, crackling and sizzling around the room, glaring and reflecting off the shiny black stone walls. It hurt, but nothing close to being burned alive, and Victor "weathered" the backlash, just as the Core had said he would.

As he grasped the crystalline globe and pulled it out of its floating position, the dungeon rumbled and shook. "Hey, uh, Core—do you have a name?"

*"I am Du."*

Victor arched an eyebrow. "Doo?"

*"Yes, Du, though with a slightly shorter 'ooh' sound."*

Victor gave it another try, "Okay, Du. What's going to happen when I put you in my vault?"

*"This dungeon will collapse. Here."* A sizzling portal of lava appeared in the air—a fiery doorway into nothing. *"This portal will take you out. Simply store me away and flee through it."*

"If you're trying to fry me with some lava, it won't work . . ."

*"No! This portal will not burn you! You have me at your mercy; I'd be a fool to harm you!"*

Victor looked at the sizzling portal and then at his vault. "How much time will I have? It takes my vault about a minute to shrink down."

*"You'll have much longer than that. Once I'm no longer on the same dimensional plane as this dungeon, it will begin to crumble from the outside in. This chamber is the heart of the dungeon space and will be the last part to collapse. I estimate it would take the count of five hundred before it fails."*

Victor stepped into his vault and set Du down near the center. He wasn't surprised when the crystal globe lifted off the ground and hovered there in the center of his vault, casting its magenta light on the metallic, rune-etched walls. Watching the lights flicker, Victor found it rather beautiful. He gave Du another hard look, straining to listen to his instincts. Nothing was setting off alarm bells, so he shrugged and stepped out, swinging the vault door closed with a heavy, resonant *clang*.

*****Alert! This dungeon has lost its Core! The collapse of this dimensional space is imminent.*****

The message *looked* like a System message, but hearing that Du was the one who'd chosen his chest rewards, Victor was starting to wonder how much of the System's duties were offloaded onto beings like Du. As he clicked the key all the way to the left, the vault began to compress rapidly, and the ground rumbled again, more violently. The lava in the lake bubbled and spurted, erupting in miniature geysers as some hidden pockets of gas were shaken loose by the tremors. Victor watched the far gate, wondering if he'd see the dungeon's destruction coming.

He'd begun silently counting when he shut the vault door, and he was at forty-seven when the vault was done shrinking. He snatched it up, slung it over his head, and, without further ado, jumped through the fiery portal. On the other side, he emerged into the very same cavern where he'd entered the dungeon.

In fact, the portal going *into* the dungeon was still there, though it clearly wasn't stable. It stretched and shrank, sizzling and popping with weird Energy bursts. Victor watched it for several long minutes, and then, with a final hissing, sizzling *zwap*, the portal shrank in on itself and burst apart in a rainbow of Energy sparkles. Just a moment after it was gone, Azforath, the ancient primal titan, spoke to him, *"You have done well, little brother. The thorn is gone from my side. The Other is distant now, no longer siphoning my might. Shall I gift you with knowledge and wisdom? This will be the reward for the small task you have performed—a nudge on the road to greatness."*

Victor hesitated. He wanted to say yes, of course, but he worried about the time. What if the ancient being did something that knocked him out for a week? What if it did something that took him out of commission for a decade or a hundred years? "Um, big brother, there are people who will need my aid in a few short days. How long will—"

Victor's words were cut short as yet *another* portal appeared before him. This one swirled with pale blue Energy that radiated peace like a calm sky over a placid beach. *"Come into my soul space, young one. In this realm, I control the flow of time."*

Suddenly, Victor's hands felt sweaty, and his heart raced in his chest. Soul space? Realm? What would he be getting himself into if he stepped through that portal? What would he be *missing out on* if he didn't? His gut said to go through—that this was a bad time to start acting like a chickenshit. Victor inhaled deeply through his nose and stepped through that swirling portal into something called a soul space where he, hopefully, would learn a thing or two from an ancient great titan, a being who claimed he could make or break entire worlds. A small, stray voice in his mind wondered if Azforath had created Ruhn.

The questions and thoughts were dashed from his mind as the portal's Energy washed over him in a cool, electric wave that made his every nerve tingle. Then he was through and came face to face with a being that radiated power like only one other individual Victor had ever encountered—the Ivid Queen, Crystal.

# 41

## AZFORATH

Victor stepped through the portal into cool air and lighting that suggested dusk was fast approaching. He stood on a grassy slope, looking down into a verdant valley marked by the checkerboard of a dozen different crops. He could see lights in farmhouse windows here and there, and in the distance, he heard the trilling twang of stringed instruments. Turning toward the sound, he saw, perhaps a mile away, lights strung up between the fruit trees in an orchard and the unmistakable movement of people as they milled about a brightly lit barn.

"Idyllic, don't you think?" The deep, melodious voice came from behind him, and Victor whirled to see a man sitting on the grass just a bit farther up the slope. He was surprisingly human-like, though there were some stark differences. His skin was a shade of red that reminded Victor of a Shadeni, but it was darker—almost black around his knuckles and eye sockets. When he smiled, the man revealed the sharp teeth of a carnivore, but his braided silver hair spoke to a certain level of refinement, much like his loose, comfortable-looking white linen pants and shirt.

"It's . . . not what I expected." Victor shrugged. What *had* he expected stepping into a "soul space"? Perhaps he'd thought he'd be in a dark chamber with a ghostly flame at the center, or—

"This is a world of my creating—a world I carry in my very soul. Have you ever seen such?"

Victor stared at the man, unable to wrap his head around the idea that he was speaking to Azforath, the titan slumbering under Iron Mountain. How could he be . . . *inside* his soul while looking at him directly? Was this just a representation of the man? He realized he was taking a long while to answer, so Victor cleared his throat and forced his vocal cords to begin doing their job. "I haven't, no. Is this"—Victor gestured toward the man reclining on the grass—"how you look in the, um, outside world?"

"Nay," Azforath chuckled, shifting to lean on one elbow. "Sit down, lad. We'll talk awhile." He waited until Victor began to comply, settling down on the lush, cool grass. "This is how I see myself, how I was in my youth. Even to those of us who've existed for eons, those early years create indelible formations in our minds. Ask yourself the question: How do you see yourself?"

Victor smiled and nodded. "Sure, I get it. Sometimes, when I look in a mirror, I'm a little surprised by what I see." Victor tilted his head to regard the distant figures near the brightly lit barn. "Are the people here real?"

"Are you?" Again, Azforath chuckled, his voice rich and deep and the sound so pleasant that Victor had to smile along with him.

"Yeah, I think so."

"So it is with those folks—people I've grown to love or care about. People who sought refuge from the travails of the world outside. They've built a peaceful existence here in my soul space."

Victor leaned back and looked up to the stars over their head, brilliant and colorful—more so than he'd ever seen, even looking up through Sojourn's too-thin atmosphere. "Are the stars real? How big is your . . ."

When Victor seemed to fumble for words, Azforath filled in the silence. "My soul space is as vast as I need it to be. I craft what I desire here. This world is complete, but those stars are but fanciful décor, I'm afraid. I could expand, but I'd do it slowly—a moon, then a nearby planet, and so on. I've yet to find a need for it. There's much to create and enjoy, even with just this single world."

"Is that why you sleep? I mean, outside? Is it because you prefer this reality to the one where . . ." Victor's words failed him again; he didn't want to be insulting by saying "real" people or places. Were those people down there really alive? How many souls did Azforath carry within his own?

"Where you come from, lad? Where things seem more real to you? Aye, I sleep because I began to spend more and more time here, among the folks I took in from one century, one millennium, one eon to the next. I built that world out there, you know? It wasn't the first, either! When I learned to pull the stuff of the cosmos together and shape it how I wished. When I learned the slow, laborious process of eons, I was fascinated by it. I built my first world and fought for it as great powers sought to invade. What fun that was! When I built the one where I rest—Ruhn, as I've heard you infants label it—I toiled to create something beautiful and unique."

"But now you build in here?"

"Now I build here where all the rules are mine to bend or change. For instance, you and I have spoken for less than a second—I've paused the passage of time here. I do this for you because you did me a favor, and though the travails of you and yours are but minor amusements to me, I have not lost my empathy. I understand your fear of being late for your 'important' event, despite the inconsequential nature of it all from my perspective."

"I appreciate it . . ." Victor trailed off, looking the titan up and down, narrowing his eyes as he fumbled with his thoughts, fighting to keep them from slipping off his too-loose tongue.

"What? *What*, lad?"

"Are you really as big as a mountain out there?"

"I *can* be. At the moment, I believe my physical form is closer to the size of a small hillock. The mountain grew around me over the eons."

Victor nodded to the handsome, maybe ten-foot man before him. "But you started out like this?"

"I did—even smaller! I was but a mewling babe when I first began the great journey of my life."

Victor laughed, amazed by how natural and easy the ancient being was with him. He imagined Azforath's mind must be strange and complex. How else could he while away "eons" and still seem an ordinary man, sitting there under a starscape of his own design, speaking to Victor? "So, the dungeon outside . . ." Victor trailed off, unable to think of a way to describe the mountain and the dungeon in relation to Azforath's soul space. "I mean, um, outside of here, was bothering you? You don't know about the System?"

"I know of the Other and its intrusion into the universe of my origin. I know it plants its greedy roots on worlds it has no claim to, though it seems most are willing to abide it for the meager services it provides—a god of convenience, it seems."

"You think it's a god?"

"Do people worship it? Do they sacrifice one another for its causes? Do they follow its dictums and preach its truths?"

Victor thought about quests and dungeons and conquests and all the other ways the System encouraged people to contend with one another. He thought about the System's classes and skills and spells and how entire universities were built with the intent of teaching young people how best to pursue them. "Yeah, I suppose it does feel like a religion in some ways."

"I've seen them come and go, though this one does seem rather pervasive. Perhaps I'll need to rid Ruhn of it, but for now, I'm content in my space. If it doesn't bother me again, attempting to leach from my Energy or steal from my hoard, I'll see what another eon brings." Azforath shifted, looking at him more directly, and as Victor looked into his dark eyes, he glimpsed the depths of the ancient titan's power again. He felt like a speck of dust before a sun's raging heat. "Well, young titan, from what world do you hail?"

"Um," Victor said, leaning on one hand and stretching his feet out on the gentle grassy slope, "from a world called Earth. My titan ancestors were called Quinametzin."

Azforath looked up at the starry sky for a few moments, and though he didn't speak or indicate that he was thinking, Victor could tell he was. How must it feel to dig through millions of years' worth of memories? After several long, quiet minutes, Azforath nodded. "I know of them." He looked at Victor, smiling that sharp-toothed smile again. "Now I see it. I find it intriguing, I won't deny it—to see a young titan walking among the lesser folks again, making his way toward greatness. How stunned they must be when you reach up from your lowly rank to snatch their pride away!" He chuckled, his deep, rich voice rolling out of his chest unhindered.

"I mean, I've won some unexpected victories, that's true, but I've been challenged pretty damn hard before, too."

"Of course, of course. Forgive my pride; it's a titan's fault, you know? There are other species, other 'elder' beings with formidable abilities, but a *titan*, boy, is a force of nature—inevitable as gravity. Your enemies, if you have any, made a mistake letting you get this far. I can see it in you—the seed of greatness has sprouted, and it will take much to snuff it out."

"Were all titans like, well, like you?"

"Ha! Did I not just mention my pride? Of course they weren't! When I walked the worlds, none matched me! Of course, there were those who might try, but we knew better; such a clash would ruin too much, destroy too many lives." After a brief pause, Azforath gestured down the hill toward the warmly lit barn. "I have friends and children celebrating below. They'll want me to join them, and it's not right to hold them outside of time without their consent. Allow me to give you some guidance in your development, and then I'll send you on your way."

Victor nodded eagerly. "I'd appreciate anything—even just speaking to you is amazing. I've met people claiming to be descended from titans, but you're the first, the only—"

"As I said, titans are prideful creatures, Victor. Not all will be eager to speak to you. Not all will be pleased by your progress. If you come upon others, ancient ones like myself, tread lightly—at least until you've grown powerful enough to defend yourself. Speaking of prideful, tell me, have you had visions? Have you been visited by the ancestor motes that dwell in your blood?"

"I have. I've also had my ancestors speak to me from beyond the veil; they've given me aid a couple of times."

Azforath nodded. "Good. They've no doubt found your manifestation of their bloodline intriguing. Ours is an ancient line—you won't find new titans in the current era of the universe. Not easily. We are beings of calamity and strife, of creation and primal forces. As we grew in power and spread our might through the cosmos, as the eons came and went, most of our kind moved on to new planes of existence. Some, like me, remained content to expand *inward*, unwilling to leave behind those people and things that grew so dear to us."

"Will that happen to me? Am I doomed to be apart from everything? A lonely titan in a world with no others?"

"Ha!" Azforath shook his head, his low chuckle bubbling forth from his chest again. "The strength of titans is our adaptability. Have you not claimed the breath of a great wyrm? Have you not learned to regrow your flesh like a monstrous behemoth? Have you not sculpted the shape of your flesh to make yourself fit in better with the little people of your homeworld? Many species might mimic one or two of these talents, but Victor, you're only scratching the surface of what you can do.

"As you grow in power, you will make yourself fit in for as long as you like! I walked among the lesser folk—a god among men—for a million years before I grew weary of such an existence. You can do the same if you survive long enough to claim your true power. You'll be a different man by the time you decide whether you'll leave this universe, slumber like me, or . . . well, or die. Many titans have lain down to sleep only to find themselves too lonely, too despondent to bother with a soul space. Moving through the veil to seek a new existence is not an unusual way for a titan to end."

"In one of my visions, my ancestor told me I had to fight the System to be a true titan."

"What is a 'true' titan?" Azforath shook his head. "I think your ancestor meant well. He likely wanted to steer you away from the easy gifts this Other throws your way. I don't believe you must wage war with the Other, however. Look at me—have I not told you that if the Other leaves me be, I will let it run its course? You must simply find a way to make the Other leave you be—to stay out of your way as you progress as you should, without the . . . limitations it imposes."

"Like the dragons do?"

Azforath leaned forward. "Have you met dragons?"

Victor nodded. "I've met one."

"Excellent! Is that where you learned that bit of elder magic I can smell wafting from your pathways?"

Victor frowned. He hadn't cast Alter Self for days or weeks. Azforath could still smell it? Or was it Wild Totem? He'd cast that in the dungeon, but it had still been a long time since. "Yeah," he replied. "My friend taught me how to alter my size, and I learned a lot by studying her spell."

"That way lies success, lad. Learn to craft your own spells. Learn to do things your own way. Learn to build your talents into an archetype of your design. Don't let the Other do it for you. Don't let it impose its limits and siphon its toll of Energy. Wage your battle for freedom bit by bit, though, lad. Don't attempt to throw off a godlike being until you can match the strength of its greedy, clutching hands."

Victor nodded. Azforath wasn't exactly giving him a guidebook to the universe, but the little he'd shared with him had given Victor some comfort. It was good to know he wasn't doomed to become a mountain-sized, walking calamity—not unless he *wanted* to. It was good to know he wasn't doomed to be alone; he could adapt to anything. It was good to know he didn't have to battle the System, at least not directly, but it was also good to know that he *could*, that it wasn't an outrageous goal if he set himself a timeline long enough.

"I won't simply give you platitudes and anecdotes in return for your help, Victor. I called you here because the dungeon was an annoyance, true, but the main reason was that I wanted to meet you. I wanted to see you with my own eyes. I wanted to feel your aura for myself. A *young* titan! How wonderful! I can see you've developed a beautifully balanced Spirit Core. The magma in your Breath Core is well paired with the blue ice, as well. I sensed you channeling the rage of the magma inside the dungeon. Have you not done so with your blue ice?"

"Um, I can use the magma because if you look closely enough, you can see that it's a mixture of fire and rage—to berserk, I need the rage."

"Have you not studied your blue ice similarly? Blue ice, Victor, is the ice at the heart of a glacier. If you think volcanos are angry, lad, you should feel the smoldering ancient rage of a glacier!" Suddenly, a beautifully tooled leather sketchbook was in Azforath's hands, and he opened it to reveal a blank sheet of white paper. He drew his finger over the surface, and tiny motes of sparkling blue light darted forth, marking the page like glittering ink. "I'll gift you with a bit more elder magic, Victor."

"I've been trying to learn about elder magic. I have some texts on it, and I've memorized most of the known runic symbols and languages associated with it."

"Good, good. This will be clear to you then. This first page is a template you can use to begin formulating your own spell patterns. I'll label the various components of the pattern and write a brief description about when and why you'd use them. I shall also draw you a pattern for Glacial Wrath—a spell much like your Volcanic Fury. Moreover, I will draw a modification that will allow you to assert your will while under the influence of such spells. I won't put the modification into your spell patterns for you. I want you to figure out where it would fit; it will be a good lesson and help build your confidence."

"Confidence?"

"With crafting spells using elder magic, Victor. You must continue to experiment. Such knowledge will be crucial when you breach the mortal stage of your development."

"Mortal stage?"

"Yes! You are currently gaining power by harvesting Energy, yes? As the Energy feeds your Core, your Core feeds your body. You grow stronger, healthier, and faster, and your intellect and the force of your will strain the fabric of your mortal vessel. When you reach the peak of that stage, Victor, you'll need to break through and craft an archetype for yourself, one that is more than mortal.

"Don't let the Other guide you on that process. You can use its tools—the template of Energy-charged runes that pattern your perception of yourself—but build the archetype without guidance. Use your knowledge of Elder magic to do it properly. You'll be a hundredfold more potent than if you accept some limited pattern for existence that the Other tries to foist upon you."

Victor folded his arms over his chest as he contemplated the ancient being's words. He was talking about the iron ranks—the "mortal stage." Crafting his "archetype" would be the steel seeker stage. Azforath was telling him to do it himself and not to allow the System to guide him through it. "You seem to know more about the 'Other' than you let on."

The ancient titan chuckled again. "True, lad. I observe. From time to time, my curiosity is tickled, and I spend a moment watching the people who clamber about the mountain where I rest." He closed the book, and the big pages fluttered as the cover came down, showing Victor that Azforath had densely populated a dozen or more pages with beautiful glittering patterns and text. "This book is for your eyes alone, Victor. Should you let the knowledge in these pages wander to the wrong hands, I'll not be held responsible for the ensuing wars."

Victor took the tome as the elder titan passed it to him, and within the leather, he felt a swirling depth of power reminiscent of the royal jelly he held in his vault. He knew better than to try placing the book into one of his storage rings, so he nodded and tucked it under his arm. "Thank you, Azforath."

"Not 'big brother'?" The titan chuckled at Victor's expression, which Victor knew damn well was mortified. Had he really been so flippant with this mighty being? True, it had been one thing when he'd felt the power under the mountain—awesome but comprehensible—the Energy and power inside this soul space, though, was another matter. Just as Victor wouldn't have cracked wise to the ivid queen, he felt he had to restrain himself in Azforath's presence.

"Yeah, I'm sorry about—"

"Fear not, lad. I appreciate your fervor and zeal. I hope you'll visit me again, but now that I've felt your Cores and caught a glimpse of your spirit, I'm sure I'll be able to keep an eye on you from afar." He waved a hand, and the pale, shimmering blue portal reappeared. "Go now, Victor. I have loved ones to attend."

Still clutching the book under his arm, Victor nodded and held out a hand. Azforath took it and, to Victor's surprise, shook it warmly—no great shocks of Energy or awful strength that massacred his bones, just a warm, friendly handshake. "Thank you, sir." The titan nodded, watching Victor with his depthless black eyes as he stepped through the tingly, almost soothing portal and back to the universe where everyone *he* cared about was waiting.

# 42

## TREASURE HAUL

When Victor stepped out of the portal, he stood in a near-silent cavern—the pedestal where he'd activated the portal into the crucible dungeon stood silent; the System runes that had once swum beneath the stone surface were gone. The lava in the cavern burbled softly, and if Victor wasn't mistaken, it was darker and thicker. Was it cooling? Was Azforath's irritation soothed to the point where his powerful Energy was no longer stirring up the mountain's wrath?

Was the mountain angry? Was the mountain an entity separate from Azforath? Victor had a feeling that was so; surely all volcanos didn't house sleeping titans. He hadn't gotten the feeling that the mountain where he'd battled Hector had been a titan, but it had definitely been *something*—an angry spirit of the earth or whatever you wanted to call it. He took a moment to open his vault and store his precious tome of elder magic inside.

From just a few glimpses of what Azforath had written, he knew the contents were far more valuable than any of the books on elder magic Ranish Dar had given him. The ancient titan had broken down the components of spell construction and written out examples, whereas the books Dar had given him were more like dictionaries of terms without any real guidance on their usage. He hoped what Azforath had written would help him decipher the book he'd found inside the Iron Prison, too. Maybe he'd end up with a few new elder magic spells.

As he hung the vault back around his neck, Victor trudged his way back up the tunnel toward the amber-ore wall where, hopefully, Bryn awaited. While walking, he contemplated the treasures he'd gained in the dungeon, from the various powerful ores to the glittering blue, baseball-sized gemstone to the Energy hearts and various pieces of armor. He had a lava king heart and hunk of meat to cook and consume, and above all that, he'd gained almost an entire tier's worth of levels.

Victor could feel the changes in himself; he'd truly been through a crucible and was stronger for it. While his enemies, especially those champions who stood between him and conquering this world, might have been sparring or practicing, he'd battled more than a hundred thousand enemies. He'd conquered hordes and mighty, monstrous foes. He'd done more fighting in that dungeon than most iron-rankers in Sojourn would see in a decade. He'd found treasures that greatly eclipsed most of his other equipment, even his relatively new armor set.

It seemed the dungeon, having lain unchallenged for thousands of years, had been eager to award him with the treasures at its disposal and, perhaps, with the challenges it had set before him. It made him wonder about the rules for dungeons. If people entered that dungeon daily, would the monsters grow weaker? Would the treasures be less potent? He had a feeling that was the case but thought it might be fun to speak to Du, the dungeon Core, about it.

He'd already sent his armor away, switching it out for his comfortable, finely tailored clothing. Lifedrinker, of course, was stored safely away, so he looked rather casual as he stretched his long legs up the tunnel's length. When he approached the amber-ore wall and the tunnel leading through it, he chuckled as a pair of Kynna's Queen's Guard snapped into combat stances at the sound of his boots crunching on some loose stone. "Relax!" He waved an empty hand. "It's me."

"Your Grace!" the woman on the right said, snapping a salute and standing stiffly with her spear pointed straight up. Her companion was quick to follow suit.

"At ease." He smiled as he approached, but the two loyal guardians shrank back, and that's when he remembered to rein in his aura; he'd let it flow freely the entire time he'd been in the dungeon and also with Azforath, who apparently hadn't been bothered in the least. The guards visibly relaxed, and the one on the left lifted a shaky hand to his brow, wiping the sweat away before it could drip into his eyes. "Sorry about that. I'm fresh from battle, so . . ." Victor shook his head. "It doesn't matter. You can come through the door with me. There's nothing down there anymore."

Victor strode through the metallic tunnel, not waiting for a response, and when he emerged from the partially open vault door, he stood and silently took in the scene. Bryn and her squire's little camp had greatly expanded. He saw a dozen other soldier types milling about, and some sort of official-looking fellow in stately burgundy robes sat at a table near a conical tent, writing in a thick tome. A massive tent had been thrown up further away, and Victor reckoned it was covering the broken body of the iron automaton. In fact, he was pretty sure he caught a glimpse of Trobban leaning over a worktable through one of the open flaps.

He'd only taken a single step out of the tunnel when Bryn came charging out of her command tent. She wore her breastplate and vambraces but no other armor and her face was alight with excitement when she caught sight of him. "Your Grace!" she called, jogging toward him. "I sensed your arrival!"

Victor folded his arms, looking down at her as she approached. He cocked an eyebrow and teased, "This is how you greet me? Where's your dress uniform? Where's my assembly with an honor guard and tribute band? I hope there's a feast, at least—"

Bryn came to a halt before him and frowned, a flicker of nervousness behind her dark eyes as she began to scowl. Still, she snapped a perfect salute and stood at attention. "I'm sorry, Your Grace, but—"

"Relax, I'm messing with you."

She blew out a pent-up breath and groaned. "You got me pretty good, there, milord." She narrowed her eyes again at the two Queen's Guards who'd paused behind him. "You should be at your posts."

"I told them to follow me. We can close the door, Bryn, or leave it open—it doesn't matter. There's nothing down there anymore."

"Nothing?"

"Nope. I'll explain later. How much time do I have before the duel?"

"As it's just past midnight, I'd say two days and a few hours."

Victor nodded. "Good. Is Florent here?"

"He is, but he's asleep. Shall I wake him?"

"Not yet. I'll speak to Trobban." While they'd been talking, a small crowd had gathered—guards, soldiers, a few scholarly types, and the man in the red robes. Victor nodded to them all, and the man in the robe approached as Victor strode toward Trobban's tent. He was tall and lanky with a bald head and eye sockets that looked to be tattooed black. The dark shading made his bright yellow irises stand out, almost maniacally, as he hurried to keep pace with Victor and cleared his throat.

"Excuse me, Your Grace."

"Yeah?" Victor looked down at him for, despite the man's height, Victor hadn't altered his size at all, and he stood head and shoulders above him and any of the other Ruhnic natives in the cavern.

"I'm Elder Trong, High Priest among the Elementalists of the Order of the Iron Mountain. We've been studying the mountain's stirring, and—"

"You don't have to worry. It wasn't the mountain waking up; it was another entity getting riled up. The threat is gone."

"I beg your pardon, but I fail to see how you can be sure—"

"How?" Victor paused and glared at the guy, instantly disliking his officious, self-important tone. "I can be sure because I spoke to the being and cleared things up. I can be sure because I am the Herald of the Mountain's Wrath, and I can feel these things." Victor didn't feel it was important to elaborate on the fact that he'd just listed a class title that he no longer carried. "Now, you can hang around here and probe about with your elemental senses or whatever, but you're wasting your time."

The man's well-tanned flesh paled considerably as Victor barked his remarks, and he stammered a little as he took a step back. "D-do you suppose we might interview you for the records? This latest event was the first rumbling from the mountain in centuries. Perhaps some details about the entity you mentioned would be—"

"You have my statement, but I'll elaborate a bit. Let it be known that I removed a dungeon from yonder tunnel because it was irritating a being with power sufficient to end this world. Said being does not wish to be bothered, and, in fact, if I thought it were possible to reach him, I'd forbid all access to this mountain. Luckily, he won't be found unless he wishes to be. I won't speak further on the matter out of respect for his privacy." Victor leaned close, and his tone shifted to a growl as he continued, "The fate of the world depends on us honoring that privacy."

He was being melodramatic, and he knew it. Azforath hadn't said any such thing, but Victor didn't like the idea of these self-important people digging into the nature or history of a fellow titan, especially one as great and ancient as Azforath. He wasn't truly worried; what he'd said earlier was true—there was no way anyone would find Azforath's resting place if the titan didn't want them to. Nevertheless, he rather enjoyed watching the man's face pale further as he took another step away from him. "Understood, Your Grace. We will focus our efforts on calming the lava flows beneath the mountain."

"Perfect." Victor clapped him on the shoulder, gave him a firm nod, and continued toward Trobban's pavilion.

When they were a dozen paces away, and it was just her and Victor, Bryn asked, "Is it true? Did you save the entire world?"

Victor chuckled. "Not exactly. I mean, maybe eventually things would have gotten to the point that the . . . *entity* would have awakened to deal with the dungeon himself, but I don't know if he would have gone on a rampage or anything."

"I was very worried when I didn't hear from you for so long, Victor—Your Grace."

Victor slowed. They were about halfway across the cavern when he turned to regard her. She looked just as he remembered her—closely shorn brown hair, a broad, strong face marked by several scars, but her eyes were different. There were dark half-moons under them, and he thought perhaps the lines between her brows were deeper. It must have been difficult to stand up to the queen's people and maintain control of this place while no one, not even she, was sure what had happened to him. "I'm sorry about that, Bryn. I didn't mean to lose consciousness for so long."

"Were you harmed?"

"Not exactly. I lost myself a couple of times, but the one that took me the longest to come back from was due to my battle rage. I fought armies in there, Bryn, and one of those armies was . . . *vast*. I had to completely let myself go, to the point where I was rage incarnate. I have very little memory of that battle and none of the time afterward. I have no idea what I got up to in that dungeon while my mind was gone."

"Well." She nodded, pressing her lips together in a thin line. "It's not your fault then. I'm glad you were able to win through."

Victor smiled, reaching out to grasp her shoulder. "Me too, Bryn. I'll see that you're properly rewarded for your loyalty—officially. Unofficially, I've got some treasure for you. We'll talk about it later, okay?"

Her lips curled upward as she nodded, blinking her eyes rapidly. He imagined she felt a mountain of stress rolling off her back. He gave her shoulder another friendly shake, then turned and hurried toward the pavilion. When he was just a dozen yards away, he called, "Trobban! Get your ass out here!"

The Artificer came stumbling through the tent flaps, his eyes obscured by many-lensed mechanical goggles and his hair disheveled. His fingers were stained with grease or oil, and they shook as he lifted a hand to wave, jittery with lack of sleep or overstimulation; Victor couldn't be sure. "You've returned! Huzzah!"

Victor laughed, shaking his head as he approached. "How's it going? Still working on this old thing?" Victor pointed toward the bulk of the automaton through the open tent flaps.

"This *old* thing is a marvel of craftsmanship! I'm learning a great deal from its study, and that's without mentioning the wealth of materials I've pulled from its innards."

"Anything useful for our project?" Victor eyed Bryn, wondering if he should ask her to leave. He decided not; she'd proven her loyalty well enough.

"Yes! Much! The actuators, vessels, pathways, and many artificial organs are elegant and, thankfully, quite undamaged by your vicious disposal of the life force within the construct. I believe even the *heart* is salvageable and, honestly, quite perfect. I'll need to employ some resizing enchantments, but I believe it and some other innards will work flawlessly with . . ." Trobban also glanced at Bryn, then shrugged and finished, "our project."

Victor nodded, then gestured to Bryn. "You can speak openly around her. She knows better than to speak of my business with anyone else. As for the giant automaton behind you, I'm glad you're gaining some insights and materials from it."

"I'm learning much, Your Grace. Whoever created this construct was a genius at storing and compressing Energy. Unfortunately, the construct wasn't exactly conscious and didn't have a Core, per se, so there are still some glaring vacancies in the list of materials I'll need."

Victor smiled and pulled his vault and key from around his neck. "I might be able to help with that. I have a few things I'd like you to examine, one of which might very well be what we'd hoped to gain from this mountain."

"Truly? An Azurite—"

"Hey! Don't spoil my surprises." Victor twisted his key, and as the vault began to hiss and tick, he quickly set it on the ground outside the tent.

"Is-is that Faecraft?"

Victor grinned at Trobban and nodded. "Yeah. I got it from a vampiric warlord from another world. Not sure how he came upon it, but maybe I'll find out when I go there to conquer them all." He said it offhandedly, but it was the first time Victor himself realized that he fully intended to go to Dark Ember to free the human chattel there.

"When do you plan—" Bryn started to ask, but the vault released an explosive jet of steam and bounced, startling her into silence as she hopped away from it.

"Not for a while, Bryn; don't worry. I'll finish up our business here on Ruhn first. And, to be honest, I owe some people on another world some help, too. I'm unsure which to tackle first, so I'll probably need to think about it for a while." As he spoke, the vault finished its expansion, and he stepped up to the round door, pausing to glance at Bryn and Trobban. "You two wait here. Bryn, kill anyone who tries to follow me in."

Victor's tone was deadly serious, and Bryn took it so. She summoned a shimmering, lightning-charged spear and took up a position right behind him, her back to the vault. "Yes, Your Grace."

Victor smiled to himself, then pulled the door wide, stepping inside the space, narrowing his eyes until they adjusted to Du's magenta light. He began gathering up the unidentified treasures he'd taken from the dungeon—the baseball-sized, glittering, sapphire-colored gemstone, the brick of lustrous silver-hued ore, the other brick of red silver-veined ore, and the strange egg-shaped crystalline gemstone that glowed and pulsed like a miniature star. As he labored to carry the heavier objects out, he instructed Trobban to turn away lest he ruin the surprise.

When all the objects were arrayed on the ground before his vault door, he slung an old cloak over them, then turned and pushed the vault door closed; he wouldn't risk anyone catching a glimpse of his other treasures. "Okay, turn around." When both Bryn and Trobban had their eyes fixed on the cloak at Victor's feet, he bent to fold back one edge, revealing the silvery ore. "It's heavy, but can you tell what it is?"

Trobban fell to his hands and knees, putting his face inches from the metal. He began to flip his various lenses, trying different combinations, uttering things like "Ah" and "Oho!" Finally, after nearly ten minutes, he looked up and flipped his lenses away from his eyes so he could lock them onto Victor's. "Are you willing to let me work with this?"

"Why? What is it?"

"Silvenite. It's a rare ore found only on worlds with incredibly high Energy saturation. It's valued for its adaptability and receptiveness to enchantment. With the correct infusions and the right enchantments, silvenite is capable of taking on nearly any property. I was planning to use vitrivine for our project's flesh—it's a kind of enchanted porcelain that is often used on finer constructs, but this, Victor, this would be far better."

"Is there enough?"

"Ha! I'd need half this much; it's very dense, as you already noted."

"And do you think the other half would be suitable to feed my axe?"

Bryn made a choking sound, and Trobban's eyes widened as he sat back on his heels. "Your *axe*?"

Victor laughed and held out his hands, summoning Lifedrinker from her container. "Haven't you met?" Lifedrinker's mirrored-black surface winked in the glow lamps set up around Trobban's tent, and her wicked four-foot-long edge seemed to seethe with sharpness. Bryn, having barely recovered from her choking incident, gasped and took a step back, and Trobban cried out, raising his hands as though in supplication.

"By the old gods! What a beautiful weapon! Is it—"

"She. She's conscious. Her name's Lifedrinker, and she's consumed many types of Energy and some metals, too. Do you think she'd benefit from a bite of that stuff?"

"M-may I?" Trobban gingerly held out a hand, his fingers trembling.

Victor frowned, for some reason hating the idea of another man putting his hands on Lifedrinker. She sent a pulse of reassurance through her haft and spoke to him, *"Blood-mate, do you doubt my loyalty?"*

Victor chuckled. "Nah, *chica*. Never." He nodded to Trobban. "Go ahead, but don't let your touch linger. She bites."

While Trobban gingerly probed Lifedrinker's axe-head, Bryn spoke in a near-whisper, "I know I saw you swinging this weapon in the queen's garden, but it was so hectic. I was so focused on staying alive that I . . . I didn't realize how beautiful it—*she* was."

Lifedrinker pulsed with satisfaction at Bryn's words, and Victor laughed. "She likes the compliment."

Trobban began flipping his lenses again, and after a few minutes, he sat back and chuckled, shaking his head. "Such a wonder! She was Heart Silver at first, am I right?"

Victor grinned and nodded. "Yeah."

"She's holding a surplus of Energy, and, to answer your question, yes, she could easily consume and make use of half this ore. Even more! I sense a great spirit within that weapon, Victor; you've cultivated something wonderful. I can't begin to predict what she'd do with such fine ore, but it would be amazing to witness."

"Good." Victor nodded and, giving Lifedrinker's haft a gentle pat, sent her back into storage. "Now, for the next!" He bent over and folded the cloak back, revealing the other ore—another brick, slightly larger, deep red with veins of brilliant silver.

"Oh, ancient wonders!" Trobban cried. "It's ferrithium ore! Victor, I'd recognize it with my eyes closed! Can't you feel the potential? Tell me, is it exceptionally heavy?"

"Oh yeah." Victor chuckled.

"It makes wondrous armor—it takes meticulous forging and some tempering with other elements, but with the right process, I could craft this brick into a pair of nearly indestructible vambraces or greaves. What's more, the metal has enormous enchantment potential."

"And Lifedrinker?"

Trobban nodded. "Again, that wondrous axe could probably make use of it, though I doubt she could absorb both metals at this time."

"I'll have to think about that then. I'll have a talk with her to see which seems better." He nodded, satisfied that Lifedrinker would see at least one more upgrade from his time in the dungeon. "Okay, next." He bent to fold the cloth back further, revealing the brilliant blue gemstone.

"Aah!" Trobban cried, slapping his hands to his head. "You've done it!"

Bryn laughed at Trobban's theatrics, but she, too, stared at the gem with mystified eyes. Victor squatted to look at the hysterical Artificer more easily. "Well? Is it an Azurite Star?"

To his surprise, Trobban's eyes began to pool with moisture, and tears slid down his cheeks as he nodded. "It is. I never dreamed I'd be in the presence of one. It's . . ." His voice cracked, and he shook his head, struggling for words.

"It's the most beautiful thing I've ever seen," Bryn breathed. "Gods! What's it for?"

"It can be used in a thousand—a *million* ways, young woman," Trobban cried. "If our dear duke is willing to part with it, though, it can be shaped into an artificial Core." He glanced at Bryn and shrugged. "For our project, I mean."

"What attunement would it have?" Victor asked.

"That will take some research; there will be an array of possibilities, but I'll need to conduct tests to see what they are." He peered up at Victor. "Are you truly willing to part with this for your friend?"

Victor shrugged. "Probably. I got it from the first chest I opened in that place."

"*What place?*" Trobban wailed.

Victor laughed. "A dungeon I had to close. Sorry, man." He reached for the cloak. "One more object. Brace yourself, buddy." As he slid the cloth away, the egg-shaped gemstone glittered like a star, its magenta veins pulsing with hidden power within the crystalline depths. "Any idea what this thing is?"

Trobban opened his mouth, gawking at the crystal. He raked his gaze over the other treasures. When he tried to speak, only choked-off consonants came out. Bryn laughed and spoke into the silence. "Whatever it is, it's even prettier than the other one."

"It's . . ." Trobban tried to say, gasping and shaking his head. He stood and walked away, his fists clenching and unclenching.

"The hell is that guy's deal?" Victor laughed. "You'd think he never saw a haul of super rare treasure before."

Bryn giggled, watching Trobban. When he finally turned around, clearly pumping his breaths to get ahold of himself, the man stopped a dozen feet away and, with his eyes closed, said, "Victor, Your Grace, you must be System-blessed."

"Why's that?"

"Because this is exactly the best possible thing you could have acquired for our project. It's an egg of crystalline sentience. It's the perfect object with which to craft an artificial mind. Your friend's consciousness will easily take root within it. More than that, she'll likely receive a significant boost to her intelligence attribute."

# 43

## A SIMPLE MAN

Victor sat on his couch, his balcony doors open, enjoying the morning breeze as he studied the book Azforath had given him. The spell patterns were complicated, even more so than the one Tes had given him. That said, Azforath's notations and footnotes were clear and helpful, and Victor knew he'd make great progress with his understanding of elder magic by studying the pages.

It was more than a simple notebook, too; the blank pages never seemed to end as he flipped through them, and he realized he'd be able to write notes and design his own spells in the tome, keeping everything he knew concerning elder magic in one place. In fact, he intended to copy down the information from the texts Dar had given him, knowing it would be an excellent way to refresh his understanding in light of what he learned from Azforath's notes.

For instance, studying the generic template, he could see mistakes he'd made with his Wild Totem spell. There were remnants of his original System-derived spell patterns that could be truncated and an entire section governing Energy input that he should add. He was eager to get to work refining the spell, but he was even more excited to learn the Glacial Wrath spell Azforath had written for him. Even better, he could almost see how to add in the modification that would allow him to "assert his will" while under the spell's influence. Would that make him less prone to losing his mind to the rage? He hoped so.

Sighing loudly, he closed the book. He had much that he wanted to accomplish, but everything on his plate—crafting new spells, eating the lava king's heart, drinking the "distillate of a Qo'lorian Essence Drifter," feeding Lifedrinker the metal from the dungeon—would take time, and he had only two days before his next duel. He doubted the heart or the distillate would take him out of commission for that long, but he didn't want to risk it. It would be disastrous if he went into some sort of fever dream that took him days to wake from.

He had an hour or so before he was supposed to meet with Queen Kynna. According to Bryn, her new chamberlain had been thrilled to hear of Victor's return and put him into her schedule first thing after breakfast. "So," he mused aloud, "an hour to kill." He snapped his fingers and summoned Arona's phylactery from his storage ring. She immediately materialized out of cold, blue-tinted mist, her wispy ethereal form hovering a few inches off the ground before him.

"Victor!" Her raspy voice echoed strangely, as though it had to fight its way through the veil that separated her from the world of the living. "Have you news?"

"Yeah, it's been a hell of a few weeks since we last spoke. I have news, and it's good."

"Truly?"

Victor nodded. "I think Trobban almost has everything he needs to begin constructing your new vessel."

"A Core? A heart? A mind?"

"Yeah, and more." Victor took a few minutes to elaborate, describing his run-in with the iron automaton near the amber-ore wall, then giving her a run-down of his time in the Crucible of Fire and all the loot he pulled out of it. As he spoke, he was perplexed to see her face growing more and more grave rather than excited or joyous, as he'd anticipated.

When he finished his tale, she looked down, slowly shaking her head. "Victor, it's too much. I know we spoke about this and that you'd be working to find similar treasures for me, but I can't even fathom the value of all these things taken together. We're friends, true, and I know I asked you for help, but this is more than I bargained for. How will I repay you?"

"Look, Arona," Victor sighed. "I'm pretty sure the dungeon Core rigged the loot in my favor, likely because I was its first visitor in a few thousand years. Taken one by one, the silvenite, the Azurite Star, the, uh, egg of sentience—sure, they're all worth a pretty penny. I've got plenty of money, though, especially considering the wealth of Iron Mountain. The real value of all those things is in how they synergize to bring together a very powerful vessel, something better than we'd hoped. What would be more valuable to me—selling off these treasures piecemeal or helping my friend recover? Would more beads in my storage containers serve me better than a powerful ally?"

Arona stared at him for a long moment, her eyes narrowed and contemplative. Finally, she said, "Have you grown more clever? I don't recall you being so eloquent, and I can't find fault with your logic."

Victor grinned. "As a matter of fact, I have!" He laughed, shaking his head. "Don't let me fool you, though. I'm still me."

"Well, I appreciate your cleverness, Victor. I appreciate your generosity, and, as I've already sworn, I will recognize my debt to you. If it takes me a year or a thousand, I'll repay you."

Victor didn't want to diminish the gravity of her promise, but he couldn't stop himself from saying, "Listen, Arona. I appreciate that. I appreciate how you feel. I'm the same way; I don't like feeling like I owe people things. Even so, I don't want you to feel like you have to, I don't know, *serve* me or something until you've paid me back some nebulous price for helping you with your vessel. I'm happy to have you as a friend and ally, but I also want you to feel *free*. Half the reason I'm helping you is because I hate how that prick, Vesavo, treated you. I want you to have agency. You get that?"

Arona drifted closer, and her wispy ethereal hand stretched out, trailing cold ghostly fingers against Victor's cheek. "Thank you, Victor."

Victor stared into her dark eyes for several seconds, something unspoken passing between them. She was acquiescing, agreeing simply to accept his generosity, but it didn't mean she didn't owe him. After a pregnant silence that stretched into near awkwardness, he shrugged and shook off the spell, blowing out a heavy sigh. "Anyway, Trobban is still gathering materials from the iron colossus. When he returns, I'll give him the more valuable treasures, and the two of you can get to work on the vessel."

"He's already created the skeleton, yes?"

"Yeah. Some kind of crystal lattice."

Arona's ghostly figure smiled, and she drifted back, turning toward the window. "Victor, I'm so excited to think that I might actually get a new affinity. I know we spoke of it, even planned for it, but a part of me didn't believe it would work out. To think that I'll soon be free of this deathly pall that's clung to my soul for my entire life! To think I'll be able to walk among those I admire without being shunned for the dark Energy in my Core!"

Victor smiled and nodded. "Do you think you'll be able to show your face around Sojourn when we're done? Will Vesavo have any claim to you?"

"He may seek to extract a price from me, some repayment for the years of so-called instruction he gave me. As I've already told you, though, the truth of the matter is that I've been little more than a slave to him; any learning I accomplished was thanks to my own perseverance. Of course, he'll argue otherwise, but that's a battle for another day. I won't dwell on it now."

Victor glanced at the clock sitting in the curio cabinet nearby and saw that his appointment with Kynna was fast approaching, so he stood and stretched, nodding toward the door. "I've got to go, Arona. I've got a meeting with the queen. I'll take you out when Trobban gets back, all right?"

"Of course. Thank you for giving me an update, Victor." Without further ado, she broke apart into cold shreds of wispy fog and streamed into her bone phylactery.

Victor picked it up and sent it into storage, then left his quarters, surprised to find Feist outside his door, guarding the elevator. "Hey, Feist. I didn't know Bryn posted you out here."

"Ah yes, Your Grace, she's attempting to catch up on some sleep. She deprived herself a bit while you were away."

"Good. She deserves a break. I'll be back soon." He could see Feist was about to ask if he should accompany him, but Victor didn't give him a chance, stepping into the elevator and closing the door. His mind turned toward Bryn and how he'd promised her rewards for her loyal service. She deserved a proper title, but he wasn't sure what it would be. He figured he could ask Kynna about it. More than that, he wanted to share some of his treasure with her, and he wondered if one of the Energy hearts he'd pulled would interest her. He snorted, shaking his head, realizing he didn't even know what her primary affinity was.

He made his way through the palace to the western wing where Queen Kynna had commandeered several parlors and galleries, setting up temporary offices for her staff as the repairs were being done to the royal palace in Gloria. The queen's staff directed him through several hallways until he found her in a small study library with big plate glass doors that opened onto a flower garden Victor wasn't sure he'd seen before. When he entered the room, the queen and two men in scribes' uniforms were huddled around a table, looking at stacks of documents.

She straightened, her face devoid of emotion, when she saw him and waved the two men away. "Leave us." When they left, the Queen's Guard stationed in the hall shut the door. The queen walked around the table, her deep blue sleeveless gown glittering with tiny sparkles like stars in a night sky, as she passed in front of the garden door. She looked beautiful and severe with her high crystal crown and perfect poise. "You had me quite worried, Victor. So long without any communication! I nearly gave up. I *would* have given up if not for the nature of the challenge we're dealing with."

"Given up?"

"On you, I mean. I almost drew a new champion from the coterie I've begun to grow thanks to your earlier victories. The only problem being that I doubted any of them would win."

"Really? Isn't the next duel against Lovania? They're just a minor kingdom between us and Bandia, right? Is their champion so strong?"

"No, he wasn't. Grenald Boranny was a man of middling ability—even my dear Foster Green could have backed him off. In fact, I was having difficulty getting Queen Fabaj to accept the duel, but two weeks ago, our negotiations took a turn; she became rather eager, pressing for a duel sooner rather than later.

Of course, my spies have been hard at work to find the reason for her change of heart, and I'm afraid it's become apparent that we've garnered the attention of the great houses. Through some political scheming, a new champion has found her way to Lovania."

"Oh yeah?"

"Oh yes. Boranny has retired, and Trinnie Ro stands in his place. She's one of the youngest duelists in recent generations to attain the rank of steel seeker. She's already built quite a reputation among the great houses, and it makes no sense whatsoever for her to represent such a minor kingdom."

Victor nodded, frowning. "She was sent to put a stop to us."

"Precisely. So tell me, Victor, are you up to the task? Can you face a steel seeker, or were your earlier assurances bravado? Please tell me now because there's a chance I can negotiate peace if I give up some territory; we've gained much from Xan and Frostmarch, enough to bargain with."

Victor folded his arms over his chest, turning to regard the garden outside the little study. The flowers were drinking up the sunlight, and fat, slow-moving bees were lazily sipping their nectar. He could smell their aroma, even a dozen yards away. It was no wonder Kynna had chosen this study as her office. If he were to remain living at Iron Mountain, he might spend some time there himself. He shook his head, turning his eyes back to Kynna. "When we talked about going all the way—even up against the great houses, did you think I didn't know there were steel seeker champions out there? Did you think I assumed there wouldn't be tougher champions than Obert and Qi Pot?"

"I don't know what I thought. I think, perhaps, I feared you assumed it would be months or years before you had to face a champion of this caliber. I feared you might have had designs on departing before we got that far."

Victor sighed and ran a hand through his hair, idly noting that it was getting a little long for his tastes. "I guess I'd begun to think we were past all that. Maybe I was naive, but I thought we'd established some trust."

Kynna turned and paced toward the garden, pausing in the light with her back to him. "I don't like being fearful. I didn't used to be. I used to be confident and sure, but I've changed. I've had my confidence eroded by inches. My father died, and my neighbors, nations who were once friendly trade partners, besieged Gloria and tried to force a duel everyone knew Foster would lose. You mention naivety—I was truly sheltered, Victor."

She turned to face him, and when she spoke, she sort of folded in on herself, gripping her left arm and rubbing her pale flesh. Victor thought he saw goose bumps on her arm, and he wondered if she'd caught a draft or if her emotions were giving her chills. "I wouldn't admit that to anyone I didn't trust. Despite my bravado, Thorn's betrayal left me reeling. I've banked everything on you, Victor, and when you disappeared, when my only word from you was secondhand from that pugnacious guardswoman you've stolen away from me, I was beginning to think I'd been a fool."

"All right, well, I'm *here*." Victor stepped closer to her. "I'm here, and I'm ready to fight whatever champion they send my way. I don't care if this Trinnie Ro is a steel seeker. She won't be the first one I've killed."

"Truly?"

Victor nodded, reaching out to grasp her bare shoulders. Her flesh was cool and smooth as a satin sheet under his rough, hot hands. She didn't pull away or recoil or act insulted by his brazen touch. Emboldened, he gently ran his palms over her upper arms, brushing away her goose bumps with the heat of his flesh. "Stop worrying, okay? I've barely begun to show these *pendejos* what I can do in those duels. If those old houses—"

"Great houses."

"If those 'great houses' want to send one of their better champions to try to take me out early, then all they're doing is saving me the trouble of fighting her later on down the road. So? When's the fight?"

Kynna closed her eyes, her body visibly relaxing as she leaned into his touch. Her voice thick with exhaustion, she murmured, "The day after tomorrow at dawn."

"When's the last time you had a good night's sleep?"

Her eyes snapped open, and she shook her head, chuckling ruefully. "Too long."

"So, here's the deal: I'm not leaving my tower until you come and get me for the duel. You don't have to worry about me disappearing or running away. I'll be there waiting. Will that help you to relax a little?"

"I . . ." She started to speak but stopped several times until, finally, she blew out a pent-up breath and nodded. "Yes, Victor. That gives me great comfort. Is there anything I can do to help you prepare? Do you need a sparring partner?"

"Not this time. The only thing I want is someone to tell me about this champion." He grinned and shrugged. "I'm curious if I'll need to wear armor or not and, I guess, if I'll need to use my best weapon."

Kynna snorted, clearly far more relaxed than when they'd first begun speaking. "You're so perplexing! Why not simply be as prepared as possible?"

"Well, as your many-times-great-grandfather explained it to me, the less I reveal in a battle, the less my enemies can prepare for what I can bring to a fight. Unfortunately, I've given away quite a lot already—people know I can berserk, they know I can heal rapidly, and if they were watching closely, they know I'm stronger than I look. I didn't mean to stand up to the veil walker in that last duel, but my rage got the better of me."

"So, your armor is a big secret?"

"Not necessarily, but if I eschew it, that forces my enemies to wonder why—can I not wear armor? Does one of my abilities prohibit it? You know, that kind of thing."

Kynna nodded, sighing softly as Victor kneaded her shoulders and triceps. "That makes sense. I'll have a dossier on Trinnie Ro compiled and brought to your chambers."

Victor gave her shoulders a final squeeze, then let go, smiling broadly. "Perfect. Now, why don't you get some rest? Let the pencil pushers handle all this shit for a while." He waved a hand at the table covered with ledgers and charts. To his surprise, Kynna didn't argue. She nodded and smiled at him with weary eyes.

"I'll do that. I feel a weight's been lifted from me, Victor. To rule is to be alone. Have you ever heard that? It's very isolating. Even when I thought I could trust Thorn, he didn't help me carry the weight—everything was always my decision, the consequences mine to bear. Foster, brave and solid though he is, could only carry so much. You're different. I feel I could pile all my troubles on your shoulders, and you'd simply shrug to adjust the weight. Do you not feel fear? Do you not feel doubt?"

"Sure I do, but not about this. When it comes to fighting, there's never any doubt in my mind."

"You're always sure you'll win?"

Victor shook his head, smiling wryly. "I didn't say that. I said there's no doubt in my mind. Live or die, I'll fight my hardest, and I'll make my ancestors proud." He saw some fear creep back into Kynna's eyes, so Victor playfully reached out to tilt her chin up. Her fiery eyes smoldered as they locked onto his, and he couldn't help noticing how her lips parted slightly as her breaths quickened. "Relax. I'm going to win."

"You . . ." She paused, reaching up to grasp his wrist, pulling his fingers away from her chin. She cupped his hand in hers. "You seem different, Victor. What happened to you in that mountain?"

"That's a long story, my Queen. I'll admit that I might be a little changed, though—for the better, I hope."

"It seems so to me, yes." Her voice was husky, almost breathless, and Victor felt he better get going before he pushed things past flirtatious into more serious territory. He pulled his hand back and stepped away, turning halfway to the door.

"So, you'll get some rest, and I'll go to my quarters to prepare, right?"

"Yes." He could tell she wanted to say more. He could see she didn't want him to leave, but Victor wasn't sure he was ready for anything like that. Of course, that made him wonder why the hell he'd been so handsy and bold with his words, but he chalked it up to having a fiery personality.

When he reached the door, he paused and turned to face her again. She looked lonely standing there, lonely and beautiful, like a sculpture made of pale, gray-blue ice. "You're a good ruler, Kynna. When we're done, all of Ruhn will know it. When we're done, they'll say your name with the same breathless excitement as Ranish Dar's."

She smiled and nodded, perhaps a little patronizingly. "And you, Victor? Is that what you desire? To have the people utter your name with awe in their voices?"

Victor smiled and pulled the door open. "I'm a simple man, Your Majesty. I just want to fight."

# 44

❖

# CORRESPONDENCE

The night before his duel, Victor's sleep was restless. He'd spent the day studying elder magic, and when Bryn brought him a dossier on Trinnie Ro, the champion he'd be fighting, he spent the evening reading all about her. As he tossed under his sheets, frustrated by the elusiveness of sleep, he regretted doing so. The dossier had been thorough, far more so than he'd expected, and he'd learned not just about Trinnie's fighting style but also about her life, and that was what was ruining his sleep.

If someone had asked Victor to write a sympathetic story about a young fighter that would make people want to root for her, he couldn't have done better than that dossier. Trinnie had been an orphan. Her father had been a champion for the Kingdom of Voth, one of the great houses on the eastern continent. When he'd lost a duel, his entire family had been stripped of their wealth and banished from the kingdom. Trinnie's mother and two older brothers had all killed themselves shortly after that. So, at age twelve, she found herself living on the streets of Khaliday, the Empire's capital.

Victor groaned, throwing off his sheet and sitting up on the edge of his bed. Why was he replaying that dossier over and over in his head? Was he trying to torture himself? In an effort to find a distraction, he began going through his Far Scribe books, looking for correspondence from his friends and loved ones to read. The first book he opened was Edeya's, and he was pleased to see a lengthy new entry from her in the book. Before he read it, he stood and summoned a comfortable robe from his storage ring and moved to the parlor, where he sat in front of the fireplace, enjoying the scent and warm orange glow of the embers, if not the warmth.

It was midnight, and the air was chilly, especially with his balcony door open as he always kept it. He enjoyed the fresh air more than he craved warmth. He sank back in the soft cushions of his chair, summoned a cup of mulled cider, and began to read Edeya's letter:

*Victor,*

*I can't believe you've been gone nearly two months already, but when I think about it and remember that you might be gone for years, it makes me sad and regretful. Why didn't I take advantage of our time together? I wish we had spent more time talking about important things—dreams, love, family—you know, the things that really matter. Instead, I bugged you about spells and sparring and . . . well, and things that won't make a bit of difference in ten years.*

*I know I'm probably not supposed to know anything about you and Valla, but I'm not blind, and I have friends on Fanwath, too, you know. I hope you're doing all right! I hope your heart doesn't ache. I hate that you're all alone on that distant world full of ancient kingdoms and strangers. Can't you visit? Surely, you're doing an impressive job there and making Dar's family proud. Shouldn't they reward you with a break soon? I've tried to speak to Dar about it, but he's never around, and when I catch him coming or going, he only offers platitudes.*

*I don't know if you can write back easily, but I hope you do. In the meantime, I'll give you an update about things here: Lam, Darren, Trin, and I have been delving into dungeons nonstop. We're all closing in on Tier Three, and even more exciting, your cousin Olivia joined us for a dungeon run last week. She's amazing, Victor! I've never seen anyone wield the elements the way she does. She melds fire with lightning and fire with earth and lightning with frost and . . . I could go on, but just know that she's incredible!*

*In the dungeon, we came to a locked metal door where we were meant to find a key to get an extra chest. Olivia melted the door. She reduced it to slag! She's only Tier Three, too. Did you know that? Imagine what she'll be like when she gets some more ranks. I hope she'll stay and adventure with us some more. I think she will; she's a little secretive, but I get the impression she's not happy with the politics at the academy where she's been working and studying.*

*I have good news about Darren! We found him another racial advancement, and he's grown his wings! They're huge! I'd be happy for him, but he's gotten a little full of himself. I suppose I can't put all the blame for that at his feet. It's the avian folk here that are causing the problem. They fawn over his "good looks," and he eats it up! Oh well, he's actually been really great. Considering how he fled First Landing in disgrace, I thought he'd have a problem with Olivia, but they've been getting along well. I'm sure most of that is due to Lesh's influence—he and Darren are always talking about the "honor of our house" and things like that.*

*Lam and I are getting along well. I told you I regretted not talking to you about love, so I won't hold back now. Lam loves me fiercely, Victor. I'm her everything, and sometimes that's wonderful, and sometimes it's a . . . lot. Do you know what I mean? Don't get me wrong! I love her too, and I never want to be apart from her, but I worry about how invested in me she is. It's a lot to carry, even if she doesn't realize it. If something happened to me, I think she'd be ruined. I suppose you saw that when I was unwell. Of course, I didn't, but I'm beginning to understand how desperate she was to see me made whole. Love like hers is wonderful and terrifying. I'm blessed, I know, but sometimes I wish I had my old friend from the mines to talk to about things like that, you know?*

*I miss you, Victor, and I hope you'll write back soon.*

*Love,*

*Edeya*

Victor closed the book with a sigh, shaking his head as he chuckled softly. "Edeya, you crazy girl." He wanted to write back to her immediately, but he had more books to get through, so he pulled another out, one he shared with Efanie, the Fae-blooded governess he'd hired to take care of Cora Loyle. There were several entries in the book, and Victor scanned through them until he came to the most recent, then settled back to read it:

*My Lord Victor,*

*I hope this note finds you well. It's been a month since my last correspondence with you, and there is much to share. I'm pleased to report that Cora has settled in nicely here at your home overlooking the Silver Sea. She's made fast friends with Deyni and Chala; they spend most days together. Your friend, Lady Thayla, has helped immensely in seeing us settled, even going so far as to include Cora in the lessons and tutelage the other girls enjoy from the experts in the area.*

*The girls learn about tracking, hunting, and animal taming from the Shadeni, and twice a week, they receive weapons training from a man in the Naghelli settlement. I met him, of course, and learned that he's a good friend of yours—Kethelket. He's humble in nature, but beneath his unassuming demeanor, he carries wisdom that speaks of extraordinary accomplishments and great trials. I've enjoyed visiting with him after the girls' lessons.*

*Of course, I've continued Cora's training in literature, mathematics, decorum, and my own brand of fencing. We've fallen into a routine, a structure that she clearly craved whether she knew it or not. Occasionally, Cora brings up her father, and we talk about him and his life, as well as the mistakes he made. You might be intrigued to learn that I'm not the only one she confides in; a few days after you left, she and Chala came to me asking if I had any objects that might represent her father. Of course, I did; I have the objects in the storage ring you gave me to hold for Cora's sake.*

*I gave her one of her father's pipes. He was well known around the Volpuré estate to be a prolific smoker, spending many evenings on the balcony of his suite overlooking the gardens with a pipe held between his teeth. Cora took the pipe, and she and Chala ran off with it. Of course, I was curious as to what they were up to, so I employed some stealth and shadowed them. To my surprise, they went down to the beach and conducted some sort of ceremony. They buried the pipe in the sand at low tide, stacking a cairn of stones atop it, and then, Chala burned a fistful of pungent herbs, and they spoke to their "ancestors."*

*I'm not sure of the ritual's origin, but I believe it was good for Cora; it seemed to give her some closure, and ever since then, she's been more open to speaking about her father and her feelings. Chala is a fierce young woman, but she's clever and crafty, too. I'm very happy that she and Deyni are friends with Cora; she's learning to be a child, a girl, and a member of a community—things she sorely missed out on growing up under Fak Loyle's strict control.*

*As for our new home, neither of us could possibly ask for a more wonderful place to live. The wilderness is wild and beautiful, and the beach and ocean offer endless opportunities for adventure for the girls. The vistas in every direction are inspiring, and I know they do much to feed Cora's soul—she dreams big, wondrous dreams, Victor, and I know that you and she might not realize it yet, but she has much to thank you for.*

*I'll write again soon with more updates. In the meantime, I hope you accomplish your goals and keep yourself safe.*

*Warm regards,*

*Efanie*

Victor found his eyes brimming with unspent tears as he finished reading the letter. He wasn't sad or ashamed or anything like that; he was just happy. He was pleased that Cora seemed to be doing well despite what he'd done to her father. As that thought crossed his mind, Victor shook his head and tried to reorganize how he viewed that situation.

He hadn't *done* anything to Fak Loyle. Fak Loyle had *chosen* to be a champion for a scumbag. He'd chosen to step into the ring with the intent to kill Victor. Was it Victor's fault that he didn't let him win? Was his life less valuable than Fak's just because he had a daughter? Wasn't it important that he put an end to Volpuré's crimes? To do so required Fak Loyle's defeat. It didn't take much effort to transfer that same logic to his current situation.

Was it his fault that Trinnie Ro had chosen to be a champion? Her dossier had painted quite a picture of her life. After the tragedy of her family's destruction, she'd competed in back-alley bloodsports, some kind of game that sounded like a cross between rugby, wrestling, and gladiator brawls.

She outlived everyone on her team time and time again until one of the legitimate leagues picked her up. Then she'd risen to stardom competing in coliseums, rapidly gaining levels through victory after victory. It didn't take long for someone to recruit her away, taking her to train in proper fighting techniques. A decade later, she'd returned as a duelist, a champion in training, and five years, a dozen levels, and twenty victories later, here she was, coming to put a stop to Victor and Queen Kynna.

"Not my fault," Victor growled. He stood and summoned a pair of pants and a shirt. Once he'd dressed, he walked to his door and looked outside. As he'd suspected, Feist was on duty, idly flipping through a slender book as he kept an eye on Victor's elevator. He didn't notice Victor staring at him until he cleared his throat, and then the young man nearly jumped out of his skin, dropping the book and exposing a page featuring a surprisingly lifelike image of a woman's naked chest.

"Oof! Er, sorry about that, Your Grace." He stooped to pick up the book and sent it away to a storage container.

"Fetch Draj Haveshi for me."

"Right away, milord? Or first thing in the morn—"

"Right now."

"Yes, Your Grace." He hurried into the elevator, and Victor closed the door. He paced around his foyer for several minutes, waiting, and when he heard the elevator opening outside, he yanked open the door and motioned for Draj to enter.

Draj was surprisingly well put together. He wore a suit, though his shirt was rumpled and his hair a bit disheveled. "Your Grace, is anything amiss?"

"Only my state of mind. Come in; I have a few things to discuss with you. I'd wait for morning, but I fight at dawn."

"Of course, of course. How might I be of service?"

Victor closed the door behind him, then led the way into the parlor, where he resumed his seat before the fire. "Sit down, Draj." He waited until the older man was sitting across from him and then spoke, putting voice to the thoughts that had been running through his mind. "I understand the conceptual reasoning for duels always being settled by the death of one champion or another. If a champion could yield to save their own life, how could any nation ever trust that their champion would give their all? Knowing that the only options are death or victory assures the combatants hold nothing back."

"That is so, my lord."

"So, here's my problem: I made the mistake of learning about my next opponent, and I find myself deeply sympathetic to her plight—the adversity she's overcome and the tough road she battled down to get where she is today. I don't want to kill her, Draj."

"Ah. Yes, the queen sought advice about this duel while you were away. It took her by surprise when her inquiries revealed the change in Lovania's champion. She wondered if any of her other champions would stand a chance against her. The consensus was no. Forgive me if this sounds patronizing, Your Grace, but Trinnie Ro is not a delicate flower that needs your protection."

"Yeah, I get that."

"If you had learned more about my brother's life, do you think you would have sought a way to keep from killing him? If you'd known that he spent three years of his youth hobbling on one foot because he kicked a Trejice viper away from our sister, saving her life but costing him a limb, would that have swayed you? If you'd known that he sacrificed most of his earnings to build institutions of learning here in the duchy or that—"

Victor sighed. "I get it, Draj. Everyone has a backstory. It doesn't change the fact that I don't want to kill this woman."

"Don't think about killing her, then. Think about keeping her from killing you. I promise you, she'll have no qualms. She wants you dead, and those who sent her want Queen Kynna and all of us other, lesser nobles dead or gone. In my case, I can hope for banishment, but I believe the queen's life will be forfeit— the queen, her son, and likely all of her first cousins and their families.

"I hope you read more about Trinnie Ro in that dossier than the historical fluff about her tragic upbringing. Did you read that she can harden her skin to the point that iron will shatter against it? Did you read that she can instantly teleport to any location she can see? She wields a ghost-cobalt glaive that can shear through solid steel. She's going to try to cut you to pieces, and she'll have no mercy in her heart for you, my Lord Duke.

"Trinnie Ro is a killing machine. Before she was a duelist, she played in the Crimson League, and she killed more men and women than anyone else on record—in a sport that allows for mercy, mind you. She didn't have to kill those people! Put aside the fantasy you've created in your mind. She must be taken seriously, and you mustn't hold anything back."

Draj didn't stop there; he continued to list the ways Trinnie Ro could kill him, and then he spoke at length about her gruesome exploits in the Crimson League. Victor wasn't sure what that even was, but he didn't care. He felt a knot loosening in his chest, and he began to breathe more easily with each barbaric exploit. It was almost like every horrifying fact about Trinnie Ro that Draj listed served to soothe Victor further, and by the time the man paused to gauge the effects of his diatribe, Victor wore a broad smile.

"Holy shit, Draj. You were the right guy to bring here tonight. Thanks for helping me see things straight. You're right; I built up a fantasy in my mind, and I think a lot of it had to do with me imagining this woman as a little girl, and, well, I've got a soft spot for little girls. I have to remember she's not that girl who lost her family so tragically anymore. She's a killer, and I need to treat her that way. Thanks, man."

"It's my pleasure, Your Grace. I am here to serve; I know a great deal about the key players in the empire. I'd be more than happy to advise you in a similar capacity anytime you need it. Was there anything else I can help you with tonight?"

"Yeah, actually. You know Bryn?"

"Your guard?"

"She's more than a guard. She's like an assistant and confidant. I want to award her some land and a title."

"Ah! Do you mean to elevate her, then?"

"Elevate?"

"To the noble class, milord. If so, you should speak to the queen. I do not doubt that she'd support your wish."

"Okay, well, you know the duchy better than anyone. Find me a good holding to offer Bryn: a hunting ground, an orchard—something like that. I'll talk to the queen about her title. Good?"

Draj nodded, smiling. "Yes, of course."

Victor stood and held out his hand. Draj hurried to his feet and grasped it. "I'm sorry I woke you up in the middle of the night, Draj, but I think it was worth it for everyone involved. You've helped me clear my head, which means everything before a fight."

"I'm happy to be of service, milord."

"All right. Get out of here. Go get some sleep." Victor clapped him on the shoulder and ushered him to the door. When he closed it behind him, he turned to his bedroom and shook his head. He wouldn't be able to sleep, not when he had to wake up in four hours to fight. Instead, he went back to his parlor and summoned his Far Scribe book. He'd write back to Edeya and Efanie, and then he'd go through his other books. He was due for a check-in with Dar and might have messages from Lesh or Gorro ap'Dommic. Hell, he might have a message from Rellia, though he'd been avoiding that book since Valla and he had split.

So, with a busy mind, he whiled away the hours corresponding with the many people in his life, near and distant. When his thoughts drifted toward Trinnie Ro and their upcoming fight, he forced himself to picture her as Draj had painted her—a merciless killer who meant to end Victor and destroy Gloria. The more he built up that blood-soaked image, the more he smiled and relaxed, and the more his correspondence took on a lighthearted tone.

# 45

## ALL OUT

When Victor stepped onto the black sands of the arena, his chest swelled with the cheering roar of the crowd. He wasn't the first to arrive. Trinnie Ro stood on the red sands, watching him with narrowed eyes, but Victor avoided looking her way. Instead, he lifted his fists and walked in a slow circle, staring up into the stands, trying to lock eyes with as many spectators as possible. He thrived on the crowd's attention; it fed his very soul and lifted his mood despite the many conflicted emotions going through his mind.

He didn't wear his armor—neither his new nor his old. He wasn't quite ready to wear the enormously heavy stuff he'd pulled from the dungeon, and if everything he'd read was true, his Sojourn set would be like paper before Trinnie Ro's glaive. Even his wyrm-scale vest, crafted lovingly by a genuine dragon, wouldn't stop that blade. No, it was better that he rely on his speed and his sturdy body to avoid being chopped to bits. Besides, wouldn't it provide a better show if he stood against the steel seeker champion wearing nothing but some comfortable loose linen pants?

The sand felt good on his bare feet, and the cool morning air tickled his naked shoulders. Holding his fists above his head forced his back and shoulder muscles to expand, exposing the incredible V shape of his torso, his enormous strength evident in the way the minor muscles flexed and contracted with the movement of his arms as he pumped one fist and then another into the air.

Victor knew Grand Judicator Lohanse would take his time to appear; he always did, so he paced back and forth, whipping up the crowd's enthusiasm, at least on his half of the arena, while he basked in the glory of it all. He made a show of not looking at Trinnie Ro. He'd missed the terms negotiation meeting, so the truth was that he was very eager to take her measure, but he didn't want her to know that. He'd caught a glimpse, which was enough—tall, wiry, wearing close-fitting leather clothes trimmed in white fur, leaning on the haft of her enormous gold-bladed glaive. She reminded him of a cat, and that wasn't something anyone wanted to see in a fighting opponent.

He was saved from the temptation to look at her again when Grand Judicator Lohanse appeared on his flying disc and boomed his usual greeting to the crowd, "Citizens! I am Grand Judicator Lohanse, and I am here to ensure all rules of law are abided by, that the agreed-upon terms are upheld, and that no outside interference mars the sanctity of this most venerated ritual of succession. Do any dare challenge my authority in this place?"

As always, a hush fell over the arena, and Victor stopped pumping his fists and lowered his arms, not wanting to irritate the man. He moved to stand near the edge of the black section of sand, looking up to his left where Kynna and her retinue sat. She met his gaze, her blazing eyes hooded beneath worried brows. Lohanse flew around the space above the sands, his gauzy, elaborate robes flowing as he went through his usual spiel. "I have read the terms of this duel of succession. Queen Kynna of Gloria, do you agree to abide by them?"

Kynna's voice rang out in an immediate response, "I do!"

"Queen Fabaj of Lovania?"

"I will abide by the terms, Grand Judicator." Victor looked toward the source of the singsong voice and saw a willowy, ebon-skinned woman with bright luminescent blue eyes. She stood near the edge of her platform, her diamond-studded crown glittering like a halo of stars trailing wispy white flames that faded into mist behind her shoulders. Those ghostly flames reminded Victor of the spirit flames that consumed his offerings to his ancestors. He wanted to stare at the woman, he was so stricken by her beauty, but he forced his attention back to Lohanse as the Judicator spoke again.

"Champions! You will not be permitted to access storage devices or use potions, tinctures, salves, or other consumable aids during this duel. Are you each equipped to your satisfaction?" Victor swore the words were exactly the same every time, even the man's mannerisms as he swooped down to hover in the air before Trinnie Ro. "Champion of Lovania?"

"I am equipped to my satisfaction," she replied, her voice clear and strong, each word enunciated perfectly. Lohanse nodded and whipped his magical sled around, gliding toward Victor.

"Champion of Gloria?"

"If you'll permit me a small indulgence, Grand Judicator, I have a weapon I'd like to make ready." Victor spoke naturally, but his voice echoed around the arena, amplified by the Judicator's magic.

The man's neutral expression faltered for just a fraction of a second, the corners of his mouth flickering downward, but he nodded nonetheless. "Very well, Champion. You're entitled to an indulgence or two before you put your life on the line."

Victor smiled and then summoned Lifedrinker from her container. Before coming to the arena, Victor had cast Alter Self, reducing his height to ten feet, which was tall but not uncommon for the people of Ruhn. That said, the axe looked enormous in his hands, and he made a show of struggling to hold the blade up, allowing her axe-head to fall to the sand. He propped the handle up on his shoulder, smiling with chagrin. Lifedrinker was more than fourteen feet long from the tip of her upward-swooping blade to the butt of her haft. Her blade was a crescent that measured more than four feet from tip to tip.

Victor smiled at Lohanse and then, shrugging, dragged Lifedrinker toward the arena wall behind him. "I'll just keep her back here, sir, in case I have need of her." The axe plowed a deep trench in the sand as he pulled her behind him, grunting with each long step.

As he walked, he heard the crowd reacting to his antics, and Victor found it easy to affect a lopsided grin. Lohanse spoke, and he knew the words were for him alone, "I'm not sure what game you play now, young titan, but if you—"

"I won't make a mockery of your duel, sir."

"See that you do not."

Victor smiled, and then Lifedrinker spoke into his mind. *Are you well, heart-slaughterer? Why do you drag me so?*

"I'm good, *chica*. Don't worry. Just a little show," Victor whispered, trusting that Lohanse wouldn't amplify the words. When he reached the arena wall, he propped Lifedrinker's haft against it, then turned back to the center where he saw Trinnie Ro watching him with a glower, still leaning against her enormous bladed polearm.

When he stood empty-handed, directly across from the other warrior, he nodded to Grand Judicator Lohanse. "I'm ready."

To his credit, Lohanse ignored Victor's lack of a weapon and nodded. "Very well." He swooped up into the sky on his see-through disc and banked in a long slow loop around the arena before he stopped directly above and shouted, "Fight!"

Victor lifted his fists and stepped back, waiting to see what Trinnie Ro would do. He'd thought about using a different weapon during the battle, something to throw off future challengers, but reading Trinnie's dossier had dissuaded him of that notion. He'd begun to suspect that she'd been chosen to "step down" into her current role in order to put a stop to him for a reason. That reason was her ability to harden her flesh to the point where few weapons could penetrate it. Everyone in the empire knew about Victor's use of a spear and, in particular, the heavy, dense spear he'd given to Queen Kynna. They wouldn't have chosen the woman before him now if they hadn't thought her armored flesh could withstand that weapon.

Nothing in his storage rings was better at breaking through armor than the spear he'd given Kynna. If he went shopping for something else, he didn't know how successful he'd be, and, besides, he hadn't had much time for something like that. So, Victor had concluded that he needed to either beat her without a weapon or use Lifedrinker.

Of course, he wanted to save Lifedrinker, but he wasn't stupid enough to leave himself without the option of winning if it came down to him *needing* her. Hence his little performance, dragging her to the wall, struggling with her weight in his "reduced" state. If nothing else, he hoped it made Trinnie Ro wonder what he was up to, which would mean at least a small part of her mind would be distracted.

He was currently channeling his Sovereign Will boost into agility and vitality. Again, he'd *wanted* to look weaker than usual, so he'd decided speed and resilience would be the order of the hour, at least at the start of the fight. It was a good thing, too, because Trinnie Ro moved like quicksilver, sliding over the sand, whipping her massive polearm around in a diagonal overhead cleave that left no evidence save for a flash of golden light as it split the air like a thunderclap.

Victor couldn't see the strike to avoid it, but he could see Trinnie. He could see the shift in her center of gravity and the tilt of her shoulders, so he ducked and glided forward to his left, and the terrible blade carved the air a fraction of an inch above his right shoulder. Victor dropped and kicked out with his left leg, but Trinnie Ro danced back with a grunt, heaving her weapon around to slice in a flat arc. Victor rolled to the side, narrowly avoiding having his leg truncated at the knee by a hair's breadth.

Victor rolled onto his feet, but he could *feel* another cleave of that massive blade coming, so he launched himself up and forward with Titanic Leap, mostly escaping the cut, but not entirely—a razor-thin slice split the flesh down the center of his back, weeping blood for a heartbeat before his regeneration sealed the cut. The wound *hurt* far more than it should have, and Victor realized her blade was likely poisoned, probably meant to weaken him or slow his healing. He'd certainly put his regeneration on display in the previous duels; it wouldn't be surprising if his enemies would be trying to counter it by now.

As he soared through the air, Victor wondered how strong that blade of hers was. Could it cleave through his titan bones? Part of him wanted to step into a blow, catch her polearm's shaft with one hand, and beat the hell out of her with the other, but not if doing so would cost him a limb or his life. He had a dozen strategies like that in mind, but for now, he wanted to keep testing, feeling out Trinnie Ro's capabilities, waiting for the right moment to—

Victor's world exploded in white light as thunder erupted through the arena, and a bolt of lightning like something thrown by Zeus himself exploded into him, knocking him out of the sky, sending him flopping and bouncing through the arena, his flesh smoking, his back blackened and scorched. The crowd let out a collective hiss of disbelief and sympathetic awe as another cacophonous crack of thunder rolled through the air, and a second blast of lightning hit Victor, drilling him into the arena as the sand beneath him turned to white-hot glass.

Trinnie Ro stood where Victor had left her, her golden glaive held over her head, her long silvery hair standing on its ends as static electricity coursed through her. She was channeling enough electricity to power a small city as lightning bolt after lightning bolt arced out of the sky, blasting Victor again and again.

Victor hated being struck by lightning. He hated it so much that when he'd read Trinnie Ro's primary affinity wasn't steel or whatever let her harden her flesh, but air, he'd almost decided to pull out all the stops and try to end the fight as rapidly as possible. He hadn't, though. He'd contented himself with the knowledge that while lightning *hurt* and tended to stun him, it couldn't kill him, especially when he was grounded, and the electricity would just course through him. In fact, after the third blast, he found himself able to grit his teeth through it, and by the tenth, he hardly noticed the new discomfort as his body worked to undo the damage.

Nevertheless, he lay still, letting Trinnie believe he was dead or stunned or wounded beyond recovery. When the world stopped thundering and the burning, jolting shocks stopped coming, he kept his eyes closed as his regeneration worked from the inside out, repairing his nerves, his tiny vessels, his organs, his eardrums, and eyeballs. With his senses destroyed by the onslaught, he opened his inner eye, turned his gaze away from his blazing Core, and saw Trinnie's aura approaching—a curtain of sharp, hungry power, eager to destroy and dominate.

Victor could feel her killing intent in that razored wave of electric death, and he watched the ripple of hate and bloodlust arc through it. He knew it would spike before she struck and wanted to wait until the last possible second. As the aura approached and the killing momentum rose to a crescendo, a wave about to break, Victor willed his body to heal, willed his nerves to reconnect and prepare for what he would demand.

Victor knew his ears were recovering. The blasted drums were reknitting, conveying the stunned babble of the crowd, the sizzling of the molten sand around him, and the distant echoes of thunder yet to fade into nothing. He opened his eyes at the last possible instant, pleased to see vivid colors and movement. He focused his gaze on Trinnie Ro and, from a prone position, cast Energy Charge, fueling it with a dark torrent of fear-attuned Energy.

Trinnie had her glaive held high over her head, ready to sweep down and cleave his body, but when Victor exploded off the ground in a streak of volatile purple-black shadows, she swung it down instinctively, hoping to split him in half even as he slammed into her. Victor was inside the arc of the cleave, though, and the haft of her weapon met him on the crown of his head, which the powerful Energy of his charge protected. He drove forward, slamming the glaive upward as he plowed into Trinnie, and dark, wailing, shadowy, fear-attuned Energy erupted from Victor's Core to protect him from the immense forces of the collision.

At first, he thought he had her. He thought he'd caught her with her guard down and that he'd shatter her bones before she could brace for the impact. He watched in slow motion, though, as if he were caught in an instant that lasted an eternity as she absorbed the impact. As he slammed into the woman's slender figure, he watched her eyes widen, and then he watched her tan, vibrant flesh crystallize with tiny flecks of gleaming metal, molecule by molecule. When the spell broke, and that instant was over, Trinnie was tumbling head over heels toward the arena wall, and Victor stood cloaked in swirling black shadows.

To her credit, Trinnie didn't drop her glaive, and when she impacted the arena wall, the thunderous report was reminiscent of a cannonball hitting home. The reinforced magical materials of the arena didn't crumble, but they cracked. Trinnie's body jerked and crumpled with the impact, but when she slid to the sand, she was whole. As the crowd roared with surprise and excitement for Victor's sudden recovery, she braced herself with her glaive and, haltingly at first, but then more smoothly, pulled herself to her feet.

Victor frowned as she began to gather electrically charged Energy into herself again, her hair dancing wildly as she reached up to wipe away a single drop of blood from the corner of her mouth. "Damn," he grunted. "She's *hard*." Growling, finding it harder and harder to hold the rage in his Core, he began stalking toward her. He flexed his neck, clenched his fists, and took a deep breath, finally feeling normal after the last barrage of lightning bolts—he wasn't eager to go through it again.

Trinnie Ro lifted her golden glaive high, and Victor braced himself, expecting a massive bolt of electricity. When she screamed and thunder crashed, though, lightning didn't fall from the heavens. Instead, Trinnie Ro vanished, and then Victor felt her glaive bite into his shoulder. He screamed in agony as it cleaved through his thick corded muscles, bit through his clavicle, and wedged to a halt in his sternum.

Victor tried to turn, but Trinnie Ro was stronger than she looked and used the length of her weapon as a lever, pushing him away, her glaive's hot golden blade grinding into his bones as he fought to grasp onto it somehow, desperate to rip it out of his flesh. It was *doing* something to him. Where Lifedrinker drained the Energy of his foes, this glaive seemed to want to impart something to him—not Energy, but something that burned and coated his bones and flesh, tainting them with its oily touch.

For the first time since coming to Ruhn, Victor felt a bit of panic, a little twinge of "Oh fuck, what if I miscalculated," and he cut the flow of Energy to his Alter Self spell. The Energy the spell had siphoned away from his Core and away from every single cell in his body snapped back into place, and he surged with renewed strength and expanded to his full, natural, nearly fifteen-foot height. The explosive growth, coupled with Victor releasing his hold on his aura, brought a gasp from Trinnie Ro, and she found herself dangling from Victor's back, hanging from her weapon, her weight acting as a counterbalance, inexorably drawing the blade out of Victor.

Victor reached over his shoulder and snatched the back of the glaive's blade before she could pull it free. He whirled and glared down at her, he holding the caustic golden metal of her weapon and she the haft. "Let go," she hissed, and Victor saw her teeth were black and needle-sharp. Before he could reply, Trinnie's hair danced on static winds, and her glaive exploded with electricity. He was thrown back, his size made irrelevant by the powerful discharge.

Victor landed flat on his back again, stunned but not out. He shook his head, realized his shoulder still ached, and glanced down to see the cut was still there, sickly black veins probing out of it into the meat of his pectoral. "Fuck," he grunted, rolling to his knees in time to see Trinnie Ro go through a metamorphosis of her own.

At first, he thought she was going to blast him with lightning again; she stood with the glaive held high, her hair dancing on the wind again, the air palpably thick with ozone and electricity, but instead of calling down lightning, she seemed to be swelling with the Energy. With each of Victor's beleaguered heartbeats, she grew, the lightning sparking brighter and brighter in her eyes as the force of a hundred lightning bolts built her up.

Her skin shimmered with the power of her invulnerability, brightening like electrified silver, and Victor began to realize something: This might be the wrong opponent to hold back on. In fact, he might have waited too damn long already. She'd done something to him, poisoned or corrupted him, and his right arm wasn't working properly. "Fuck that," he grunted, growling as he ground his fists into the sand, pushing himself up. "If it's time to go all out, then it's time to go all out."

# 46

❧❦❧

# LOYALTY

Victor knew his plan to hold back all of his abilities, to hide the nature of his Core and beat Trinnie Ro without revealing what he could do, was a lost cause. He wasn't sure it was even much of a loss; it was clear that the powers that be, the ones who'd decided to send Trinnie Ro down to fight him, had guessed or learned plenty about his skills. It wasn't as if Victor's battle in the palace at Gloria had been a secret. They'd tried to keep a lid on things, but people will gossip, and there had been a lot of servants whose whereabouts during the battle hadn't been accounted for.

That said, was he suffering for nothing? Shouldn't he have maybe gone all out from the first second of the battle and tried to end things quickly? Had it just been stubbornness that made him try to play his game? Now, he had a corrupted wound splitting his right shoulder and an opponent powering up, displaying that she wasn't a slouch when it came to steel seekers. Victor could feel the Energy flowing out of her, and it was on par with anything he'd seen from Ronkerz's Big Ones.

Hoping to seal up his wound and put an end to things, Victor cast Iron Berserk. He expanded with size and power, surging to more than twenty feet in height, exploding with hard, cable-like muscles, and grunting an almost involuntary war cry as his chest expanded. The rage coursing through his pathways felt good and right, and Victor could feel it fighting against the corruption in his chest, pushing it back, knitting his flesh together—if not perfectly, then enough to allow him to move normally.

Trinnie Ro was still expanding, still coursing with electrical Energy, crackling and sizzling as sparks and ozone-rich air pulsed around her. She held her golden glaive high, and it gleamed so brightly that Victor couldn't look at it directly. It made him want to pick up Lifedrinker, but some part of him still hoped he could finish this battle without showing all his cards. Instead, he stalked toward her. He was now a good five or six feet bigger than even her charged-up form, and while she was still screaming soundlessly, channeling her torrents of Energy, Victor wound up his right fist and smashed her in the chest.

Electricity coursed through him, but not before Trinnie Ro was flung back, stumbling, arms cartwheeling, her "power-up" rudely interrupted. As for Victor, he bared his teeth and let the lightning-charged Energy run through him, dispersing in the sand, melting it to glass at his feet. Trinnie, eyes wide, perhaps surprised by his size or the strength of the blow, readied her glaive and then, in an explosion of lightning, disappeared, only to crackle into existence behind Victor, her glaive hacking sideways at his exposed flank.

Victor punched down, his knuckles impacting the flat of the blade, sending it down to his thigh, where it sliced deep through his flesh and muscle and ground against his femur. He was his full titanic size now; the bone was like a tree trunk but harder than steel. The glaive skittered over it, and meanwhile, Victor backhanded Trinnie Ro across the bridge of her nose, sending her reeling. He stalked toward her, snaking out a hand to snatch the electrified haft of her glaive as she raised it.

Trinnie tried to pull it away, but Victor's strength was inexorable, and he jerked it to the side, exposing her midriff to more vicious punches and jabs as he drove her back toward the wall of the arena. Victor was beyond words or taunts—he growled and grimaced, punching and kicking, constantly gripping her weapon to keep her from retreating outside the range of his blows. Of course, she could release the polearm, but he knew that wasn't an option; she wouldn't drop her golden glaive any more than he'd drop Lifedrinker involuntarily.

Victor was lucid; his rage was a cool, calculated one, and he knew his blows weren't doing any damage. Each time his fist or foot impacted Trinnie, her skin hardened like diamond, and she grimaced, but that was all. He wondered how long she could keep it up. Was it effortless, that armored flesh, or did it take Energy? Was she depleting her Core, or would she easily outlast his rage?

Growling, Victor closed with her and caught her triceps in a grapple with his right hand while still wrestling with her over the glaive with his left. Then he focused on the arena wall some twenty yards behind her. Grinning with grim brutality, he cast Energy Charge. Dark shadows enveloped the two of them, and he exploded over the sands, driving her to impact the wall. The enchanted marble split, the world echoed with the thunderous crash, and Victor slammed his knee into Trinnie Ro's abdomen, screaming with frustration at his inability to harm her.

Trinnie Ro, for her part, grimaced and grunted, and then she erupted with electricity, sizzling with the charge of her Energy as she snapped out of existence, only to reappear behind Victor, hacking her glaive in a blinding X across his back, flaying him to the bone. "Just die," she hissed, her voice sizzling like the electricity that coursed through her veins. Victor bunched his legs and, using Titanic Leap, launched himself away from the shattered marble, vaulting over her as his flesh worked to knit itself back together.

His healing was slow and imperfect. Each cut took longer to knit, and Victor knew her glaive had done something to him. He could feel the oily corruption sliding along his bones, getting under his skin, twisting and breaking down the tiny vessels as his skin came back together. It was a horrifying sensation, and if they weren't already trying to kill each other, if he hadn't already tried shattering Trinnie's invulnerable flesh, he would have gone mad with the frustration of it all. As it was, he found a large part of him begging for release, begging for him to let go of his control and let his rage *really* take over.

As he closed with Trinnie, he ran through his other abilities in his mind, seeking a strategy to deal with her obstinate, unbreakable form and her deadly lightning-charged abilities. Seeking inspiration, he knew he was a fool for holding back *that* particular ability, so he cast Inspiration of the Quinametzin. He supposed he hadn't used it thus far in the hopes of saving it or not revealing it. He also had to consider that he couldn't channel Iron Berserk, Inspiration of the Quinametzin, and a *third* powerful ability like Banner of the Champion.

Still, inspiration was what he needed, and as the glow of that golden-hued Energy entered his rage-filled vision, Victor began to calm down and think around his rage rather than with it. Perhaps unsurprisingly, the first conclusion he came to was that he had to change his tactics. Why was he trying to fight this woman with his bare hands? Was Lifedrinker such a secret? He'd already exposed her. Veil walkers and steel seekers were observing the battle, and they could learn much simply by studying Lifedrinker with their inner eyes, with their Energy sense.

Victor stopped in his tracks and watched Trinnie Ro approach. He needed to break with her long enough to pick up his weapon, so he watched her, waiting for the telltale surge of electrical Energy. He doubted she'd come at him directly. No, she'd teleport and hit his flank. Victor would, of course, try to avoid the blow, but he figured he might need to eat at least one more painful cut before he could get his hands on Lifedrinker—before he could feel her encouraging weight and power and start to turn things around.

Queen Kynna Dar watched Victor and felt her world begin to crumble. Just as the black lines of corruption ate at his flesh, leaving his cuts half healed and his moves lethargic, she could feel the impending gloom encroaching on her queendom.

She couldn't fault Victor, could she? He was giving his life, after all. Had he been a fool set on his own destruction? Was his weapon a bluff? Could he not wield the mighty axe? Hadn't he done so in her garden? The questions raced through her mind as she watched him slam Trinnie Ro against the arena wall again, recoiling as her wicked glaive sliced him.

Kynna felt sick about Victor's likely doom but also for the disloyal part she'd had to play—disloyal but not traitorous, she comforted herself. She'd done nothing to influence his performance, only hedged her bets, guarding the fate of her queendom in the event he'd overplayed his hand, which seemed more and more likely. Kynna glanced at the guardswoman whose promotion, requested by Victor himself, had come across her desk that very morning. Bryn. Her eyes were red beneath the visor of her helm, but she didn't weep. Not yet.

A commotion behind her and the stammered words "Imperial Highness" startled Kynna out of her melancholy reveries, and she stood, clutching her thick formal gown as she turned and prepared to curtsy. Sure enough, Grand Prince Troyssas was entering her viewing box, her guards practically prostrating themselves in his presence as he stepped past them. Kynna curtsied low, tilting her crown and staring at the man's glittering crystalline slippers as he approached.

"Kynna." He chortled, no hint of formality in his tone. "Do relax. I've simply come to pay my respects; I doubt I'll stay to see the end of this sad display."

Kynna straightened, fighting her bristling pride and irrational desire to defend Victor to this man, perhaps the fourth most powerful on the planet. "It's very kind of you to think of me, Your Imperial Highness."

"Nonsense. You've done much to offer entertainment over the last months. What a wonderful surprise it was to see you come out from beneath the bootheels of old Groff and Vennar. Ha! I bet they rue the day they encircled Gloria, hmm?" He stepped past Kynna, his bulk like a small planetoid beside her, pulling against her like gravity. He peered down into the arena, watching for a moment as Victor, again, leaped away from Trinnie Ro, trailing buckets of dark, black blood. "What a strange champion. He certainly took you far, in any case. Far enough to negotiate a proper outcome to this contest, at least."

"Yes, Your Imperial—"

"*Highness* will do, dear Kynna."

"Yes, Highness."

"So, what was the settlement? Iron Mountain and a hundred years of peace? Something you can live with, at least, yes? A bit of a pity you won't have your vengeance; Bandia will escape Gloria's wrath for the moment." He winced and moved a massive, thick hand to his blush-covered cheek, suddenly holding a jade-inlaid fan to shield his eyes. "My, but he *does* bleed, does he not?"

"He's full of surprises, Highness. I wouldn't count him out—"

"Come, enough fantasies. Take your medicine, love. He's a brute—a barbarian with a berserker's talents. His healing's been dealt with, and, as you see, even his rather unique bloodline isn't enough to overcome a proper steel seeker with talents and equipment to match."

Kynna looked past Troyssas to the arena floor and saw Victor backing away from Trinnie, his hands out, somehow managing to avoid most of her hacks and cleaves without further injury. Troyssas wasn't wrong, though; the damage had been done. Victor's vibrant, tanned flesh was tracked with black veins, and his cuts hung partly open, spilling dark, stained blood to the sands. They were on the black side, so it wasn't obvious how much he was bleeding, but when Kynna squinted, she could see the damp, glittering nature of his blood on the sands.

She felt eyes on her and glanced to her left where Bryn stared, eyes wide, horror marring her expression. She must have realized what Troyssas meant about Iron Mountain. Kynna had negotiated very favorable terms, indeed. If Victor were to win, Lovania would be her subject state, but if he lost, Kynna simply had to give up her most valuable duchy—Iron Mountain—and swear a non-aggression pact. No one could blame her. The terms were too good to pass up; after all, she had her people, her family, to consider.

The terms were, in fact, *too* good, and Kynna knew why: the imperial family had made a point of pushing this duel forward. They'd created openings for other champions, clearing the path for Trinnie Ro's placement with Lovania. They wanted Victor killed and Kynna's ambitions along with him. Kynna met Bryn's gaze, daring her to speak, but the woman knew her place; she jerked her chin back to the arena, watching the man she'd come to admire fight to the last. How long would it be? How long could a man, even one as great as Victor, function with such injuries?

Something in Kynna made her want to argue with Troyssas. Perhaps she simply didn't want her guards—and Bryn—to hear her blithely accept Victor's fate. "Are you sure you must leave, Highness? Victor may yet surprise us."

"Nonsense! He's suffered an unfortunate turn of fate, finding himself up against Trinnie Ro, but misfortune is what it is. She's quite thoroughly adept at countering his strengths. Her glaive poisons the berserker's blood, canceling his regeneration, and her durability is without peer; even his prodigious strength cannot harm her. What other little tricks does he have? He was mediocre with that spear, and, for some reason, he eschews his axe, not that it could harm Trinnie Ro's flesh. He's let things go too far, in any case. I doubt he could even pick that weapon up in his current condition. No, I think the most we can hope for is a mercifully quick death for the poor man. I'm sorry for your loss."

"... can do much more than that ..." Bryn's whisper was muttered between clenched teeth, but Kynna heard her. If Troyssas heard her, though, he didn't react. Likely he hadn't registered the noise of vocal cords so far beneath him. He fluttered his fan and turned toward the steps leading down from Kynna's viewing platform.

"Thank you again for looking in on me, Highness."

The imperial prince turned and favored her with a thick, burgundy-lipped smile, fluttering his perfumed fan again, this time wafting some of the jasmine scents toward Kynna. "Again, I'm sorry you won't have your vengeance for Thorn's betrayal, but mind your opportunities, dear Kynna. Perhaps a place at the imperial court is in your future. If nothing else, this barbarian has reminded people of Gloria's past greatness."

Kynna curtsied low again and watched the enormous man's bulbous figure descend the steps. Shame turned her neck hot as she straightened and turned back to the arena. None of her guards, none of her attendants looked her way. It was as though they could feel the guilt radiating off her. Why was she guilty, though? Should she have bet everything on Victor? Should she have refused terms that so blatantly favored her? Should she have tried to avoid the duel? Should she have given Victor time to prepare for such an opponent? Hadn't she asked him? Hadn't she *told* him how dangerous Trinnie Ro was?

She sat down, resting her elbows on her knees and staring at the glittering, sapphire-studded silken slippers on her feet. She was happy that, at least, she hadn't allowed Tomorran to attend the duel. Better that he hear of Victor's demise than to see it. The crowd had taken on that weird, shell-shocked nature that often occurred when a fight was one-sided. It was almost as though they were reluctant to cheer for Trinnie Ro—as if the torture she was doling out was shameful. Instead, they "oohed" and gasped, even moaned, with each new spray of black-tinged blood that her golden glaive wrung from Victor's flesh.

Kynna had grown so used to those resigned, wincing collective gasps that when the tempo changed, and an underlying current of excitement bubbled up through the enormous arena, Kynna glanced up, her eyes wide. "What is it?"

"He picked up his axe," Bryn said through clenched teeth, her hands white-knuckled where they gripped the balcony railing.


*"Blood-mate! You bleed, and your touch is cold and soft! What ails you? Guide my edge to the foes that beset you!"*

Victor couldn't help the mad smile that split his bloodstained lips as he felt Lifedrinker's eagerness. He was hurting, no doubt about it, but he hadn't played all his cards yet. It was clear that Trinnie Ro thought he had. She was content to wear him down, bleed him out, and poison his body while she was at it. Victor had taken his sweet time getting to Lifedrinker. He'd danced a good long time with Trinnie Ro, trying to get her to reveal her cards. Was she done? Was this the extent of it?

She'd shown him her teleportation ability. She'd shown him her glaive's wicked, quick edge that could taint his very blood. She'd powered herself up with lightning-attuned Energy, making herself nearly titanic in size and fast and strong, to boot. Finally, she'd shown him how she could call lightning from the heavens to blast the ever-living shit out of him. Wasn't that enough? Did she have to have something more held in check? He'd tried to get it out of her if there was something. He'd let her carve the hell out of him, poisoning him down to the marrow in his bones. She hadn't done anything else, but maybe she didn't realize she needed to.

"Okay, *chica*. Don't worry yet. Just cut this *bruja* for me." With those words, Victor hefted his wonderful axe and strode toward Trinnie Ro, content to let his reflexes, instincts, and Lifedrinker run the show for a while. He'd been nursing his rage, letting it fill his pathways, but no more. He could feel the corruption in his bones and knew even his Quinametzin constitution was struggling with whatever taint his tormentor's glaive was leaving behind with each cut and gash. He wondered how long he would have lasted without his titan blood, without his titan's pride that wouldn't easily allow poison to take root.

Trinnie Ro's glaive flickered like a golden serpent's tongue, and Victor's forearms twitched, lifting Lifedrinker's prodigious blade into its path. For the first time, metal on metal rang through the arena, and blazing golden sparks flew as Lifedrinker carved a sliver of metal from the poisoned weapon's edge. Victor's grin turned savage, and he licked his bloody lips as Trinnie backpedaled, her eyes wide with concern for her precious weapon. "What's the matter?" he grunted, breaking his rule about shit-talking.

"If you think an axe will save you, fool, you should step outside yourself to see your ruined flesh. You're dead; you just don't know it yet."

Victor hocked a loogie, spitting a thick black wad of bloody phlegm onto the sand. "What, *this*? I'm Quinametzin, *pendeja*; your poison isn't going to end me." With that, Victor darted forward and began to weave Lifedrinker in a dizzying array of feints, hacks, thrusts, and cleaves, driving Trinnie back as she had to work extra hard to keep the edge of her glaive from meeting Lifedrinker's hungry blade. Their metal rang and howled as they clashed, and the spectators' reactions took on a new life as it became more and more apparent that Victor wasn't out of the fight.

Cheers resounded with each clash of the mighty weapons, and when Trinnie tried to teleport to Victor's flank, attempting to catch him off guard, the crowd went wild when Lifedrinker was there, ready for that golden blade. With Victor's guiding hands, she rebuffed the attack, and the glaive rebounded, a new notch at the top of its sword-like edge. Trinnie scowled and redoubled her efforts, and their battle went on.

The fight was far from one-sided, and there was some truth to the idea that Victor had waited too long. He was weakened and slowed by the toxins coursing through his body. Even as his Quinametzin constitution worked to eject the poison, it seemed to multiply on itself, thickening in his blood and spreading through his marrow—the source of that infection being his split clavicle. He had an idea for how to purge himself of the poison and turn the tables, but Victor was reluctant. He wanted to see how far he could go as he was. He wanted to see what Trinnie Ro was made of. Could their dance bring out the Paragon of the Axe?

Grand Prince Troyssas of Khaliday held up his thick hand, and Ambassador Voolian clamped his mouth shut. Troyssas turned to Brinnit, the captain of his personal guard, and barked, "What's happening in there?" Clangs rang out, and the crowd was energized. He could feel it from there.

"I'll check, Highness." Brinnit took the stairs up to the imperial box three at a time, and Troyssas contemplated returning to his seat to view the rest of the match. Surely it was nearly over, but why the sudden change in tone? It had been a massacre; the foreign berserker had been on his last legs when he'd gone to taunt Kynna. Gods! That little wretch, Trinnie Ro, had better not be squandering the opportunity he and his sister had fed her.

"Is something the matter, Your Imperial Highness? If there's aught that I can do to improve your experience, you have but to ask. Perhaps you'd enjoy viewing the rest of the battle from the comfort of my airship? I noticed you came through the teleporter, and I'm sure I have more comfortable accommodations than those in the viewing boxes." Voolian mewled, his worthless, obsequious flattery falling on deaf ears. Troyssas was focused on the stairs, watching for Brinnit's return.

She reappeared almost immediately, descending to the breezeway in a single light-footed bound. "The barbarian has picked up his axe and seems rather skilled in its use."

"He still bleeds?"

"He does, Highness."

"And Trinnie?"

"Unscathed, Highness."

"Enough, then. Escort me to the portal chamber."

"As you say, Highness." Brinnit snapped her fingers, and Troyssas's guards melded out of the stonework around him, forming a protective wedge and marching along with his enormous, rolling steps as he left Voolian babbling about how pleased he'd been to chat with him again. In all honesty, Troyssas couldn't recall a single word of their conversation; it had been as meaningless as breathing or taking a piss.

He glanced at Savinicus, his Master of Revels. "See that my baths are well staffed. I'll be going in for the night."

"Of course, Highness, any particular flavor?"

"I require soft comforts tonight, Sav. Ensure one of my singers is there." Troyssas shuddered, appalled by the sliver of stress that had wormed its way into his mind. How *dare* that barbarian last as long as he had? Some folks just didn't have the *decency* to die when the time was upon them. He caught Brinnit eyeing him, her expression hard, as usual, though she usually had the good sense to drop her gaze when he caught her looking. "What?" he barked.

"Will all be well if he doesn't die?"

"Gods *damn* it! Why would you ask that?" Troyssas threw out a thick, meaty fist, blasting one of his guards into the wall with the crunch of shattered bones. Two of his retinue slowed to help the poor fool recover, but Brinnit didn't flinch.

"I ask because I saw the glimmer of a paragon on his blade. If the poison doesn't do him in, he may well cut Trinnie Ro, regardless of her diamond-hard flesh."

"*Damn* you for saying so!" Troyssas pouted. He stopped in his tracks and folded his enormous arms over his bulging chest, contemplating things. If Kynna Dar's champion managed to win, she'd be one step closer to challenging Bandia. If she won that contest, then she'd own a coastal kingdom, which would open the way to challenges on the eastern continent. She could be a dozen well-planned challenges away from threatening one of his borders.

She claimed she was aiming to conquer Bandia because of Thorn's betrayal. If that were the case, her little conquest would end there. If not . . . if not, then the great houses had champions that would make Trinnie Ro seem a child. No, things weren't lost, even if that barbarian managed to win the day, however unlikely that might be. "Brinnit, you will stay and observe the rest of the fight. Carpecus," he said, turning to his chief advisor, "I'll need you to make a report to my sister. We may have much to discuss."

Victor's rictus smile grew wider and wider as he began to drive Trinnie Ro back. His axe hummed through the air, an instrument of death that weighed thousands of pounds and moved like the flicker of a murderous thought. Trinnie's glaive was a nuisance, a feather-light obstacle that he could bat aside, cut through, or dismiss as the ghostly edge of his paragon began to appear, slipping past Trinnie Ro's guard and slicing through her impossibly hard flesh. Panic entered her mean-eyed glare, and instead of asking him why he wouldn't simply die, she began to pant for breath, baring her sharp black teeth in ever-increasing stress.

Victor was past the point of sympathy. He never hesitated to follow up his attacks, watering the sands with Trinnie's bright red blood. As more and more shreds of golden metal flew through the air and the cuts on Trinnie's flesh mounted, Victor found himself feeling better.

Slowly but surely, his body was pushing the poison out, even without him burning it from his veins with an infusion of magma. His Spirit Core was flaring brightly; he'd only used about half his Energy to maintain his Iron Berserk and his Inspiration of the Quinametzin. He'd saved most of his trump cards: his Volcanic Fury, his Glacial Wrath, his Aspect of Terror, even his Banner and Wild Totem.

He'd gone through hell for nearly thirty minutes, but had it been worth it? Would saving all those tricks up his sleeve and not exposing his Breath Core pay off down the road? Anyone who fought him now would know that Lifedrinker was a force to be reckoned with. They'd know he was a master of the axe. They'd know that while poison might weaken him, it would take a hell of a corruption to kill him. Was it time to stop caring? Was it time to just put his cards on the table and straight up beat the hell out of all comers?

Trinnie Ro was tough, but was she the *toughest*? They'd brought her down to put an end to him, but had they held stronger champions in reserve? Victor knew damn well the great houses wouldn't leave themselves defenseless. If they gave Trinnie Ro to a lesser house, you better believe they thought their own champions could end her. All those thoughts ran through his mind as his frustration fed the fury of his lethal combinations, and he pushed Trinnie Ro into a fatal error.

When she charged herself with lightning, and Victor knew her teleportation was imminent, he watched the corners of her eyes where she would tell him where to strike. Sure enough, just for a fraction of a second, the whites tilted to the right, and Victor whirled, hacking Lifedrinker in a broad, screaming cleave, the Paragon of the Axe extending her edge by six feet. Trinnie Ro flashed with lightning and reappeared in Lifedrinker's path, and Victor cleaved her in half, splitting her just above the hips in a shower of crimson droplets.

As half of Trinnie Ro fell to his left and the other toppled to the right, Victor lifted Lifedrinker high and roared into the crowd's answering cheers. He was just starting to feel normal again, and he knew his roar was amplified by his Voice of the Angry Mountain. He could feel it shaking the ground around him. He could see the arena walls where he and Trinnie had cracked the marble, showering dust and debris down onto the sands. His voice echoed and reverberated back to him, and, to Victor's rage-addled mind, it made him imagine other titans were answering his cry. He screamed all the louder, and the people in the stands went wild with his enthusiasm.

When he turned to look at Kynna, he saw her standing, her face stunned, her eyes wide. He'd done it, and she couldn't believe it. He laughed at the expression and shook Lifedrinker in victory, and the axe screamed with him, her bloodlust unquenched. *"Let us kill all these fools, blood-heart! Let us dance on their bones!"*

Victor laughed and shook her harder in response, so proud of his wonderful axe, so amazed by her ability to outclass that golden glaive. His heart was swollen with his pride for her, and as he screamed his victory cry, tears filled his eyes, and he choked out a softer declaration, just for her, "I love you, *chica!* Thank you for saving me so many times."

# 47

※

# WHAT THE HEART WANTS

When Victor recovered from his influx of Energy, it took him several seconds to remember where he was. His knees were resting on hot black sand, and Lifedrinker sat before him, her blade baleful in the mid-morning sunlight. Recognizing the stupor of being drunk on Energy, he wasn't surprised to see a System message waiting for him:

*****Congratulations! You have achieved Level 82 Warlord and gained 24 intelligence and 17 vitality.*****

"Champion," a familiar voice said from behind him, "will you claim a prize from your fallen foe?" It was Lohanse, and as Victor recognized his voice, everything fell into place, and he remembered where he was. He squinted up at the stands, unsurprised to see less than half the seats occupied. How long had he been senseless? With a grunt, he stood, gripping Lifedrinker's haft like a lever to haul himself up.

He looked at Lohanse, resplendent in his fine ceremonial robes. "You know what I'll claim."

Suddenly, the air felt thick, and the murmurs and noise of the stadium faded, sounding like they were coming to him through a thick veil of water. Lohanse spoke, and his voice's pitch made it clear that only Victor would hear his words. "I would beg a favor, Victor. I knew Trinnie Ro's father well. Will you leave her body whole, that she might travel untroubled through the veil?"

Victor frowned. "The champion?"

"Yes, he was. A very good man."

Victor nodded to Trinnie Ro's broken body, lying in two halves, her flesh unnaturally pale. "You think it makes a difference?"

"I know not what ritual you perform with the hearts of your foes. However, watching you pull those grisly trophies, I've witnessed shreds of spirit clinging to the organs. Do you deny it?"

Victor shook his head. "I don't."

"So? Will you honor my request?"

Victor's lust for blood and death was thoroughly satiated, and the idea that Lohanse, a man of immense power, was asking him for a favor meant something significant to him. He clenched his jaw and nodded. "I will."

"Will you claim a different trophy, then?"

Victor let his eyes drift over Trinnie's ruined body again. He stared at the golden glaive lying not far away. Should he take the weapon that had tormented him so? Would he ever use it? He frowned, considering an idea that danced through his mind, and then nodded. "I'll take that wicked polearm of hers."

As Lohanse moved to pick up the weapon for him, Victor touched Lifedrinker's haft. "I'll speak to you soon, *chica*. I have gifts for you."

*"I will wait for you, battle-heart."*

Victor smiled grimly, sending her away to her storage ring. When Lohanse stepped toward him, Trinnie's beautiful glaive in his hands, Victor studied the long, sword-like blade—it was already whole, having mended itself of the damage Lifedrinker had dealt it. "Does it live?" he asked.

Lohanse nodded. "I believe so, though it doesn't speak to me."

"Then I'll put it with Lifedrinker; it won't suffer in that storage device."

Lohanse nodded, offering Victor the haft of the polearm. "Your axe is something remarkable, young man."

"She is," Victor agreed, touching the golden glaive's haft, wincing slightly at the cold, electric tingle that ran through his fingers. He sent it to storage, wondering if the two weapons would be aware of each other in there. He looked up and saw most of the remaining spectators streaming out of the arena. Kynna's platform was empty. "Looks like it's time to go."

"Aye, lad. The people who waited around for you to regain consciousness hoped to witness another brutal heart-taking."

"Ah." Victor nodded, then turned toward the tunnel leading back to his ready room. He took one step before he felt a heavy hand on his shoulder.

"I promised you a debt, and I'm a man of my word. I'll offer you a word of caution for free, however. Will you hear it?"

Victor turned to regard the veil walker, arching a heavy black eyebrow. "I will."

"Know this, then: The great houses have taken note of you. Trinnie Ro wasn't here by some obscene coincidence. There will be schemes within schemes to keep Gloria from rising to power again. If Queen Kynna intends to do more than conquer Bandia in retaliation for Thorn's betrayal, then you should expect danger around every corner, behind every curtain, and, certainly, at every duel. It might be time to stop playing games."

Victor absently rubbed his right shoulder where Trinnie's golden glaive had sliced through his flesh and bone. He contemplated the man's words for a moment, more in a show of respect and to let Lohanse know he was taking his words seriously than because he felt he needed the warning. After a moment, he looked at the veil walker in his depthless, power-filled eyes. "I came to that conclusion during the battle, Grand Judicator. I appreciate the warning nonetheless."

Lohanse nodded, then released his grip on Victor's shoulder. "Until your next battle, then."

Victor turned and stalked down the corridor into his waiting room. When he arrived, he was a little surprised to find only Bryn waiting. He'd thought Kynna would be eager to congratulate him, though he had to admit, she'd looked a little distraught at the end of the fight. Had the battle taken a lot out of her? Had she thought Victor would lose? He'd be lying if he hadn't had some doubts during the fight. How would the witnesses have felt? "Hello, Bryn."

"Your Grace! Congratulations!" She still wore her helmet, but Victor could see her eyes were bright with good cheer. "I knew you had more fight in you!"

Victor chuckled. "Ah, so there was some speculation about my demise?"

"The atmosphere in the queen's box was grim for a while there, milord. The queen has returned to Iron Mountain to arrange the festivities."

Victor frowned. "Shouldn't they already be arranged?"

"Indeed, milord. I believe it was an excuse to leave and gather her . . . *wits*."

"Was she stunned by my performance?" As he approached Bryn, Victor realized he was towering over her, so he cast Alter Self, bringing himself down closer to ten feet so he'd be comfortable in doorways and on the furniture back at the palace.

"I believe she suffered a wide range of emotional responses to your performance." Bryn moved to the door, pulling it open for him. "I'll gladly give you more details back at your palace, Your Grace, but . . ." She gestured to the glowing crystals near the clock on the wall. Victor got her meaning; this wasn't the place to speak openly. He nodded and followed her through the door into the tunnel, where he found half a dozen more of the queen's guards waiting to escort him to the portal.

Back at the palace, Victor made his way directly to his quarters. He wanted to meet with Kynna, and he wanted to get an update from Trobban, but more than anything, he wanted to have a long hot soak in his bath. He was tired—not so much physically as mentally. He'd worn himself out worrying about fighting Trinnie Ro, and now that it was over, he felt as if he'd shed a mountain of stress, and all he wanted to do was soak and forget about the whole damn thing. When he stepped out of the elevator and Bryn exited behind him, he turned to regard her. "You should take the rest of the day off."

"I . . ." She looked as if she wanted to say more but stopped to breathe or think, and then she just nodded briefly. "Thank you, Victor."

"Oh," Victor said, holding up a hand, "one thing before you go." He reached into his storage ring and summoned out Trinnie's golden glaive. "I got this for you."

Bryn gasped and took a step back, shaking her head vehemently. "I cannot!"

"The hell you *can't*. I want you to have it. I don't know if the queen or Draj Haveshi has spoken to you yet, but I'm also going to, um, *elevate* you. I'm going to award you some land and a title."

"Victor!" Again, Bryn shook her head, waving both her hands in negation. "I've done nothing to earn—"

"Bullshit you haven't!" Victor thrust the glaive toward her, noting how it seemed to caress his flesh with tiny electric tingles. "Bryn, you've been by my side on Ruhn since day one. You put your life on the line more than once, and I intend to hold you to that standard for the rest of my visit here, and that could be years. I demand a lot from the people who work for me, and in return, I like to think I offer appropriate rewards.

"Now, this glaive represents something important to me—Trinnie Ro was a hell of a fighter, and I learned a lot while fighting against this weapon. I want it to go to someone who will respect and use it, not stick it on a shelf or hide it away in a storage ring. It's a conscious weapon, Bryn. Don't insult . . ." Victor paused and considered the feelings he was getting from the glaive through his hands. He grinned and nodded. "Don't insult *her* by refusing."

"Her . . ." Bryn's voice was full of wonder as she stretched out trembling hands to grasp the glaive's haft below Victor's. When she felt the weapon's electric touch and accepted the weight of it, her eyes flew wide and Victor could see the smile on her face through the grill of her visor.

"There. Now, I don't know exactly where your land will be, but you'll need to hire an estate manager anyway, 'cause I'm not letting you go. Not yet."

Bryn reached up and touched her helmet, sending it away to storage, and Victor saw her big brown eyes were streaming with tears. She blinked them several times, then fell to a knee, pressing her forehead to the glaive's haft. "I swear, Victor, Your Grace, I swear I will serve you faithfully with this weapon."

Victor stepped forward and rested a hand on her shoulder, looking into her eyes. "I know you will, Bryn. Now stand up and go enjoy the rest of your day."

"Your Grace, there's something I should tell you."

Victor arched an eyebrow. "Yeah?"

"Yes." Bryn stood, then glanced around the little antechamber between the elevator and Victor's quarters. "Can we step inside?"

Victor's curiosity was piqued, and he nodded, pulling open his suite door and stepping inside. The rooms were dim; the curtains on the balcony were drawn closed. He didn't go and open them; instead, he pulled the door shut and stood with his back to it, regarding Bryn. "What is it?"

"While you were battling, a visitor came to the queen's box, one of the Grand Princes—Troyssas."

"That's . . ." Victor thought about the name, trying to remember where he'd heard it. "That's one of the emperor's sons?"

"Yes, milord."

"And?"

"He spoke to the queen, and, well, their conversation made it sound like she'd arranged favorable dueling terms, perhaps at the expense of your preparation."

Victor sighed and reached up to scratch his nails through the stiff stubble along his jaw. "Elaborate."

"She arranged terms that permitted Gloria to continue with her as the queen. Her only loss, should Trinnie Ro have won the duel, would have been this duchy."

Victor sniffed and nodded. "So when she learned about Trinnie Ro, instead of backing off the duel or delaying it, she accepted some favorable terms to make it happen immediately. That's the gist of it?"

"Yes, Your Grace." Bryn looked down, something like shame in her eyes.

Victor forced a smile, then reached out and rested a hand on her shoulder. "Thanks for coming to me with this, but don't mention it again, okay? If you're worried about the queen's loyalty, then don't be. She's loyal, but first and foremost, she's loyal to her family. After that, she's loyal to her nation. There are probably a few more things in between that and me. I'm aware of that, and I'll keep my eyes open, okay? Don't get yourself in trouble sticking your neck out."

Bryn nodded, sniffing and wiping at her nose. "Did I overstep? Was it wrong to doubt the queen's—"

"The only thing I'm worried about is someone misunderstanding *your* loyalty, Bryn. I'm counting on you to keep your eyes open, but caution is always paramount. Understand? I can protect you from much, but not everything."

"Understood, Your Grace." She straightened the glaive, haft resting on the floor by her boots, and brought her other fist to her chest in a smart salute. "Thank you . . . Victor."

Victor smiled and turned to open the door for her. "My pleasure. Enjoy the rest of your day." He watched her leave, then shut the door and went to his balcony, pulling the curtains wide. He inhaled deeply, sighing with pleasure as he took in the view of Iron Mountain. His place on Fanwath was lovely, and he enjoyed the view of the Silver Sea it provided, but this was on another level. Iron Mountain was otherworldly in its majesty and evoked something in his chest that the sea couldn't match.

He turned and went into his bathroom, which also featured a wall of glass that provided a view of the mountain. He ran hot water into the enormous tiled tub, then undressed and sank into the hot water. He felt good. He felt good about Bryn and was only moderately disappointed to learn that Kynna hadn't prioritized his safety. Could he really blame her? She was given a chance to have her cake and eat it, too. If Victor won, her conquest continued. If he lost, she was mostly left intact with a kingdom facing hundreds of years of peace.

Even so, it stung a little when he remembered her words before the fight—how she'd said it felt like he could share her burdens. It had seemed as though they'd made a connection in that moment. Had he imagined it? Maybe it was real, but to a woman who was closing in on a hundred years old and who had a million responsibilities, maybe that connection hadn't been as meaningful. "And that's life," he sighed, slipping deeper into the hot, soapy water.

He wondered how long it would take to arrange the fight with Bandia. He doubted they'd be eager to do battle, having seen Victor beat Trinnie Ro—a steel seeker. He figured Kynna would need to apply some pressure and maybe some subterfuge. It might take months to set up the duel in that case. In a way, Victor hoped it wouldn't take that long; he was eager to get things moving and finish up with his battles on Ruhn. He had people he wanted to see and . . . *obligations* he wanted to complete.

Khul Bach was waiting to be reunited with his kin, and Victor owed the War-lord of Coloss a visit. Even more than that, Victor wanted to make good on his implied promises to Nia, Agnes, and the other surviving thralls from Dark Ember; the people living under the horrific rule of the undead "great lords" deserved a chance at freedom. By comparison, this burgeoning war of succession felt almost petty. Still, Victor owed Ranish Dar, and the master Spirit Caster wanted his granddaughter to rule the empire, so it was a task he had to face.

"I wonder," he mused aloud, "if I should eat that lava king heart." His mouth filled with saliva at the prospect, and a grin spread his lips as he dunked his head to rinse soap from his short, stiff hair. Why shouldn't he? It was as good a time as any. He had the "distillate" to drink, too. "And Lifedrinker has some metal to consume!"

Anticipation making him hasty, he leaped from the tub, thankful for his absurd, cat-like reflexes as he caught himself sliding on the wet soapy tiles. He dried off and pulled on his pants, then, gripping his vault key necklace, he left the bathroom, only to stop in his tracks when he saw Kynna sitting, perfectly at ease, on the sofa that looked out on his balcony. Victor dropped the vault, letting it bounce against his sternum as he fumbled through his storage rings for a clean shirt. "Your Majesty," he sputtered, settling for a black cotton shirt with silver buttons.

"Victor, I'm sorry I let myself in." She gestured to the open balcony doors, and he wondered if she meant that was how she came in. Could she fly? He supposed it only made sense; she was a high-level iron ranker with the resources of a queen—she probably had a dozen ways to fly.

"Uh, no problem." He stood back, buttoning his shirt, and she remained seated, her face focused on the view outside the window. Victor realized she didn't wear her crown. Was that the first time he'd seen her without it? He was pretty sure it was. "I figured you'd summon me to speak with you."

"I would have, but I couldn't wait. I'm overwhelmed by strange emotions. Will you sit?"

Victor stepped forward, walked around the couch, and sat beside her, leaving a cushion between them. "Everything all right?"

"Yes, I believe so. Do *you* feel that everything is well?"

Victor nodded, stretching out his legs and propping his feet on a cushioned ottoman. "I didn't enjoy fighting Trinnie Ro—I prefer my opponents to be less . . . *heroic*—but it's over, and I'm ready to move on."

"Are you? Do you not harbor any doubts about the nature of her appearance? Do you not feel that I should have, perhaps, objected to the change in champions? I could have delayed the duel. I could have—"

"You asked me if I could beat her. I told you yes. There's nothing more to talk about."

Kynna looked at him, her eyes locking on his. They burned white, as always, but seemed softer—like incandescent bulbs in fog. "Do you mean that? Would it matter if I told you that I was offered very favorable terms, enticing me to push the duel forward?"

"Do you feel guilty about it? If so, Your Majesty, that's between you and your conscience. I came to fight for you, and that means against any champions that stand in your way. I've accepted that. If you haven't, perhaps you should reevaluate your commitment to this campaign. I mean to conquer Ruhn for you. I can't go hiding from this or that champion and expect it to happen anyway. So, yeah, if you're wondering if we're good, we are. You do the politics bullshit, and I'll do the fighting."

"You . . ." Kynna licked her lips and shook her head slightly. "People thought you were losing. I have it on good authority that Grand Prince Troyssas boasted of champions that could make Trinnie Ro seem a mere gifted child. The great houses haven't been involved in duels, not in recent memory, so I don't know how braggadocious he's being, but Victor, you *seemed* to struggle with Trinnie Ro!"

Victor thought about being honest with her. He thought about setting aside bravado, but when he heard about the "grand prince" talking shit, his

Quinametzin pride bristled, and he chuckled, waving a hand dismissively. "Just because I put on a good show doesn't mean there was any real danger. I'm ready to face whatever steel seekers they throw at me. Now, Your Majesty, I have a, um, natural treasure to consume and may be out of it for a few days. Is now an appropriate time to do something like that?"

"Now?" She reached a hand across the cushion between them, lightly brushing his knee with her fingertips.

Victor frowned and stood, pacing to the balcony. He wasn't sure why. Was he irritated that she'd called his performance into question? Was he more bothered about her political scheming than he let on? Was he just uncomfortable with the idea of taking their relationship beyond professional? Maybe he was still hung up on Valla. Whatever it was, he did a good job of signaling his reticence because, as he stared at the mountain, Queen Kynna stood behind him and spoke to his back.

"I'll leave you to it, then, Victor. You have my gratitude—our *nation's* gratitude. I'll have your trophies delivered to your chambers, as it seems you won't be attending the celebratory banquet this evening."

Victor didn't turn around. He nodded, gripping the marble balcony railing, and stared at the mountain, drawing strength from it. "I appreciate that. I hope you understand that I'm weary."

"Of course. I should have thought of that. Please seek me out when you're rested."

Victor closed his eyes and breathed deeply, listening to her steps retreating to the door. When he heard it open and then click closed, he exhaled, sighing heavily. He hoped he hadn't insulted her too much. He was his own person, though, and he might not know what his heart wanted, but he was reasonably sure, at least at that moment, that it wasn't Kynna Dar.

# 48

## A VISITOR

*On wings of fiery rage, the lava king soared through his domain, his blazing eyes hunting for the interloper. This was his hall, his kingdom. This was where his ash queens laid their eggs, this was where his father and his father before him had fought free of their shells, and this was where he had fought for the right to call himself king! His domain was deep under the earth, caverns through which lava rivers and lakes stretched farther than the eye could see. His domain was vast, his dominance absolute, and any fool that thought to breach his defenses would feel his claws and taste his fiery breath.*

*He banked, channeling more Energy into his wings, surging forward faster than any creature with his bulk had a right to move. He passed through a great natural stone arch, his wings scorching the stones on either side. Once through, he swooped up toward the mile-high domed stone ceiling, and from that lofty vantage, he scanned his largest cavern, his eyes piercing the darkness, snatching out the blues and greens of things with blood too cool to dip into his molten domain.*

*"There," he growled, diving toward four green and blue figures. They were large and bipedal, and they clutched their steely fangs in their forelimbs like so many of their kind. It didn't matter. The lava king gathered a great lungful of air, expanded his chest, and, with a spark from his Breath Core, doused the cool-blooded fools with an avalanche of lava. By the time he set down on the steaming, ticking stone shelf where they'd stood, naught but bones and some bits of charred flesh remained.*

*The lava king turned to face the center of the cavern and roared his victory, signaling to his brood and his mates that their subterranean world was safe once again. He settled his great bulk on the hot stone and folded his forelegs beneath his chin as he lazily allowed his fiery wings to fade. Absently, he stretched his neck to snatch up one of the hot bones, a bit of flesh still clinging to it. He crunched it, savoring the hot marrow, and then swallowed it whole. Life was good.*

When Victor woke from his vision, he felt so good that he laughed, realizing his cheeks were already sore from the smile plastered on his face. He stretched and rolled over and lay there for a good minute, trying to figure out where he was. Slowly, as the décor of his ducal suite began to register with his sleep-addled mind, he remembered he was in Iron Mountain and that he was Victor—a Quinametzin titan from Earth. He remembered eating the lava king's heart, and then he remembered his vision, and the smile returned. What a life! He chuckled again but then noticed, on the edge of his vision, System messages that he'd somehow brushed aside:

*****Congratulations! You have gained a new Feat: Flight of the Lava King.*****

*****Flight of the Lava King: Your species is gifted with the ability to channel Energy into powerful wings capable of providing flight to even the great, scaled, densely boned bodies of your kind. This ability is innate and requires only the fiery Energy in your Core to function.*****

Victor blinked, staring at the message for several long minutes. It was the same ability his Sojourn armor set provided. However, if it proved to be anything like the flight he'd experienced in his vision, then it would be far more versatile and last a good deal longer.

The System had written the message as though Victor were a lava king. Was that how it was when his titanic nature absorbed the ability of his vanquished foes? Was that what a titan was—a conglomeration of the species it absorbed? Victor stretched out his arms, clenching his ring-covered fingers into fists, turning them left and right. He hadn't grown scales or anything. He brought forth his status page:

| Name: | Victor Sandoval | | | |
|---|---|---|---|---|
| Race: | Quinametzin Bloodline: Epic 5 | | | |
| Class: | Warlord: Legendary | | | |
| Level: | 82 | | | |
| Breath Core: | Elder Class: Advanced 7 | | | |
| Core: | Spirit Class: Epic 3 | | | |
| Breath Core Affinity: | Magma: 9, Blue Ice: 9 | Breath Core Energy: | | 6100/6100 |
| Energy Affinity: | Fear 9.4, Rage 9.1, Glory 8.6, Inspiration 7.4, Unattuned 3.1 | | Energy: | 43812/43812 |
| Strength: | 580 | Vitality: | 819 (867) | |

| Dexterity: | 280 (302) | Agility: | 303 (325) |
|---|---|---|---|
| Intelligence: | 220 | Will: | 673 |
| Points Available: | 0 | | |
| Titles & Feats: | Titanic Rage, Ancestral Bond, Flame-Touched, Greater Titanic Constitution, Titanic Presence, Desperate Grace, Unyielding Challenger, Elder Magic, Born of Terror, Battlefield Awareness, Battlefield Presence, Aura of Command, Epic Quinametzin, Mountain's Resilience, Behemoth's Regeneration, Blood Supremacy, Wyrm's Fervor, Warborn Mind, Flight of the Lava King | | |

"Still Quinametzin," he sighed, arching his back until it popped. He rolled to the side of his bed and sat on the edge, looking around his suite. It was dim; most of the curtains were drawn. Other than that, everything looked much the way it always did. He didn't see any urgent notes on his bedside table, nor were people clamoring at his door. He didn't *feel* as if he'd been out all that long, so hopefully he hadn't missed anything important.

He stood and padded into the bathroom, where he studied himself in the mirror. He looked the same. With a glance to either side of him, ensuring nothing flammable was too close, he concentrated on the new knowledge in his mind, a reflex much the same as extending a limb. Hot Energy poured out of his Breath Core, and wings of smoldering flames sprouted from his back, stretching out to either side of him. They were enormous, and he'd misjudged the space in the bathroom.

One wing stretched out over his tiled bathtub enclosure, but the other stretched through the doorway into his bedroom, scorching the frame. Not only were the wings made of smoldering fire, but they *dripped* magma. Sizzling pools grew on the marble floor and the rug outside the door, in his bedroom, instantly began to burn. Victor laughed and stopped the flow of Energy to his wings, and they flickered and faded. He summoned a thin trickle of Blue Ice into his lungs and, with a whistling exhalation, doused the fire in the doorway.

He was pretty sure the materials used to finish his quarters were enchanted to self-repair, but if they weren't, it wouldn't be hard for one of the artisans on his household staff to mend the damage. Glancing at his status sheet, he studied his Breath Core Energy Levels:

**Breath Core Energy: 6022/6100**

Part of the Energy he'd expended was from the Blue Ice, but even ignoring that, he could see he'd be able to maintain his wings for a long time. "Flight," he sighed, shaking his head with a grin. He cleaned up and got dressed, and the grin faded as he remembered one of the main reasons he'd wanted the ability to fly: so that he could do so with Valla. He bent to pull his boots on and shook his head, banishing the thought. He'd write to her soon, but he was doing better, in his opinion, not thinking about her all the time.

Dressed and feeling refreshed, he walked through the sitting room, past the dining area, and into his library and study. He'd set up his vault in the room, and it sat where he'd left it, dominating most of the free space. Victor took the key from around his neck and put it into the lock, twisting it until it clicked several times, and steam hissed out of the airtight seal. He pulled the door wide and smiled when he saw Lifedrinker at the center of the space, lying on the vault floor, bathed in the dungeon Core's magenta light.

She was still working on the hunk of silvenite he'd given her. After Trobban took what he'd needed, there'd been more than half of the brick of ore left, and it was clearly difficult for Lifedrinker to process. Victor could still see the ore beneath her mirror-smooth black blade, and it looked as though almost all of it was yet to be consumed by the axe. Tiny spiderweb tendrils of the silvery ore were threading into her axe-head, but Victor couldn't see what effect, if any, they were having on her.

He stepped close and gently gripped her haft. "Good, *chica*, take your time." She didn't reply, but he felt satisfaction and the warmth of love radiate from the weapon, and he stood there for several minutes, gently holding her. One upside to his ill-prepared duel with Trinnie Ro was that he'd grown even closer to the weapon. When so much had failed him, she'd been there, reliable and ready for anything. "When have you not?" he asked, feeling moisture gather in his eyes.

With a contented sigh, he turned and rifled through one of the satchels he'd left in the vault until he closed his fingers around the "concentrated distillate of a Qo'lorian Essence Drifter." He didn't know how much it would affect him, but he figured it was as good a time as any to find out. As far as the queen or anyone else knew, he was still out of it after having consumed his "natural treasure." If this thing knocked him out for a while, so be it.

He took the distillate and left, closing and locking the door to his vault behind him. He went to his parlor and stood before the mostly closed curtains to his balcony, staring over the canopy of trees toward the enormous majesty of Iron Mountain. With a crooked smile, he saluted the mountain. "Here's to you, big guy," he grunted as he tossed back the little potion.

The liquid's effect was immediate, and it wasn't gentle. Victor felt every muscle in his body go rigid, like a thousand spasms all at once. He couldn't speak or cry out, so taut was his every muscle. All he could do was spread his arms and arch his back, struggling to inhale the smallest of breaths as he felt like he was being stretched on an invisible rack. Even his fingers seemed as if they'd flee their sockets, they strained so hard to stretch and widen. He suffered through the pain for several minutes, and then, like a spring being released, his muscles relaxed and rebounded, and he fell to his knees, gasping in relief.

He didn't feel any different, though it would be hard to tell after that session of torture. All he was sure of was the relief in his trembling muscles. The potion was supposed to boost "one or more attributes permanently," so Victor opened his status sheet, looking to see what had changed:

| Strength: | 680 | Vitality: | 819 (867) |
|---|---|---|---|
| Dexterity: | 280 (302) | Agility: | 303 (325) |
| Intelligence: | 220 | Will: | 673 |

There it was, plain as day: He'd gained exactly one hundred strength. "Holy shit," he gasped. Considering he gained thirty-six unmodified attribute points with each legendary-class level, he wasn't going to complain about a potion that gave him a free hundred points. He'd tried talking with Du, asking him about the awards and the suspicious synergy of them all, but the dungeon Core hadn't uttered a word since taking up residence in Victor's vault. Victor thought maybe it couldn't—maybe it needed to be placed and given a new home before it could interact with people.

"Or maybe he's just a cagey little *pendejo*." Victor chuckled. He stretched, relieved that his limbs and muscles were feeling normal again. "That didn't take long." Considering that the potion's effects had been near instantaneous, he contemplated laying low for a while, avoiding more responsibilities by pretending to be recovering longer than needed. With a heavy sigh and the weight of unknown duties on his shoulders, he walked over to the door to his suite and opened it, unsurprised to find Feist slumped on a stool, flipping through another smutty pamphlet.

The fighter almost knocked his stool over as he leaped to his feet, stuffing the leaflet into his belt. "Good, uh, morning, Your Grace."

"Is it?" Victor hadn't looked at the clock.

"Aye, well, good enough for me, milord. I had a lovely breakfast, and my girl, Tienna, she promised me a massage if I didn't get in trouble with Lady Bryn again and avoided being kept late to review my drills. It doesn't hurt that she was hired on here in the palace as a scullery—"

Victor held up a hand. "That's enough detail, Feist. Where's Bryn?"

"The, uh, baroness is watching over that craftsman you hired. She said you asked that he and his project be guarded at all hours, and Lady Bryn's only hired on two others that she trusts so far, so—"

"Go and get her. You can take her place."

Feist hurriedly saluted, then jogged across the little room to the elevator. Victor watched him push the button to open the doors, then nodded and closed the door. He put on a serious face with the guy, but in truth, Victor thought Feist was pretty funny, and though the man probably had ten years on him, he reminded Victor of himself when he was younger . . . and *stupider*. He chuckled, shaking his head as he walked over to his little kitchen. The cold-cupboard probably had less food in it than Victor's storage rings, but he thought he'd take a look.

He'd barely taken out a pitcher of fresh-squeezed juice—pale blue and sweet—and was pouring it into a tall glass when a knock sounded at his door. "That was fast," he muttered. Had he locked it? "Come in!" he called. The latch clicked, and Victor heard the door open, but he didn't hear Bryn's usual bootheels clicking on the marble. When he looked up, he nearly dropped the pitcher, but his fingers were deft, and he caught it before it shattered on the countertop.

A woman stood there. A woman with blonde hair, very blue eyes, and wearing a smile that spoke volumes. She stepped forward, a long leg swishing out of her flowing yellow skirts, her little matching slippers silent on the floor. When she was standing in the center of the front parlor, looking directly at Victor, she gripped the outer layer of her skirts and performed a delicate curtsy. Her blonde ringlets danced with the motion, the yellow ribbons in her hair fighting to hold them in place.

"Milord, Victor," she said, her bright, crisp voice clear as a crystal chime as she straightened.

"Holy shit. *Tes?*" Victor's legs were already moving as he spoke, carrying him around the kitchen counter over the thick rug and into the parlor. He would have stopped and waited for her to respond, but he didn't need to—her eyes welcomed him, and the smile spreading her perfect, bow-shaped lips was too much for him to resist. He stooped and snatched her up, smashing her against his chest as he turned in a circle, swinging her dangling legs out as she laughed.

When he set her down, her cheeks flushed, and she fanned herself, looking up at him. "Such liberties!"

"Oh, come on. You could have thrown me through that wall over there if you didn't want me to hug you."

"True," she laughed, turning to inspect his quarters. "What a lovely setting." She walked toward the sitting area near the balcony, peering out at Iron Mountain. "There's the mountain where your ancient kin sleeps, hmm?"

"You know about him?"

"I have him to thank for my visit."

"Huh?"

"He's an ancient primordial—a being who follows his own rules. When he contacted and met with you, it opened some doors for me . . . *politically* speaking."

Victor was having a hard time wrapping his head around the fact that Tes was standing before him, speaking to him almost as if nothing had happened since the last time he'd seen her. "Jesus, Tes, I can't believe you're standing here!"

"Well, I am, so please try to believe." She giggled and twirled, looking past him toward the door. "Someone comes."

Victor stared at the door for a moment, and then, sure enough, knuckles rapped on the wood. Now that he was concentrating on it, he recognized the pattern as Bryn's. He looked at Tes. "Does anyone know you're here?"

"Naturally! I greeted many staff as I walked through your palace. Best you don't announce me as anything other than an old friend, though."

Victor walked over to the door and opened it. Bryn stood there in her usual uniform, though he noted a new star-patterned embroidery on her collar. "Hey, Bryn, I think I called for you a little prematurely. I didn't realize I had a guest in the palace."

"You do? Shall I escort . . . *them* up?"

"No, no. She's here already. I'll introduce you after we finish catching up. I'm sorry about dragging you up here for nothing. Go ahead and go back to whatever you were doing, okay?"

Bryn's eyes narrowed, but her face was nearly expressionless as she responded, "Of course, Your Grace. Nothing is amiss?"

"Nothing with me. Is everything good with the, um, queen and Trobban and all that?"

"Everything is fine, Your Grace. Based on how you spoke yesterday, I thought you'd be out longer."

"*Yesterday?*" Victor laughed, shaking his head. "I thought it would be longer. Anyway, it's good to know I didn't miss much. I'll call you soon." At his words, Bryn nodded, and Victor closed the door.

"You care about her," Tes observed, still standing near the balcony windows. She'd pulled the curtains wide.

"She's been great."

"Good. You'll need allies."

"Ahem," Victor cleared his throat, still feeling off balance. "Care to elaborate on that?"

"Oh, *Victor*! What a sticky mess you've gotten yourself in!" She sighed, shaking her head. "I have some leeway to speak, thanks to *him*"—she pointed toward the mountain—"but my hands are still a bit tied. Nevertheless, I'm here and can guide you for a while. We'll see you through this . . . I *hope*."

"Through *what*?"

"Well, you're determined to battle your way to the top of the food chain on this world, yes? I won't lie and say I haven't been watching you from time to time."

"Yeah, I guess I'm determined. I made promises to—"

"Well, my dear, sweet titan, you've made promises that will prove difficult to keep. There are very powerful, very wealthy people ruling the great kingdoms of this world, and they have vast resources. Do you think you're the only warrior from another world who's found himself a position as a champion here? Men and women are lining up to kill you, sweet boy."

Victor didn't love her patronizing turn of phrase, but she had a way of delivering the words with that sweet smile and tone that disarmed his flickering anger before it could take root. He shrugged. "They can't be veil walkers. I've fought steel seekers before."

Tes smiled and stepped closer to him. She was larger than she had been most of the time on Coloss—giant-sized—but she still had to stand on her tiptoes to look more directly into his eyes. Her lips curled up on the right side in a crooked smile as she *tsk*ed. "Love, you aren't the only person in all the worlds connected to Ruhn who has a potent bloodline. You aren't the only warrior to have the blessing of a strong Core and legendary classes. There are some true monsters readying themselves to face you—men and women unlike any you've faced before. At least one of them has an elder bloodline."

Tes flickered in and out of focus for the briefest moment, and Victor saw her true form. A great blue-scaled dragon's head flashed before his eyes, her white fangs exposed in a wicked, leering smile, her glittering sapphire eyes like jewels with the light of a blazing star at their heart. "If you take my meaning," she said, back to her human-appearing self.

"A dragon?"

"Let's not get ahead of ourselves. The way I see it, you've got some time to prepare. It'll be a while before you face the first of Ruhn's great houses. Their machinations will take time, their schemes to obstruct your queen's progress. Oh, what a pit of vipers you've gotten yourself mixed up with!" She sighed and tilted her head, arching an eyebrow. "How would you like me to spend some time with you here? I know you've been studying elder magic. I can . . . *tutor* you."

"Shit, seriously? *Fuck* yes, I'd like that!" The idea of having Tes there to help him again filled Victor's chest with unmitigated joy. He *loved* her style of "tutoring." She was straightforward and pleasant and spent *time* with him when he'd been on Coloss. Of all the "mentors" he'd had, Tes was more than his favorite—he wouldn't deny that he'd been smitten by her. He could put that aside, couldn't he? He could focus and learn from her. *Right?*

"Good! Thanks to yonder titan," she said, pointing out the window at the mountain, "and thanks to your wandering spirit—you visited me, do you remember that?"

"W-what?"

"Yes! Your spirit came my way during some fever dream or another. Anyway, thanks to that little fact—you contacted *me*, technically—the Celestial Envoys have granted me permission to visit. I'm not allowed to reveal my true nature to others, and I'm not allowed to intervene, but I think some gentle guidance and a little tutoring are well within my limitations."

Victor laughed and stooped, reaching for her, wanting to pull her into another sweeping embrace, but she took a step back. "Easy, now!" She laughed. "We've much work to do and . . . well, we need to keep things *professional*. I'm so impressed with your growth, Victor; I truly am. You've made tremendous strides in so many ways. You're truly a man of great accomplishments. Nevertheless, if I'm going to teach you, you must take *me* seriously, as well."

Victor nodded, a little embarrassed but too happy, too *relieved* to have Tes there, to care. She was a lifeline for him, someone he trusted implicitly—more than Arona, more than Queen Kynna, more than anyone else on Ruhn—even more than Ranish Dar. No, the truth was, he felt that way, *especially* about Dar. How wonderful would it be to have a mentor again whom he wasn't second-guessing, whom he didn't think might have ulterior motives? He *still* wasn't sure Dar expected him to win all these duels. As far as he knew, Dar had plans based on either outcome—success or failure.

"Good!" Tes nodded, turning back to the balcony. "Let's start with a review of where things stand. You can tell me about your allies here, your equipment, and the things about you that have changed. I can see *much*, but I can't see *every-thing*. Truly, Victor, you impress me! So?" She produced a crystalline decanter. "Would you have a drink and sit with me? I might have a tale or two to share with you, as well."

Victor smiled and nodded, moving to the couch where he sat. She walked over and settled beside him, tilting her knees so they pointed his way. She set the decanter on the table beside them and produced two crystal glasses. She put them on the table and nodded. "You pour."

"Oh, sure." Victor reached for the decanter and pulled the stopper. The heady scent of potent alcohol and something cloyingly sweet filled his nostrils. "Smells good."

"It is! And," she said, leaning forward and smiling as she slapped his knee, "it would kill most people even to have a sip. You've advanced your race past epic, though; I can feel it. You'll be fine."

Victor's eyes widened, his mouth set in a stupid grin; he felt as if the drink was a peace offering. It was Tes acknowledging that he'd changed, that he was ready for more from her. They might be embarking on a student-mentor relationship for now, but he was more than just a student to her, and she was showing him as much. He poured the honey-colored liquid into Tes's glass, and the potent fumes wafted into his nose. He smelled fire, rain, and something like cherry blossoms in that eye-watering haze. "Nice."

After he poured them both a finger of the stuff, he handed one of the glasses to Tes and then tapped his against it. As their glasses clicked together with a crystalline chime, she said, "To old friendships made new again."

Victor nodded. "To old friends and warm hearts."

She smiled, and they drank. Victor took just a tiny sip, afraid he'd get drunk too quickly, but it went down easily, and despite Tes's earlier words, it didn't seem all that dangerous. Still, he set the glass down and turned to look into Tes's eyes. "I'm so grateful that you came."

"I love that about you, Victor—how you wear your heart openly for all to see. Now, tell me everything, and you can start with the shadow on that big heart. What steered your course to Ruhn, and where has Valla gone?"

"Ah." Victor's smile faltered. He leaned back, contemplated picking up and draining his glass, then sighed, shaking his head. "Things started to get difficult for us when we got to Sojourn . . ." So, he and Tes sat together, and he told her everything. For the first time in as long as he could remember, he bared his soul to another person, sharing his fears, his doubts, and his heartache. Tes listened and, to his relief, didn't offer any platitudes. She nodded and commiserated, and before long, their conversation turned to Ranish Dar and Victor's mad quest to make Kynna Empress of Ruhn.

Before he got far, though, Tes asked him to back up and tell her about what he'd done since Coloss. Victor nodded, and he recounted his time on Fanwath, his conquest of the Untamed Marches, and how he and his allies had traveled to Sojourn to save Edeya. In a way, it was cathartic to sit there rehashing everything he'd done, all he'd been through, and all he hoped to do. It helped him to remember that he *had* accomplished a lot. He might have gotten himself into a "vipers' nest" there on Ruhn, but just because he had some tough *pendejos* lining up to fight him, that didn't mean he couldn't find a way to win.

So, he talked, and then Tes talked, and they planned, and they plotted, and before he knew it, the night had grown late, and they were both drunk and laughing. Victor's chest was filled with joy as he shared all his troubles, and that shared weight made them light, and he forgot about them for the first time in a very long while.

# ABOUT THE AUTHOR

Plum Parrot is the pen name of author Miles Gallup, who grew up in Southern Arizona and spent much of his youth wandering around the Sonoran Desert, hunting imaginary monsters and building forts. He studied creative writing at the University of Arizona and, for a number of years, attempted to teach middle schoolers to love literature and write their own stories. If he's not spending time with his dog, you can find Gallup writing, reading his favorite authors, or playing *D&D* with friends and family.

# RESPAWN YOUR CURIOSITY

*follow us on our socials*

 podiumentertainment.com

 @podiumentertainment

 /podiumentertainment

 @podium_ent

 @podiumentertainment

www.ingramcontent.com/pod-product-compliance
Lightning Source LLC
Chambersburg PA
CBHW030924120726
47906CB00002B/476